seeking
the center

leslie spitz-edson

Cuidono • Brooklyn

Seeking the Center
© 2016 Leslie Spitz-Edson

Cover Image: "Pond Hockey" © Wilkinson Visual

ISBN: 978-1-944453-02-2
eISBN: 978-1-944453-03-9

Cuidono Press
Brooklyn NY
www.cuidono.com

To Mike, and to our children

Agnes stretched back in her seat, her feet frozen on the floor in front of her, her hands fisted in the pockets of her parka, her bag slouched on the seat beside her precisely as she had dropped it so many hours ago. Her eyes, tracking the frozen landscape through the rain-slanted bus window, were like fingers drawn across a chain link fence. There was nothing for them to lock onto—just the white crust left over from an early October snow-fall, bleeding into a veil of cold fog between the lips of the prairie and the smoke-colored sky. The highway kept coming, etched into the land, straight as an engineer's pencil against the side of a ruler. At its edges, though, it broke up into bits, and you could see where tufts of grass and floes of grainy earth had infiltrated the smooth certainty of the asphalt.

Agnes put her hand to her mouth and yawned, lulled by the constant hum of the bus motor and by her own inertia. Her eyes, though, were open, and she wasn't dreaming—certainly not of the job that Jo had gotten for her in town. That job, she knew, was scarcely a stab in the dark. For Jo, living in town and working at the Indian Jewel Box beckoned like city lights, like fashion runways and luxury apartments and rich boyfriends, and other figments of her imagination. But for Agnes—it's not that she didn't want any of those things. Maybe she did. She just didn't know.

A gaudy billboard flashed by, announcing a casino grand opening. Agnes shifted in her seat. She had no illusions that living in town and working at the Indian Jewel Box would start her down the path to a beautiful future. Girls like her never had the type of future that Jo envisioned. Their future was pretty much the same as their mothers' present. And what's the point of a future if it's already being lived by somebody else?

The corrugated metal roof of Compass Point Marine & RV glinted in a sudden slant of sunshine that sliced through the clouds at the western horizon. The "O" in *Compass* was designed to look like the compass on a map. Slapped onto the top corner of the sign, like the Good Housekeeping Seal of Approval, was a large, red Canadian maple leaf. Agnes smirked, but she couldn't deny it: Compass Point was a beautiful store. It was everything that Donny's back home wasn't, from its snow-white linoleum floor—like the smoothest, sweetest sheet of ice she'd ever skated on—to its huge, squeaky-clean plate-glass windows and the delicious smell of new rubber tires and vinyl upholstery. Agnes had gone there once a long time ago with Dad when he was thinking about trading for a bigger boat. Afterwards they'd stopped for lunch at the A&W, just the two of them, and Dad had let her order a coney dog with fries and a root beer float. On that day, everything had sparkled with a thrill that bordered on dangerous. Holding Dad's hand, she'd felt that she could go anywhere and do anything. But that was years ago, when she was just a kid. She didn't know any better, then.

Dad didn't want her to move to Wapahaska. He was afraid that she would never come back. From Wapahaska she would be lured to Thompson, or some other big city, a place that had mutated, like the cannibal Windigo of the old stories, into a silent, howling flash-freeze, parched and ravenous. But instead of feasting on her flesh, it would feast on her spirit. Agnes was well aware of the dangers, though, and they didn't lurk in any particular geographical location. Being young, female, and brown-skinned meant that she was expendable, and set her up for the worst anyone *anywhere* cared to dish out. Huddling in fear at home in St. Cyp was no guarantee of safety, much less of vanquishing Windigo and feeding her *own* spirit.

But even though she was nearly twenty-one, and could go wherever she pleased, she loved her Dad and had wanted his blessing. Luckily, Dad's mother, Agnes's kookum, was afraid of nothing. Maybe not even Windigo. And Kookum was on her side.

"Lazare, Agnes is a grown woman," said Kookum.

"Mary was a grown woman. Look what happened to my Mary," Dad replied. All these years later, he still choked up when he said her name out loud.

"They are different people, Mary and Agnes," Kookum replied.

"She should never have gone," said Dad.

"To move is in our blood, Lazare. And Wapahaska is not so far. Plenty of people move there from here. Janet's boy is living there. Remember?"

"It swallowed her alive," lamented Dad.

"You can't change the mother's course by trying to chart the daughter's."

"I want to keep her close. She belongs here."

"Lazare, this will always be her home. She carries it inside. She's beginning to know herself. But she needs to find her boundaries."

Kookum wouldn't give up, and finally Dad had admitted she was right. It was more a vote of confidence in Kookum than in Agnes. But Dad had agreed to let Agnes go, so she'd accepted Jo's offer to share an apartment and taken the job at the Indian Jewel Box. She'd bought a bus ticket, packed up, and left.

The only other person who might have gotten her to stay was Vin. She still carried a little dog-eared snapshot of the two of them in her wallet. It was from when they were really little. They were standing in the dust, in front of some ramshackle wooden stairs. Maybe they were the stairs of the trailer they had lived in back then. She didn't know. They both had big, dark eyes, uncombed hair, and clothes that didn't quite fit. Vin was probably about four, or maybe just barely five, but he was holding her hand protectively, and aiming a tough, little-boy stare at the camera. Agnes, a couple of years younger, her brow wrinkled, was looking up at him—the brother she so admired—for reassurance.

The bus pulled into the depot. Agnes stood up and stomped her feet. She picked up her bag and climbed down the steps to the platform. Waiting for the driver to open the baggage compartment, she felt tiny, her white puff of breath slight and small compared to the billows of bus exhaust swelling like demons in the failing light. She claimed her suitcase and lugged it over to the local bus stop. When the bus came she climbed aboard and paid her fare. She could feel the other passengers eying her dark hair and skin, her worn bag and parka, and her brand new suitcase, which, out of necessity, was partially blocking the aisle. She ignored them and once again directed her gaze out the window.

Sprawled at the next junction was the Ex. It was deserted this afternoon, its white, wooden gate chained and padlocked, but the muddy, tire-track road stretched beyond the gate, slicing through the emerald grounds. Rainwater pooled like mercury in its hoof-prints and wheel-ruts. Generous bald patches on the grassy fields showed where footsteps had overflowed the pavement, where the earth had been abraded by hoards of fair-goers. Agnes herself had visited the Ex many times, as had most everyone she knew.

It used to be that after it rained they'd spread old pieces of plywood across the low spots. If you could get enough kids jumping on one of those you could really raise some spray. "Tidal wave!" you'd yell, and you'd jump up and down and ride the plywood, arms outspread, as if you were on a surfboard, watching the muddy water swirl and splash. Mostly the grown-ups would just pull their necks down into the collars of their jackets and keep walking. Some might betray themselves with a sort of secret smile, remembering that when they were kids, they did the same thing. And there always seemed to be a white lady—maybe a schoolteacher or someone like that—who would start to scold you, to try to teach you so that you'd know better.

But you'd just follow the lead of the older kids, avoid eye contact at any cost, and run away as fast as you could.

The low rectangle of the arena backed up to the show rings, which were easy to spot from a distance, their two-rail fences hovering like white halos in the twilight. The dark shapes behind them were the barns. The concession stands squatted together in a group, their windows shuttered. The awkward, cantilevered roof of the grandstand loomed over the racetrack, dark against the sky—it looked like you could knock it over with your pinky. The grandstand was metal now, but it used to be wooden, and when you climbed up the side of it, monkey-style, it would sway a little, chirping like baby songbirds as the wood scraped wood. The fence around the track was chain link, with splintery slats.

Dad's work was fixing cars and boats and tractors, but his love was horses. He'd always wanted to work with horses. *It's in my blood,* he always said. That's because long ago his people bred the best horses, horses that were coveted by the white settlers and, even before that, by the buffalo hunters. But it takes money to get started breeding horses, and it takes time, and before Kookum came to stay, he'd been raising two kids alone. He'd taken whatever job he could find. He did well, too, eventually buying the small garage where he worked. He'd consoled himself with the idea that cars and trucks now are like horses used to be, and motorboats like the *canots du nord*, the old trading canoes—so that his work now served the same purpose as his ancestors' used to. But, of course, cars and trucks aren't the same as horses, and so for special occasions like the Yearling Sale or the stockyards' Customer Appreciation Day, Dad would take a day off work so he and Agnes and Vin could go to the Ex. It was a holiday for him, and Agnes and Vin were supposed to look out for each other. He'd warn them to stick together and give each of them a pocketful of dimes and quarters. They'd run from stand to stand, buying all the corn dogs, cotton candy, and fry bread they could eat until they ran out of money. Then they'd chase each other around the animal stalls until it was time to meet Dad in the stands for the show.

Those days were gone now, at least for Agnes. Probably some other kids were jumping in the puddles, sneezing in the hay jump, pinching their noses in mock disgust at the smell of the manure, and gorging themselves on fried food. Some other little kids were climbing up the grandstand, begging their dads for pennies to use in the gum machines. Some other kids were playing tag in the big field behind the arena.

Agnes remembered the arena, too. She'd been there a few times when she played peewee, for tournaments and clinics and things like that. Those memories never failed to conjure, all too pungently, the familiar boy-smells that had colored so much of her childhood. And yes, *colored* was the right word, because at times they constituted an almost visible haze: the sharp odor of sweat, the rankness of sore-throat breath whenever they opened their grossly inarticulate mouths, and the putrid aroma of unlaundered socks and underwear surreptitiously recovered from piles on the bedroom floor and reworn. She remembered driving down with the MacKenzies once, crushed in the backseat with Owen and some other boy. It must have been Tommy Oliver. When Owen's dad turned abruptly into the parking lot, causing them all to lurch sideways, the boys had exaggerated the motion, slamming into her, hard, and laughing hysterically. It had hurt—mostly because they were ganging up on her, their teammate—and it made her angry. She knew it was because she was a girl, but there wasn't much she could do about it just then. Later she'd find a way to get even.

But those days were gone, too. The bus passed the arena as if it wasn't even there, and continued on, more and more slowly, into less familiar territory. Large, open lots gave way to small yards, each with its own little bungalow. The streetlights pushed away the grandness of the sky with their sickly glow, and the close-cropped lawns, cars, and pickups lay trapped in their pinkish smother. Soon the streets narrowed even further into a gauntlet of shiny storefronts and two- and three-story brick buildings. The driver, leaning across the steering wheel, labored over every turn.

Agnes sat up straighter and read the signs with growing curiosity: Jeannie's House of Beauty, Town Locksmith, Hal's Hobby Shop and Crafts, Martin Realty, Double-A Appliance Repair, T.T.'s Tavern, Dottie's Breakfast and Dairy, Fresh Florist & Garden Shop. On a corner by itself was the Police and Fire Department, flanked by a paved lot filled with cop cars and graced by the spotlit, stenciled motto, "Public Safety Is Our Business and Yours." Lemaire's Memorial and Funeral Home was an old Victorian set back from the street, its circular drive lined with boxy evergreens. Agnes watched the street signs carefully, too, and when the bus came to the stop that Jo had specified, she took a deep breath and hauled her suitcase down onto the street. She went through Jo's directions in her mind and trudged off to find her new home.

"It's almost six," Agnes said to Jo. "It's my turn to close up. You can go, if you want."

"I'll stay and help," Jo answered.

"I can do it alone," said Agnes. "You've shown me a couple of times."

"I know. But maybe it'll get busy," said Jo.

"No it won't. You've got that big project due next week. I figured you'd want to get out of here. What's up?"

"Well . . . " said Jo, with a dramatic pause.

Agnes rolled her eyes.

"Remember that guy who was in here on Tuesday?" asked Jo.

"No."

"The one who ordered that kitty-cat charm for his sister?"

"Mmm, sort of. Maybe," said Agnes.

"I called him to tell him that it came in," said Jo. "He's going to pick it up today."

"So?"

"He's a hottie."

"Oh, come on, Jo. Do you really believe for one minute that the charm is for his sister?"

"Yeah. Why not?"

Agnes shook her head. "I don't think so."

"He's a Prairie Wolf."

"I rest my case."

"He seemed nice."

"*Highly* doubtful."

"Why are you so down on hockey players all of a sudden?"

"It's not *all of a sudden*, Jo," said Agnes.

"Sure it is. You always liked hockey players."

"No, I like *hockey*. There's a difference. Hockey is an awesome game. Fun to play, fun to watch. The guys who play it, on the other hand—it's all about them, and their game, and their numbers, and their, you know, *anatomy*—"

"Aren't all guys like that?" laughed Jo.

"Yes, they are. But when they travel in packs it gets magnified. Glorified. Trust me, I know what I'm talking about," said Agnes. "You deserve better."

"You know, Owen MacKenzie plays for the Prairie Wolves, too," said Jo.

"I know."

"Aren't you ever going to look him up?"

"No. Aren't you ever going to stop *asking* me if I'm ever going to look him up?"

"Why won't you?"

"Why would I?" asked Agnes. "Anyhow, if you're not going home early, I will. That way you can be alone with your hockey player."

"No! Please stay!" said Jo. "Oh, look, here he comes."

Agnes retreated to the small office in the back of the shop. She had no interest in Jo's flirtation, and anyhow, there was plenty of work to do. Just this morning they'd unpacked a box of hammered silver bracelets and beaded earrings made by some artist in Winnipeg. Then it had gotten busy and they'd left the box sitting on the desk overflowing with cascades of tissue paper. Agnes got to work cleaning it up.

It was true, though, what Jo kept reminding her: Owen MacKenzie was living in town, playing center for the Prairie Wolves. But even though Kookum had given her his phone number—inexplicably, Kookum had always loved O—Agnes hadn't even remotely considered calling him. She and Owen had known each other forever, but their friendship—if that was the right word for it—had mostly caused confusion.

She didn't even know who he was anymore. Was he the sweet kid who had invited her under the bleachers after practice to share his prized, vending-machine Oreos? Or was he the kid who had slammed into her in the backseat of the car with Tommy Oliver, shrieking with laughter? Was he smallest in size but first in line to take with issue with that monster Dub Hawkins who crashed her crease during that long-ago playoff game? Or was he the obnoxious jerk who all but ignored her after she had made the very awkward trip with his parents and little brother to watch him play junior hockey out in Shellbrook?

She didn't know. And the most confusing part was that she didn't know which Owen was worse: Oreo Owen or Obnoxious Jerk Owen. She hated them both. She really did.

She peeked out. Jo's guy was gone. She grabbed the vacuum and dragged it out of the office with her.

"I guess I'll go home, then," said Jo, looking discouraged.

"Oh, man up, Jo," said Agnes. "There are still, like, twenty guys left on the team."

"The good ones are always taken," said Jo, shaking her head. She got her coat and boots from the back and left.

Agnes stayed in the front of the store now, going from table to table, shelf to shelf, making sure the displays were in order. The Indian Jewel Box sold a sort of mishmash of Native and "Native-inspired" jewelry, accessories, and clothing, some crafted by real artists and others not. Most were reasonably tasteful, anyhow.

Some of the profit went to the craftspeople, which was a good thing, and occasionally Edie, the owner of the store, sold things on consignment. She'd even sold clothing that Jo, who was studying fashion design, had sewn herself. Usually, though, Jo's designs weren't "Indian enough" for Edie.

After Agnes had finished refolding some thin, poor-quality woven sashes, she straightened a display that included a pair of gorgeous, Nehiyawak moccasins. Their beaded design was circular like the prairie: the four quadrants—in red, black, white, and yellow—were the four directions, in perfect balance. Agnes ran her finger over the impossibly even beadwork, and then she went to stand behind the counter. Bored, she started tidying the shelf under the register, throwing out trash and making a neat pile of the remaining catalogs and magazines.

The bell jingled. Agnes looked up to see a middle-aged white woman in a long, camel-colored wool coat. She had a leather handbag hanging over her arm and was carefully made-up with teased, dark hair that flipped up from under her deliberately angled hat.

"Hello," said Agnes.

"Oh, hello," the woman said. She seemed surprised to see Agnes.

"Can I help you?" Agnes asked.

"Uh . . . is Mal not here?"

"No, she's off today. But I'd be happy to help," Agnes said.

The woman shook her head. "I don't know how Edie can have you girls here alone . . . " her voice trailed off.

"Us girls?" Agnes asked.

"You and . . . the other one," the woman said.

"Do you mean Josephine?" asked Agnes.

"I don't know her name," the woman said, "but I was hoping to talk to someone . . . with more experience."

"There's no one here but me, at the moment," said Agnes.

"Well, I guess I'll come back some other time," said the woman, nervously.

Or you could try asking me, thought Agnes.

"Have a nice evening," the woman said as she left the store.

Agnes shrugged. She *was*, apparently, experienced enough to help a couple of *other* customers who came in just before closing time. Then she locked the door, vacuumed, and took her time closing out the register. When she left the store it was well after seven o'clock and the sky was black. Yellow light from the storefronts fell across the shoveled sidewalks. They'd had another light snow, and probably the cold was here to stay. It was refreshing, anyhow, after so many hours in the stuffy shop. She inhaled and imagined that this was a real city, like the city her mom had gone to, with cars crawling along the shiny streets, their turn signals blinking like Christmas lights, and people hustling along the sidewalks on their way to restaurants and concerts and theaters. She was starting to like it here. She hadn't done much yet except go to work, but she loved the traditional handicrafts that they sold. She loved the paycheck, too, small though it was, and sharing an apartment with Jo was much more entertaining than living with Dad and Kookum.

Instead of going straight home, Agnes turned right and walked towards Duncan Street, where most of the shops were concentrated. She was beading a purse for Kookum, after a traditional design that she'd learned from her auntie out at Catfish River, and although she wasn't the best beader ever, she knew that Kookum would like it because she'd made it just for her. Now that she was earning some money, though, maybe she could buy store-bought presents for Dad and Vin.

Vin had finally gotten a good job up north, working as a mechanic for a mining company, but maybe he'd get a few days off for Christmas, enough to drive down and visit. He'd be happy because he was working. They'd tease each other and play pranks and dance with their aunts and uncles and cousins. Hopefully, *hopefully*, he'd be there. She wouldn't let him out of her sight the whole time.

She stopped to look at the window display at Walt's Western Wear. A headless mannequin wearing blue jeans, cowboy boots, a flannel shirt, and a fringed, suede jacket dangled a cowboy hat from its left hand. She couldn't afford to buy any of those things, but arranged on a striped trade blanket below were an assortment of wallets, key rings, bandannas, fancy lighters, and a vest. Jo could help her put together a better vest than that! And there was still plenty of time before Christmas. Maybe she could add some beading on the pockets—

"Ag, is that you?" said a voice from just behind her right ear.

She spun around.

"Jesus, O, you scared the shit out of me," she said.

Owen smiled, that bright-eyed, lopsided smile of his. "Always the lady," he replied. God, she hated him. "How about a hug?" he said, opening his arms.

They hugged. His wool jacket was scratchy against her face.

"Wow, you look great," Owen said. "What are you doing here? Shopping?"

"I live here," said Agnes.

"No kidding!"

"Yeah. I'm working at the Indian Jewel Box."

"Wow, why didn't you tell me?" he asked.

She didn't answer. God, he was an idiot! Could he seriously not figure out why she hadn't told him? And how could he not have known? There's no way his mom didn't tell him—Janet MacKenzie and Kookum had been friends for years. He must have forgotten. That would be just like him.

He asked, "Do you want to grab a sandwich? I'm headed out for dinner."

"Uh, no thanks. I'm on my way home."

"Where are you living?"

"On Second Ave. I'm sharing an apartment with Jo—Josephine."

"Oh yeah? Josephine Gervais? She's here too?"

"How many other Josephines do we know?" asked Agnes.

"Hey, you should come out and see a game sometime," Owen said.

"Yeah, maybe," answered Agnes.

"Seriously. We're not bad. It would be fun if you came." There was that goddamn smile again, the one that made her think he actually cared about her. But really he smiled at everyone like that. She looked away into the shop window. He started to rummage around in the pockets of his jacket.

"Here, Ag," he said. "Give me your number. I'll put you down for two tickets on Saturday. You can bring Jo. Or whoever you want."

Whomever, she thought.

He pulled an old gum wrapper out of his pocket and handed it to her.

She said, "Gosh, thanks, O."

He didn't get the sarcasm. "Do you have a pen or something?" he asked.

Agnes found a pen in her bag and wrote her number on the wrapper.

"Come on, I'll walk you home," he said.

"Well, okay, thanks," she conceded. In her mind she could hear Kookum going on and on about him. Kookum thought Owen was a gentleman because he called her "Miss Sophie" and held the door open. She didn't seem to realize that those things weren't worth a pile of crap.

"Yeah, honestly, Ag, we're not bad," Owen was saying. "We just got a new goalie. Robbie Bancroft. Have you heard of him? You should check him out. He's real quick and pretty small, like you—well, small for a guy—but not as consistent. But lucky for him they've been going in for us, so he's picked up a couple wins. Hopefully it helps get him going. I think he's got a confidence problem. Don't tell anyone I said that, okay? I just think he doesn't stay with it long enough and then as soon as something goes wrong he'll just hang it up."

"But other than that, he's good." Agnes laughed.

"Yeah. But don't tell him I said—oh, yeah, I see. I'm making him sound terrible. But he's mostly been okay for us, so far."

"Are you playing on the top line?" Agnes asked.

"Naturally," he said, and smiled.

She rolled her eyes. "Who're you playing with? Anyone good?"

"So far mostly Don Mrkonjic and Freddie Brennan," he answered.

"What are they like?"

"Donner's a good guy. Older. Real strong. Goalies hate him. He's like—what are those things called that stick in your clothes?" Owen didn't wait for Agnes to answer. "Brennan, well, he's a character. He's always talking about—well, I'd better not go there!" Owen laughed. "But he's fast and he's got some skill. We live by the two-on-one." He winked.

And die by it, most likely, thought Agnes. She asked, "Any good defensemen?" Vin used to play D.

"Yeah, Hammer's good. Hampton, that is. But you've probably never heard of him. He's older, too. Bald. Completely. Not a hair on his head. Jordie Carroll, though, maybe you remember him—I used to play against him in juniors. He played out in Everett. Reminds me of . . . what's his name? Oh, yeah: Alex Scott. Remember him, from midgets? Anyhow, Jordie couldn't *ever* stop me. I remember one time I passed it to myself right through his legs and then chipped it into the net. Old Jords had *steam* coming out of his ears! But then when we get here, he pretends like he doesn't remember. Like I'm making it up. So for a long time, like, every practice, I had to put the damn puck through his legs. In the dressing room I had to, like, roll some tape through his legs, or shoot a rubber band, or whatever. It turned into a big joke. He's got a hard shot though, even next to Hammer. And you know, Hammer's called *Hammer* 'cause he can really pound it."

"Otherwise you'd have to call him Baldie," said Agnes. "Or Bubblehead."

Owen laughed.

Agnes couldn't help it. Owen's enthusiasm was drawing her in. He went on and on, describing all the different guys on the team, making her laugh. Soon they were standing in front of her building.

"This looks nice," said Owen.

"It is pretty nice. We're up on the second floor," Agnes said. She pointed up at the building. "That's our window. We have a good view of the street and everything."

"Cool. Well, see ya, Ag. I'll let you know about the tickets."

"Okay," she said. "See ya."

Owen was true to his word, and on Saturday night, two tickets for the Prairie Wolves' game against the Silver Lake Blue Ice were waiting for Agnes at the arena's box office. The temperature had plunged and the evening was moonless and dark, but like a giant space station adrift in an empty black cosmos, the arena was oblivious to anything beyond its walls. Inside, there was no day or night and it was never too hot or too cold. Once the game began, it lifted off and spun away, leaving the real world far behind.

Agnes and Jo stepped through the doors and then stopped to get their bearings. Back home, there was nothing like this— no big arena and no professional team. They didn't even have a junior team. The concourse was infinite. It stretched on, both to their left and to their right, until, in both directions, it turned, so that you couldn't see the end of it. Its walls, painted in the Prairie Wolves' white, gray and purple, were studded with brightly lit signs and broad concession counters. People streamed by them, in both directions, talking, eating, and drinking, their voices merged into one continuous roar.

"Wow," said Jo.

"Yeah," said Agnes. "I've never seen so many people."

Across the wide hall from where they were standing there was a group of fans wearing player jerseys and team caps. They were busy greeting friends who were just then arriving. The guys slapped each other on the back and shook hands, and the girls hugged, took off their hats, and smoothed their hair. They seemed perfectly at home, as if they met here often. Agnes wondered what their lives were like, and what kind of jobs they had that allowed them to come out like this. Back home there weren't very many jobs. Of course, there weren't very many interesting things to spend your money on, either.

"Let's just walk around the place once, okay?" Agnes said to Jo.

"Okay."

They took off their hats and gloves, unzipped their jackets, and joined the stream of humanity flowing around the hall. They started to feel more comfortable. There *were* a lot of people, but when you started looking at them, they didn't seem that different from the people back home.

A group of older, white couples stood across from one of the hot dog counters. The men, leaning back on their heels, thumbs in their belt loops, sported beer bellies and flannel shirts. The women wore polyester stretch pants and comfortable walking shoes. Agnes figured they were farmers. During the summer they'd be discussing tractors and the price of wheat, but tonight they were talking players and penalty kills, groin injuries and goals against, all in the slow, drawn-out manner of country people.

"Could be," one of the men intoned. "I just feel like he's kinda lost a step since a year ago."

"Always been a slow starter," answered another. "It's early. He'll get there. Anyhow, the team needs him in the dressing room. They got so many young guys, this season."

Speaking of young guys, a hockey game is a perfect opportunity to scope them out, and it didn't take long for Jo to put up her antennae. A pair of scruffy looking Native guys who were hanging around one of the concessions sipping beers gave them the eye. Jo studiously ignored them.

"Bums!" she said, under her breath. "Wash your hair, at least. It's Saturday night!"

"Try wearing a belt, too," Agnes added, "Your ass is going to get real cold hanging out like that on a night like this."

They kept walking.

"This bunch looks a little better," said Jo.

"I'll take the one in the black jacket," joked Agnes.

"Somehow I knew you would," laughed Jo. "I like the redhead."

"You can have him. He's a little too freckled for me," said Agnes.

"It's a good thing we have different taste in men," said Jo.

"It is," said Agnes. They kept walking.

"Hey Jo, look," said Agnes. "Now *those* are my kind of men!" She nodded in the direction of a group of five or six eight-year old boys, too young to have assumed the masculine mantle of cool, so excited to be there that they were practically shooting sparks out of their eyeballs.

"Well, you could do worse," said Jo. "They're not going to lie or cheat on you, anyhow."

A couple of the boys got sucked into a display of Prairie Wolves souvenirs, while the others kept walking. "Tyler," called the harried dad who was serving as chaperone. "Tyler and Jake! Hold up a minute! Come on back here!"

Agnes smiled at him—the poor, hapless dad.

"Wow, I love her bag," said Jo, "don't you love her bag?"

A thirty-something couple was walking towards them. He wore a pink, button-down oxford, a yellow sweater, and a brown leather jacket. She carried a big, shiny handbag.

Agnes made a face. "Not my style," she said.

Just then two kids bolted up to the couple. "Dad!" the girl shouted, "can we have our ice cream now? Please!"

The mom shook her head and just kept walking.

"Sandy?" the dad called to her, looking helpless.

She didn't look back. Sighing, he pulled his wallet out of his back pocket and opened it up. He handed the girl a bill. The kids took off like twin cannonballs.

Jo raised her eyebrows.

"Maybe he'll buy us ice cream, too," suggested Agnes.

"He probably would. He looks a little lonely right now," laughed Jo. Then she said, "Oo, don't look now."

Another group of guys was headed their way. They were tall and ruddy and athletic—just Jo's type. Even Agnes had to admit they looked good. As ever, Jo tried to walk the fine line between dash and discretion. She smiled at one of them ever so shyly. The guy looked right through her, but one of the others remarked, not even under his breath, "Look at the tits on that squaw, I'd like to give her a go." Agnes hoped that Jo hadn't heard him, though she didn't know why. It wasn't as if they both hadn't heard it before. But since kicking the guy in the balls wasn't exactly an option, they just kept moving. Neither of them said anything.

Standing along the wall by the drinking fountain, trying to look inconspicuous and imposing at the same time, were two policemen. Their eyes were shifty but blank. Agnes felt herself tense up at the sight of them. She'd heard the stories about the policemen in town and they weren't good. Public safety her ass. Maybe for the *white* public. Those greasy-haired bums with the low-hanging pants had better look out.

It was a relief to see a wholesome, young family coming towards them. The mother held a little one, and two older boys in youth team hockey jerseys held their father's hands. One of them was jumping up and down, pointing in succession at the cotton candy stand, a glass display case full of vintage, autographed hockey sweaters, and Ulf the Wolf, the Prairie Wolves' mascot. The other boy was quiet, seemingly mesmerized by the endless stream of people moving past him. Agnes smiled and waved at him, and as they passed each other his head swiveled to hold her gaze until they lost each other in the crowd.

Two Native kids were walking with an older couple that Agnes guessed were their grandparents. The old faces were familiar and beautiful. She thought she could see in them traces of the life they had led—the life she had heard about from her own grandparents. That life was gone now. Instead of hunting or working the traplines along the frozen rivers, stopping to carve their grandkids a hockey stick out of a willow branch, they were living in town, taking them to watch a game on artificial ice. Were their lives easier now? Were they happier? And what about the children's parents? Were they gone, too, like the buffalo, or the birchbark canoe? Like Agnes's mom?

Agnes noticed that Jo had been quiet for some time. "Are you okay, Jo?" she asked.

"Yeah, you?"

"I'm good," answered Agnes. "What do you want to eat?"

"I don't know yet. Maybe I'll just start with a beer."

"Sounds good," said Agnes.

They nearly bumped into a girl coming out of the restroom. They both recognized her because she came into the shop sometimes. But she linked arms with a big, thick-necked guy wearing a Prairie Wolves jersey, and if she noticed Jo and Agnes at all, she ignored them. As the couple walked away, Jo pointed at them and said, "Hey Agnes, look at that!"

The name on the back of the guy's jersey was *MACKENZIE*. As in *Owen* MacKenzie.

Agnes shrugged.

"That's crazy—don't you think?" asked Jo.

"I don't know," replied Agnes.

"It's like he's famous or something," said Jo.

"He *is* famous," said Agnes. "I mean, in Wapahaska, anyhow."

But it *did* feel funny to see some random fan wearing an Owen MacKenzie jersey. And just exactly how it was that skinny old Owen, her long-ago teammate, had grown up to become the star center for a professional hockey team, was kind of a mystery. It hurt her, too, in a deep, inexplicable way. But she wasn't going to admit any of that, not to Jo or to anyone else.

They stood in line for beer and then went to their seats, which, as it turned out, were fantastic—just a few rows behind the Prairie Wolves' bench. Whatever else you might say about it, being friendly with star player Owen MacKenzie just might have its benefits.

The lights dimmed, the buzzer sounded, and the P.A. announcer cried out, "Ladies and gentlemen, please welcome your 1993 Wapahaska Prairie Wolves!" The house lights flashed, purple spotlights swept the ice, and music blared. One by one the players jumped out of the gate and started circling the rink.

"Where's Owen?" yelled Jo into Agnes's ear. The din swallowed up her voice.

"There," yelled Agnes, pointing. "See? Number eleven."

Jo hollered, "Do you know anyone else?"

"No," yelled Agnes.

"Who's he?" asked Jo, pointing.

"Who?"

"The blonde guy."

"I don't know. Forty-one. Torris. Look him up in the program."

"He's kind of cute," yelled Jo.

"Nah," answered Agnes.

"You don't think so?"

"You just like blonde guys, Jo. You always have," yelled Agnes, who was watching the goalies lumbering around in their huge pads, wondering which was the one that Owen had mentioned.

"What?" Jo yelled.

"You always go for the blonde guys," yelled Agnes.

"What's wrong with that?" asked Jo.

"Nothing," yelled Agnes in Jo's ear. "But if he was wearing his helmet, you'd never have noticed him."

Jo didn't answer. She wasn't offended, she was just tired of yelling. She started leafing through the program. "Forty-one. Clay Torris," she informed Agnes. "LW. Six feet, zero inches. One-hundred ninety-five pounds."

"There you go," said Agnes.

Jo closed the program and looked down at the skaters again. "*He's* a big boy."

"Who?" asked Agnes. She'd been watching Owen—she hadn't seen him skate in a long time. "Oh, yeah, Hampton,"

Agnes yelled back at Jo, reading the name of the guy that she'd pointed out. "Owen told me about him. He's one of their defensemen. They call him *Hammer*."

"He must be, like, six-four or something."

"Yeah, maybe," said Agnes.

The buzzer sounded and all but the starting players left the ice. Rink workers unrolled a purple carpet and a young woman with a microphone walked out to the end of it.

"Ladies and gentlemen!" the P.A. announcer proclaimed, "Please join me in welcoming Brittany Trimble, a senior at Quarry Lake High School, and winner of the CJBY *Sing Saskatchewan* contest! Please rise as she sings our national anthem!"

The crowd stood restlessly as Brittany tossed her hair, gazed heavenward, and sang in an exaggeratedly slow, overly embellished fashion, milking every one of her proverbial fifteen minutes. *Look out, Nashville*, thought Agnes. As Brittany reached the anthem's last line the fans commenced the customary applause, and as soon as her lips began to form the shape of the penultimate word the crowd turned as one to pull their seat bottoms down and settle in. Then they reached for their beers.

The puck dropped and after a scramble it squirted out towards the Wolves' goal. A Blue Ice winger skated clear of the scrum, found the puck, dangled it around a lone, helpless defender, and dished it over the goalie's shoulder. Not ten seconds in, the Ice had already found the back of the Wolves' net. A groan went through the crowd, or rather, half of the crowd—the other half still had beer cups up in front of their faces and had missed the play.

The P.A. announcer proclaimed, "Blue Ice goal scored by number fourteen, Jonas Vytchek, assisted by number twenty-nine, Elliot Marsh! Time of the goal, seven seconds."

Ouch.

They need to work on their faceoffs, thought Agnes. And their defensemen need to skate. As for their goalie, he should find another team—for his own good.

Meanwhile, play had started again. Sometimes getting a goal scored on you early can really get you going. Not this time. The Wolves continued to sleepwalk and after some back-and-forth the Ice managed to set up in the Wolves' zone, where a botched clearing attempt went straight to an Ice defenseman who blasted it into the net.

If the Wolves had been her team—which they weren't—Agnes would have been mortified. Not so much because they'd fallen behind, but because rather than getting them fired up, the two measly goals against, not ten minutes into the game, were breaking them. On the bench their heads were hanging, their shoulders sagging, their coach pacing and barking. On the ice they seemed to be skating in wet cement. They couldn't make it through the neutral zone to save their lives, and so they were trapped endlessly on defense, forcing their goalie to stand on his head, and in spite of the poor man's best efforts they were losing 5–0 by the end of the second. At the beginning of the third a fight broke out, but even that seemed rote and passionless. Apparently the guys were so demoralized that they couldn't even give their sticks a solid whack on the boards in recognition of their teammate's sacrifice.

Sometime around the middle of the third, Agnes saw Owen glance up from the bench to where she and Jo were sitting. He was probably wondering whether they were still there, considering the pitiful crap his team had put on display so far. When he looked up, a bunch of the other guys followed suit. Agnes rolled her eyes and shook her head. Checking out the girls in the stands was *not* going to improve their play. Jo, on the other hand, who was, to put it mildly, not much of a hockey fan, had been more focused on the bench than on the ice for nearly the entire game anyhow. So when Torris, the blond guy, looked up at them for the second time, she gave him a shy smile and a little wave. Agnes looked away.

By that time the game was entirely out of reach. It ended, mercifully, about seven and a half minutes later. The only Prairie

Wolves' goal was Owen's—a lucky bounce sprung him on a breakaway, and he laid a flashy deke on the opposition goalie to spoil his shutout. Few saw it because the arena had largely emptied by then. People had better things to do on a Saturday night than sit around and watch their team get humiliated. Agnes and Jo, though, stuck it out until the bitter end.

On Monday afternoon Owen came into the shop.

"Hey, Ag. You made it to the game." He smiled his trademark smile.

"We did. Which is more than I can say for *your entire team.*"

"That's pretty harsh."

"You guys sucked."

"True. What about my goal, though?"

"What about it?"

"Pretty slick, right?"

Agnes made a face. "You were totally out of position," she said.

"Aw, come on, Ag. It's not like me being *in* position would have made any difference."

"Owen, you're a *centerman.* And you're a goddamn *alternate captain*—you're not supposed to be out there *freelancing* for God's sake."

"You sure know how to hurt a guy, Ag. But that goal was dedicated to you." He winked.

She rolled her eyes.

"Oh, come on, Ag. I can score one for you if I want to."

He was smiling that big smile at her, like a kid, and she couldn't help but smile back, just a little.

"Come again this weekend," he said. "We're at home on Sunday. I guarantee we're going to win!"

"Maybe," she said.

"I'll put you down for two tickets again."

"Okay. Thanks, O."

"Cool," he said. He was still smiling.

She shook her head. Perfect timing: the door opened and Agnes turned to greet the new customer. Owen fiddled with some bracelets on a display rack, and then left.

Owen made good on his guarantee—on Sunday the Prairie Wolves beat the Red Devils of Hawkridge. There were four different goal scorers and Owen had two assists. The one on the power play was especially sweet: a pass through the defenseman's legs to Brennan in the slot.

The team as a whole showed more fire, too. Apparently the Devils were a particularly hated rival, and starting on the very first shift the hits came hard and fast. One particular Red Devil, who—in both size and skating ability—bore a striking resemblance to a silverback gorilla, seemed to be deployed exclusively for the purpose of slamming opposing players into the boards. Some of the Wolves' bigger guys, like Mrkonjic, Hammer, Eichenhaus, and Jorgensen, did their best to counter him, and every time they nailed someone the crowd voiced its approval with a bloodthirsty roar.

The Wolves won more puck battles than they had during last weekend's drubbing, but they were far from dominant. They were lazy about going to the harder areas around the net, where the Devils' D were relentless in their cross-checking, tripping, and general pushing and shoving. But what really bothered Agnes was the way that Owen and his linemate, Brennan, were continually harassed with absolutely no repercussions. Would no one stand up for his teammates? They clearly couldn't rely on the ref to keep gorilla-guy and his accomplices honest.

On D, the Wolves could've really used Vin. He wasn't big, but he was a good skater, a tireless defender, master of the poke check. He'd lean into you, lift your stick, chirp you to distraction, and he blocked shots like crazy. He also had pride and killer instinct—qualities that the Prairie Wolves were severely lacking. Case in point: the Red Devils were missing a couple of their key players, but even so, thanks to their tough play they managed to stage a comeback late in the third and nearly take the game. The Wolves hung on, though, and that was just enough to keep Agnes interested. Tuesday, with her whole day off ahead of her, she decided to go and watch them practice.

Agnes opened the door to the practice rink with anticipation and, yes, even joy. The place was cavernous, cold, and unnaturally white. There was no bright sky, there were no pale, winter sunrays streaming from behind a fringe of dark trees to kiss the tarnished ice, and there was no rough log where you could sit while you pulled on your skates, surrounded by hand-me-down snow boots and shovels and discarded layers of clothing. Rather, the indoor rink was artificially, aggressively clean and empty, the light even and undifferentiated, the space finite and separated from the world outside by a hard membrane.

Though perhaps not beautiful, it seemed entirely right to Agnes. For her, a game of hockey was a whole unto itself, a complete entity encompassing desire, intent, action, and consequence. But although separate from the everyday, it wasn't completely apart. The membrane between was occasionally, curiously, porous.

Agnes appreciated the sensuous beauty of outdoor ice—variable, uncharted, marked only by the elements—but she also loved the clarity and the symmetry of the red lines and blue lines, the circles and dots and hash marks. They lent their own structure, delineated their own universe, in which order could be born of chaos—bounded by certain laws, as was Nature herself—and then be dissolved once more. The indoor hockey rink was like a giant graph on which dramas would be plotted and improvised, commenced and concluded, all in the perpetual-motion aesthetic of the game that was, to Agnes, the most beautiful game on the planet.

But before the game could begin, before the drama could commence, there was practice, and that, for Agnes, was where it all came together—or fell apart. Practice was where bodies and minds learned to accommodate themselves to those laws, those natural laws of hockey. For it was only after the players had absorbed them, and had become secure in their positions and paths, their orbits and trajectories, that the magic of creation could begin.

She stepped inside. A coach was taking shots at one of the goaltenders, easy ones at first, aimed at the glove or the blocker, to get him warmed up. Agnes loved the sound of the puck popping into the glove or bouncing with a thud off the big, rectangular, padded blocker into the corner. To her goalie self, these sounds signified a save made, a puck steered to relative safety. She felt a kinship with the guy behind that big, caged goalie mask—whoever he was—and felt his saves as her own.

Agnes was so absorbed in the goalie's practice that at first she scarcely noticed when Owen and a couple of other guys hopped onto the ice, arranged themselves in a sort of circle, and started snapping a puck around. The clack of puck on stick was musical, though, and she couldn't resist it. Her hands itched for the feel of it. These guys had hard shots, though: hard and fast. Even Owen. Yeah—especially Owen. At the moment, his back was to her, but the force of the guys' passes and the subtle shuffle of their skates to get in position for the next one pushed their circle slowly clockwise, so that soon he'd be looking right at her. She tried to stay out of sight, because she really wasn't sure that she wanted him to know she was there.

Meanwhile, more players emerged from the dressing room. She could see them come trudging down the hall across the ice from where she sat. Some started skating right away, some hit the ice to stretch first, and others eased into the session leaning against the boards, shooting the breeze with their teammates. Little by little the noise increased. Each player added the slithering of his skates, the resonance of his stick meeting a puck, and the thwack of frozen rubber on the boards to the general racket.

After a few minutes of random activity, the boys started their first, lazy, warm-up laps, some working with their sticks as they sailed around the rink, loosening up their hands and wrists.

Their pads, helmets, and practice sweaters sheathed them in exoskeletons of anonymity—even their facial features were bleached out in the glaring light. But Agnes didn't need to see Owen's face or name or number to recognize him on the ice. She'd been secretly in awe of his clean, smooth skating since they were kids, and she'd know it anywhere. He was deceptively fast, and his turns were effortless. He was always square to the play. There was never a flailing arm, never a misplaced motion, just one unbroken, arching, curving line after another, perfectly paced, perfectly balanced. She remembered skating with him when they were younger, trying to match his stride and his movements. She could come close then, but she wouldn't be able to now.

Soon the coaches appeared, and at the whistle the players gathered in a knot around them. Then they lined up to begin the first drill. They worked on breakouts, east-west passing, drop passing, and, finally, defending the two-on-one. *With a D-corps that virtually specializes in giveaways*, thought Agnes, *they'd better pay particular attention to that one!*

For an hour or so she lost herself in the rotating patterns and ceaseless motion. The players shed the cool mien of guyhood to reveal the open, hyper-aware faces of boys and the ferocious abandon of men. They hurled themselves down the ice, an initial giddyap catapulting them forward, skates splayed for maximum bite, arms pumping. Frozen pucks thumped into gloves and clattered along the boards, sticks smacked, bodies banged, men cursed and hollered, the Coach's whistle shrieked, and skates whooshed like a firehose as they skidded to a stop in front of the whiteboard.

Agnes remembered how intensity mounted during a good practice, and how, even as it tired her, it psyched her up for the coming contest. She knew that the boys got each other even more revved up in the room, post-practice, and as ugly as their little pranks and jokes and rituals no doubt were, she imagined that they must also be, paradoxically, beautiful. Beautiful in function, if not in form. But she'd never know for sure.

When the whistle blew for the last time, formal practice was over. The polyphonic clatter thinned as the players started to leave the ice. Agnes stood up and made her way out, too. In the lobby, she glanced across the signs announcing classes and pickup games, and the bulletin board where people posted notices about used hockey gear, lost and found items, and teams forming. Then she buttoned her coat and stepped out into the frozen afternoon.

The door closed behind her. All was still. Back when she used to play, that stillness had been accompanied by a wonderfully loose, post-workout buzz. Today she just felt stiff from sitting so long in the cold air of the rink.

When Owen came into the shop the next day, Jo was in the back and Agnes was behind the counter.

"Hey, Ag," said Owen. "I saw you at practice yesterday."

"Well, yeah, I had the day off."

"Got any pointers?"

She laughed.

He gulped. "You still play?"

"Me? Nah," said Agnes.

"Why not?" he asked.

"Where would I play?"

"I don't know. Pickup?"

Agnes wrinkled her nose. "Too loose. Not like a real game."

"What about a women's league? There's got to be some kind of women's league you could play in."

Agnes didn't answer.

"You're too good for a women's league, eh?"

"I didn't say that," she said.

"You're too *tough* for a women's league. *That* I would believe."

"What? Women aren't tough?"

"I didn't say that."

"Just give it up, Owen."

Owen said, "You're good. You like to play. Why aren't you playing?"

"You wouldn't understand."

"Try me."

"Okay. I *used* to be good. I *used* to play with *you*. The great Owen MacKenzie. Now look at me."

"What do you want?" he asked. "To win the goddamn Stanley Cup?"

"Don't you?" she replied.

He looked puzzled.

"You just don't get it, do you?" she asked. "How would *you* feel if you kept working, training, trying as hard as you could, and everyone around you kept getting bigger, and stronger, and you just stayed the same? I mean, first they put you in goal, and then you're playing with a bunch of girls. *Girls*, dammit! How'd *you* like to have to play with a bunch of girls?"

"I like playing with girls," joked Owen.

She gave him a dirty look.

"I'm sorry, Ag."

"Let's just not talk about it," she said.

"Okay," he agreed. He didn't want to upset her. He wanted to make her laugh again. It had almost knocked him out the first time. But he couldn't think of anything funny to say just now.

He leaned on the counter and looked up at her. In a low voice he asked, "Busy after work?"

"No."

"Have dinner with me, okay?"

She hesitated.

He said, "I want to get your pointers, from practice."

She still didn't answer.

"Come on, Ag." He put his hand on her arm and gave it the gentlest squeeze. "Don't make me beg. That would be embarrassing."

She rolled her eyes. What was this shit he was suddenly laying on so thick? "Okay," she said. "Meet me here at seven. Knock. Loud. The door will be locked and I'll be vacuuming."

"Great! See you then." He stood up straight again and winked at her.

Agnes watched him as he turned and left the store.

"What was *that* all about?" Suddenly Jo was right beside her.

"Nothing."

"Oh, come on. It was like you two were linked by some magnetic force."

"It was not."

"Do you think I'm blind?" asked Jo.

"We're just going to have dinner," said Agnes.

"I thought you didn't want to date him!"

"We're not dating. He just wants to ask me what I thought of their practice yesterday."

"Oh come *on* Agnes! He couldn't care *less* what you thought about their practice! He's all, looking into your eyes and holding your arm and then when I come out here you've got that misty look."

"What?!"

"That *misty* look."

"Bullshit," said Agnes.

"He just asked you out, right? And you said yes, right? That's a *date*! You're dating."

"We're just friends!"

"That's ridiculous!"

"And not even very good friends."

"Shh! Here comes a customer," whispered Jo. "You'd better go to the office and compose yourself."

Agnes didn't move.

"Go!" said Jo to Agnes. Then she turned to the customer. "Can I help you find something, ma'am?"

Agnes went back to the office, closed the door behind her, and put her head down on the desk.

2

"Dad?"

Lazare looked around from under the hood of a car.

"Vincent?" His heart lightened at the sound of Vin's voice, but then it sank like a stone. Vincent wasn't supposed to be here. He was supposed to be nearly four hundred miles to the north, almost as far as Reindeer Lake, working at a mining camp. Something had gone wrong. Lazare sighed, but opened his arms. "Come here, son."

Vin walked into the garage and they embraced.

"What are you doing back here, Vincent?" asked Lazare. Vin was a handsome kid. Like Agnes he had his mother's high cheekbones and pointed chin, but already at twenty-three he looked haggard.

"Dad, I got into some trouble."

"Again? What happened?"

"I couldn't help it. The guys were up to see me. Lance got into it with a guy at a bar. He called us filthy Indians. I had no choice. What am I going to do? Let the guy kill us?"

"What were they thinking, going up there? You had a good deal up there. They should've left you alone."

"They're my friends," said Vin.

"Some friends!"

Lazare looked at Vin and shook his head. When would the boy grow up? He stepped away and leaned over the engine again. He fiddled with the dipstick. His hands were calloused and stiff with the cold. His fingers were stained with grease. His back ached from standing on the hard concrete floor, from twisting awkwardly, from lying on the creeper and straining upwards, day after day after day. But mostly his heart ached from knowing that his son was unsettled and unhappy. He asked Vin, "What are you going to do now?"

"I was hoping you'd have some work for me, until I can find something else."

"I don't know, son. I can't pay you much."

"That's okay," said Vin.

"You'll live at home."

"Thanks, Dad."

"You'll follow my rules."

"Okay."

"Right?" said Dad.

"Yes, Dad."

"Go over to the house and see your grandmother. Get something to eat. Then come back and give me a hand with that outboard over there."

"Thanks, Dad."

"Go on." Lazare shooed him toward the door.

The fast-falling, December darkness was accompanied by a searing cold, but Agnes barely noticed. She was spending more and more of her free time at the rink, and more and more time with Owen. They weren't really dating, but they weren't really *not* dating, either. He seemed intent on making her remember why she liked him, and, predictably, she was falling for it. He was funny, and he laughed a lot. He didn't drink too much—at least not as much as a lot of the other guys did—and he was nice to Jo, too. Sometimes after work Agnes and Jo would go to T.T.'s Tavern to meet up with him and some of the other Prairie Wolves.

One evening Jo came home late after closing up the store.

"Where've you been, Jo?" asked Agnes.

"Guess who stopped by the store just now?" asked Jo.

"I don't know. Who?"

"Come on, guess!"

"Santa Claus?" asked Agnes.

"You're no fun at all," Jo complained. "It was Clay. Clay stopped by the store!"

"Who?"

"You know, Clay—from the Prairie Wolves."

"Oh, yeah. Torris." Agnes wrinkled up her face.

"You don't like him?"

"He's a terrible skater."

"So?"

"So, he needs to work on it."

"I don't care about that," said Jo.

"Maybe you don't, but he should."

"It's just a *game*, Agnes."

Agnes shook her head.

"He asked me out," Jo said.

"You hardly know him."

"You sound like my mother."

"Sorry, but you don't. How old is he?"

"I don't know. We're just going to T.T.'s, anyway."

"Oh."

"Yeah. Are you going?"

"Tonight? Yeah. We were going to go together, remember?"

"Oh yeah." Jo seemed uncomfortable.

"What's wrong?"

"Well, Clay said he'd pick me up."

"Maybe he could give me a ride, too?" asked Agnes. In spite of the cold, she liked being outside and she liked walking to T.T.'s with Jo. It wasn't very far. But it was dark and she didn't want to walk alone.

"I guess I can ask him," said Jo.

"That would be nice."

They finished getting ready and Clay arrived. He wasn't one of the more sparkling personalities on the team. In fact, he wasn't very memorable at all. But now he seemed more lively than Agnes had remembered, and he offered her a ride without Jo having to ask. *A true gentleman*, thought Agnes.

When they got to his car, Jo started to get into the back seat with Agnes.

"Sit up here with me," Clay said, patting the seat beside him.

"Okay," said Jo, and she slid out of the back seat and moved to the front.

Clay turned the key in the ignition and revved the motor. "So you're really into hockey, eh?" Clay asked, looking at Agnes through the rearview mirror.

"Why do you ask?" said Agnes.

"I've seen you at games and practices. Most of the girls just come to the bars afterwards," said Clay.

"She used to play," said Jo.

"Oh yeah?" he said.

"Yeah," said Agnes.

"You didn't play, did you Josie?" asked Clay.

"No. I did some figure skating when I was little," said Jo.

"Hockey's more of a man's sport," said Clay.

"Yeah," agreed Jo.

Agnes winced. She had just as much right to play hockey as anyone else, but she didn't feel like arguing with Jo's new flame. They couldn't get to T.T.'s soon enough for her liking.

T.T.'s was far from the only bar in town, but it was the tavern of choice for the Prairie Wolves hockey team. The place was dark, with colorful neon beer signs shining in the big, plate glass window, a jukebox, and an old-fashioned, wooden bar along the wall. The Wolves typically commandeered three or four of the large, round tables, which they'd pull together and surround with dozens of T.T.'s knobby wooden chairs. Then, having left their mark on the décor, they'd turn their attention to the evening's business: celebrating, commiserating, or simply forgetting about previous or upcoming games, picking up girls, and eating. Not coincidentally, T.T.'s was one of the few bars in town that served a full menu up until closing time.

When they walked through the door, Agnes saw Owen stand up and wave her over.

"Do you want a beer?" he asked.

"Sure, thanks, O."

When he got back with the beers, Agnes asked him what he knew about Clay.

"He's okay," Owen told her.

"Really? He orders Jo around. And he said that hockey is a man's sport."

"A lot of people think that. That doesn't mean he's some kind of axe-murderer."

"No, but it might mean that he's a jerk."

"Jo seems to like him," said Owen.

"She doesn't know any better."

"That's a nice thing to say about your friend!"

"Look, O. I love Jo. I really do. She's the greatest. But she has bad instincts when it comes to guys. Are you sure he's okay?"

"Sorry, Ag, I don't really know him. He's only been around a couple months."

"Hey, Mac, what's goin' *down*?" Jamie Barber, also known as Barbie, his hockey nickname, swung a chair around and pulled it up behind Agnes and Owen.

"Not much, brotha." Agnes didn't know where the *gangsta* act came from, but in any case Jamie couldn't get enough of it, and Owen played along. Jamie was a good guy, though—he was the Wolves' captain and deservedly so. He was older than most of the guys, and he wasn't flashy, but he always seemed to have matters in hand. And most importantly, he had heart.

"Now that was a *game*, last night, eh?" said Jamie. The Wolves had just returned from a road trip. They'd lost the first two games, staged a comeback in the third period of the third game, and won it 4–2—although the fourth goal was an empty-netter.

"Yeah, you and me, man, we da bomb." They high-fived each other.

Agnes rolled her eyes. From what she'd heard they'd mostly played badly, and based on what she knew about hockey players—which was probably more than any self-respecting girl should—they'd no doubt embarrassed themselves *off* the ice as well.

Jamie continued. "Did you hear Stanton got called up?"

"No way. Old Stanislav?" answered Owen.

"Haha, that's right."

"Two months into the season and it's bottom of the barrel for the Bandits!" They laughed, but then Owen continued more seriously, "He's got a wicked shot, though."

"Yeah, the sneaky bastard. He always seems to be in the right place at the right time," said Jamie.

"He's not afraid to *go* to the right place," said Agnes.

"True," said Jamie.

"He probably actually *works* on his shot," said Agnes.

"I bet he does," said Jamie.

"Thank God *you're* not our coach, Ag," said Owen, "or we'd be having shooting practice right here in the bar!" He was laughing, so she just rolled her eyes.

"She's coaching you, though, eh Mac?" Jamie winked at Owen. "Go hard to the net, buddy, that's my advice."

Agnes just shook her head. It was standard fare, and coming from Jamie, it was all in good fun. Never mind that she and Owen weren't *actually* dating.

Jo and Clay came over from the bar, beers in hand. Clay had a shot glass, too.

"Hey, guys," said Jo.

"Hey Jo," said Owen. "By the way, I'm driving home for Christmas. Do you want a ride? Ag's coming, too."

"Well, okay, Owen, yeah. Depending on my work schedule. Thanks."

"I'll reserve a seat for you." He grinned.

"Hey, Torris, did you hear old Stanislav's getting called up?" Jamie yelled up at Clay. The jukebox had just come on and the place was getting loud.

"Yeah, I heard Darnwell's got a separated shoulder," Clay yelled back.

"Ouch!" said Owen.

"I wanna get called up too," cried Jamie.

"Ain't gonna happen," said Clay.

"True," Jamie admitted. "You're first in line, Macker," he said to Owen.

"Then he'd better get his shit together," said Agnes.

"Whoa, you really are a slave driver," Jamie said to her. "She's all whips and chains, eh boy?" He gave Owen a playful shove.

"Yeah, yeah. You got me there," said Owen, turning a little pink.

At least he had the decency to be embarrassed, thought Agnes, but only because she was sitting right next to him. One-track minds, these boys had. No wonder most of them ended up going nowhere.

When Owen walked Agnes home later, he asked, "So I need to get my shit together, eh?"

"Yes, you do," Agnes said.

"You don't mince words, do you?"

"Do you want me to?"

"Sometimes it might be nice," said Owen.

"Okay. You're a rock star, O, a fucking rock star. That's why your name's engraved on the Stanley Cup."

"Oh, come on, I mean, I'm a good player."

"Sure you are, O. You're a really good player. Probably the best on the whole entire team."

"Do you think?" he asked.

Agnes smirked. "O, you really shouldn't drink so much."

"You're all about what I should and shouldn't do, aren't you?"

"Someone's got to keep you in line."

"Okay, coach, so tell me, what should I work on?"

"You could work on your shot, like Stanton."

"I do. All the time."

"Okay, you could work on positioning. Get yourself back quicker on D."

"You're talking about the other night—"

"You give up too many chances."

"I'm an offensive player, Ag."

"Bullshit. It's a weakness. You've got to work on it. It's not going to fly in the NHL."

"Jesus, Ag."

They stopped in front of her building.

"Are you going to make it home okay?" she asked him.

"Nah, I'm pretty fucked up. I'd better stay at your place tonight," said Owen.

"Fat chance."

She did kiss him on the cheek, though, a quick one on her tiptoes, and then she skipped up the stairs to the apartment, smiling to herself. She got into her pajamas, turned on the TV, and curled up on the sofa.

When the sound of the key in the lock woke her, it was almost three o'clock in the morning.

"Jo?"

"Oh, hey Agnes."

"You're home late."

"Yeah."

"Everything ok?"

"Yeah."

"Really?"

"Yeah."

"I guess I'll go to bed," said Agnes, getting up and turning off the TV.

"Goodnight, Agnes," said Jo.

"Goodnight."

"Oh, Agnes?" said Jo. "I think I'm going to stay here for Christmas."

"What?"

"I can get some work done on that repeating fabric designs project."

"Really, Jo? You were just telling me how excited you are to see your new niece."

"Yeah, but—"

"What's the real reason?" asked Agnes.

"I just told you. I've got work to do."

"Bullshit."

"Okay. Clay's brother and his wife live over in Belfort. Clay wants me to go to their place with him."

"But you hardly know him."

"I know."

"Jo, don't do it."

"He says he'll miss me," said Jo.

"You just started dating, like, today. How much could he miss you? He's a grown man. He'll be okay without you for a couple of days."

"I don't know."

"Besides, your parents will *really* miss you if you don't come home."

"I guess maybe you're right. I'll have to tell him. I don't think he'll like it."

"Too bad," said Agnes. "He'll get over it."

Agnes looked out through the windshield and smiled to herself. It felt good to be on the road, her eyes aimed northward with nothing to block their view. Back in town, the clouds were gray, but out here in the early prairie twilight they were smoky blue and the snow beneath them shone white and pure. Blasts of wind kicked up the powder and shook the occasional stand of naked trees like the angry brooms of a witches' coven. The car, too, shuddered, even as it motored on, a speeding comet in a darkening cosmos.

She was on her way home for Christmas. Soon she'd be eating Kookum's bannock, meatballs, and stew, stomping her feet to the rhythmic scraping of Uncle Bert's fiddle, and basking in the color and light that was Christmas at home. Vin would be there, too. His job up north had fallen through, which was too bad, but the upside was that he'd be home the whole time that she was there. She was proud of the vest she'd made for him. Maybe he would wear it on Christmas Day.

Jo was acting more like herself than she had for a while, and Agnes was relieved. They'd barely left town, and she'd already achieved full motor-mouth mode. Her barrage of questions, thought Agnes, was like the first shift of a hockey game: the opponent comes out hard, cycles the puck, and pounds shot after shot on goal. The defending team is pinned in its end, forced to block the hard shots, the players' legs turning to jelly, trying vainly to clear, to put an end to the mauling. But for once Agnes wasn't in goal—Owen was. And he was doing well, actually, managing to give an answer, however noncommittal, for just about everything Jo could shoot his way.

"Too bad about yesterday, Owen," began Jo.

"Yeah," O said.

"I mean, I hate that Dubchek guy."

"Yeah. He's tough to play against."

"Did you see him push Marcel?"

"Uh, no, I'm not sure," said Owen.

"He just pushed him right over."

"Yeah, that happens."

"Doesn't that make you mad?" asked Jo.

"Well, it's not really my job to get mad," he offered.

Jo fell silent, briefly. Then she asked, "Which team do you think is better, the Mercuries or the Miners?"

"Um, well, the Mercuries are rivals. They play real hard against us," answered Owen. "The Miners have a better record, though, I think. So I don't know."

Jo continued, "It's kind of not fair. I mean, if Sal hadn't broken his stick they probably wouldn't have scored that last goal."

"Yeah, maybe not," said Owen.

"Doesn't that make you mad?"

"Well, guys'll take advantage, when something like that happens. I'd do the same thing. It's part of the game. Anyhow, we didn't know it was going to be the game winner."

"Hmm," said Jo. "What was wrong with it, anyhow?"

"With what?"

"The stick," she said.

"Oh. I don't know," said Owen. "Maybe he leaned on it too hard. Maybe it had a crack in it from before. Maybe someone slashed him."

"Shouldn't he have checked it before he played with it?" asked Jo.

"Well—"

"I can't believe they just keep playing even if someone's stick is broken! It just doesn't seem fair."

Owen said, "It's just part of the game."

"What if someone tripped on it?" asked Jo.

"That never happens," said Owen.

"But it was just lying there for the longest time."

"Yeah, they're not going to stop play just for that," said Owen.

"I guess you just have to skate around it."

"Yeah."

"But, Owen, what I don't get is—"

Jo must have known less about hockey than anyone in the western hemisphere. Her questions kept coming, and Owen kept answering. He had the patience of a saint—Agnes would have cracked long ago. Finally Jo lapsed into silence, and all they could hear was the hum of the engine and the prairie bluster jostling the car. The town was far behind them now. The clouds had broken up some, and a couple of stray ones hung like giant puffs of smoke in the light of the rising moon.

Agnes leaned her head back. She wanted to turn and look at Owen, but she also didn't want to. And anyhow, she didn't really need to look at him to see him. She could sense his easy breath and the beam of his clear, gray eyes on the flat runway of the road. She could see him draw his fingers through the wave of sandy hair that spilled across his forehead, rest his elbow on the door, and curl his long, bony fingers around the steering wheel.

Jo's voice came from the backseat. "Are you asleep, Agnes?"

"No. Are you?" Agnes answered.

Jo giggled, but she didn't follow up with another question.

The frigid wind spit furiously through every seam of the car.

After a while Owen said, "Hey, Ag?" He said it quietly, just to her.

"Yeah?"

"Remember when we drove out to Sebby's parents' place that weekend, for that graduation party?"

"Yeah."

She waited for him to say something about it, but he didn't. Finally she asked, "What about it?"

He took his time answering. "That was a good trip," he said.

"Yeah," she whispered, and she stole a quick, sideways glance at him. It was dark now, and she could only see fragments of his face in the moving patches of reflected light. Still, she could see that he was smiling. Not that crazy, lopsided smile. Just a small, quiet one. She looked away again and sank into the darkness, glad that he was busy at the wheel.

Anyhow, it was only the driving that made him remember that other drive, to Sebby's parents' place by the lake. Otherwise, he wasn't the kind of guy who'd remember the tender glint of the water in the long twilight, the jolt of electricity as her eyes met his, or the warmth of his hand on the small of her back. He wasn't the kind of guy who'd remember things like that. He was a hockey player, for God's sake.

Owen dropped Jo off first, and then drove the few blocks to Agnes's street. Agnes recognized Uncle Bert's car and cousin Gene's old pickup parked in front. Owen stopped in front of a neighbor's house and got out of the car. Even though Agnes's bag wasn't at all big or heavy, he grabbed it out of the trunk for her.

"Thanks," Agnes said, reaching out to take it from him.

"I've got it, Ag," he said. But he didn't close the trunk and he didn't start walking toward the house. He just stood there.

"Thanks for the ride, O," Agnes said.

"Sure thing. Hey, I was thinking, do you want to go for a skate?"

"Now? It's kind of dark for skating, isn't it?"

"Our rink is pretty well lit."

She'd almost forgotten about Owen's backyard rink. When they were younger they'd always skated on the pond in the little patch of woods at the end of his street. It was easy to get to for Agnes and Vin, because their house was just on the other side of the trees, and there was a path that went straight through. But when Owen and his brother Evan got to be teenagers, they figured out how to build a rink in their own yard. Agnes had rarely skated with them there. Evan must have put it up without Owen's help this year.

"It'll be fun. Get your skates," said Owen.

"Um, I want to hang out with my family for a bit," said Agnes. "I want to see Vin. I haven't seen him in ages."

"Okay, I can pick you up later," said Owen. "Just call me when you're ready."

Agnes considered.

"Come on, Ag," Owen said. "It'll be fun. It was a long drive. I want to stretch out a little."

"But why do you need me?"

"Gosh, Ag, I don't know. I don't *need* you, I guess, I just . . . want your company. I think it would be fun, that's all."

"Okay, O. But you don't have to pick me up. I'll borrow Dad's car and drive over later."

Owen closed the trunk, and they walked to her door. He didn't wait around to say hi to Kookum, or Dad. He put her bag down on the stoop and gave her a clumsy hug. "Merry Christmas, Ag."

"Merry Christmas," she answered. He was already jogging down the shoveled driveway to the street.

Agnes opened the door and took a deep breath. She smelled bannock baking and stew simmering in the big iron pot. Everything was scrubbed clean for the holiday. The big brown sofa sat against the wall to her right, its cushions full and fluffed. On it were three smaller cushions that Agnes had made covers for last year, trimmed with beads and appliquéd in cheerful red ribbon. Dad's armchair sat near the head of the sofa with a striped blanket folded over one of the arms. The woven rag rug had been newly beaten—its colors were rich in the lamplight. But the room was empty and the Christmas tree stood bare and lonely in front of the window, the boxes of ornaments unopened. Agnes heard voices in the kitchen.

"Hello!" she called out. Kookum came hurrying out to greet her.

"Welcome home, Agnes," she said. She put her hands on Agnes's shoulders. "How was the drive? Are you tired?"

Agnes kissed her grandmother's soft, wrinkled cheeks. "No, I'm fine, Kookum. Merry Christmas."

"Merry Christmas," Kookum replied. "Come into the kitchen, Agnes."

Agnes left her jacket on a chair and followed her. Uncle Bert, Dad's brother, was sitting with Dad at the table, his hand wrapped around a mug of coffee, and cousin Gene was standing next to him. Dad stood up.

"Agnes, I'm glad you're home. It's a joy to see you," he said. He took her head in his rough hands and kissed both her cheeks.

Bert and Gene also greeted her. Gene was like a brother. His mother was Agnes's auntie, her mother's sister. He and Vin had been especially close when they were younger. In fact, Vin had lived for a while with Gene's family at Catfish River. But Vin was conspicuously absent now.

"Where's Vin?" Agnes asked.

Dad turned to sit down again. "He went down to Barney's with some of his friends."

"Not with Lance, and those guys?" said Agnes.

"Yes. You know how he is, he likes to go out and celebrate, with his friends."

Agnes felt a flash of anger. "I'm not a little girl, anymore, Dad," she said. "I'm almost twenty-one. I know what he's doing and it's *not* celebrating. He's got nothing to celebrate. And they aren't his friends. They're just a bunch of losers he *calls* his friends."

"Agnes," said Dad.

"It's the truth," she said. "You know it. You all know it." She looked around at them. Bert and Gene looked kind of embarrassed. She turned back to Dad. "Why'd you let him go? I *really* wanted to see him. I haven't seen him in *ages*. But by the time he gets back he'll be—"

"I'm gonna go, uncle," said cousin Gene to Dad. "They're probably still at Barney's place. I'm going to go down there and get him."

"No, Gene," said Dad.

Agnes's heart went out to Gene. "I'll go with you," she said to him.

"No you won't," said Dad.

"I want to see him," said Agnes.

"Agnes, you're as tough as anyone but you don't want to get mixed up with that bunch, trust me," said Gene.

"Gene's right," said Dad. "Agnes, I know you're not a little girl anymore. But Vin—"

"I wanted to see him. Doesn't he care about me?" Agnes asked.

"Of course he does, Agnes," said Dad. "Boys," he continued, looking at Gene and Bert, "leave Vincent be. Go home to your own families. Vincent knows it's Christmas. He knows Agnes is here."

Dad stood up, which meant that it was time for Gene and Bert to go. They wished Kookum and Agnes goodnight and let Dad walk them to the door. They embraced.

"Goodnight," said Dad. "See you tomorrow." They walked out and he closed the door behind them.

"Agnes, get cleaned up and we'll have some dinner," said Kookum. "There's a whole pot of stew here that wants to be eaten."

The three of them ate, silently, and then Agnes cleared the table. Dad and Kookum sat talking together, but Agnes made sure that the sounds of the water and the plates and silverware clanging together drowned out their voices. She didn't want to hear their lame talk. The white suds puffed up in the sink, glistening like the shop-window snow back in Wapahaska, its hills and valleys filled with storybook villages and happy children and mothers carrying packages. When Agnes looked up, though, she was staring into the dark window over the sink and the reflection of her own scowling face, framed by sadly cheerful red curtains.

When Dad hugged her goodnight, Agnes didn't even feel like hugging him back. She didn't know who had disappointed her more: Vin, who, even if he did come back from Barney's sober, which wasn't likely, had already ruined their Christmas, or Dad, for letting it be this way.

Agnes and Kookum were left to decorate the Christmas tree. As Agnes hung the lights she remembered some of Vin's past "celebrations" with Lance and the boys. Like variations on a theme, they all followed the same basic storyline. A couple of years ago the car they'd been riding in slid off the road, careened through some brush, and slammed into a tree. Luckily the car hadn't been going very fast, and no one had been seriously hurt, but they'd frozen half to death before they woke from their drunken stupors. They were lucky the R.C.M.P. happened to spot them— lucky to spend the night in jail. Another time they'd been drinking down in Barney's uncle's shed and they'd managed to set the place on fire, destroying a boat the uncle had been building. Vin had needed to work to pay him back, and that had taken the place of training that summer. It had killed Vin's ambition as far as hockey was concerned, and in the years since he'd found nothing to replace it.

Kookum knew what Agnes was thinking about. "Your father's right, Agnes," she said. "Vin has to find his own way."

"But Kookum, I just want us all to be together. Why does he have to do this to us?"

"He's not doing it intentionally, dear."

"I'm worried about him, Kookum."

"I am too."

Kookum opened a box of glass ornaments and they began to hang them on the tree.

"He's a lot like mom, isn't he?"

"In some ways he is. And that's not a bad thing. She was a good person, Agnes, but she had it hard. Vin's had so much love. From your father, from me, and from you, too. And from your mother. One day he'll learn to draw on that love."

Agnes sighed. She wanted to believe what Kookum said. She just couldn't see a clear path from where Vin was now, to where he ought to be. And Vin himself—was he even looking for a path? Or was he content to drift wherever the prevailing winds might take him?

Kookum said, "Tell me about life in town, Agnes."

"There isn't much to tell."

"How is Jo?"

"She's working hard in school. She's dating this guy, Clay Torris."

"Oh? What's he like?"

"I don't know. I don't get a good feeling from him."

"Are you playing?"

"No, Kookum. You know I'm not. I left my gear here."

"That's a shame."

"There's no point in playing anymore," said Agnes.

"It's not all about *points*, you know," said Kookum.

Agnes chuckled. She said, "I mean, it was getting me nowhere."

"I can't imagine that," answered Kookum. "Everything leads *somewhere*. And you seem so much happier when you're playing."

Agnes shrugged. "I don't know."

"But you did call Owen."

"I ran into him by accident."

"Owen is a good boy."

"He has his moments."

"It was nice of him to drive you girls home."

"He's good with things like that," said Agnes. "And he was driving up here anyway. He didn't have to go out of his way or anything."

She opened another box of ornaments. "Kookum, why do you always try to get me together with Owen?"

"I'm not trying to get you together with him, dear. You were close already as children. Janet's been a good friend for many years. She raised her boys to be kind and thoughtful. Hardworking. You're a smart girl, a talented girl. Owen is the kind of boy you should be with."

"But he's not exactly the way you think he is. He's not even very mature."

"He's young, dear," said Kookum. "So are you."

"I don't feel young," said Agnes.

Kookum laughed. "You're not old enough to know what young is," she said. "You have things that weigh on your heart. We all do. But you have plenty of time to grow. And so does Owen."

They set aside the empty ornament boxes and Kookum went to put on her nightgown.

"Are you coming to bed, dear?" she asked.

Agnes and Kookum shared one of the two bedrooms in the small house, and Dad had the other. Vin had always slept in the attic.

Agnes asked, "Kookum, do you think Dad would mind if I borrowed his car? Owen invited me to go skating tonight."

Kookum looked at her. "That sounds lovely, Agnes. You go right ahead and take the car. I'll explain to your father."

"Thanks, Kookum."

"Thank you for helping with the tree, Agnes. And try not to worry about your brother. He's a good boy, too, at heart. He'll find his way."

"I hope so."

"Now go enjoy yourself, dear."

Owen had lived in the same house for as long as he could remember: a square little bungalow with a triangle roof. Nothing fancy—just a regular house, the same as all the others on the street. Mom had a sewing room in the attic, under the peak of the roof, and when she wasn't at work or doing housework, she liked to sit there and sew or knit, and look out onto the street. Dad was usually in his basement workshop—that is, when he wasn't deploying snowplows or trash trucks or other utility vehicles for the village. Tonight, yellow light shone through the curtains in the front window, the bushes were trimmed with multi-colored lights, and a wreath with a red ribbon hung on the door. The roof was frosted in white.

Owen parked on the street so as not to block the family car in the driveway, grabbed his bag from the trunk, and walked around back—no one who knew the family ever used the front door. The side of the house was dark and the rink lights were off. Evan must be out somewhere. Owen crunched through the snow and up the four steps to the back porch. He flipped the switch and the rink lights came on. As always, the door was unlocked and he pushed his way in. The dark kitchen tunneled him toward the glow of the living room where his parents sat waiting for him.

"Owen!" said Mom. "Welcome home!" She was built tall and lanky, like he was, and she had his sandy hair and gray eyes.

He hugged her and greeted his dad with a handshake and a quick embrace.

"How was the drive, son?" asked Dad.

"Easy," said Owen.

"Can I make you a sandwich?" asked Mom.

"No, thanks. I can do it."

His parents followed him into the kitchen. Dad asked him a couple of questions about the team, but he soon said goodnight. Mom stayed to talk for a few minutes.

"Did you end up driving the girls, too?" Mom asked.

"Yeah," said Owen.

"I'm sure they appreciated it," she said.

"Doesn't make sense for them to buy bus tickets when I'm driving up here anyway," said Owen. "And the bus takes about three times as long. How are things here?" he asked.

"Everything's fine. Evan's doing well. He's loving the apprenticeship—and the money. He's out spending it now, I guess." She smiled. "He's been spending a lot of time with Cindy—you know, Tommy's sister."

"Oh. Nice. What about you, Mom?" asked Owen.

"Keeping busy," she said. "You know, this is always a hectic time at work." Mom was a social worker, and people's problems always seemed to come to a head around Christmas. "How are you?"

"Good," he answered.

"Are you happy with your playing?"

"It's getting there."

"What about the other guys?"

"They're alright."

"I can see I'm not going to get much information out of you tonight," she said, smiling. Sometimes Mom still treated him like a little boy, but he didn't really mind it. "How's Agnes?"

"She's fine."

"Sophie was a little worried about her moving away from home."

"I think she's doing okay, Mom," Owen said.

"That's good. You'll keep an eye on her, right?"

Owen snorted.

"What?" Mom asked.

"You have no idea how pissed off she'd be if she thought I was, like, *keeping an eye on her.*"

"It's just what friends do," said Mom. "Anyhow, she's more like family, really, isn't she? I know I didn't even need to ask you."

"No, you didn't," he said.

"Well, remember to turn off the rink lights when you come up. I'm going to bed."

"Yeah. Goodnight, Mom."

Owen fixed himself a sandwich and poured a glass of milk. He sat down at the kitchen table, looking at the lit rink through the glass panes of the back door. He felt like he was still on the road—the seconds ticking by on the kitchen clock were like the telephone poles zipping past on the highway.

Funny that the weekend at Sebby's parents' place had popped into his head. It was a long time ago, now. He'd planned to go with Sherry, his girlfriend at the time. But it had turned out that she couldn't go until the next day, so she'd arranged to get a ride with someone else and he'd been left to drive a couple of the guys. It had been Mom's idea to ask Agnes if she needed a ride. By then, Agnes had been playing on girls' teams for a couple of years and they hardly ever saw each other. When she'd slid into the passenger seat beside him, though, the whole car had filled up with her. She wasn't very chatty, or even very nice—not in the way that most girls were—but when he'd managed to make her laugh it was like the sun coming out from behind a cloud. She'd made him forget about Sherry, that was for sure. Even though Sherry had shown up the next day, he couldn't remember anything he'd done with her. All he remembered from that weekend was Agnes.

The first thing had happened that night, soon after they arrived. He dropped his stuff in the cabin and walked down to the shore right away. He took off his shoes stood at the lake's edge, his feet going numb in the icy water. He heard a twig snap, and when he looked around, he saw Agnes coming out of the woods. She didn't see him. She pulled her sweatshirt over her head and dropped it in the sand. Then she pulled her white tank top, which had hiked up a bit, back down over her stomach. She stepped out of her shoes and bent over, her bare arms reaching down to roll up her jeans. Her long, jet-black hair fell in a heavy mass, its ends brushing the earth. When she stood up and swung it back again the sunlight fell on her, and she seemed to catch fire. Maybe she felt his involuntary reaction, because she suddenly turned toward him. Their eyes met.

And that was it. Nothing else happened. He was frozen in place, and she looked away again and waded a short distance into the pool of molten silver that was the lake. She splashed it onto her arms and face. Then she stood up again, and they both just stayed where they were, staring out at the long, straight line where the water meets the sky, listening to the birds' goodnight calls. Neither one of them said anything. Time just sort of stopped, as if nothing had come before, and nothing would come after. It was just *now*. After a while, though, she turned and waded back to shore, the water swirling around her feet. She picked up her shoes and sweatshirt and walked back into the woods. He followed a minute later, thinking he might catch up with her along the path, but she was too fast for him.

The next morning a bunch of them went out for a swim. During a game of keep-away she caught the ball and he challenged her, grabbing her bare mid-section under the water and then dunking her by leaning on her shoulder while she tried to hold the ball away from him. He got the ball, of course—his reach was much longer than hers—but somehow she managed to grab him and slam her foot into him. Lucky for him it was underwater, where she couldn't generate much force, and, even luckier, she missed his private parts, where she could have done some damage anyway. When she popped up out of the water, wet and sputtering, she'd grabbed him by his hair, pulled his face close up to hers, and hissed, "Don't you *ever* do that again." Someone had yelled at him to throw the ball, and he must have thrown it to someone, but he couldn't remember. It was like he'd blacked out.

Later that night, though, at the bonfire, he found himself walking around behind her for some reason, and without even thinking he put his hand on the small of her back as he passed. She spun around so quickly that he half expected her to kick him again, with more painful results than before. It would have been worth it, but she didn't. She just gave him a look and turned away.

Then, of course, he had to get back to Sherry, and the next day Sherry rode home with him, and Agnes rode with someone else, and after that everything changed. He went off to some hockey camp, and then away to juniors, and Agnes—well, he wasn't exactly sure what she did next.

He was done eating his sandwich, so he put his dishes in the sink, grabbed his jacket and hat and gloves, and stepped out onto the back porch. He pulled the snow shovel and his old skates from the familiar jumble of winter gear by the back door and headed down the stairs to the ice.

Agnes drove around the block once. Sure enough, the light was on in Owen's backyard, and she could see him, a tall, dark figure, alone on the ice. She drove around the block again, parked a couple of houses down, grabbed her skates out of the car, and walked along the edge of the road. When she was still hidden in the shadow of the neighbor's trees, she stopped. Owen was skating, his hands in his pockets, lazy and nonchalant. Without the bulky hockey gear, he just looked like himself, and you could see how agile he was. Every twist of his torso, every shift of his hips and shoulders, every turn of his head propelled him precisely. A series of smooth, twirling turns sent him one way, and some flashy, staccato crossovers brought him back. He tried a figure-skating spin, and even a little loop jump, and then he glided, his slender frame floating in the fuzzy light, waiting for another move to take him.

The clean, scraping sounds of his blades brushed against her face like whispers. She wanted to call to him, to walk over and join him, as if everything was as smooth and silvery in her world as it was in his. But she couldn't pretend and she couldn't lie to him: her ice was different. It was like the corner ice, where the gate opens for the zamboni. It was uneven and stained with dirt from the outside. She didn't want him to see that rough, ugly ice. If he did, he'd never want to skate with her again.

The cold clawed at her face. One layer at a time, it crept beneath her clothing, too, through her flesh and into her bones. But she couldn't walk away while Owen was still out here, waiting for her. So she waited for him. Finally, after what seemed like hours, he slid to a stop and stepped out of the rink. She heard him up on the porch, saw the darkness settle as the rink lights went off, heard the door open—raspy and grating on the ice-crusted porch floor—and then heard it close. Then she turned around and walked back to the car.

Towards morning there was a pounding on the door. Kookum or Dad must've been up already because right away Agnes heard the door open, and she heard voices. She could see that Kookum's bed was empty, so she got up and peeked into the living room. As she stood there in the dim light a mass of cold air slithered through the open front door and across the floor, settling around her legs like a snowdrift. She shivered.

Dad's friend Carl Beamer stood stooped over in the doorway. He'd retired from the R.C.M.P. years ago, but he still looked out for his neighbors—especially those who, like Dad, had been so welcoming when he was first posted here. And since he'd shed his official status, he'd come to be appreciated by nearly everyone. Even Vin, who hated all policemen, respected Carl Beamer. Now Vin was draped over him like the old bearskin that cousin Gene's dad always bragged about—the one he'd shot that winter up by the Narrows when he was just a kid. Vin's left arm hung down over Carl Beamer's left shoulder, and his head dangled over the right. Dad was pulling Vin's arm over his own shoulders, in order to transfer the boy's weight onto himself on that side. Vin's eyelids fluttered open and closed. His hair was matted and his face smeared with blood. There was a brown splatter down his shirt, which was torn apart at one shoulder. He wasn't even wearing a coat. Dad and Carl Beamer dragged Vin across the small room and lowered him onto the sofa. Kookum kept his head from slamming down onto the armrest and arranged a cushion beneath it.

It sounded like Vin was trying to say something, but his mouth couldn't form the words.

"Where'd you find him, Carl?" Dad was asking, real softly, so that Agnes could barely hear him.

"Down in front of Hale's," answered Carl Beamer. "Whoever was with him ran off when they heard us coming. He knows his name, knows his address. Don't think he's hurt too bad. Might want to get him checked out, though."

"Carl, thank you," said Dad. He took Carl's hand as if to shake it, but then his left hand followed the right and he just held Carl's hand for a moment, in both of his, and looked at him. It didn't seem to make Carl uncomfortable in the slightest. He had a good heart.

"Would you like a cup of coffee, Carl?" Kookum asked.

"No, thank you, Miss Sophie. I'd better get home."

Carl left and Agnes went back into her room to put on some clothes. When she came back into the living room Dad was starting a fire. Kookum was cleaning the blood off of Vin's face.

"Let me do that, Kookum," said Agnes.

"Agnes. I didn't know you were up." She handed her the washcloth. "I'll make some coffee."

Agnes pulled a chair over and sat down next to Vin. The bruise on his cheekbone was dark purple and his blood had congealed into a dark, sticky paste where it had oozed through the broken skin. He didn't even flinch when Agnes dabbed at it. The bruise over his left eye was bigger and rounder—a big blue bump, really, as if he'd been struck with a blunt object. His lip was split and so swollen that it looked like it would burst open again. Otherwise his face was smooth and relaxed, like a sleeping child's. Agnes was sorry that she'd felt so angry with him. She stroked the thick, black hair that stood up from his scalp like soft bristles. She got her hairbrush from the bedroom and worked it tenderly through the matted parts. When she got around to a spot on the right side, he suddenly jerked away from her.

"Sorry, Vin, I'm sorry," she whispered. His eyes were open now, but they had a strange, empty look. She said, "Vin, it's me, Agnes. Are you okay?"

"Agnes, yeah, I'm alright," he whispered. He smiled a little bit.

"Vin, did you hit your head?" she asked.

His eyes closed again.

"Dad, look," said Agnes.

Dad came over and Agnes parted Vin's hair so Dad could see the big bump on the side of his head, just above his right ear.

Dad shook his head. He bent over and put his hand on Vin's chest, his face right up close to his son's. "Vincent?" he said. "Son, can you hear me?"

Vin just kept on sleeping.

✳

When Owen picked Agnes up for the drive back to Wapahaska, Jo was already in the car. That's how Agnes knew she had hurt him. He didn't want to have to talk with her alone.

"Did you have a good Christmas?" That was all he said when he took her things and threw them into the trunk. He didn't even comment on the extra bag and the hockey sticks. She got a huge lump in her throat and had to try hard not to cry.

She had planned what she would say. She would tell him that she was embarrassed for him to see her skate, because he was such a good skater and she hadn't skated in so long. Of course, it was bullshit, but it might have allowed for some feeling of normalcy between them. But that was all before Carl Beamer had dragged Vin home in the middle of the night, bloody and unconscious.

Vin was in bad shape even now, more than twenty-four hours later. He'd barely gotten up from the sofa and he hadn't eaten at all. She'd insisted on sitting with him through most of the night in case his mind suddenly cleared, so she was dead tired. She could still see his bruised face and his fluttering eyelids that tried and tried again to open, but in the end stayed shut.

Agnes didn't want to talk about Vin, and she didn't know what else to say. She finally remembered to ask Jo about her new baby niece, but then fell back into silence, barely noting Jo's reply. The three-hour drive was so tense that even Jo didn't say much of anything. By the time Owen finally stopped the car in front of their building, tears were coursing down Agnes's cheeks and she just sat there, trembling, her lips pressed together, until Jo had gone upstairs. Then she got out of the car and walked over to Owen, who was standing by the open trunk.

"O, I'm sorry," she whispered.

"It's okay," he answered.

"No. I really wanted to skate with you, O. I really did."

She looked up at him. He didn't even look like himself. It was like he was all twisted up. Maybe it was because she was looking at him through her tears.

"I was worried about Vin. He went off somewhere with those loser friends of his and Dad didn't know what to do. And it was Christmas, and all. I didn't want to ruin it for you, too. And then they brought him home all bloody and he had this big bump on his head. He hardly even knew me." She dropped her head into her hands and started to sob.

Owen put his arms around her and pulled her close. "Don't cry, Ag. It's okay."

"No, it's not okay. You don't even know. I'm sorry, O. I'm sorry for everything. I just don't want to ruin it for you," she said, her words muffled in his embrace.

"Ruin what for me? You don't know what you're saying," said Owen. "Take a breath. It's okay."

Owen's words just made her cry even more, her face buried in his old, soft sweatshirt. But he just kept holding her, rocking her back and forth real gently, like a baby, and after a while she started to calm down. She wanted to stay there forever, feeling his heart beating and his arms tight around her.

"Take a breath, Ag," he said again. "It's going to be okay."

She looked up at him. Her eyelashes had little sparkling teardrops in them. She said, "Owen, you're not wearing a coat. You'll get cold out here."

"Not while I'm holding you," he said.

Her tears welled up again.

"I love you, Ag."

She shook her head. "No, you don't."

He loosened his hold on her. "Go on, Ag. Go inside and get some rest."

She pulled her bags and sticks out of the trunk. "I'm sorry, O."

"It's okay. See ya."

"Yeah."

"See ya, Ag."

Agnes walked slowly to the door of her building. She heard the trunk slam, and then the car door, and then he drove away.

3

"Hey guys, what'll it be?"

There was a new waitress at T.T.'s. She was perfect. She looked exactly like every girl Owen had dated in high school: blonde hair, blue eye shadow, a push-up bra, and a low neckline. Her name was Sissy.

"I'd like a Molson, please," said Agnes.

The waitress wrote down her order but otherwise didn't acknowledge her. Her eyes raked the motley collection of guys— some with girlfriends but most without—and came to rest on Owen. "Don't I know you from somewhere?" she asked.

"I don't know, you might," he answered, with a smile.

Encouraged, she twirled her ponytail around her pencil, and then chewed on the eraser for a split second before she continued, batting her impossibly long eyelashes. "You wouldn't happen to be one of those Prairie Wolves, would you?"

Agnes shook her head. Out of the corner of her eye she saw Jamie Barber raising his eyebrows. Even Jamie's girlfriend, Hillary, who was old enough to have a nursing career and a nine-year-old son, smiled and rolled her eyes a little. Meanwhile, Owen had put both his elbows on the table and was leaning across it toward the waitress, probably explaining what a great hockey player he was, and why, if she didn't already know him, she should.

After Sissy came back with everyone's drinks, Jo and Clay showed up.

"Hey, where've you been, man?" one of the guys called out to

Clay. "I thought you'd been traded."

"Sorry to disappoint you," he said.

Uncharacteristically clever reply, thought Agnes. She made room for Jo next to her.

"Hey, Jo, thanks for closing up tonight," she said. "How'd it go?"

"It was really slow. I thought I'd never get out of there."

Clay called to her, "Hey, Josie, come on over, I got you a chair here."

"Coming," she answered. "See ya, Agnes."

Agnes shot a dirty look in Clay's direction, but he didn't see it. She scooted out of her chair and went over to sit by Jo.

"You doing okay, Jo?" she asked.

"Yeah."

"Why do you always do everything he says?"

"What do you mean?"

"You were sitting next to me, then he snaps his fingers and you're over here."

"I didn't think you'd mind," Jo replied.

"It's not about *me*. What about *you*? Where do *you* want to sit?"

"I don't know," answered Jo. "I came here with Clay."

"Okay, fine," said Agnes. She went back to her original seat next to Owen.

"We're gonna kick their ass," Ducks Johnson was saying.

Agnes took a sip of her beer.

"I know I'm personally gonna kick some," said Jamie.

"I'm not so much worried about their top line," said Owen. "Or even the second. It's the bottom six. That guy Holtzauer is a barbarian, and Cointreau—I played against him in juniors, and—"

"He's a douchebag," finished Ducks.

"You just gotta ignore him," counseled Jamie.

"I know it, man, but he's really got it coming. Someday." Ducks pounded his fist in his hand.

"I didn't say he doesn't deserve it," said Jamie, "but we have to concentrate on winning some games."

Agnes was surprised to hear the seriousness in his voice. It often seemed to her that no one on the team cared at all about winning.

"You're right, Jamie," she said. "You can't worry about every bastard and what he says about your mother. Just hit him with a good solid check and move on. If he keeps asking for it, and you gotta give it to him, just be smart. Keep your eyes on the zebras."

"Expert advice from the lady," said Ducks, sarcastically.

"Oh, she knows what she's talking about," said Owen. "Back when we played together, a lot of guys tried to get her off her game. Nine out of ten, *they'd* end up in the box."

"Oh, come on, Mac, she's a girl. You can bet she was more trouble than she was worth," said Torris.

"Don't be so sure," countered Owen. "You get a whole different perspective when you're down on your ass looking up at her."

Everyone laughed.

"I'm not kidding," said Owen. "I've been there. Literally *and* metaphorically."

"Meta-what?" laughed Ducks, in mock confusion.

"Yeah, talk English, Mac! We're just dumb hockey players," said Hammer.

"That's what we're trying to make them *think*," said Barbie, winking.

Suddenly Agnes was aware that the waitress was looking down at them. "Owen MacKenzie, can I get you anything else?" she said in a sugary voice. "Boys? Anything?" She looked around the table.

"Uh, yeah, thanks, another beer," said Owen.

"Same here," said Jamie. "Want another, Hill?"

"No, I need to get home to Jackie. The babysitter has school tomorrow."

"I'll take you home, babe," Jamie said to her.

"Thanks," said Hillary.

"My pleasure—excuse me, waitress?" said Jamie. "Cancel that beer, will ya?"

"I'll take his," said Ducks.

"Another shot for me," said Clay. "And a beer. Jo? What about you?"

Barbie and Hillary got up to leave, and Agnes followed suit.

Owen said, "Ready to go, Ag? I'll walk you home."

"That's okay, O, you just ordered a beer. I can get home myself."

"Nah. Let's go. I'll just settle up with the waitress."

Owen and Agnes stepped outside and their faces prickled. Wapahaska was in the middle of a days-long arctic blast barreling straight down from the Yukon. Owen turned up his collar and Agnes wrapped her scarf tighter. They both put on their gloves.

"It's nice of you to walk me home, O," Agnes said.

"It's nothing," Owen replied.

"I still feel really bad about the other night."

"Don't worry about it. You weren't in the mood for skating. I understand."

"No. That wasn't it. It's just, you're too good for me, O."

"What?"

"You are."

Owen didn't say anything.

Agnes said, "I really appreciate what you said tonight."

"What did I say?"

"You know, that I know what I'm talking about."

"Well, it's true, Ag. Maybe you're not as big or strong, but you're way smarter than a lot of those clowns. And you do know what you're talking about."

"When it comes to hockey, anyway." She smiled at him.

He smiled back. "Yeah, when it comes to hockey."

A frigid, penetrating gust of wind just about froze them in their tracks.

"Jesus," said Owen.

"Yeah," agreed Agnes.

They turned the corner and the wind eased up. Owen said, "You brought your gear back. Are you going to play?"

"I think so."

"Nice."

Agnes shrugged. "Just pickup."

"It's a start."

They walked for a while, side by side, in a sort of suspenseful silence. Agnes looked at Owen. His curls were mostly hidden under a knit cap. His face was still a boy's face, smooth and pale, with a fine nose—never been broken. Also, he had the clearest gray eyes she'd ever seen. They were like water. Looking at them sideways as she was now, in the streetlight, they were translucent. He turned toward her and she had to look away. A kind of panic came over her.

She asked, "Did you get her phone number?"

"What?" asked Owen.

"You know, the waitress. She reminds me of, what was her name? Sherry?"

"Yeah, Sherry," he said.

"You always go for that same type of girl."

"Aw, that's not true, Ag."

"She really zeroed in on you, too," said Agnes.

"She probably zeroed in on a hundred different guys tonight."

"Maybe. But there's only one Owen MacKenzie, wearing the 'A' for the Prairie Wolves. The net's wide open, Mac. Get your stick on the ice."

Owen didn't say anything for a long time. Then he said, really quietly, "As a matter of fact, I did get her number."

"Good," Agnes answered. "I think you owe it to yourself."

"Ag, now you're pissing me off."

"I mean it, Owen, I really do. You owe it to yourself."

They were in front of her building now, and they stopped dead on the sidewalk. Agnes turned around to face him. He was looking at her all squinty-eyed, and one wave of hair curled out from under his cap, like a spark in the streetlight. She touched it with her gloved finger. The cap was cute, too. Probably his mom had knitted it for him.

Agnes said, "O, thanks again for standing up for me. I'd go seriously crazy without you." She turned and ran up the stairs to her apartment.

Owen kept walking, picking up speed. It was cold as hell. His eyeballs were practically frozen in his head, and he half expected to see his breath freeze solid in front of his face, drop, and shatter on the sidewalk below. He'd heard plenty of tall tales like that from the old pioneer days.

He made it back to T.T.'s, pulled open the heavy door, and walked up to the bar.

"You're back," said Sissy.

"I got hungry," said Owen.

"What can I get for you?" she asked.

He pulled off his cap and gloves and sat down. "Grilled cheese?" he asked.

"Anything to drink?" asked Sissy.

"Do you have a glass of milk?"

"That's awfully wholesome of you," she remarked. She smiled. He smiled back at her. "I'm working tomorrow."

He unzipped his jacket and watched her while she reached under the counter, poured him a glass of milk, and walked back to the kitchen to give the cook his order. She was wearing a white shirt unbuttoned enough to show a lace top underneath, tucked into a pair of tight jeans. Her little black apron, stuffed with pencils, straws, and a pad to write on, was tied around her waist in the back. Her blonde ponytail bobbed up and down as she walked. When she came back she asked him, "Do you have a game tomorrow?"

"No, just practice." He took off his jacket and had a sip of milk.

She brought him his sandwich and while he ate it she cleared some tables and waited on some other people. He knew she was watching him, though. He could almost feel her eyes studying him, and he could almost hear her brain wondering about him. It was fairly typical. Girls liked him—they always had. He liked them, too. He ate as slowly as he could, to give her some time to think about it. He didn't feel like going home alone tonight, that was for sure. When he was done with his sandwich she came back and asked, "Can I get you anything else?"

"No, thanks, Sissy. That was perfect."

She smiled. He'd remembered her name. She took her pad out of her pocket, wrote up a check, and put it face down in front of him. She picked up his empty plate and glass.

"When do you get off work?" he asked.

"Any time now," she said. "It's pretty slow."

"Can I walk you home?" he asked.

"Sure."

Sissy's place was close by, up a flight of narrow stairs on the second floor of an older, yellow-brick building. It was tiny—all one room. Even the bed was in that same room, hiding behind a screen. "Come on in," she said.

She turned on a lamp by the sofa. There wasn't much in the place, but what there was, was orderly and clean. The lamplight made it feel cozy.

"Can I get you something? A beer, maybe?" Sissy asked.

"No, that's okay."

"Oh, yeah, I forgot. You've got to work tomorrow."

"Yeah, and you're *off* work now, right?" he said. "So you don't need to get me anything." He smiled at her.

"You have a nice smile," she said. "Take off your coat. Sit down." She motioned toward the sofa. "If you don't mind, I'm just going to get out of these waitress clothes. I've been wearing them, like, all day."

"No, I don't mind," he said. "Can I give you a hand?"

She giggled. "Sure."

He followed her behind the screen.

Owen's eyes opened. It was dark except for the glow of the lamp out by the sofa. Somehow he'd allowed himself to doze off. Sissy was sleeping on her side next to him, breathing lightly. With her button nose and kiss-shaped lips she looked like a little girl, or a doll, even. The only thing was, she had all this makeup on around her eyes. He didn't know why girls did that. She had these big, crazy, baby-blue eyes anyway. It's not like he wouldn't have noticed them without the paint. He put his hand on her bare, white shoulder.

"Sissy?" he whispered.

He stroked her arm and gave her hand a gentle shake.

"Sissy?" he said, again.

"Mmm?" She stirred.

"Sissy, I've got to go. I've got to get to work in the morning."

"What?" she said. She reached for him but he had already rolled over to get out of bed and was gathering his clothes. "Oh, okay," she said. She sat up and watched him, holding the sheet up to cover her breasts.

"You don't have to get up," he said. "Go back to sleep."

"That's okay," she said.

Owen said, "I didn't want to wake you, but I didn't want to just . . . leave."

"Yeah," she said. She got up and walked naked into the bathroom. When she came out again she was wearing a bathrobe.

He grabbed his wallet and put on his shoes and jacket and knitted cap. They walked to the door and she opened it for him.

"Goodnight, Owen," she said.

She looked up at him like she wanted him to kiss her, so he did. "Goodnight, Sissy," he said.

He walked down the steep steps, out into the glare of the streetlights and the stinging, arctic air.

The next day Owen came into the dressing room to find a new guy sitting in Campbell's stall, his dark head bent over the blade of a stick. He was naked from the waist up, and in every visible dimension he looked to be about twice Owen's size: feet, knees, hands, wrists, chest, shoulders—even his head. At the sound of Owen's step he looked up. His face was wide and open. An inch-long, silvery scar marked his left cheekbone, and his nose had clearly been flattened a couple of times. Whatever curiosity Owen might have had about where Campbell ended up drained right out of him.

The new guy set his stick aside, stood up, and held out his hand.

"Claude Doucette," he said. He was an inch or two taller than Owen, and though intimidating, his muscular arms and broad chest seemed not so much a product of the gym as of his natural habits and condition.

Owen grasped the hand he offered, which was as big as a platter. "Owen MacKenzie," he said. And then, as it dawned on him, he continued, "Wait, I know you who you are, you're I'm from St. Cyp. Aren't you from up around there, too?"

"That's right. Up around Blue Lake," said Doucette. "But I lived in St. Cyp. Played there."

"Right. I remember hearing about you."

"What'd you hear?" Doucette asked, with a wink.

"I wasn't even in high school yet," Owen said, "but I remember people talking . . . guys thought it was really cool, how well you were doing in juniors."

"Yeah, not bad for an Indian, right?" Doucette chuckled.

"For any of us," said Owen. "It's what we all wanted to do. But, yeah, I'm sure some people saw it that way."

Doucette said, "I've heard about you, too. The Steers' coach—where I just come from—he says you're going to turn this club around. That is, if you don't get called up first. You've been here, what, two seasons?"

"One and a half."

"How's it been?"

"Not bad," Owen said.

"We're still in it, right?" said Doucette.

"Yeah. Figuring out what to work on, anyhow," Owen answered, with a grin.

A man's high falsetto echoed in the cinderblock corridor outside the dressing room. *What's love got to do, got to do with it? What's love, but a second-hand emotion?* Jamie Barber strutted into the room behind his Tina Turner impression, partially clothed and sporting a puck-sized greenish bruise on his left bicep.

Gyrating for comic effect, he held his right fist up to his mouth like a microphone. *Who needs a heart when a heart can be broken?* Barbie saw the new guy and stopped in his tracks. Suddenly businesslike, he adjusted his breezers and offered his hand.

"James Barber."

"Claude Doucette."

They shook hands.

"Glad to have you on the team, man," said Barbie.

Owen envied Barbie's composed yet loose bearing. His relatively short, pale, wiry body was in stark contrast to Doucette's big, beefy, brown one, and he was a perpetual motion machine, which was, likewise, particularly noticeable against the backdrop of Doucette's quiet posture.

"Thanks. Glad to be here," said Doucette.

"Hey, wait a minute. *Doucette*," said Barbie. "Was that your old man used to play for the Rebels?"

"My uncle," said Doucette.

"Yeah? No! Eddy Doucette was your uncle? He was the greatest, man. When he came to town, I'd sneak in just to see him play. Well, I'm not gonna lie—I snuck into most of the games. Didn't have any money. But old Eddy Doucette was a fuckin' freight train! He stopped for no one. He'd back a goalie right through the twine. I'm not kidding!" He aimed that last admonition at Owen and then he turned back to Doucette, who was smiling sheepishly. "And he could dangle. Whoa, boy! Could he dangle! Around this guy, around another guy . . . " Barbie bent his knees as if he were skating, dangled a make-believe puck with a make-believe stick, and zig-zagged his way through the opponent's defense. "See, I was only about, well, maybe eight, nine years old, and the Rebels were our biggest rivals for a couple of years there. So I had to be kind of secret about being such an Eddy Doucette fan. But he had such a way about him. I mean, he was a crazy player, just crazy—but he was sort of calm, too, in a certain way. Dignified, maybe, is a way to say it."

"That was Eddy," said Doucette.

"It's funny. He had a reputation as a fighter. A real tough guy. And you knew he was tough, because of the way he played. I mean, he laid it all out there, you know? But I only ever saw him fight a guy once."

"Didn't have to," said Doucette.

"He quit pretty young, didn't he?" asked Jamie.

"Yeah," said Doucette.

"Do you know why?" Jamie asked.

Doucette shrugged. "Think he just wanted to come home."

"He was the greatest," Jamie continued. "The perfect combination of heart and skill and just plain toughness. Really missed him when he was gone. But now we got his nephew, eh Mac?" He gave Owen a playful punch on the shoulder. "Un-*freakin'*-believable! It's great to have you here, Deuce! Fantastic!" He held out his hand to Doucette again and they shook on it.

*

Agnes sat down on the metal bleachers, a couple of rows up. On the other side of the glass, just a few feet in front of her, Owen flew by in a blue practice jersey, his arms pumping, his stick-blade skimming the ice. He leaned into a turn, skidded to an ice-shaving stop, and sprung off again. Stopping short in the slot, he tapped his stick on the ice, settled a pass, and fired a quick wrister. There was a lump in Agnes's throat, as big as a golf ball. She swallowed it.

The last few skaters finished the drill, and then they glided toward the coach, sticks across their knees, breathing hard. Their faces glistened with sweat and their eyes shone as they joked and jostled one another. Agnes couldn't hear what they were saying, but their easy camaraderie made the lump in her throat bloom again. Not so long ago she was just like them, feeling the rush of air on her hot, moist skin, feeling her muscles strain, then soften, then strain again. But now she was sitting here on the damn bleachers, pulling her sweater close around her, her ass slowly turning into a block of ice. Kookum was right—she should be playing. She rubbed her hands together and reached into her coat pockets for her gloves.

When she looked up again, an unfamiliar player caught her eye, standing in the far corner of the rink.

Wow.

No wonder the Wolves had traded for him. Whomever they'd dealt, he was worth it. He was big and awesome. *Awesome* as in *inspiring awe.* He'd be immovable in front of the net, terrifying chugging toward you along the boards. He'd tower over every guy out there. But there was something else about him, too.

He was just standing there, in line with all the other guys, waiting his turn, his gloved hands resting on the butt end of his stick. He answered a teammate's question with a nod and shifted his weight from skate to skate in the impatient, endearing way of all hockey players. But Agnes couldn't even *see* the others anymore. When the new guy's turn came, his skates crunched hard down the wing and he traded passes with a teammate in a two-on-one breakaway drill. He wasn't very fast, but a guy like him hadn't been acquired for his speed. He didn't try to shoot, either—he dished a solid pass to his counterpart on the left wing, who shot and missed. Then, his turn complete, he circled behind the net and glided to the half-wall to line up again. His skin was honey-colored, like hers. His black hair, wet with sweat, curled up over the rim of his helmet in the back.

Agnes watched him through the whole hour or so of practice. He was a better skater than the stereotype of guys his size. He didn't try anything fancy—probably didn't want to be conspicuous—but she could see that he had soft hands. He was working hard, too, clearly trying to make a good impression in what she figured must be his first or second practice with the team.

After the formal practice broke up, a group of seven or eight guys gathered in a semi-circle, waiting to take shots on one of the goalies. Agnes leaned forward to watch. She'd been hurt when her bantam coach put her in goal—she prided herself on her skating and her accurate shot—but she'd wanted to play so she'd managed to do a decent job of it. All she had to do was think of something that made her angry, which was rarely a problem, and then she'd grit her teeth and make up her mind that nothing would get by her. And often nothing did.

Owen finished taking faceoffs at the far end and Agnes saw him glide down to join the group of shooters in front of her. They spotted each other at the same moment. She wondered fleetingly whether he'd gone back to track down that waitress last night, but she smiled anyway at the sight of him. He smiled back, one of those big, goofy grins of his. Yeah, she was pretty sure he'd had that waitress. She shook her head. God, she hated him. She really did.

The new guy had turned around just as Owen was coming toward him, and he must have seen Agnes and Owen smile at each other. He looked up at her and his eyes seemed to linger for a split second. Then, maybe the coach said something, because he turned right back to the ice. He wasn't paid to be a sniper—whoever he was—but when the puck came his way he one-timed a real hard shot top-shelf past the frozen goalie. His new teammates burst out with whoops and cheers. He skated around the half circle, exchanging fist bumps, but he didn't look back up at Agnes.

You had to think that something had happened to change old Claude Doucette—dubbed "Deuce" by Barbie—from what he was once, to what he was now. In Owen's memory he'd been known as an explosive player, fast and skilled. But with the Wolves he rarely showed it. It was only sometimes at the end of practice, when the guys were horsing around, that Deuce would let some of his skill show. And maybe once every few games he'd dish a real sweet pass that a linemate might try to muscle into the net. Usually, though, he was the one doing the muscling. And, when called for, the intimidating and the fighting.

Deuce didn't say much, and he mostly kept to himself. He seemed to be above the lace-slashing antics of the rest of the dressing room. He wasn't the oldest guy by a long shot—Barbie probably had ten years on him—he just seemed older. Like he'd seen things, maybe. Or like he saw things, or saw different things, or saw things differently, maybe, than the other guys did. To Owen, it seemed that a lot of the guys went through the daily routine in a semi-conscious haze, but Deuce wasn't like that.

One day Agnes showed up again at practice. Owen saw her come in and climb up onto the bleachers. Deuce must have seen her, too, because all of a sudden he skated over to Owen and asked about her. Owen didn't know how Deuce got the idea to ask *him* about Agnes, or how he got the idea that they even knew each other. Owen had scarcely seen her since that night he'd walked her home after Christmas, and even if he had, how would Deuce know? Old Deuce hardly ever came out with the guys except on road trips.

"That girl up there, she your girlfriend?" Deuce asked Owen.

"Who?"

"Her, up there," said Deuce, gesturing in Agnes's direction with his head. There weren't any other girls up there, anyhow.

"Nah, just a friend from back home," said Owen.

"You're not dating her?" Deuce asked.

"No."

"But you used to," Deuce said.

"Mm, no," said Owen.

"No?" Deuce asked.

"No," Owen repeated.

"Really? You two aren't dating?"

"No."

"But you're going to," said Deuce.

"Going to what?" asked Owen.

"You know, ask her out," said Deuce.

"No, man, trust me, we're just . . . she's just an old friend, I promise."

The whistle blew and the drill started up again. After a while Deuce slid to a stop in line behind Owen.

"What's her name?" asked Deuce.

"Who?" asked Owen.

"That girl up there."

"Agnes."

"Agnes what?" asked Deuce.

"Agnes Demers."

"How do you know her?" asked Deuce.

"I told you, she's a friend from back home."

"You two used to go out together?"

"No."

"What's she like?" asked Deuce.

"What do you mean, what's she like?"

"You know, what's she like?" he asked again.

Owen had no idea what to say. "She's . . . I don't know." He shrugged.

The whistle blew.

A few minutes later, Owen found himself standing alongside Deuce again.

Deuce began to ask him, "What's she—"

"Look," said Owen. "We played together when we were little. Went to school together. She's—I don't know what to tell you. I don't know her that well, okay?"

"Okay," said Deuce. "But you'd like to. Get to know her, I mean."

"Goddamn, Deuce. No, okay? Why do you keep asking me?"

"No reason," he said. He winked.

The Prairie Wolves were settling into the long haul of the season, the crucial stretch in the deepest, darkest part of winter when the rink, though paved with ice, starts to simmer with an acrid brew of blood, sweat, and testosterone. It's not quite time for "desperation hockey"—that comes later—but it *is* the moment when any team with a claim to greatness has to plant its skates in the ice, grab itself by the balls, and wrestle its demons to the ground. Whether the Wolves had the faculties, the focus, or the fortitude to do any of this was still a matter of debate. What wasn't debatable was that their sloppy play early in the season had left them short on standings points, and if they didn't start winning some games now, they'd be teeing off before the snow melted.

Agnes still went to see the occasional game, and some of the practices, too, but she didn't hang around with the team anymore. She didn't hang around with anyone anymore. Whenever she went out she saw Jo with Clay, and Owen with Sissy, and she didn't know which made her feel worse. Clay sucked up all of Jo's good humor, and most of her time and energy, but at least he seemed to *like* her. He called her all the time, bought her presents when he was on the road, and took her out when he was at home. Owen, on the other hand—did he really *like* Sissy? Chances are, he would never even have gotten together with her if Agnes hadn't pushed him into it. What *was* it about guys, anyhow? Owen had obviously noticed Sissy that night at T.T.'s, but given the way she'd extended her feelers, there's no way he *couldn't* have noticed. Every guy in the place had noticed. She might as well have been Marilyn fucking Monroe in the floating dress—it had nothing to do with Owen *liking* her. Sissy herself must have known it. She must have known that Owen was just passing the time. It's what most of these guys did.

One night when Agnes did go out with Jo and Clay, they were at T.T.'s and she had to use the washroom. When she was walking down the hall, heading back to their table, she happened to glance sideways into the little nook with the pay phones, and there they were, Owen and Sissy, flat against the wall, feeling each other up. And Sissy was right in the middle of a shift. Classy.

Instinctively, Agnes had turned to hockey for consolation. But the pickup games she'd played this winter had come up short. Most of the guys tried to be welcoming—after all, they needed *someone* in net. But she might as well have been one of those printed, practice-net goalies: her female, brown-skinned presence was somehow inconvenient, and so they tried to ignore it. But after dark, when the kids had gone home for dinner, she'd head out to the neighborhood rink. Like the goalie gear she'd left in her bag, Owen, Sissy, Jo, Clay, and even the disappointing pickup guys were forgotten. Beneath the film of snow the ice was solid. She'd dig in, drawing power from every stroke, grinding, crunching, ripping, and hurling the puck at the net until sweat filled her eyes and it was time to go home.

✳

The whistle blew: icing.

Shit.

Still breathing hard, Owen squared up for the faceoff. The linesman judged him to be out of position, so he kicked him out of the circle and Owen ended up having to line up next to that douche Cointreau.

So far, the Prairie Wolves had the edge. The score had been 2–0 in their favor since the first, and Owen had one of the goals and an assist on the other. The Cold Front had been frustrated all night, unable to get anything going, and their fans were getting restless. Meanwhile, Cointreau had been taking every opportunity to get in Owen's face: cross-checking, late hits, and, of course, crude commentary on Owen's mother, grandmother, aunt, sister—which Owen didn't even have—and anything else he could think of. He'd already gotten two minutes for roughing, but that only seemed to encourage him. Now it was midway through the third and Owen made up his mind to make a play and put the game away for good.

"Watch me, kid, I'll show you how it's done," he said to Cointreau.

Freddie Brennan won the faceoff and pushed the puck back to Owen, but Cointreau was in his face and he was forced to play it around behind the net to Don Mrkonjic. Donner tapped a pass forward to Jorgensen, who won it along the boards and chipped it out to Brennan, speeding out of the zone. Owen followed, still shadowed by that douche Cointreau. He managed to shake loose long enough to corral a pass and take a shot, but the goalie had anticipated well and caught it right in his gut.

Owen stopped hard in front of the net with Cointreau on his heels. The douche cross-checked him, hard, for about the thousandth time that night and said, "Eh, MacKenzie, I can see you're gettin' in some good shooting practice these days."

Owen turned around to look him in the eye, "Fuck off, why don't ya?"

"Yeah, I bet it's goooood shootin' with that filthy Indian cunt," he sneered. "Goes in real easy—"

Owen felt something inside of himself explode. "I'm gonna *kill* you, you motherfuckin' bastard," he snarled, and he launched himself into Cointreau, shoving him so hard and so unexpectedly that the douche lost his balance and fell down on his ass. He sprung up again in a flash, mad as hell.

"Ya wanna go?" he sneered.

"You fuckin' got it," said Owen. But before he could shake off his gloves, the linesman was there pulling Cointreau away and Owen felt Donner's arm across his chest, pulling him in the opposite direction. "Easy, Mac, come on, calm down," Donner said.

"Fucking bastard!" Owen spat out, "I'm gonna kill him, I swear I'm gonna kill him!"

"Easy, Mac," said Donner. "Easy. It's okay. We're up, eh? We got this one," he said, skating him toward the bench.

This time both guys ended up in the penalty box for roughing.

"Hit ya where ya live, eh MacKenzie?" Cointreau hollered at him, above the noise of the crowd.

"You can fucking go to hell," hollered Owen.

"I hear she's a real—"

"Shut your goddamn filthy mouth," Owen shouted back at him.

The puck dropped and right away gloves were on the ice—Doucette was in a dance with Holtzauer. The two of them skated around each other, sizing each other up. Deuce pounced first—he grabbed Holtzauer's jersey and pulled him into his fist. His normally placid face was red and wrinkled and he was snarling like some kind of demon. Holtzauer didn't stand a chance. Deucer kept coming at him and he went down to the ice. Deuce just turned his back and skated off like the fucking five o'clock express, head bowed, through a chorus of stick-tapping.

When Owen was back on the bench, Jordie Carroll asked him, "What'd he say to you?"

"I don't know, man." Owen shook his head.

"Aw, come on, Macker, what'd that douchebag say? I've never seen you go off like that."

"Yeah, Jords, I don't know what happened, man. I'd just had it, I guess."

"Well, Deucer showed'im. Fuckin' awesome smackdown. No one's gonna mess with *you* anymore."

Owen sat hunched over, chewing furiously on his mouthguard.

"Oh, you're up," Jordie said.

Coach was giving Owen a nudge. "Ya ready?" he asked.

"Yeah, I'm ready." Owen hoisted himself up and swung his legs over. Time to put it out of his mind.

Next thing he knew, there was that douche Cointreau again, skating right beside him.

"Good thing you got ol' Chief there to look out for you, eh MacKenzie?" he sneered.

"Aw, shove it, you fuckin' hoser," Owen answered, shaking his head.

Cointreau laughed and skated off.

"Hey, Agnes, will you give me a hand with this?" asked Jo.

"Sure," said Agnes.

Jo was trying to maneuver a length of filmy, baby-pink fabric off of a bolt and around one of her mannequins.

"What's the matter with your arm, Jo?" asked Agnes.

"Nothing."

"Is it okay?"

"Yeah, it's fine."

"It doesn't look fine."

It was Sunday afternoon and sunlight was pouring through the big, front window. Agnes was doing some long overdue cleaning while Jo worked on a project for her dress design class.

"I guess I must've hurt it somehow," said Jo.

"Maybe you should get someone to look at it," said Agnes.

"No, it'll be okay."

"What is this you're working on, anyway?" Agnes asked.

"It's my mid-term project for *Construction 2: Bodices, sleeves, and collars.*"

"The fabric's not very practical for this time of the year."

"Not around here, but maybe somewhere else," said Jo.

"Like Cancun?" asked Agnes.

"Sounds good to me."

"Me too." Agnes smiled.

"It drapes real nice, too," said Jo.

"It does," said Agnes.

"Hey, Agnes, what's the deal with Owen and that waitress?" asked Jo.

"Sissy?"

"Yeah."

"Oh, you know. He always goes for that type of girl."

"You're not that type of girl," said Jo.

"Exactly," said Agnes.

"No, no," said Jo. "I mean, he really, *really* likes *you*. And you're not that type."

Agnes said, "We're just *friends*, Jo."

"That's so *obviously* not true, Agnes. What happened? Did he just suddenly ask her out, like, out of the clear blue sky?"

"Yeah. I guess she was just too perfect to pass up."

"Weird," said Jo, shaking her head.

"He's a hockey player, Jo. He's a guy. There's nothing weird about it."

"Something happened when we were home for Christmas," continued Jo. "Did you two have a fight or something?"

"No," said Agnes.

"*Something* happened."

"I just . . . don't like him in that way, okay?" Agnes said.

"I don't believe you."

"Give it up. Okay, Jo?"

Jo continued to work on her dress. She said, "I can't decide whether to drape it softly around the shoulders like this, or maybe off the shoulder? Or make it more structured: maybe in straight pleats . . . yeah, sort of a cup sleeve made of lots of tiny little pleats, and a low, straight neckline. Kind of boxy. What do you think?"

"I'm not sure I even know what you're talking about," laughed Agnes.

"That's okay. I'm just thinking out loud," said Jo.

She pinned a few pleats in the fabric and stood back to look at it. "Hmm," she said. "Maybe if I got something different—maybe a satin—for the skirt. Or some kind of print. I don't know."

"Speaking of Sissy, this would look great on her," said Agnes.

"Yeah, it would," said Jo.

They both laughed.

"Oh, guess what?" asked Jo.

"What?"

"I almost forgot to tell you. When I talked to Clay last night, he told me that Owen almost got into a fight."

"Really? On the ice?"

"Yeah, the other night in Fitzgerald. That's what he said."

"What happened?"

"He pushed this guy down. He wanted to fight him. Don had to hold him back. Clay said Owen was so mad he was still yelling at the other guy in the penalty box."

"No kidding," said Agnes, wide-eyed.

"Then the new guy got in a fight."

"The new guy?" Agnes asked.

"You know, the really big guy. Claude Doucette. From home."

"Wow, cool, I've got to start going to more games," said Agnes.

"Yeah, Clay said he really clobbered the guy. It's funny. He doesn't seem like someone who would do that kind of thing. But Clay said—"

"Wait, how do you, I mean, do you know him?" asked Agnes.

"Claude Doucette? I've met him. What's the big deal?"

"No big deal," said Agnes.

"You've got a thing for him," said Jo, with a sly smile.

"I do not."

"I can tell by the look on your face."

"I do not," repeated Agnes. "It's just that I've been hearing about him since I was a kid. Vin and his teammates used to talk about him all the time—he's, like, two or three years older than them. When Doucette was in midgets they'd go watch him play. They'd be like, 'Did you see that pass by Doucette?' 'Did you see how he set up what's his name?' 'Did you see how he dangled around that D?' Then they'd head straight out to the pond and try to copy everything he'd done."

"Clay doesn't seem to think he's any big deal."

"Clay doesn't know as much as he thinks he does. Back home, Claude Doucette was a *really* big deal. Not very many Native guys stick in juniors, much less go pro and stick there, too. And I've seen him skate in practice and he looks good to me."

"Aha! So you do have a thing for him!"

"I do not!"

"Do you want me to tell him you're interested?"

"What? God, no, Jo. Just stay out of it, *please*!"

Jo chuckled. "Don't worry, I wouldn't say anything. I never see him anyhow. He doesn't come out with the other guys. It was just once, when I was meeting Clay, he happened to be there, too."

"What's he like?" asked Agnes.

"He seemed real nice, low-key. You know, just a typical homeboy. Just shook my hand, asked if I was from around here."

"What'd you say?"

"Obviously, I just said, 'No, I'm from St. Cyp,' and he said, 'Oh, that's a real nice town, I went to school there,' and I said, 'Yeah, it's okay.' I'm guessing he's from one of those families out by Blue Lake."

"And then what?"

"I think he just asked, 'What are you doing here,' and I told him, 'Going to school and working at the Indian Jewel Box,'" said Jo.

"And then what?"

"I don't know. I think that's when Clay said, 'We gotta go,' and we left."

"He's not very sociable, is he?" asked Agnes.

"I thought he seemed sociable," said Jo.

"Not Doucette. Clay."

"Oh," said Jo. "Yeah, he likes it better when it's just the two of us."

"What about you? Do you like it better?"

"I don't know. Sometimes."

"Sometimes?" asked Agnes.

"Sometimes I like it and sometimes I don't. Sometimes it would be fun to hang out with the team more, like we used to. But now he usually wants to leave early, and go back to his place, or to dinner, or to some other bar. Anyhow, you're never there anymore, and I don't really know anyone else."

"Well, why don't you tell him you don't want to go? You should try to sit with Jamie and Hillary—"

"He gets kind of tense, and then he'll sort of grab me, and say, 'Come on, it's time to go—'"

"Is that what happened to your arm?" asked Agnes.

Jo hesitated. "He didn't mean to hurt me. He just doesn't know his own strength."

Agnes didn't know what to say. "I think you should let a doctor look at it," she said slowly, and then, "Is this the only time that he's . . . hurt you?"

"No."

"What the hell, Jo? That's not good. He's not worth it."

"I don't know what to do about it," said Jo.

"Tell him you don't want to see him anymore."

"But, that's not really true . . ."

"You want to be seeing someone who's always hurting you?"

"He's not *always* hurting me."

"Just *sometimes*? Come on, Jo."

"Agnes, he really cares about me."

"Bullshit. If he really cared about you, he wouldn't hurt you."

"Can we just change the subject?"

"Okay, Jo. But think about it. Okay?"

Agnes decided she'd better keep a closer eye on Jo, so the next night she skipped her pickup game and asked the happy couple if she could join them at T.T.'s.

"I thought you were too good for us now," Clay said.

Agnes pretended like he wasn't being an asshole and said, "No, I miss you. I miss the guys. Besides, Jo told me about how Owen lost it the other night. I want to hear all about it."

"Oh, yeah. Mr. Cool, eh? Donner had to pull him off the guy and then Deuce had a go with Holtzauer. Really cleaned his clock, too."

"What made him go off like that?" asked Agnes.

"Macker? I don't know. The guy probably just told him he was sleeping with his sister or something."

"Owen doesn't have a sister," said Agnes.

"Exactly. Nothing to get himself hurt over. Let Deuce do the heavy lifting. That's what he's there for."

When they walked through the door at T.T.'s, the first thing Agnes saw was Owen leaning on the bar like he owned the place, flirting with Sissy. Ugh. She was immediately sorry she'd come. She stood uncertainly just inside the door, about to turn around and walk back home.

"Hey Agnes! Come on over!"

It was Jamie to the rescue. He and Hillary were both waving at her. Jamie made her sit in his chair while he went to get another.

"Where've you been?" asked Hillary. "I've missed you. We need to keep up some kind of female presence at these gatherings."

Agnes laughed. "How's Jackie?"

"Good. You know—school, road hockey, eat, sleep, repeat. He's got Jamie out skating with him every chance he gets, too. He's going to wear the poor guy out."

"It's great that Jamie's so good to him."

"Yeah, sometimes I think Jamie cares more about Jackie than he does about me," Hillary said.

"Did I just hear my name?" Jamie asked, scooting up a chair between them.

Hillary laughed at him.

"You know what they say," he continued, "the only thing worse than being talked about is not being talked about. Where've you been keeping yourself, Agnes?"

"Oh, you know, just been going to work and stuff," she said. "What's new with you?"

"Not much," said Jamie.

"The Wolves are hanging on," said Agnes.

"Yeah, by our fingernails," laughed Jamie. "Or our claws, I guess."

"*You* had a bit of a hot streak going," said Agnes.

"Yeah, I've always been streaky. Mostly cold ones, though, unfortunately. You talked to Owen lately?"

"No," she said.

"He could use some of your sage advice, because he's really been losing it out there."

"I heard," answered Agnes. "You'd think that getting laid regularly would have the *opposite* effect."

"Mmm, mm," said Jamie, shaking his head.

"It's supposed to be good for guys. Or so I hear," Agnes continued.

"So you're okay with him and Sissy . . . ?" asked Jamie.

"Well, if it's in the name of better hockey, I'd have to say yes," she answered, only half joking.

"You got a heart of stone," he said. He grabbed a fork off the table and sang into it, "*No, you'll never break, never break, never break, ne-ver break: this heart of stone! No, you never gonna break this heart of—*" He stopped short and said, "Oh, hey, would ya looky there? It's Deucer! Where's he going dressed so fine?" He stood up and waved. "Hey Deuce, over here!"

Agnes looked in the direction that Jamie was waving. Holy shit. Claude Doucette was standing just inside the door, and his eyes were riveted on her. Her face caught fire. Thankfully, he looked away quickly. He must have heard Jamie shouting at him. Agnes's eyes were locked onto him, though. She couldn't help it. It wasn't just his size. It was his gaze, the crown of dark curls, the wide cheekbones, the full lips. All of a sudden, she felt a little bit sick to her stomach. He was headed her way. He was wearing a brown leather jacket, a red shirt, and a bolo. He was dressed like her dad on his way to the Ex, for Christ's sake! But it suited him. It *really* suited him.

Jamie and Doucette shook hands, and Jamie slapped him on the shoulder in a friendly way. He said, "What brings you out tonight, Deuce? We don't usually get the honor." He didn't sound the least bit sarcastic, either. "Have a seat." He motioned to his chair. "I'll buy you a beer. You too," he said to Agnes. "Should've done that before."

"Nice to see you, Hillary," Doucette said, shaking Hillary's hand. "And you're Agnes, right?" he continued, offering his hand to Agnes.

She nodded, wondering how he knew her name.

"Sorry," laughed Jamie. "I seem to be socially challenged tonight. I figured you two had already met. Agnes, this is Claude. Claude, Agnes. Deucer here saved Macker's ass the other night."

"I don't know," said Claude. "He was pretty fired up. Looked like he could've taken the guy."

"It's good of you to give him the benefit of the doubt," laughed Jamie. "But I'd say he was in a little over his head, eh Agnes?"

She smiled. "He's not a fighter," she said.

Jamie went to the bar to order a round.

Claude sat down in Jamie's chair.

Hillary said, "I need to check in with the babysitter," and headed over to the pay phones.

Claude looked at Agnes. "Glad to finally meet you, Agnes."

"Glad to meet you," she answered.

"I've seen you around," he said.

"I've seen you."

"I'm, uh, a little hard to miss," he said, smiling a little.

"Not a bad quality to have," she answered.

Neither one of them knew what to say next.

"You're hard to miss, too," tried Claude. But it didn't sound right. He looked down at his hands for a second. Then he looked up again. It was his first close-up look at her, and it was worse than he'd thought. She was impossibly young. Her eyes were dark brown and perfectly almond-shaped, and her skin was very smooth and golden, glowing in the dim light of the bar. His stomach was all butterflies. He thought of his own scars and smashed-in nose and almost got up and walked away.

But she was asking him, "How do you like it here so far?"

He answered, "I like it pretty good. It's a good group of guys. Real nice arena."

"The team's looking better since you got here," she said.

He didn't answer.

"Honestly, they didn't have much heart before. Except for Jamie."

"Yeah, Barbie's okay. Real good guy."

"But you're, well, you've really . . . "

She didn't know how to finish her thought. She was finding it a little bit hard to breathe. He was just looking at her, calmly— at her face, into her eyes, not at any other part of her. He was no typical hockey player. He was a whole different animal. He wasn't a cocky kid. He was a man.

Jamie approached, beers in hand, with Owen trailing behind him. Jamie motioned toward Agnes with an elbow. "There she is," he said to Owen.

"Oh, hey, Deuce, how's it going, man?" Owen said. He leaned over Agnes's chair. "Hey, Ag."

"Hey Owen," said Agnes, looking up at him. It was as if ten years had passed since she'd first walked into the bar this evening and noticed him flirting with that waitress. She'd forgotten they existed.

"Haven't seen you in a while," Owen said.

"Yeah," she answered. "I know."

"Everything okay?" Owen asked. He glanced at Deuce, who, he thought, was sitting just a little bit too close to her.

"Yeah, O, everything's great. You?" she asked.

"Good, yeah, great, everything's fine," he said.

"Glad to hear it," said Agnes.

There was a silence, just long enough to be awkward.

"Yeah, well, um, see ya around, Ag."

"Yeah, O, see ya."

Owen glanced at Claude again, straightened up, and walked back to the bar.

"So, Agnes," Claude said, "how come you're so interested in hockey? I see you at practices a lot."

"Uh, well, my brother always played."

"Oh yeah, who's your brother?"

"Vincent Demers."

"Hmm. Where are you guys from?"

"St. Cyp."

"Yeah? Vincent still play? I don't think I remember him."

"He doesn't play anymore," she said.

"My brother used to play, too," said Claude. "We used to play together. Long time ago, now." Claude reached out to pick up his beer.

"Ouch," said Agnes. "That looks painful." Without thinking she had reached out and intercepted Claude's hand before it got to the beer mug. She held it and turned it to catch the light so she could see it better. His knuckles were a mess, covered with scars and abrasions.

He pulled his hand away. "I know, ugly, right?"

"Claude, no, I don't think it looks bad at all. Here, let me see again."

He was mesmerized by the sound of her voice saying his name. It was so soft, mostly just an "oh" sound rolling off her tongue. He offered her his hand. She held it and ran her fingers lightly over the scarred knuckles. He saw stars. In fact, his whole body tingled, as if with some strange medicine.

"Is this from the other night?" Agnes asked.

"Yeah, well, some of it. You know. It adds up."

"It's good of you to stick up for your teammates like that."

He didn't answer. She knew it was a dumb comment. That was his role on the team. Still, he'd done *that*, for Owen?

"Where are you from?" she asked, reaching for her beer.

"Blue Lake area," he said. "You ever been up there?"

"Once or twice," said Agnes, "but we usually go down river, or to Big Lake. My dad used to put in up there."

"He like to fish?" asked Claude.

"Yeah, fish, camp, you know."

"You like that kind of thing?"

"I do," said Agnes. "I love being with Dad, just the two of us, on the water. Just feeling it move under the boat, kind of soft and strong at the same time. And just listening to the wind, the birds."

"Ever go up there anymore?" he asked.

"It's been a while. I've been busy, you know? School, work, other stuff. Dad wants to get into horse-breeding, so he helps at Haslund's whenever he has the chance. Spends less time up there."

"It's real peaceful up there," said Claude. "Just me and the eagles, you know? There's a whole family of them, the place I like to go. Sometimes I think they know me, they know what I'm thinking. That's when I know I'd better come back down again." He smiled.

She smiled back at him.

He took a deep breath.

"I, uh, Agnes, I was thinking I'd go over to that Italian place across the street. It's a pretty good place. And get some dinner. It'd be good to have some company. Do you want to, maybe, join me?"

Agnes tried to steady her voice. "Um, yeah, I'd like that."

The Italian place was cozy, with dim lighting and red and white checkered tablecloths. Agnes wasn't very hungry, so she mostly twirled her spaghetti around her fork while she watched Claude eat a basket of garlic bread, a salad, and a huge dish of lasagna.

"So, what're you doing down here?" he asked.

"My friend Josephine helped me get a job at the store she works at. It's called the Indian Jewel Box."

"Do you like it?"

"It's okay. I needed some kind of job, you know. I wanted to get away from home for a while. I mean, I get along fine with Dad and Kookum, but sometimes you just need some space."

He nodded. "So what were you doing before? School?"

"Yeah, college."

"So, you must be, like, nineteen, twenty? I mean, if it's okay to ask."

Agnes laughed. "Yeah, it's okay to ask. I'm twenty-one. Just had my birthday."

He nodded. "Sorry, you just look pretty—I mean, you're a real pretty girl, Agnes."

Agnes looked down at her spaghetti. If anyone else had said that to her, she would have laughed in his face. It wasn't the kind of thing most guys said.

"So you were living with your dad and kookum?" he asked.

"Yeah. And sometimes Vin. He kind of . . . comes and goes."

"And your dad is . . ."

"Lazare Demers."

"He runs Prairie Wind Motors," said Claude.

"He owns it *and* runs it," Agnes replied.

"Right. And your kookum?"

"Sophie. Parenteau."

"From . . . ?"

"Back near Prince Albert."

"Same family that ran the post down on Fish Lake?"

"Yeah, I think that was Kookum's dad. But she spent a lot of time in town, too."

"What about your mom?"

"Her name was Mary Agnes. Just like me. She was from Catfish River."

"So, your friend who got you the job—she's a friend from home?"

"Yeah. Jo. You've met her. One time when she was waiting for Clay Torris."

"Oh, yeah. I remember." He took a bite of lasagna. Then he asked, "What about Mac—I mean, Owen? He's a friend, too?"

"Yeah. He went to school with me and Jo."

Claude was looking at her intently, and she looked right back into his eyes. Owen was the last person she wanted to talk about right now.

"Jo and I went to school together, all the way up," Agnes said. "She's my best friend. She always stayed friends with me, no matter what."

"No matter what?"

"We were a little different than some of the other families. Like sometimes Kookum used to sew my clothes. And you know, I lived with Dad and Kookum, right? No mom. And Vin got in trouble a lot at school, so everyone thought he was a juvenile delinquent or something."

The waitress came by and Claude asked her for the check.

"Do you want to go back across the street?" Claude asked Agnes.

"Not really. Do you?"

"No. Can I drive you home?"

"Sure. Thanks," she said.

The air outside was sharp as a knife.

"It's a cold one," he said.

Agnes put on her hat and gloves but Claude just had the leather jacket.

"You must be freezing," she said.

"Nah. Got blankets in the truck just in case. But I don't have far to go tonight."

He drove an older pickup, painted a dull red. It was parked on the street nearby. "Mind if we drive along the river?" he asked. "Just to get out of town for a minute."

"Well, okay, sure," she said.

He opened the door and she climbed in. Even though the air inside the truck was as cold as a freezer, it smelled oddly sweet and summery, like tall grass and tobacco. Claude got in the other side, drove a few blocks, and took a right turn onto the riverfront road. Soon the houses ended and the land opened up. The river itself was iced over and covered with snow, so the only way you could tell where it was was by looking at the brush sticking up through the swelling drifts along the bank. On the other side there were some bare trees, and then the wide, flat swath swung around a slow bend to meet the sky.

Claude stopped the truck by the side of the road. "Little easier to breathe out here," he said.

"Yeah."

"Look."

The sky was buzzing with light, but you could only see a piece of it through the windshield. "Let's get out and look," Agnes said.

They got out of the truck. A band of greenish light spiraled across the heavens, bleeding from the purple sky in a sobbing, shuddering beat.

"The old chiefs are dancing tonight," Claude said, green flickering across his face like firelight. He said it just like he was seeing it.

"Claude?" she whispered.

"Yeah, Agnes?" He turned away from the sky to look at her.

"Nothing," she whispered. "Sorry." She'd just wanted to see his face.

They picked their way through the crumbles of packed snow along the side of the road. He sort of had his arm around her, behind her, without really touching her, as if he were protecting her from something back there. The snow was tinged baby pink and mint green, like cake frosting. It glittered. Except for the colored light, which throbbed faintly, erratically, everything around them was completely still.

Claude stopped walking again and looked up. Agnes looked up, too. Beyond the aurora the sky was studded with stars—absolutely plastered with them. Some sparkled and some shone, but which were closer or farther away, which were being born or dying, she couldn't tell.

"They make me dizzy," she said.

"Me too."

She let her eyes linger on him. His big body was a dark silhouette against the bright sky, and the thought occurred to her that maybe she shouldn't be out here, alone, late at night, with a guy she had only just met. But it didn't seem like they'd only just met. And the light that washed across his upturned face seemed to shine both inside and out. She felt safe with him. He was just like those old chiefs.

A car drove by very slowly, and Agnes watched it, nervously, out of the corner of her eye. On frigid nights like this, the police were known to pick up people who seemed out of place—as did nearly every Native person, in their view—and take them on a one-way tour, far out onto the prairie. She looked back at Claude as the car drove on. He didn't seem to have noticed it.

"Agnes. I should get you home now," he said, as if he expected her dad to be waiting at the door for them, enforcing a curfew.

They walked back to the truck and he opened the door for her. When they got to her building he parked and walked her up the stairs.

"Thank you for dinner, Claude," she said.

The way she said his name made him shiver.

"And for the drive," she added.

He shuffled his feet. "Can I call you some time?" he asked.

"Yeah." They exchanged numbers.

"Good night," he said.

"Yeah, good night." They looked at each other. Then she fished her key out of her bag and turned it in the lock.

When she was inside she stopped and stood there, her back up against the door, listening to his boots going down the stairs. Then she ran to the window and watched him get into his truck and drive away.

4

Jo looked at Clay across a table full of spent take-out containers, an empty wine bottle, and a couple of glasses glinting in the lamplight. "Thanks for dinner, Clay. It was delicious."

"No problem, babe," he said.

"I'll help you clean up and then you can drive me home," said Jo.

"Don't worry about cleaning up right now. Come here and sit with me," Clay said, walking over to the sofa.

"You promised you'd drive me home after dinner," she said.

"I will, Josie. I will. Just sit with me for five minutes," he said. "I want to tell you something." He sat down.

"Okay. Five minutes. But whatever it is, you had all evening to tell me." She didn't feel great about giving in on this, but she was relaxed from the food and the wine and they'd had a nice evening, so far. She sat down next to him. "What is it?"

He said, "I wanted to tell you, that . . . " He leaned in close to her and started to unbutton her blouse.

"Clay, no."

He kissed her and pushed her back against the cushions. She tried to sit up, but he pushed her down again. "Come on, baby," he said, and he kept working on the blouse until it was all undone.

Jo said, "We already talked about this."

"We did?"

"You know we did."

"I don't remember." He tugged her blouse out from her jeans

and slipped his hand underneath it, around her waist to the small of her back. She tried again to sit up.

"Clay—"

"Relax, baby. I know what you want." He unhooked her bra.

"No!" She tried to push him away.

"I said, I know what you want, you little Indian *bitch*," He kissed her hard, forcing her head backwards.

She struggled to turn her face away. "Clay, I have class tomorrow. I have to give a presentation—"

He jerked her head back toward him and shoved his tongue into her mouth. His hand moved down to the button of her jeans. She grabbed it, but she wasn't strong enough to pull it away. He unsnapped the button.

"Clay. I had to work all day today. I need some time—"

"Face it, babe. You're never going to be a designer." He unzipped her jeans, slid his hand inside, and leaned on her, hard.

Jo panicked. "Stop! You're hurting me!"

"What's the matter?" He pulled his hands away, laughing at her.

"Why are you doing this?" she gasped.

"Doing what?"

"You *promised*. Doesn't that mean anything to you?"

"I just want to have a little fun, babe, come on."

"This isn't fun!"

Clay's face darkened. "There's some other guy, isn't there? Some guy in your class." He had her wrist now, and he squeezed it.

"Ouch! Clay, let go!"

"*There's some other guy*," he said again, through gritted teeth.

"There isn't."

"There better not be." He gave her wrist an extra hard squeeze and flung it away.

"Clay, why do you do this? There's no other guy! You know me. I'm not like that."

He sprung up and towered over her, fists clenched. "When I'm away on a road trip. That's when the other guy comes in, right?"

"No! What are you talking about?"

He turned away. "What's his name?"

"If you're not going to drive me, I'll walk!" Jo said. She stood up and started toward the washroom so she could get herself together.

Clay followed her. "What's his *name*?" he asked again.

Jo took a deep breath. She turned around to face him. "Do you really think I'm having dinner with you and then going off to see some other guy? Come on. I told you I would eat with you, but I have to get up early tomorrow and give this presentation. It's important. There's no other guy. Nothing. Just you and my schoolwork. That's all. Now *please*. If you really love me—"

"Okay, Josie. Okay. You win."

"It's not about winning or losing. It's just . . . just drive me home, and I'll see you later, okay?"

"Tomorrow?"

"Sure, tomorrow."

Somehow, Jo made it through the morning. When she got home, Agnes was sitting on the sofa, eating lunch and leafing through a magazine.

"How'd it go?" Agnes asked.

"Pretty well," said Jo, plopping down next to her.

"Only pretty well?"

"Yeah. Agnes?"

"What?"

"Things aren't going so well, with Clay," Jo said.

"Did he hurt you again?"

"He thinks I'm seeing some other guy."

"What? That's crazy. You're the most loyal person on earth. He doesn't know you very well, does he?"

"How can I make him believe me?" asked Jo.

"I don't get what makes him think that way in the first place," said Agnes.

"The only other guys I see are when I'm out with him," said Jo, "and they're his teammates. There're only a couple of guys at school—"

"And they aren't interested in girls," said Agnes.

"Yeah," said Jo. She smiled. Then she remembered that she'd promised Clay she'd see him tonight. Suddenly she felt really tired. "Have you heard from Claude yet?" she asked.

"No."

"You never told me about your date," said Jo.

"There's not much to tell."

"Tell me anyhow."

Agnes smiled. Jo had an insatiable appetite for this sort of thing. She said, "Okay. We were talking there at T.T.'s and he asked me to have dinner with him. So we went across the street to that Italian place and then we went for a drive along the river. The stars were out. And the Chepuyuk, too—all green and purple and sort of pulsing. It was beautiful."

"Sounds romantic."

"Then he drove me home."

"That's it?"

"Yeah."

"He didn't kiss you or ask you back to his place or anything?" asked Jo.

"No. He asked if he could call me some time. But he didn't kiss me goodnight or anything."

"Weird," said Jo.

"Maybe he wasn't really attracted to me."

"Then why'd he ask you out in the first place?" asked Jo.

"Maybe he just wanted someone to eat dinner with."

"And to look at the stars with?"

"I don't know," shrugged Agnes.

"Maybe he thought you were too young for him," said Jo. "He's kind of ... older."

"Maybe, but he asked me, and I told him I'm twenty-one. That's not too young."

"He asked you how old you are?"

"Yeah," said Agnes. "He even grilled me about my family and everything."

"Wow. Old school. He's probably visiting your dad right now, asking for permission."

"Haha," said Agnes.

"You never know."

"I guess he just didn't like me all that much," sighed Agnes.

"But you like him?"

"I *really* like him."

"He's not your type at all," said Jo.

"Are you kidding me? He's *totally* my type," said Agnes. "He makes me feel kind of woozy. I can't even explain it."

"Wow. You've got that misty look again, almost like that time at the shop when Owen asked you out," laughed Jo.

"Don't remind me!"

"Sorry. But you know, Agnes, you should be careful. Maybe he's got a girl back home. A lot of the Native guys do."

"I don't think so," said Agnes.

"How would you know?"

"It just doesn't seem like it."

"I'm telling you, Agnes. You say he's this great, famous hockey player. He's making a lot of money—especially compared to the guys back home. Why wouldn't he have someone up there? It would be strange if he didn't, actually."

"But having a girl at *home* never stopped a guy from messing around with a girl *away* from home. All guys do that. Native or not. It's just a fact."

"True."

"He's just not attracted to me."

"Is that really what you think?"

Agnes shook her head. "No."

"Maybe he's just busy."

"What should I do, Jo? I really want to see him again."

"You're serious, aren't you?"

"Yes."

Jo shook her head. "I'm surprised. I thought you and Owen would end up together for sure. You seemed so perfect."

"We weren't. Believe me."

Jo looked at her. "Agnes, you shouldn't do anything. I think Claude'll call you. You've got to be patient. He's just a little slow. You know. Indian time, and all that."

They both had a chuckle over that one.

"I hope you're right," said Agnes.

One by one, the Prairie Wolves hit the ice. Claude took a lap, easily working a puck from backhand to forehand and back, again and again. He stickhandled around some imaginary pylons, flipped the puck up onto the blade of his stick, and bounced it up and down a few times. His wrists felt good this morning. Everything felt good. Loose. He glided over to where Owen was standing, etched a circle around him with an outside edge and came to a stop.

"She's a good girl," Claude said to him.

"Who?" asked Owen.

"Daisy." Deuce was handling the puck again, easy and soft on the tape. Backhand to forehand to backhand to forehand.

"Who's Daisy?" asked Owen.

"Agnes. *Mary Agnes*," Deuce said.

Owen was annoyed. "Why'd you call her Daisy?"

"She's more like a Daisy than an Agnes."

"No way," said Owen.

"Sure she is."

"Not with me she isn't," said Owen.

"Well, she's not with you. Right?" Deuce was still playing with the puck. Backhand, forehand, backhand.

"Uh, right."

"You said she's not your girlfriend."

"That's right."

"You're definitely not dating her."

"No. Are you?" asked Owen.

"No."

"No?" asked Owen again.

"No. Workin' on it, though. You know." He winked and skated off.

Owen didn't put the puck in the net once during the entire practice. Not that it mattered very much to anyone but him, but he was normally pretty focused, and even on bad days he had a few tricks he'd use to get himself going. Agnes had taught him that. She'd crouch in the goalcrease and egg him on. Sometimes it was game seven and he had the OT winner right there, on his stick. Sometimes she'd challenge him to put it blocker-side, or five-hole, or whatever. But today he was hopeless. The guys thought it was hilarious—the pucks going high, or wide, or fanned on altogether—and they took full advantage of the opportunity to air out all of their most time-honored, predictable, inane jokes.

"Lookin' good today, eh Macker? You couldn't find your asshole if it was plastered on your forehead," Barbie hollered at him.

"Hey, hot shot! Old donut hole over here can't make a save *with* the puck, let alone without it," said Eichenhaus, jostling Bancroft in the crease.

"C'mon, Macker, you know where to put it," called Newtower, making a crude gesture.

Owen didn't get off a single decent pass, either, and that *did* matter, because it rendered every drill completely useless.

"Mac, you're looking like a pile of shit," said Mrkonjic, his winger.

"Whoo, faggot, whatcha doin'? Passing to your mama in the stands?" called Brennan.

"Boys! Fucking focus or I'm gonna sit ya," yelled Coach. Not that his admonition had any effect whatsoever.

As soon as the formal practice was over, Owen stepped off the ice.

"You alright, Mac?" asked Sammy, the trainer.

"Yeah, yeah. A little tired today, that's all."

In the dressing room, Owen sat in his stall as the other guys trickled in. Like all the rest, he unlaced his skates, unwound the tape, pulled off his jersey and pads and breezers, underclothes and jock, layer after layer until there was nothing left to peel away and the sweaty heat from his body pulsed out of him and joined the sweaty heat from all the other guys' bodies in one big sweaty, stinking fog. Normally, he didn't even notice. Normally, after practice he thought only about himself—about *his* workout, *his* skating, *his* shot. In fact, he relished thinking about those things, and he tried to prolong those last, concentrated moments before they dissipated into the unfocused, everyday, off-ice world.

Today, though, he wasn't thinking about any of that. As he glanced around the room at his teammates, stripping most *un*dramatically to the beat of some old, heartsick, R & B dirge courtesy of James Barber, their benevolent but aging captain, it suddenly struck him how weak and pathetic they were, each and every one of them. Ice packs and bandages were strewn evenly across the benches and floor like used-up confetti and streamers. Bruises and scars and stitches disfigured every body without discrimination or exception. Each guy was quartered in his own little stall, identically outfitted from the outside in and the inside out. Yeah, some guys were bigger or smaller, taller or shorter, more or less hairy, dark or fair. But each had two arms for shooting, two legs for skating, and, invariably, between the latter—almost like some kind of sick joke or bizarre after-thought—a drooping set of genitals. They were all in the same leaky boat, paddling and bailing like crazy, subject to the same faint hopes, the same corporeal dangers and, ultimately, the same miserable and unexceptional fate.

Except, possibly, for one guy.

And that guy was Deuce. His stall was almost directly opposite to Owen's, and he sat there now looking very relaxed, his warm-toned skin glowing with sweat, his shoulders broad and well-formed, his pecs softly rounded. He opened and closed his fists and inspected his knuckles, his biceps twitching. He looked over at Owen and their eyes met for an instant. Owen blinked and looked around for his water bottle. Deucer picked up his own water bottle and squeezed the last of its contents into his mouth. He stood up and hung his helmet on the hook to the right of his stall. Then he bent over to pick up a piece of discarded clothing and turned to head into the showers. Involuntarily catching a glimpse of the big man's profile as it jiggled past, Owen dropped his face into his hands.

A couple of days ago, Deuce had been the same as Owen, the same as any of them: a bruised, battered body, suiting up and suiting down every day—sometimes twice a day—in an unremarkable, mundane parade of preparedness. But ever since Owen had seen him with Agnes, Deucer's bruised, battered body was suddenly, maybe, possibly, *quite* possibly, in a different category altogether.

Still, Owen sat there in his stall with his head in his hands, trying not to think, trying not to imagine. Deuce had said that he and Agnes weren't seeing each other, but he'd made his intentions clear. Owen had seen how close they were sitting at T.T.'s. He'd seen them talking. He'd seen them looking at each other. He'd seen him helping her on with her coat. He'd seen them disappearing through the door together. Deep in the roiling pit of his stomach, he knew how much Agnes admired the size and strength and toughness that Deuce embodied. It was something that he himself could never match.

Something smacked Owen on the head. A roll of tape hit the floor beside him and spun away. He stood up and headed to the showers.

*

Finally, Claude called Agnes, and they made a date to meet after practice on Tuesday, Valentine's Day. It was an unusually sunny, warm day—that is, for Saskatchewan in mid-winter—so after lunch they took a walk. Claude gave Agnes a little heart-shaped box of chocolates and they sat on a bench out of the wind and shared it while they watched some kids skate.

"That little girl is just like me when I was that age," said Agnes, "tagging along after her brother."

"You close to your brother?"

"Yeah. But he hasn't been around much the last couple of years. He's kind of been hanging out with a bad crowd. You know."

"That's too bad."

"Lately he's been working for Dad. But that never lasts long. He can't keep it together."

"I'm sorry."

"It's okay. I just miss him the way he used to be."

"Used to be different, eh?"

"Well, *things* were different. I mean, back then he was just a kid at school, looking out for his sister. Now, when he gets in a fight it's at a bar and he's fighting some white guy—so of course *he* gets the worst of it."

"There's a lot of guys that do it on purpose, you know," said Claude. "Just go out and bait a guy like that. He shouldn't listen."

"I told him that. But he feels justified for doing all the stupid stuff he does because he doesn't have a mom. But, you know, I don't have a mom, either, and I don't go out and get myself in trouble all the time."

"What was she like?"

"My mom? I don't know. She left when I was really little."

Agnes tried to think back, but the only thing she could remember was the trailer they lived in back then. It was gloomy and dank and it kind of teetered. It was full of noises, too: clattering and crashing and sobbing. Maybe everyone's mother made those noises, but their trailer was so small that everything got all clogged up in it. All the bad stuff just hung there. Maybe that's why she went away.

"They say she looked like me," Agnes said.

Dad still kept an old high school photo of Mom in his wallet. It must've really hurt him when she went away. He'd gone looking for her, but aside from maybe Kookum, no one knew whether he'd found her or what. He came home alone and never went looking again.

Claude put his arm around Agnes, and she scooted closer to him. She closed her eyes and listened to the kids shouting.

After a while she looked up at him and said, "I've got this special ointment. I got it from Kookum. It'll help your hands heal."

"Thanks," he said.

They watched the rosy-cheeked kids playing tag, falling down, sliding across the ice, and scrambling to their feet, again and again. One little boy grabbed onto his dad's leg and tried to drag him down, too. They were both laughing their heads off. Agnes brought her legs up onto the bench and pulled Claude's arm tighter around her. She felt his breath in her hair.

After a while Claude said, "My arm's falling asleep."

"I'm sorry," she said.

"It's okay," he said, shaking it out.

"I guess I'm just getting cold," she said.

"Do you want to get a cup of coffee or something?"

"No. Let's go to my place," said Agnes. "I'll give you that ointment."

They stood up and she looped her arm through his. The sun had sunk beyond the naked trees, and the violet dusk was settling around them. As they left the park, the cries of the kids playing faded into the occasional whoosh of a car going by, or voices coming from somewhere out of sight.

✳

"Come on in," Agnes said to Claude, unlocking the door to her apartment. "Jo's not here. She's working until seven." She closed the door behind them. "Hang on, I'll get that ointment."

She took off her parka and hung it over a chair. Then she disappeared down the dark hall.

"Nice place," said Claude, walking over to the front window, a big rectangle of pale light in the dusky room.

"Well, it's pretty basic," Agnes's voice floated out behind her, "but I love the window. I like to see what's happening outside."

She came back into the living room. "Take off your coat," she said, sitting down on the sofa. She motioned for him to sit beside her. "Come here. I'll help you with the ointment."

He obeyed, and sat somewhat stiffly while she got up on her knees beside him and opened the jar. She took his right hand, dabbed a bit of the ointment on his knuckles, and rubbed it in. It had a fresh, piney smell and a slight sting. She massaged his hand for a minute or two, and then took up the left.

"That feels real good," he said.

"That's the idea."

"Agnes. You're like a flower. One of those yellow ones, shaped like the sun. What are they called?"

"I don't know." She smiled.

He took the jar out of her hand and put it on the table. He put his hands on either side of her head and stroked her hair and kissed her mouth—just one, soft kiss. She wrapped her arms around his neck and kissed him long and slow, until finally she could feel him start to kiss her back. His hands settled on her hips.

"How'd you get this scar?" she asked, touching the scar on his cheekbone.

"High stick, I think. Back in juniors. Looks pretty bad, right?"

She kissed it. "No. I like it."

She leaned on him and pushed him down beneath her so that they could stretch out together and she could feel his hands on her body. They were still cool from being outside, but that just added to the chills that were flowing through her in waves. Anyhow, after a while they started to warm up. He was real gentle, real slow. They were just about getting to second. But then, when he had his hands up inside her sweater in the back, about to unhook her bra, he stopped cold and said, "Uh, Agnes. I have to ask you a question."

"No, can't it wait?" she breathed.

She was lying on top of him, all of her weight on his chest and he sat up suddenly, just like that, like she weighed about five ounces, and so she found herself sitting upright, too, straddling his legs. She started to slide her hands up under his shirt. His stomach was hard and smooth.

"Wait, Agnes." He caught both of her wrists, gently, in one hand.

"What?" she asked. She wrapped her arms around his neck and kissed him again.

"I'm sorry. I've got to ask you this."

She looked at him.

"Are you—were you and Mac, I mean, Owen—"

"Owen? Really? You're thinking about Owen right now? Jesus, Claude!" She scrambled off of him and got to her feet as quickly as she could.

"But," said Claude, "sometimes it seems like you two are, maybe—"

"Well we're not."

"I just didn't want to, you know—"

"Just forget it. It's too late now."

She turned her back to him and crossed her arms over her chest, biting her lip and blinking at the streetlights that pierced her dark reflection in the window. She heard him get up, grab his jacket from the chair, and walk out. He stopped outside the door and waited there for a long time. She started to shiver madly. It was cold, standing there alone after lying in his arms. Finally she heard him walk down the stairs, and saw his figure melt into the darkness of the street. Then she threw herself down on the sofa and buried her face in the cushions.

Agnes lay face-down on the sofa for a long time. Jo didn't see her until she walked over to turn on the lamp.

"Oh my God, Agnes! Are you okay?"

"No."

"What happened?" Jo dropped to her knees next to Agnes.

Agnes looked at her. "Jeez, Jo, sorry to scare you. Nothing happened. I'm fine."

"You look terrible," Jo said.

"Claude and I, we had a fight."

"He didn't . . . hurt you?"

"No, he wouldn't do that," said Agnes. "He asked me about Owen."

"So?" Jo stood up.

"We were right in the middle of, you know, making out. What was he thinking?"

"Well, maybe the timing was off, but I'm not surprised he wants to know about you and Owen. I mean, everyone knows that you two have sort of a . . . thing going on."

"We don't have a thing going on!"

"Oh, come on, Agnes."

"But me and Claude, here we were, you know? And then all of sudden, bam! He just sits up and *I have to ask you about Owen.*"

"So what did you say?"

"I just pretty much kicked him out."

"Really? And he just left?"

"Jo, he's a pussycat. I had to think up some dumb scheme just to get him up here in the first place. And now he's gone."

Jo raised her eyebrows. "Well, I'm going to have something to eat. Clay's picking me up soon. We're going to T.T.'s. You should come. It'll cheer you up."

It was a skeleton crew at T.T.'s that evening. A lot of the guys were missing in action because of Valentine's Day, but Jamie was there because Hillary had gone to visit her sister with Jackie. Agnes was happy to see him because he was always in a good mood and it was always infectious. Tonight turned out to be different, though.

"How'd it go with Deucer the other night?" he asked. "I'm sorry I didn't introduce you at first. Somehow I figured you'd met."

"I knew who he was," she said.

"He seemed to know you, too."

"Yeah."

"So, what'd you two end up doing?"

"We had dinner. He's from home, you know, so we have some things in common."

"He's a real class act."

"Yeah. He seems nice."

"My buddy on the Steers told me about him. Said he was out of the game for a while. Not sure why. But someone over there must have remembered him, because they invited him to their camp last fall."

"Oh yeah?"

"Yeah. It was a real break. You know, it isn't easy for a guy like him. Everyone thinks of him as a fighter. Probably even in juniors he never got the coaching to do much else. But he worked his way back. Picked up his game. And here he is."

Agnes didn't say anything.

"I mean, he's no Rocket Richard, but he's done good for us so far."

"He has," Agnes agreed.

"I think it'll get easier for him if he can just hang on this first year or two. I hope we can keep him around."

Agnes put her head down on the table.

"What's the matter?" Jamie asked.

"I'm not feeling too good."

"Are you sick?"

"Maybe."

"Can I give you a ride home?"

"Would you?"

When they got into the car, Jamie said, "Sorry if I was too nosey in there."

"That's okay."

"I know it's none of my business."

"It's not that," Agnes said.

"Are you sure you're alright?" Jamie asked.

"Yeah, Jamie, thanks. I really appreciate the ride."

"Anytime," said Jamie.

As soon as Agnes got home she went to the phone and dialed Claude's number. No answer.

She brushed her teeth, put on her pajamas, and tried Claude again. There was no answer.

She turned on the TV, watched the last period of the Trader's game, and called Claude again. There was still no answer.

She got into bed, and after tossing and turning for forty-five minutes she got up and called him one last time. There was still no answer.

Owen stuffed his gloved hands into his pockets and raised his shoulders tighter to his ears. He'd been walking for a while and now it was late—last call. He rounded the corner and, pitting his weight against the stiff gale, pulled open T.T.'s heavy door. The wind slammed it shut behind him. He walked over to the bar.

"Hey, Sissy," Owen said. He took off his gloves and cap and laid them on the dark, glossy wood. Then he slid onto a barstool.

"Hi," she answered. "What can I get you?"

"Nothing."

"You've got to get something," she said.

"Okay. A beer," he said.

"What kind?" she asked.

"Whatever you got."

She brought him a beer.

"It's been a while," she said.

"I've been thinking about you," he offered. "You look great, really great. It's good to see you."

"It's Valentine's Day," she said.

"Oh yeah?" He unzipped his coat and slid his fingers through the curl that hung down over his forehead.

Sissy went to the other end of the bar to give a guy his tab, served someone a basket of fish 'n' chips and a bottle of ketchup, and made her way back to Owen.

"Need anything else?" she asked him.

"Are you free after work?" he asked.

"No. I have other plans," she said.

"Okay," he replied.

A large party got up and left, and Sissy went over to clear their table. It took a long time. There were about a hundred empty glasses and bottles, plates with half-eaten sandwiches and congealed gravy, crumpled up napkins and jars of condiments missing their tops. When she had filled three bussing tubs, carried them into the dish room, and wiped down the table, she rinsed off her hands, straightened her apron, and went back to Owen at the bar.

She said, "How come you never call me?"

He was finally starting to warm up. He took off his coat and laid it over the stool next to him. He said, "Last time I called you, you were working, remember?"

"Yeah, I guess," she said. "I had to work a double that day."

"And then I was on that road trip," Owen said.

She picked up his beer and wiped away the circle of water

underneath it. Then she put it down again. She leaned on the bar. "How come you never take me out?" she asked.

"Where do you want to go?" he replied.

"What about that party?" she said.

"What party?" he asked.

"You know, the one the guys were talking about. The one at—what's her name?—Hillary's house."

"Hill and Barbie's party?"

"Yeah," said Sissy.

"What about it?" asked Owen.

"Why don't you ask me if I want to go with you to that party?"

Owen looked up into her baby-blue eyes, the dark lines painted painstakingly around their edges, the lashes so long they cast shadows. Is that really all she wanted—to go to that goddamn party? Her hand was resting on the bar and he put his hand on top of it, softly, and sort of stroked around her knuckles. Her hand was warm and kind of clammy. He smiled up at her and said, "Do you want to go to that party with me, Sissy? Hill and Barbie's party?"

She smiled back down at him. "I'd love to, Owen," she said. "Hang on a minute, I almost forgot. I've got to get these guys some coffee." She pulled her hand out from under his, grabbed the pot and went to pour some coffee at a table near the window. When she came back she asked, "Are you ready for your tab?"

"Yeah," he said. His beer mug sat on the bar where she'd left it, pretty much untouched.

"I'm about ready to head out myself, Owen," she said. "I'd love a walk home." She smiled at him again.

"You got it," he said.

"Agnes! Wake up!"

It was Jo.

"What?" Agnes opened her eyes. It was dark. She closed them again.

"Someone's at the door!" whispered Jo, shaking her.

"Don't answer it," said Agnes, half asleep.

"Agnes!" Jo urged again.

By now Agnes was awake enough to hear the knocking. Maybe it was Claude. It must be. She threw off her blankets and reached for her sweatshirt. "I'll get it," she said.

The knocking was insistent. From the living room Agnes could hear a voice, too. "Agnes! Are you there? It's me, Vin."

"Vin!" Agnes unlatched the door, flung it open, and threw her arms around her brother.

"Whoa," he laughed, as he stumbled backwards a little.

His jacket carried the cold and the sharp smell of snow. Somehow they'd ended up out in the hall, and the floor was icy under Agnes's bare feet, but she didn't care. She looked at Vin. His face was all healed.

"You look great, Vin!" She gave him a hockey-style face wipe.

"Maybe we should go inside?" he said.

She pulled him into the apartment. "Jo, it's okay, come say hi, it's Vin. Vin, are you hungry?"

She ran to the refrigerator, opened it, and inventoried its contents in her head. There were some leftovers and some stuff for sandwiches, too.

"No, I'm okay. You don't have to feed me."

Suddenly it occurred to Agnes that it was somewhat unusual to go visiting at three o'clock in the morning. She closed the refrigerator. "What are you doing here? Is everything okay?"

"Yeah, everything's fine. Sorry to show up in the middle of the night like this. I didn't leave until kind of late."

"You came from home?"

"Yeah."

"Everyone's okay?"

"Yeah, yeah. Dad says hi, and Kookum, too. Oh, that reminds me." Vin put his hand into the pocket of his jacket and pulled out a small plastic bag. "This is for you. From Kookum." He dropped it into Agnes's hand.

Agnes prodded the bag with her fingers. It was full of tiny glass beads. There were different shades of red, orange, and rose, two or three shades of green, and an iridescent black.

"These are pretty. What are they for?"

"She didn't say. I figured it was something between the two of you," said Vin.

"No," said Agnes. "Not that I know of."

"Oh, well. Give her a call and ask her."

"Yeah. What are you doing here, anyhow?"

"Dad asked me to leave."

"Aw, Vin, what happened?"

"Nothing."

"But he needs the help, and you need a job. Couldn't you make it work somehow?"

"Not this time."

"How many times will there be?"

"Come on, Agnes—"

"It's hard on Dad, you know?"

"Well, he's hard on me."

"Bullshit."

"You know him. He's got all these rules. He's always judging me."

"He cares about you. It's for your own good."

"I'm twenty-three years old. I know what's for my own good!"

"The hell you do."

Vin didn't answer.

"If he's trying to keep you away from Lance and those guys, you'd be better off doing *exactly* what he says. And you know it."

"Agnes, they're my friends. I have to be there for them."

"Are they there for you?"

"Sure they are."

"Well, yeah, if it means punching the shit out of some guy at a bar. But if you need them to give you some space or support you when you're trying to do something *real*, they're fucking useless. Worse than fucking useless."

"So they've got no self-control. I know that. Neither do I."

"Yes, you do. You don't have to be just like them."

"But when someone says something, I—"

"Just ignore it. Just walk away."

"That's easy for you to say," said Vin. "You're a girl. No one expects you to stand up for yourself."

"And I don't really give a shit, what they expect or don't expect," replied Agnes.

He didn't say anything.

"What are you going to do now?"

"I was kind of hoping that I could stay with you for a couple of weeks, maybe look for some work around here."

"I don't know, Vin. My rules about who you can hang out with are just as strict as Dad's. Stricter, even."

"Don't worry," he said.

"You know I'm not joking," Agnes warned him.

"I know."

"It'd be fun to have you around for a while." Agnes looked over at Jo, who was standing at the entrance to the short hallway in her long white bathrobe, her arms crossed in front of her chest.

Vin said, "I can sleep on the sofa."

"You'd pretty much have to," said Agnes. "What do you think, Jo? Is that okay?"

"Well, yeah, okay," said Jo.

"Just for a couple of weeks," said Vin.

"It's a deal," said Agnes.

"I'll go get my stuff," he said, and he was out the door.

"Thanks, Jo," said Agnes. "I appreciate it."

"Well, he's your brother. But you know, we're not really supposed to have three people living here."

"I know. Don't worry. Vin isn't perfect, but he's not a freeloader. He won't want to stick around if he feels like he's a burden."

Jo went back to bed and Vin came in with his duffel bag and bed roll. Agnes got a towel from the hall closet, tossed it at his head, and sat down facing him, cross-legged, on the sofa.

"You been playing?" he asked her.

"A little."

"Pickup?"

"Yeah."

"How's it going?"

"Same as always. Just trying to fit in."

"I know what you mean," said Vin.

"At least you're a guy," she replied.

He shrugged.

"So Dad and Kookum are okay?" she asked.

"Yeah. The garage is getting a lot of business. Dad's working at Haslund's, too. He's real busy."

"And Kookum?"

"She's doing great. It's funny. Dad hardly ever talks about you. I think he misses you too much. But Kookum, she talks about you all the time."

"What's there to talk about?"

"You know—the shop, what kind of stuff you guys sell and all that. She talks about your playing, and about Jo, and her classes. She talks about MacKenzie, too. You're not going out with him, are you?"

"What if I were?" Agnes asked.

"Are you?"

"No."

"She'll be sorry to hear that." He grinned.

"Yeah, she's always loved old O."

"He's not too bad—for a white kid."

"Vin, come on."

"Seriously, he's just a little thick about some things."

"You're a little thick about some things, too," said Agnes.

"Kookum said you went out with him when you were home for Christmas. She said you were out really late with him."

"Is there anything she *didn't* tell you about my personal life?"

"What else is there to tell?" asked Vin.

She threw a cushion at him. "Good night, Vin," she said.

"Good night, Agnes."

Agnes tried to be very quiet going back into the bedroom, but she needn't have bothered. As soon as she climbed into her bed she heard Jo whisper her name from across the room.

"Agnes?"

"Are you still awake?" Agnes answered.

"Agnes, when Vin was knocking on the door, I was afraid it was Clay."

Agnes propped herself up on her elbow and stared through the darkness in the direction of Jo's bed.

"Did you two have another fight?"

"Not really, but—"

"What do you mean, *not really*? Jo, you've got to break up with him."

Jo didn't answer.

"You have to, Jo. It's crazy. When I heard Vin knocking I was *hoping* it was Claude. But you're afraid of *your* boyfriend."

"I know, it's just, he seems to need me so much. I know he cares for me. He doesn't mean to, but I'm afraid he's going to hurt me."

"How can he care for you, and then hurt you? That isn't normal."

"He still thinks I'm cheating on him. I don't know what else I can do to reassure him."

"It's not your job to reassure him. If he doesn't trust you, that's his problem. He should just break up with you."

Jo was quiet for a few seconds. Then she said, "I just don't know what to do."

"Don't worry, Jo. I'll help you. We'll figure it out. We'll just go step by step."

"Okay," she whispered.

"Now go to sleep, okay?"

"Yeah. Thanks, Agnes."

"Goodnight, Jo."

5

Jackie was visiting his grandparents, the Wolves were beginning a homestand, and Jamie and Hillary were hosting their annual party for the team at her place. They'd been doing it since before Jamie became captain, and for a team in which most of the guys were young and single, with bare-bones apartments and barely-stocked refrigerators, an evening in a house with carpet on the floor, a fire in the fireplace, and a table full of home-cooked food satisfied a real craving. Their anticipation had been growing since their first glimpse of the schedule back in the fall when they scoped out the mid-winter homestands and placed bets on the likeliest dates for the big event. Hillary cooked, Jamie played DJ and dishwasher, and the guys brought the beer—along with that little something extra that gave each year's gathering its unique flavor.

Jamie still shook his head when he remembered the year the Wolves brought a five-game winning streak into the evening and took an eight-game losing streak out of it. And the year that Perry brought both of his identical twin sisters—the one who was dating Jonner *and* the one who wasn't—leading to a quasi-Shakespearean comedy of mistaken identity. And then there was the year that Jamie first became captain, and the party happened to be on his birthday, and some of the guys arranged for Hammer to jump out of a psychedelic birthday cake while the third line plus Tonkins plus Phil, the backup goalie, performed an inspired cover of the Jackson Five's *I'll Be There*, complete with platform shoes and afros.

No one knew what this year's edition would bring. Jo called Clay to tell him that she was getting a ride with Agnes and Vin, and that she would see him there. He didn't like it, but Agnes cheered her on and Jo made it through the phone call with flying colors. Vin's situation, though, troubled Agnes—after a few short, unproductive days of job hunting, he was already discouraged. What had happened to the relentless warrior she remembered from his playing days? Was he nothing more than the creation of a little sister's unconditional admiration? As for Agnes herself, the more she thought about what Jo and Jamie had said, the worse she felt about what had happened between her and Claude. She hadn't called him again, and she hadn't heard from him, either.

Still, she was excited when Vin pulled his old Dodge up in front of Hillary's house. It was tiny but cozy, and even though Christmas was long past, a string of lights twinkled merrily along the line of the roof. Agnes's heart beat faster when she noticed Claude's red pickup parked across the street.

Agnes, Jo, and Vin filed up the shoveled walk and went inside, adding their boots to the pile by the door and hanging their parkas over the back of the sofa. The living room was nearly empty, but they heard voices in the kitchen. Agnes went first, carrying a plate of bannock—after months of practice, hers was almost as good as Kookum's—and Vin carried a case of beer. The kitchen was jammed with people.

"Hey Agnes," said Jamie, "Glad you could make it."

"It's nice of you to have us," said Agnes. "Jamie, this is my brother, Vin."

"Hey man, welcome," Jamie said. They shook hands. "Jo, good to see you. Come on in, grab a beer, guys."

"Agnes," said Hillary, "Jackie was so upset when I told him that you'd be here and he'd miss out on seeing you. You two must have had a lot of fun the other day."

"We did," she answered. "I'll take him again soon. Stick and puck with Jackie is a welcome change from pickup."

Vin was opening bottles of beer for himself and Jo. "Agnes, do you want a beer?"

"No thanks. Not right now," said Agnes.

Claude had appeared in the doorway between the kitchen and the little dining room. As always, he was just a little more formal than any of the other guys—he looked well-scrubbed and his forest green, flannel shirt was tucked into his jeans. His belt had a shiny buckle. Agnes got goosebumps, and she started toward him through the crowded room. His eyes followed her the whole way. He seemed to be just as nervous as she was.

"Hey, Claude."

"Hey, Agnes."

"I tried to call you," she said. "You didn't answer."

"I had to go home," he said.

She looked at him. "I just wanted to say, I wasn't being fair. I mean, the other day, when we were at my place."

"It was my fault," he said.

"No. You had the right to ask me. I just didn't want to talk about it, not then."

"I know. Bad timing," he said. "Should've asked before. Meant to. Just got a little carried away."

They both smiled.

"Maybe we can get together again sometime?" he asked.

She nodded and looked back at Vin. "Come here, Vin," she said. "Claude, this is my brother Vincent. Vin, Claude Doucette."

"Wow, Claude Doucette," said Vin, offering his hand.

"Good to meet you, Vincent," said Claude.

"Excuse me," said Agnes. "I'm going to give Hillary a hand."

"I remember you," said Vin. "I used to watch you when you played midgets."

Claude chuckled. "That was a long time ago."

"Yeah. I was pretty young. But you had like, forty goals one of those seasons, right?"

"Something like that."

"A lot of them were real pretty, too."

"Well—"

"And now you play for the Wolves, eh? What's it like?"

"It's a lot harder to score, that's for sure."

"Yeah, well, where've they got you now? Fourth line? Maybe half the minutes you had back then?"

"It's a tough league. And I'm bigger, slower—of course they're going to use me different. But I always loved to play. Glad to be playing now."

"How's it working out with MacKenzie?" asked Vin.

"Mac's a good kid, good player."

"I played with him one year in midgets."

"Oh yeah?"

"Yeah. He was good, but there were guys who played better."

"Really?"

"He got a lot of good breaks, though," said Vin.

"I bet he did," said Claude. "He's on the ice early most days. Real focused. Stays late taking draws, shooting. Not every guy does that kind of stuff."

Vin didn't answer.

"What about you?" asked Claude.

"Me?"

"Yeah. What're you doing?"

"Now? Looking for a job."

"Agnes told me a little about you," said Claude.

"Oh yeah? What'd she say? That I'm a bum?"

"No, she told me she's missed you the last couple years, that's all. It's good that you came to visit her."

"She's a good kid," said Vin.

"She really cares about you. Looks up to you."

"Nah."

"She does," Claude said.

Vin smirked. "I'm not much of a role model."

"Well, she doesn't need a role model so much these days, maybe. But there's a lot of kids that do."

"Hey, I just remembered," Vin said. "You played with the Lumbermen, right?"

"Right."

"You took down Gill Harris. You gave him what was coming to him."

Claude shrugged.

"The bastard. He deserved it. That late hit on McIntyre—it was ugly. And that wasn't the first time. He was real bad to us Indian guys. I would've killed him myself if I got the chance."

Claude shook his head. "I didn't mean to hurt him like that. It was a mistake."

"It's part of the game. Anyhow, you taught him a lesson."

"I don't know," said Claude. "He's going to do what they tell him to do. Just like the rest of us."

"He's playing again, you know," said Vin.

"Yeah. What about you? You ever play anymore?" Claude asked. "Agnes said you played good hockey."

"I used to be okay."

"What'd you play?"

"D, mostly."

"But you don't play anymore?"

"No, it's been too long. Rusty."

"What's it been? Three, four years? That's not too long."

"I don't know."

"You're a young guy. What else have you got going?" asked Claude.

"Not much," admitted Vin.

"Boys, the food's on the table," said Hillary to Vin and Claude, shooing them out of the kitchen. "Help yourself." Then she said to Agnes, "Why don't you get them set up in the living room? It's getting too crowded in here. Jo, will you get the salad out of the fridge?"

"Sure, Hillary. Should I grab some dressing, too?"

"Oh, rats. I don't think there is any. I was going to make some." Hillary pulled a couple of bottles and some spices out of the cupboard. "I'll just toss it all together," she said.

Jo stood beside her, watching.

"I really like your place, Hillary."

"Thanks, Jo."

"You and Jamie, do you think you'll get married?"

Hillary smiled. "Gosh, I don't know, Jo."

"I'm sorry, I didn't mean to get personal. It's just that, you seem like such a perfect couple."

"Well, we're really lucky. But I'm sort of married to my son right now, you know? And if Jamie gets traded, I'm not sure I could just pick up and go with him. I've got a good job, and Jackie's in school here. We have our own lives."

"Hmm. You just seem so perfect."

"No, not perfect. Doing okay, though, so far. What about you, Jo? How's school?"

"Pretty good. I'm trying to get going on my final project."

"What is it?" asked Hillary.

"It's supposed to be a dress or outfit that expresses a Saskatchewan sense of place or identity," Jo said.

"Wow, and you have to sew the dress, right?"

"Yeah, with sketches and everything. And you're supposed to use contrasting materials, and all this other stuff," said Jo.

"Sounds hard."

"The hardest part is coming up with the concept. Usually I get really psyched for these things. But not this time."

"Oh yeah? How's everything else? I haven't seen much of you lately."

Jo shrugged. "I'm okay."

"I noticed that Clay's not here."

"I drove over with Agnes and Vin. I told Clay I wanted to cool things off a bit, you know."

"He seems like a pretty intense guy," said Hillary.

"Yeah."

"Sometimes it's good to just be with your friends."

"Right."

"Okay," said Hillary. "Here's the salad. Will you put it on the table? And get yourself something to eat. I'll try to get out there in a minute."

Jo helped herself to some chicken casserole and went into the living room. Agnes was sitting in an armchair, looking up at Vin and Jamie, with Claude on an ottoman at her knees. Jo perched on the arm of Agnes's chair.

"Vin knows hockey," Claude was telling Jamie.

"Oh yeah? Maybe there's an opening at the rink. Can you run a blademaster?" Jamie asked Vin.

"Yeah, sure," said Vin. "I can drive a zamboni, too."

"He's a good mechanic," added Agnes.

"Cool. Hey, Ducks?" Jamie called over his shoulder to where Ducks was talking with some of the other guys. "Did they ever find a replacement for Peters?"

"I don't know, Barbs," said Ducks. "I think they wanted to sort of hold the place for him while he's in the hospital. Hoping that he'll be back, you know."

"Yeah, but he'll be out for a while, eh?" Jamie said.

"I think so," agreed Ducks.

Jamie said to Vin, "Todd Peters is an older guy. He's been there forever, but he's been sick. Maybe you can sub for him, get your foot in the door that way. I mean, it's not the best job in the world, but if nothing else comes up, it could hold you for a while."

"Sounds good," said Vin, nodding.

Hillary called to Jamie, asking him for help in the kitchen.

Vin said to Jo, "I'm going to get some more of that chicken dish. Do you want anything?"

"I don't know. I'll come with you, though," said Jo. "We'll leave the lovebirds alone."

They walked into the dining room.

"What's going on with those two, anyhow?" Vin asked Jo, motioning back to Agnes and Claude.

"I think they're sort of at the getting-to-know-you stage," answered Jo.

"Awesome," said Vin, nodding and grinning.

Jo made a face. "What's awesome?"

"He's like, freaking *Claude Doucette.*"

"Come on, Vin. Name one person who's ever heard the name *Claude Doucette.* I mean, outside of St. Cyp."

"Where are *you* from, Jo Morin Gervais?"

"I know where I'm from," she answered.

Vin said, "You have to admit, if they got together they'd have some seriously awesome hockey-playing kids."

"The same would apply if she *got together* with any one of these guys, right?" said Jo, making finger quotes around *got together.*

Vin didn't answer.

"Anyhow, it's not about breeding hockey players," said Jo. "It's about what's best for Agnes as a person."

"My point, exactly," said Vin.

Claude had been quiet, emptying his plate and studying Agnes. He knew he was staring at her like an idiot, but he kept doing it anyhow. He'd nearly driven off the highway remembering the afternoon at her place, but that was nothing compared to being near her now. Her hair shimmered, her delicate silver earrings reflected the light, and her fuzzy, white sweater looked so soft. Now that Vin and Jo were gone, she was looking at him, too, and he thought he ought to say something.

"You look beautiful tonight, Agnes," he said.

She looked down at her plate. "How was your trip home?" she asked.

"It was good. Took care of a few things," he said.

"Were you visiting someone?"

"Yeah. My mom."

"Does she live alone?"

"Yeah. She does real good, too. She's a strong person. But I still need to check on her. Make sure her heater's working. She's not going to tell me if it goes out."

"You're a good son."

"Well, there's only me, now." Claude took Agnes's empty plate out of her lap and started to get up. "You want anything?" he asked.

"No," she said. "Wait. Put those down for a minute, okay?"

He put the plates on the floor. She scooted forward in the armchair so that her face was very close to his. She put her hand on his knee.

"Claude, Owen and I never—Owen was never my boyfriend. We just kind of grew up together. His mom helped us a lot after my mom left, and she and Kookum are still friends. Owen's a friend, but he's real different. I mean, he's going to be a great player, and I'm just someone he knows from home. Just an old friend. That's all."

"Yeah?" He wanted to believe it.

Agnes nodded.

"Okay," Claude said. "I mean, Agnes, here's the thing. I'm not like Mac. I'm just a big body. There's hundreds of guys like me. Lining up behind me. I can't do anything to hurt the team."

Agnes knitted her brow. She'd always respected players like Claude, but until now she hadn't considered that their sacrifices might go beyond the physical. She said, "Claude, I think you're selling yourself short. But I understand. Jamie told me about how hard you've worked to get back."

"I wish he hadn't told you that."

"Why?"

He shrugged.

"I'd be proud. I'm proud to know you. I just wish it didn't have to be so . . . "

As they sat there together, knee to knee, their faces inches apart, searching each other's eyes, Owen came through the front door and saw them. He froze. Sissy was a step ahead of him. "Come on, Owen," she said. "What're you waiting for? Take off your boots. Give me your jacket. Come on, let's go."

Owen didn't move.

"Come *on*, Owen," Sissy said again.

"What?" Owen snapped out of it and followed Sissy into the kitchen. He blinked in the bright light.

"Hey Macker!" said Barbie. "You're late! What'cha been up to?" He winked, but then he said, "What's the matter? You don't look too good."

"No, man, I'm good," Owen replied. "This is great. Hey Hill, it smells great in here. I'm starving!"

"Well, grab a beer," said Hillary. "The food's in the dining room. I've got another lasagna coming in a minute."

"Wow, this is the life, eh Barbie?" Owen said.

"You don't hear me complaining, that's for sure," Jamie answered.

Claude came into the kitchen with his and Agnes's plates. "Hillary, thank you for dinner. It was real good. What do you want me to do with these?"

"Just put them in the sink," she said.

"Sink's pretty full. Can I put some of this stuff in the dishwasher for you?"

"No thanks. Jamie'll do it. You go enjoy yourself."

Claude put the dishes in the sink and followed Owen into the dining room. "Hey Mac, how's it going?"

Owen didn't look at him. "Alright, you?"

"Good, thanks."

"Yeah, looks like you're set up pretty well," said Owen under his breath.

"What's that?" asked Claude.

"Nothing, man. Nothing." Owen took a plate and started serving himself. Claude grabbed a soda. The two men sat down on a couple of chairs along the wall.

"Good of Hillary to have us all," said Claude.

Owen nodded.

"I just met Vincent—Vin Demers. You know him?" asked Claude.

"A little."

"You ever play with him?"

"Yeah, one year. We overlapped one year in midget," answered Owen.

"How's he play?"

"He played pretty good D, back then. He has a short fuse, though. Gets himself in a lot of trouble. It's really tough on Ag— on the family."

Claude was quiet for a while and then he said, "I was just talking to Agnes."

"You mean Daisy?" asked Owen.

"I mean Agnes," said Claude.

"I noticed," Owen said.

"Hope you don't mind," said Claude.

"Why would I mind?"

"She's a good girl."

"You said that before."

Claude was quiet for a minute, looking down at the soda can in his hand. He swirled it around, one way and then the other. He said, "Look, Mac, as far as Agnes goes, I don't want to—"

"It's okay, man," Owen said.

"She told me you're friends from home?"

"Yeah. I already told you that, didn't I?"

"Yeah, you did. How do you two know each other?"

"We played together when we were kids, in the woods, and all. Skated in the winter. Played some shinny, you know, that kind of thing."

"Yeah? You and Agnes?"

"Yeah. And my brother, and her brother, and the other kids. But yeah, Agnes . . . she came out there a lot."

"She did?"

"We played some pond hockey."

"Oh yeah?" asked Claude.

"Yeah, we played bantam together, too."

"No kidding! You and Agnes?"

"Yeah. Peewee, bantam."

"I didn't know she played," said Claude.

"She didn't tell you?" asked Owen.

"No."

Agnes appeared in front of them. "Tell him what?"

Claude stood up to offer her his seat. Just then Ducks called to him from across the room. "Hey Deucer, come here for a minute, will ya? You gotta tell us about this guy Norton."

Claude looked at Agnes.

"Go ahead," said Agnes. She sat down next to Owen, and Claude went to talk with Ducks and the other guys.

"What were you talking about?" Agnes asked Owen.

"Nothing much," said Owen.

"Bullshit."

"If you must know, Deuce asked how we met, and I told him we used to play together."

"You told him I used to play?" asked Agnes.

"Yeah."

"Hockey?"

"Yeah. What's the problem?"

"Why'd you do that?"

"He asked how I knew you," said Owen.

Agnes buried her face in her hands.

"Oh, come on, Ag. I figured he knew. You're probably giving him all sorts of pointers. I mean, you two are in pretty deep, right?"

"What do you mean, *in pretty deep?*"

"You know what I mean."

"No. I mean, yes, but that's not really—"

"I saw you two just now, sitting over there. What do you think I am, blind? Why do you fucking lie to me? Jesus Christ, Agnes."

Owen's words bit into her. His face was all scrunched up like it had been that time outside her building when she'd sent him off to call Sissy. But this was worse. He was angry. Owen *never* got angry.

He didn't move, or change expression, and she just sat there, waiting for him to say something else. Finally she asked, "Owen. Are you okay?"

He blinked. "Yeah, Ag. I'm great. Just great."

He got up and headed to the kitchen. She followed him.

"Owen, wait. Please."

He turned around so quickly that his fork shot off of his still-full plate and clattered onto the floor. He ignored it. "Look, Ag, I just need some time, okay? I need some time to get used to this." Then he turned back around and disappeared into the kitchen.

"Hey, Macker, can I get you something?" Barbie asked him.

"No, thanks, Barbs. Great party. I gotta run, though. Say goodbye to Hill." He put his plate in the sink.

"What's the rush?"

"I, uh, got a couple things to take care of."

"Okay, see you tomorrow. Oh wait—what about Sissy? Hill's showing her Jackie's new room."

"Sissy? Oh, yeah. Barbs, could you help me out, man? Tell her I had to leave. Tell her it was an emergency or something. She's really been looking forward to tonight. I don't want to mess it up for her."

"Yeah, no problem, Mac."

"Thanks, man. I owe you one."

Owen grabbed his jacket off the pile, jammed his feet into his boots, and walked out the door. He ran into Clay tromping up the walk.

"Mac," Clay said. "Jo in there?"

"I think so."

Clay stumbled in the door and, without taking off his boots or coat, stomped into the kitchen, where Jamie was on dishwasher duty. Hillary and Sissy had just returned from Jackie's room and were leaning against the counter, talking. Hammer was taking a beer out of the cooler.

"Jo here?" Clay asked.

"Oh, hey Torris, you made it, good to see you," said Jamie, turning toward him.

"Jo here?" Clay asked again.

"She's probably in the living room," said Hillary.

Clay left the kitchen.

"He's lit," said Hammer.

Hillary raised her eyebrows at Jamie. He dried his hands and he and Hammer followed Clay into the dining room. "Torris, have something to eat," Jamie said. "The lasagna's *molto squisito*—made from scratch."

"Where is she?" Clay's voice was loud enough to carry clearly back into the kitchen. Hillary looked at Sissy with alarm and followed the men into the living room, where Jo was talking with Vin, Agnes, Claude, Ducks, and Dan Jorgensen, one of the team's defensemen, and his girlfriend, Junie.

"Josie, come on, let's go," Clay commanded.

Jo looked frightened but she said, "Hi Clay, come on over." She reached her hand out to him.

Clay repeated, "Josie, come on. It's time to get going."

Jamie said, "Clay, relax, have something to eat. You just got here."

"But *she's* been here long enough," Clay answered, giving Vin a hard stare.

"Clay, I'm right in the middle of a conversation," said Jo.

Clay's voice rose. "Then excuse yourself and—"

"Why don't you join us?" she continued.

"Don't interrupt me!"

"You're interrupting me," said Jo.

"She *said* she wants to stay for a while," Vin said to Clay, through gritted teeth.

"You stay out of it," bellowed Clay.

"Whoa, whoa, guys," said Jamie. "Clay, come and get something to—"

"I'm *not hungry!*" shouted Clay, and he kicked over a small side table, flinging a couple of beer bottles and an empty plate onto the floor.

"Alright," said Jamie. "Give me a hand, boys." Hammer, Claude, Dan, and Ducks helped Jamie muscle Clay over to the door. Vin would've joined them, but Agnes held him back.

"Hill, we're taking him home," called Jamie, as the three men pushed Clay out the door.

Jo started to shake and ran out of the room. Agnes followed her down the hall and into the washroom. She closed the door behind them.

Jo slumped down on the toilet seat lid and started to sob. Agnes sat on the rim of the tub and tried to reach her arm around Jo's shoulders. She didn't know what to say, so she mostly just let her cry.

"Shh. It's okay, Jo."

Finally Jo choked out, "I was so scared."

"I know. But you were brave. You really stood up for yourself. I'm proud of you, Jo," said Agnes.

Jo let out a sharp cry and started sobbing again.

"Shh, Jo. Calm down, it's okay."

"I ruined the party!"

"No you didn't. Clay ruined the party."

Jo gasped for air. "But if I hadn't, if I didn't drive here with you guys . . . "

"Jo, you can drive with anyone you want. It's Clay's fault for showing up drunk and trying to drag you away like some kind of caveman—"

There was a knock on the door. "Agnes? Jo?" It was Hillary. "Can I come in?"

"No, no!" whispered Jo, and she shook her head violently. But Agnes got up and opened the door. Hillary came in and closed it behind her.

Jo said, "Hillary, I'm so sorry, I ruined your party."

Hillary knelt down in front of Jo. "You didn't ruin the party! First of all, it would take a lot more than one guy knocking over a table to keep this team from partying. Second—" and her tone became more serious, "Clay's got no business storming in here like that. He was totally out of line. But don't worry, Jamie's taking care of it. It'll be okay."

"That's really nice of Jamie," said Jo. "But Clay can be . . . I don't want Jamie to get hurt."

"Don't worry," said Hillary. "He's got plenty of help. They'll all stay together until Clay calms down. I promise."

Jamie and Ducks helped Vin get some part-time work at the rink.

"I know it's not much," Jamie told him. "But it's something. And you can use those free hours to look for something better."

Vin was happy to be working, and, even more, for the vote of confidence that Jamie had given him. To celebrate, he invited Agnes and Jo out for pizza. Agnes was game, but Jo said she wasn't feeling well. She was still shaken up from what had happened at the party.

"Come on, Jo. That was two nights ago and you haven't done anything but mope around the apartment. It'll cheer you up to get out a little," said Agnes.

"I don't feel like it. You guys go. I just want to stay home and take a bath and watch TV."

"Okay. We'll give you a call to check in," said Agnes.

Agnes and Vin left and Jo took a nice long bath, got into her coziest sweatpants, and turned on the TV. The phone rang. She wouldn't have answered it, but she figured it was Agnes.

"Hello?"

It wasn't Agnes. It was Clay.

"Hey, Josie."

Her face got hot and her heart started to pound.

"You there?" he asked.

"Yes," she said.

"Listen, I'm real sorry about what happened the other night."

Jo didn't answer.

"You still there, babe?"

She started to hang up, but she knew he'd just call again, so she brought the phone back up to her ear.

"You still there?" Clay asked again.

"Yes."

"You know, Josie, I just had one too many. I missed you. I didn't mean to cause trouble."

"You knocked over their furniture! You broke their plate!"

"I know, I know. And I apologized, believe me, I did."

Jo's breathing was quick and shallow.

"You there?" Clay asked.

"Yes."

"Look, Josie, I'm really sorry. I was out of line, I know. I just, I love you so much, baby. I hate to see you with another guy—"

"I wasn't *with* another guy, Clay. I was just talking to some friends. At a party. What were you thinking?"

"I don't know, baby, I just snapped, you know? It was a mistake, I didn't mean it. I didn't mean any of it."

Jo started to shake.

"You there, Josie?"

She closed her eyes.

"Are you there?" he asked again.

"Yeah," she whispered.

"Come on, please, you have to forgive me. I didn't hurt anyone. I was just a little upset, that's all. 'Cause I love you, baby, I really do."

Jo squeezed her eyes shut. Her tears etched cold tracks down her hot face.

"Come on, baby, forgive me. Okay?"

"Okay," she whispered. And she hung up the phone.

She went into the bathroom, put cold water on a washcloth, and held it over her eyes, her elbows on the sink. She took some deep breaths. Then she went back to the sofa to watch some more TV while she waited for Agnes and Vin to get home. But just when the program got interesting, someone knocked on the door. She jumped to her feet.

"Hey, Josie, it's me," called Clay through the door. "Wanna go out for a drink?"

Her heart started pumping like some kind of crazy machine that wasn't even a part of her. She took a breath and tried to keep her voice even.

"Oh, hi, Clay," she called back at the closed door. "No thanks, I'm not feeling so hot. I was just getting ready for bed. Maybe I'll see you tomorrow, okay?"

"Aw, that's too bad, baby. Sorry you're not feeling well." He paused. "Maybe a little drink'll help you feel better, eh?"

"No. I don't think so. Thanks again, though, Clay. Goodnight."

She stood there looking at the closed door, waiting for his response. He was quiet for a few seconds. Finally he said, "Okay, babe. See you later."

She heard him walk down the stairs. She turned off the TV, turned out the lights, took off her sweatpants, and got into bed. The sheets were so cold that they raised goosebumps on her flesh. She pulled her elbows and knees in close to get warm and tried to slow her breathing. After a long time she started to relax. She stretched out and sunk into the soft mattress.

But just as she was slipping into unconsciousness she heard knocking again. Her heart raced. There was no way to ignore it—the pounding got louder, faster, more frantic. She got up, put on her bathrobe, went into the living room, and switched on the light.

"Hey, baby, it's me!" came Clay's voice from the other side of the door. His words were slurred. "Wanna get a drink?"

She didn't answer.

He pounded the door again. "Come on, baby," he hollered.

"Clay, I told you I'm going to bed. I was already in bed. Maybe tomorrow."

"Aw, come on, Josie! Don't make me wait! I wanna see you *now*." He pounded on the door some more.

"Clay, stop it, you're going to wake the neighbors!"

"Then why don't you let me in, baby? What's going on in there anyway?" He kept pounding.

"Stop it, Clay! Please!"

"Who's in there with you? I bet it's that guy from the party, right?"

"No, Clay. No one's here. It's just me. I wanted to go to sleep early tonight."

"Don't lie to me! Come on, open up! Open up!" He was shouting now, and pounding. The door rattled and jumped until Jo thought it would fly off its hinges.

"Okay, okay," she said. "I'll open the door. Just *be quiet. Please.*"

She opened the door. "See, there's no one here but me. I told you."

Clay shot past her and tore around the apartment, switching on every light, peering into every corner and even rifling through the closets and checking under the beds, while Jo stood trembling in the living room in front of the gaping door.

Clay burst back into the room.

"See, Clay? I told you. There's no one here but me," Jo said.

It was as if he didn't even hear her, didn't even see her.

"What's back here?" he snapped, and as he swung around to look behind her mannequins they toppled onto the floor, along with the beginnings of her final project. He kicked one of them as it lay there.

"Clay, that's my project!" she protested, and she bent over to rescue it.

"Get away from there! You're never gonna be a fucking fashion designer anyway," he shouted.

"Yes I am!"

He grabbed her arm and jerked her up and away from the mannequins. Then he pointed at Vin's duffel bag, which was sitting under the window. "What's that over there?"

"That's just Vin's bag, he's staying here while he—"

"*That's just Vin's bag,*" Clay repeated in a high, mocking voice. "You fucking Indian whore!" He slapped her across the face and she fell backwards onto the floor.

At that moment, Vin appeared in the doorway with Agnes behind him.

"What did you say?" shouted Vin.

"There you are!" Clay yelled back. "I'm gonna kill you, you goddamn Indian son of a bitch!"

But Clay was slowed by whiskey and Vin was on fire. He leapt across the room and hurled his fist at Clay's mouth. The blow turned Clay around by a few degrees, and his countering punch only grazed Vin's cheekbone. Vin drew his arm back again and slammed his knuckles into the hard bone of Clay's brow. Blood started oozing from the corner of Clay's eye and he stood there blinking, stunned.

Agnes pointed at the door and yelled at him, "Get *out*, Torris! Get out, *now!*"

Reeling, Clay fingered his busted lip as he stumbled toward the door. He couldn't see clearly—it was as if he'd been plunged underwater. He blinked again and again until finally, out of the murk, a police constable materialized, holding a gun. Like a suspect in some low-budget crime drama, Clay slowly lifted his hands. No one else moved a muscle. Agnes's command hung there like a frozen echo. Otherwise there was dead silence in the room.

The constable looked from face to face. Vin stood inside the door to his left, wearing a jacket and a knit cap, his partially untucked shirt hanging down over his jeans on the right side and a welt rising on his cheekbone. Jo, the right side of her face a bright crimson and starting to swell, blood dripping from her nose, huddled crookedly on the floor against the back of the sofa, her bare legs and feet showing from under her white bathrobe, which she was adjusting as best she could to cover them. Next to Jo stood Agnes, wearing her parka, hat, and gloves and carrying a flat, white cardboard box with the red lettering *Pizza! Eat it while it's hot!* Almost directly in front of the constable stood Clay, halted on his way to the door, his jacket unzipped, his lip busted, blood oozing from around his eye and splattered down his shirt, hands up in the air, and the stench of alcohol on his breath.

"What happened here?" asked the constable.

No one answered.

"Whose residence is this?" he asked.

Agnes and Jo looked at each other and slowly raised their hands.

Vin and Clay Torris ended up being hauled off to the police station, but not before a second officer, Constable Darcy, grilled everyone about the evening's events. When the door had finally closed behind the four men, and the echo of their footsteps on the stairs had died, Agnes turned to look at Jo.

"Are you okay?" Agnes asked her.

"I think so," Jo answered. Like a hockey player clipped by a high stick, she touched the blood tickling her upper lip and then examined her bloody fingers. Then, unlike a hockey player, she dropped her face into her hands and started to sob.

"Shh, Jo," said Agnes. "It's okay." She hugged her and they stood there for a long time, Jo crying into Agnes's shoulder.

Finally, Jo asked, "What are we going to do now?"

Agnes answered, "We're going to the police station to get Vin."

The slogan on the outside of the police station, "Public Safety Is Our Business and Yours," had always struck Agnes as goofy, but inside, the PR campaign was nowhere in evidence. It was all business. Long, straight halls of polished, gray linoleum met at right angles with other, identical halls. Every once in a while there was a closed metal door with a frosted glass window, or a bulletin board enclosed in a locked, glass case—otherwise the brownish-yellow tiled walls were bare. It was hours after dark, but you'd never know it. The fluorescent light glared on, constant in its hum and flicker. Agnes thought of Vin, trapped somewhere in this cold maze of hallways, and the old stories flooded her mind, stories of Riel and Big Bear and Poundmaker, the leaders of her people, and how they'd been imprisoned, trapped outside the sun, the cycles, and the seasons—outside of life as they knew it—until they withered. She was afraid for Vin. Everyone knew that even now, a hundred years later, the police could hardly be expected to extend justice to a Native man.

When Agnes and Jo finally reached the reception area, they were surprised to find Jamie there. He was surprised to see them, too—Clay had called him for help, but he hadn't told him the whole story. Jamie was horrified to see Jo's face and her bruised, swollen right arm, which had been injured when she fell.

Suddenly one of the adjoining doors opened and Constable Darcy stepped into the waiting area.

"Mr. Barber," he said, walking toward Jamie and shaking his hand. "Tom Darcy."

"Good to meet you, sir," said Jamie.

"Right this way," said Constable Darcy, ignoring Agnes and Jo.

"Thank you, sir," said Jamie.

"You boys going to make the playoffs this year?" the constable asked him, as they walked back toward the door.

"We're going to try, sir," answered Jamie.

"It's been a long time since this town won a cup," Darcy said.

"Yes, sir, it has."

"Getting hard to hold our heads up at the provincial meeting," continued the constable.

The two men walked through the door and closed it behind them.

Almost an hour passed. Jo and Agnes didn't speak to each other and no one spoke to them. Finally, the door opened and Jamie came out. Constable Darcy looked out at Agnes and Jo.

"*Ladies,*" he said, with just a hint of sarcasm. "This way." They followed him into the room.

"Have a seat," he said.

Agnes and Jo sat on two chairs facing the desk. The constable sat down behind it and shuffled some papers. Then he looked at them.

"Miss Demers," he said, "your brother is free to go. But he's been advised that assault is a serious offense and had the circumstance been different—had we judged that the evidence could sustain a criminal charge—such a charge may have been laid against him.

"As for Mr. Torris, his license has been suspended for twenty-four hours on suspicion of driving while intoxicated."

Agnes looked at Constable Darcy in disbelief. She said, "Wait, he gets off with a twenty-four hour suspension of his driver's license, after what he did to Jo?"

The constable looked at her. "Given the circumstances, I don't believe that pursuing an assault charge against Mr. Torris would be productive, either for the Crown, for Miss Gervais, or, frankly, for your brother."

"But—" began Agnes.

"Anything else?" asked the constable, pushing out his chair.

Agnes closed her mouth.

"Alright then," said Constable Darcy, and he saw them out of the room.

The day after the police released him, Vin quit his job at the rink and decided to leave town. Agnes begged him to stay, but he insisted that he didn't want to cause more trouble for them and that he had to move on. He wouldn't say where he was planning to go. Maybe he didn't know himself. Agnes hadn't heard anything from Claude since the day after the party, when he'd stopped by the shop to ask how Jo was doing. He'd asked if he could call her, and she'd said yes, but he hadn't. She was tired of wondering why. Worst of all, Jo was completely down and out. Her face would take a while to heal, and she refused to leave the apartment except to go to the clinic. They gave her a sling and a bandage for her wrist and told her that she could use her hand as much as she was able to tolerate the pain. But as soon as she got home, she changed back into her sweatpants, took up residence on the sofa, and stayed there.

"Jo, you've got to get back to work," said Agnes.

"I'm not going out looking like this," said Jo.

"I don't mean at the shop—Maya and I can fill in for you there," said Agnes. "But you need to work on your project."

"But I'm not supposed to use my wrist," said Jo. "It hurts."

"Well, you have two hands, don't you? At least get up and put your stuff in order. It's still just lying all over the place over here. Come on. I'll help you."

"I don't feel like it," Jo said.

"You've got to," Agnes insisted.

"No I don't," said Jo. "Clay was right. I'll never be a fashion designer."

"You're not going to listen to what that goddamn bastard said, are you?" asked Agnes.

Jo looked like she was going to cry.

"Sorry, Jo."

"It's okay. It's just that I have no ideas," said Jo.

"Well, how do you normally get ideas?" asked Agnes.

"I don't know," Jo said. She turned on the TV.

Agnes gave up. She put on her coat, hat, and gloves, and she left. Out on the street she was greeted by the burning-oil smell of an old junker and a scene as dull as a faded black and white photo. The sky, the clouds, and the endless piles of snow wore no color—only a million shades of barely differentiated gray. The stunted street trees were stripped of leaves and life, the cars were rimed with road salt, and the people themselves were ashen. If Jo's assignment meant having to find inspiration in this shitty province, no wonder she was stumped. Was there any color *anywhere* in March in Saskatchewan? Even the Easter displays in the shop windows seemed grimy, the chicks downtrodden, the bunnies mangy.

Agnes thought of the beads that Kookum had sent to her, sparkling with warm, bright color. Maybe she should give those to Jo—they might inspire her. It was a good idea, but Agnes didn't want to give the beads away. She liked to look at them and imagine the things she could make with them. Maybe she could find something else for Jo. She turned around and started walking toward Nelson's Knitting and Notions. It was a small shop and kind of hit-or-miss, but maybe this time she'd get lucky.

As she passed, she glanced into the window of the Sports Corral, with its display of sweatshirts, sweatpants, trainers, and jerseys. It was a sparse arrangement with no back panel, and her eyes wandered beyond it into the store itself, where she could just make out a large, familiar figure. She went inside to investigate. Sure enough, it was Claude.

"Hey, Claude," she said, as nonchalantly as she could.

"Agnes," he said. He seemed glad to see her. "How are you?"

"I'm okay," she said. "What are you doing?"

"Just picking up a few things. I'm driving home after the game tonight."

"Oh," she said. "Where've you been? I've missed you."

"Me, too, Agnes. I miss you, too," he said. "When I get back, I'll—"

"Can I help you?" asked the sales girl. They'd ended up at the register.

"Thanks," said Claude. He dropped an armful of things on the counter. Among them were two Prairie Wolves sweatshirts. One was a women's sweatshirt—the Wolves' royal purple was replaced with pink and the stylized wolf traced in glittery silver. The other one was tiny—toddler-sized.

Agnes looked at Claude in disbelief. He was completely unaware, casually pulling his wallet out of his back pocket. She heard herself say, "Have a nice trip." Then she bolted to the door.

Claude's voice, oblivious to the abruptness of her departure, followed her. "Thanks, Agnes. Good to see you."

When she'd made it outside, she stopped. She literally didn't know which way to turn. She'd forgotten all about going to Nelson's, so she just started walking.

She'd seen the proof with her own eyes, but she still couldn't believe what a cheater Claude was. Jo had been right. He was going home to some other woman. Thank God she'd kicked him out before they'd gone any further. He'd had the nerve to ask her about Owen? She and Owen had scarcely even touched each other, *ever*, and here he was, the father of some other woman's child—some other woman that he still cared about enough to buy presents for!

It was humiliating to remember that night at the party—how she'd apologized and tried to be so goddamn nice and understanding. What did he think she was? Didn't he respect her enough to tell her the truth? She thought about the way he'd looked at her. She knew he cared for her. But if he had a *family*? Ugh, no. *That* was out of the question.

And where the hell had he been, anyway? If she hadn't run into him, he probably wouldn't have even told her that he was leaving town. Who knows how many more days would have passed while she waited for him to call?

She thought about their afternoon together and felt like she'd been kicked in the gut. She almost started to cry. She really liked him. She wished she'd stayed in the store with him just now. She wished she'd talked with him, smiled at him, somehow found a way to be alone with him again before he left town, even if just for one short hour. She knew it wasn't right but she couldn't help it. She couldn't let it end this way.

✳

Two days later, when Agnes figured Claude would be back, she went to the Wolves' practice. She took a seat and watched as the guys strode onto the ice, but Claude wasn't among them. And when they began their first drill, some other guy was taking his place on the fourth line.

Where the hell was he? She'd traded shifts with Maya so she could see him, and he wasn't even here. She left and started to walk home but she'd only made it as far as the park across the street when the thought hit her that maybe he was at practice, but he just wasn't on the ice for some reason. That worried her. She decided to wait there until the guys started coming out. She was too keyed up to do anything else, anyhow.

After most of the other guys had gone, she went to wait inside at the dressing room door. Suddenly it flew open and Owen came out.

"Owen!" she said. It made her feel better just to see him.

He kept walking, though, as if he hadn't seen or heard her, his gym bag slung over his shoulder.

She had to run to match his stride. "Owen!"

He kept walking.

"Owen, please, wait," she begged.

He stopped. "What?"

She hesitated. "How are you?"

"What do you care?"

"I care. I care a lot."

"I'm okay," he said. He didn't look okay. He looked the same as he had at the party. She'd forgotten how angry he'd been. It wasn't like him.

"Really?" she asked.

"Yeah," he said. "I mean, what choice do I have, anyhow?"

"O, I'm sorry. I didn't know you felt this way."

"Well, I do, okay? Or I did. I don't really know anymore."

"I'm sorry, Owen. This is really hard."

"Hard? Come on, Agnes."

"It *is*."

"You're killing me. Just absolutely fucking killing me. You stand me up, lead me on, lie to me, fucking order me around. But it's hard. For you. Jesus. At least now I know where I stand."

"Is Claude okay?" Agnes asked.

Owen started walking again.

"Where is he?" she asked.

He didn't answer. She followed him through the double doors and into the parking lot. He opened the trunk of his car and threw the bag into it.

She asked, "He didn't get cut from the team, did he?"

He turned to face her.

"What is it about him anyhow? Why do you like him?"

She shrugged. "He's a real sweet guy."

"Sweet?" Owen was incredulous.

"Yes. He is. He's saved *your* ass on more than one occasion."

"I would've been okay."

"Bull*shit* you would have!"

"So what. That's pretty much his job. Anyhow, I don't think you're sleeping with the guy because of *my* ass."

"I'm not—see, how can you say that? That's the difference between you and him."

"Look, I'm sorry, okay? But I just don't get it."

"You don't get what?" asked Agnes.

"I don't get why you like him."

"Well, he's . . . he reminds me of home, I guess."

"But he's not *from* your home. I know that because, if you remember, *I am* from your home."

"Not really," said Agnes.

"Yes really," answered Owen.

"You're from my *town*. But *he* reminds me of home."

"What? Why? Because he looks like your dad?"

"He doesn't look like my dad!"

"You know what I mean! Come on, Agnes."

She didn't answer.

"Anyhow," he said, "if you miss home so much, why don't you just go the fuck back there?"

"I didn't say I *miss* home. I said he *reminds* me of home."

"Why do you stay here just to be reminded of home?" asked Owen.

"What?"

"I mean, if you want to be reminded of home, why don't you just go home?"

"You already said that," said Agnes.

"No, I didn't. Anyhow, you never answered."

"You don't even know what you're talking about," said Agnes.

"Yes, I do. Why are you even here if you're just going to be dating a guy like him?" asked Owen.

"I'm not dating a guy *like* him, I'm dating *him*."

"That's what I don't get," Owen said.

"You're so damn thick sometimes!"

"No, Ag, you're the one who's thick. It's pretty simple, actually. The girl I'm in love with is in love with some other guy, and I'm having a hard time with it. Okay?"

Agnes opened her mouth and closed it again. She said, "I'm not—that's why this'll just never work. Don't you see? You're going to be a big, big player. You can't be messed up with people like me."

"I'm not messed up with people *like* you, I'm messed up with *you*," he said.

"Haha. Good one. Look, O, I need your help."

"Now you're just avoiding the issue," he said.

"I am not."

"To hell with it, Agnes. My hockey career has nothing to do with our relationship."

"Yes it does. It has everything to do with our relationship."

"No. You're wrong. And if you're looking for Deuce— Claude—no. He didn't get cut. Why would he get cut? I think he just has some kind of . . . family issue, or something like that."

"Owen, he's seeing another girl. I know it. Another girl, back home."

"You just got finished telling me how sweet he is."

"Yeah, he's probably sweet to her, too," said Agnes. "That's why he didn't call me for, like, days, and that's why he was buying her that stupid pink sweatshirt at Sports Corral. I'm sure of it. Even Jo said so. She said all the Indian guys do."

"What? You're crazy."

"You don't understand, O. I'm not crazy. You've got to help me find out what's going on. You've got to talk to him for me."

"No way! What am I? Detective for hire? You're out your fucking mind!" He walked around to the driver's side, got in, and slammed the door. After a few seconds he rolled down the window and stuck his head out. "Do you need a ride somewhere?"

She shook her head.

6

By the time Cilla heard the truck creeping up the snowy road, she had gotten Toby's breakfast dishes cleaned up, pushed his new, brightly colored high chair to its place in the nook by the side of the bathroom, and was getting him dressed. He heard the truck, too. He squirmed out of her grasp and slid off the bed. Before Cilla knew it, he'd pulled the door open and was out on the stoop, in nothing but his diaper and a t-shirt, shrieking at the top of his lungs. The truck door slammed and Claude's voice called, "Hey Tobes, old champ!" Through the tiny window, Cilla saw Claude lift Toby high above his head and spin him around the little clearing. She went and stood in the doorway, waiting for them to finish. When Claude saw her he looked sheepish and immediately put Toby down. "Hey, Cill. Sorry, we got a little carried away there, didn't we old champ?"

Toby reached his arms up to Claude, "Again, again!"

"Later," said Cilla. "Toby, you need to finish getting dressed. It's cold out here."

"Go ahead, Tobes. Do what your mama says. Go on." Claude made a shooing motion with his hands. Toby shot him a stormy look, but he obeyed, reaching up to grab the railing and stomping up the wooden stairs. Claude grabbed a plastic shopping bag from the cab of his truck and followed them inside.

Cilla lifted Toby back up onto the bed where he stood with his hands on her shoulders while he stepped into his tiny blue jeans.

"Why don't you sit down, Claude?" Cilla said.

Claude had been sitting for hours, but the trailer's ceiling was uncomfortably low for him. He grabbed a chair, unfolded it, and sat down at the table. "I brought you something. Maybe Toby wants to wear it today." Claude pulled a Prairie Wolves sweatshirt out of the bag and held it up.

"Yeah, wanna wear it! wanna wear it!" screeched Toby.

"Claude, you shouldn't have," Cilla said.

"Sure I should," said Claude. "There's one for you, too."

"You *really* shouldn't have. I don't need it, Claude."

Claude didn't answer. Cilla helped Toby thread his arms through the sleeves of his new sweatshirt. The little boy looked down at the design on his chest and traced it with his finger.

"Hungry?" Cilla asked.

"No, thanks," said Claude, even though he hadn't eaten. He knew she couldn't afford to feed him, too. "You should come with us, today, Cill. Get out of here for a few hours."

Cilla hesitated. "No, Claude, thanks, it's better if just the two of you go. I've got to study."

"Alright. What do you think, champ? Just you and me? We'll do some skating and I'll buy you a hot dog and then maybe we can go—"

Toby started jumping up and down so that Cilla had to jerk her head away to avoid having her teeth knocked out.

"Sorry, Cill." Claude smiled.

"Okay, you're done," Cilla said to Toby. "Go."

Toby scrambled down from the bed and started sucking on his sippy cup, suddenly too shy to get any closer to Claude. Cilla wanted to open up a chair and sit for a while, but she didn't want to stretch things out, so she just stood there, Toby clinging to her leg. Claude stood up and pulled an envelope out of his pocket. He held it out to her.

She shook her head and pushed his hand away.

"Yeah, Cilla. He's growing fast. He's going to need some things. You too, buy yourself something nice, Cill, please?"

She shook her head again. Claude said, "If you don't need

it now, just put it in the bank, okay? Save it for later, for Toby. Please," he said. "For me."

He took Cilla's wrist and put the envelope in her hand, closing her fingers around it. He put his hand on her shoulder. She closed her eyes. "You okay, Cill?" he asked.

She nodded, but tears started to slide down her cheeks. Claude put his arms around her and held her until she stopped shaking. Toby was still clinging to her leg. "I'm sorry, Claude," she whispered. She pushed him away.

"Cill, it's okay. You're doing great. Just do your schoolwork. Don't worry about us. We're going to have a great time, right, Tobes?" Claude sat down on the chair again, leaned over, and looked Toby in the eye. Toby squeezed Cilla's leg tighter. Claude continued, "And we'll bring back some dinner, and we'll all eat together, okay? Toby, what's your mama's favorite dinner?"

Toby didn't say anything, but his eyes were fixed on Claude.

"Pizza?" asked Claude.

"Yeah!" shrieked Toby, and he jumped up and down in celebration.

Claude and Toby stopped to get some breakfast, and then they picked up Toby's new skates. Finally, they got to the rink.

After they had skated for a while, Claude bought Toby some pretzels from the vending machine and they sat on a bench to rest.

"Can you open it, Tobes?"

Toby tried to open the pretzel bag.

"Help!" he said.

"Okay," Claude said, taking the bag. "See, you grab each side like this, and then you pull. Try it."

He handed the bag back to Toby, who tried again, but still couldn't open it.

"Jeez, Claude, don't torture the kid," said a woman's voice.

Claude looked up. It was Tess, of course. He'd know her voice anywhere. She looked tired, but she was laughing at him. Even in the chill of the ice rink she was wearing a short-sleeved, grass-green t-shirt and jeans. Her two black braids hung down from underneath a knit cap almost to her waist. He smiled. He'd forgotten the odd way that her impressive, womanly curves utterly failed to disguise the angular girlishness of her frame. He stood up to greet her just as she squatted in front of Toby.

"Are you really Toby?" she asked. "Wow, you've gotten big! I'm Tess. Remember me?"

"Tess!" he answered.

"That's right," she said. "Tess. How are you, Toby?"

He didn't answer.

"Do you like to skate?"

He still didn't answer.

"I bet you're a really good skater, right?"

He nodded, his eyes big and serious.

"Runs in the family," she said.

She stood up again and smiled at Claude.

"He's cute," she said.

"Yeah," he answered.

"How are you, Claude?" Tess looked up at him. She wasn't short, but in his skates Claude towered over her.

"I'm doing good, Tess. You?"

"Okay. Still thinking about you, sometimes."

Claude looked down at his feet. "How's the hockey club?" he asked.

"Good. Got a lot of kids."

Claude smiled. "You're doing a lot of good."

"That's the idea. Still could use some help, though."

Claude looked at his feet again. "Tess—"

Tess put her hand on his arm. "It's okay." She tousled Toby's hair. "You boys have a good skate, okay? See ya."

"See ya, Tess," said Claude.

He watched her walk away and then he sat down again next to Toby.

*

The morning after he got back, Claude was on the ice early. He left his stick and helmet on the bench and took some easy laps around the rink, first one way and then the other. He felt alright, considering that he hadn't slept much in the past forty-eight hours. The manufactured stillness of the rink, the cleanness of the ice, the crisp scrape of his blades: those things soothed him somehow. His limbs warmed and he started to loosen up. Then, all of a sudden, there was shouting—angry fragments of words that slammed off the hard surfaces of the empty rink and echoed so as to be almost unintelligible.

The fragments shifted into focus and converged like the patterns in a kaleidoscope.

"Come here, you two-timing bastard!"

Claude jerked his head toward the source of the cry and his body spun around, too. Mac was charging onto the ice.

"Yeah, you! Motherfucker!" Mac hollered.

Claude stopped short, confused. Maybe it was a mistake, or a joke. But no, there was no one else on the ice, and Mac's face was red and screwed up into an ugly grimace. He came flying towards him and skidded to a stop an inch away. He raised his bare fists.

Claude said, "What the hell, Macker? What'd I do?"

"You know what you did! You know *damn* well!"

Owen grabbed Claude's jersey at the neckline and twisted it hard, yanking him in close. He slammed his other fist into Claude's jaw. In his surprise, Claude hadn't braced himself. He might have fallen, but Owen was still hanging on to his sweater and his momentum was going the other way so that the opposing forces neutralized each other. Claude shook off his gloves, dug a blade into the ice, held off Owen's arm, and jabbed his fist into Owen's cheekbone. That seemed to fire Owen up even more. He twisted his arm free and landed two quick ones, on Claude's mouth this time. Claude felt the bite of his teeth into the soft flesh. His blood was flowing now and he felt himself heating up. He tried to control it—he didn't really want to hurt Macker—but what was he going to do? Let the kid have his way with him? He grabbed Owen's sleeve and punched him hard on the side of the nose. He probably could have gotten him again but Owen, though struggling hard to free his arm, was more or less trapped, and Claude's rage ebbed as suddenly as it had surged.

The two men hung on each other, neither wanting to concede anything, fighting to stay upright and to forestall any more punches. By now there was more shouting and some of the other guys skated out to separate them. Blood dripped from Owen's nose and his left eye was already swelling, but he hadn't noticed yet. He was still seething. As soon as their grip loosened he shook off the guys trying to hold him and lunged at Claude again. His teammates pulled him back and held him more securely this time.

Claude was in shock. He'd been afraid all along that something like this might happen, but it still seemed unreal. Hadn't he tried to talk to him? He'd talked to both of them. He'd been real slow and cautious. He'd tried real hard not to screw things up. Hell, he'd hardly even touched her, in spite of her own best efforts! What else was he supposed to do?

Coach was there now, yelling at both of them and sending them back to the dressing room. Claude didn't need to be told twice—he skated back ahead of Mac, hanging his head, wishing he could disappear. He was afraid, really afraid, that this was the end of the road for him.

Owen stood in the shower for a long time, feeling the hot water stream over him.

"Hey Ag, here! I'm open!" Owen tapped his stick on the ice.
But she didn't pass—she sped past him and shot it herself.
"Aw, come on, Ag, I was open!"

She laughed at him and skated over for a playful hip check.

"Come on guys, break it up, break it up!" called Tommy. He dished the puck to Ian and they played keep-away, getting some good passes off until the puck took a bounce and rolled back toward Owen. He and Agnes tried a little give-and-go, and he took a shot at the two tree branches that served as their goal but the puck bounced wide. She hooted with pleasure. "See? That's why I never pass it to you!" She glided around him in a big circle, laughing at him again.

Tommy skated over. He was rolling his eyes. "You two are sick. I gotta go. Promised the old man I'd help him with some stuff."

"Same here," said Ian.

"See ya," said Owen. Agnes was already halfway around the little pond. He dug in and followed her. "Hey, Ag!"

"Yeah?"

"Those guys are taking off."

"Okay." She spun around so that she was skating backwards, looking back at him. Her dark hair swam down from under a white knitted hat and she was smiling a big, open smile, which was pretty rare for her, and incredibly beautiful. Owen got a prickly feeling all over his body. He felt like she was daring him to do something that he would never have the guts to do. She turned back around and he just kept following her, like a goddamn idiot.

The steam kept rising. Owen inhaled deeply, and then exhaled.

Deuce hadn't even showered. He'd wanted to talk, but Owen didn't want to listen. It wasn't his job to hear him out, much less to accept an apology or offer forgiveness. That was for Agnes to do, if she cared to. His job was done and he felt great. His blood was coursing through his veins at twice its normal speed. Finally Deuce had just disappeared.

"Oh, no," cried a much younger Tommy, skittering along the ice in those giant skates he'd inherited from his brother. He pushed his cap up out of his eyes. "Look who's coming!"

Owen skidded to a stop. Yes, they were coming, making their way along the trampled path through the brush, Vin first and then his little sister, Agnes.

The other boys didn't like it so much when they came to play. Vin was moody and overbearing, and Agnes was a girl, a good skater, and a show-off. Still, when Owen saw her his heart jumped. He took off skating in a tight circle, as fast as he could.

There was a knock at the door.

"Oh no," thought Jo, and her heart sank.

But the knocking was gentle. And it was the middle of the morning. The Wolves were probably skating right now. She had to assume that Clay was among them.

"Yes?" Jo called, in a strong voice, to the closed door.

"Ag? It's me, Owen."

Jo opened the door.

"Oh, Jo. Is Ag—oh, Jesus, Jo, what happened? Are you okay?"

Jo turned away from him quickly. She didn't want him to see her, and she didn't want to meet his eye. The spot where Clay's hand had struck her cheek still had an angry, purple center to it, spotted with red where it had been abraded. Around the edges it mellowed to a smoky yellow that faded into the color of her skin.

"It's a lot better than it was," she said, but her voice was shaking. She had a bandage on her right wrist.

Owen stepped inside and closed the door behind him. He said, softly, "What happened, Jo? Did you fall?"

"No, well, yeah, I, uh . . . he hit me, and then I fell."

"Who hit you?"

"Clay."

"You're kidding," he said.

Jo put her face in her hands.

Owen put his hand on her shoulder. "I'm sorry Jo, I know you're not kidding. I was just . . . surprised."

"I know."

"Gosh, that's terrible."

"It's okay," said Jo.

"Can I do anything for you? Can I get you anything?"

"No, Owen. I'm fine. Just resting. Thanks, though. If you're looking for Agnes, she's at the shop."

"Yeah. I need to talk to Agnes." He hesitated. "I don't want to leave you here, though. Maybe you should come with me."

"That's really sweet, Owen. But I'll be okay."

"Don't open the door."

"Don't worry." She turned around to thank him, and then she saw his face. "What happened to *you*?"

"Nothing," he said. "Just, you know, hockey. But you take it easy, okay, Jo?"

"Yeah," she said. "Thanks, Owen."

He ran down the stairs and all the way to the Indian Jewel Box. By the time he got there his face was beginning to throb.

Agnes was behind the counter.

"Owen, what're you—holy shit, what happened to you?"

"Nothing. Listen—"

"It doesn't look like nothing to me!"

"It's not important. I was at your place just now looking for you and there's Jo, all bruised up. She said that Torris hit her. What happened?"

Agnes told him.

"Coach should know about this," said Owen.

"Jamie knows. Shouldn't you be at practice right now?"

"Uh—"

"What's going on with you?"

"Nothing."

"Bullshit. Tell me."

He shrugged. "I got into it a little with Deuce. Now, listen—"

"Wait. What? You got into a fight with Claude? Why? What happened?"

"Nothing."

"Come *on*, O. Tell me!"

"I just didn't like to think of him treating you bad, that's all."

"Are you insane? He could've killed you!"

"Nah."

"Jesus Christ, O. You are. You're completely insane. Are you going to be okay?" She reached out as if to touch his face, but he backed away. That made her feel worse than anything.

"Sorry," she said. "But it looks awful."

"Look, Ag, relax. It's just a goddamn black eye. But I don't think we should leave Jo alone in that apartment."

Agnes looked at Owen. She wasn't surprised at his words—he was his mother's son, after all, and old Janet MacKenzie had been looking after girls like Jo since before he was born—but there was something else about him right now. Something new. That is, apart from the black, swollen eye and crusty nostrils.

"Owen," she said, "I can't babysit Jo. I have to work. I'm working *her* shift today, because she doesn't want to be out in public looking like that."

Owen sighed. He had gone looking for Agnes so he could tell her that he'd made Deuce pay for cheating on her. He was going to tell her that he loved her. He was going to sweep her off her feet—if such a thing was even remotely possible where Agnes was concerned. But now he knew that that wasn't going to happen. Not today. Owen saw her on the pond, with that big smile on her face. She turned her back to him and skated away.

He said, "Ag, why don't you and Jo stay at my place for a while? I have an extra room. We won't tell anyone, but even if Torris finds out I don't think he would bother her at my place. Maybe he'll cool off a little."

"I don't know, O. That's really nice of you. But she's working on a big project right now. She'll have to bring all her sewing stuff. Your place'll look like a fashion show."

"So?" he shrugged.

"But what if you have the guys over?"

"I don't *have* the guys over, Ag."

Agnes hesitated. "What about Sissy?"

"I'm not seeing her anymore," said Owen.

"No?"

"Come on, Ag. I think you guys should do it. Just for a while. Let things blow over."

"What in *God's* name were you thinking, MacKenzie? What in God's *fucking* name?" asked Coach.

Owen hung his head. He and Deuce sat side by side on metal folding chairs in Coach's windowless office, like overgrown schoolboys in front of the headmaster. Coach sat behind his desk, arms crossed, leaning his chair back against the wall. On the desk were a binder and a couple of pencils. On the wall hung a calendar: March. Games for the first couple weeks of the month were already marked with big red L's and W's. There were considerably more of the former than the latter.

Coach's voice bounced off the cinderblock walls.

"You boys are on the *same team*. Now I understand that you might have your *personal* differences. I don't give a shit about that. That's your business. But you got no business pounding on each other's goddamn ping pong ball heads when the team's trying to make the fucking playoffs for the first time in five years! Ya understand me? I already got one drunken son of a bitch *benched* by the front office for God's sake! Christ! A little self control! That's all I ask. Shit, if *any* of you boys had any of *that* we wouldn't be in this position in the first place, now would we?"

Coach took a breath and continued. "Now. I gotta ask ya, do you boys care about this team? Do you care about your team-mates? Do you care about the organization? Do you care about the *glorious* game of hockey? Because if you do, then show some respect. That's all I ask. Doucette!"

Claude jumped.

"What in the name of *God* did you do to get MacKenzie here so fired up?"

"Well, Coach, I—"

"I told ya already, I don't give a shit. I don't wanna know. But *you* need to know that I can't have you boys fighting *each other*! That's not why you're here. You know that. Am I right, Doucette?"

"Yes, Coach, you're right. I know it."

Coach looked at him for half a minute, his lips tight, his eyes narrow, letting Claude sink into the quicksand silence. Finally he continued, more quietly, "I know you know it, Doucette. I know you do. Your skin may be a few shades darker than mine but you're no dummy. You been around the block a few times and believe me, I respect you for it. I honestly do. But you put me in a hard place, a hard fucking place. You know that, right?"

"Yes, Coach." He hung his head.

"Barber seems to think the team *needs* you." Coach paused. "We're taking a chance on you, you know that, right?"

"Yes, Coach. I do, and I appre—"

"Now MacKenzie here's got some growing up to do, too, don'tcha, kid?"

"Yes, Coach," said Owen.

"Team's put a lot into your game, son."

"Yes, sir."

"You're gonna exercise some self control."

"Yes, sir."

"And if you got a problem with one of your teammates, what're you gonna do?"

"Well, Coach—"

"I'll tell you what you're gonna do." Coach's voice began a steady crescendo. "I'll tell you what you're gonna fucking *do*. You're gonna work it out, right? You're gonna play nice, and then you're gonna *work it out*. *Off* the ice. On your *own* time. *Without* getting yourself *killed!*"

Coach waited for the cinderblock echo of his words to die away. Then he let his chair fall forward onto all four legs. He sighed. "Now," he said. "Do you boys think you can hold it together long enough to make a go of it on this road trip and win some goddamn *hockey* games?"

"Yes, Coach," they answered, nodding.

Coach frowned at them. He made a sarcastic, mock bowing motion. "Well, thank you, boys," he said. "Thank you for playing the goddamn game you're paid to play. 'Cause I gotta tell ya, I got a whole dressing room full of you hothead, knuckle-brained boys! You two oughta be the *least* of my problems! Now. Let's shake on it."

The two players looked at each other.

"I said *shake hands.*"

They shook hands.

"Alright. Now get up and get on outta here! That's right. Get up! Go!"

Claude and Owen unfolded themselves from the chairs, and Coach stood up and shooed them out, shaking his head. "You gonna act like kids, I gotta treat you like kids. Jesus Christ!"

Agnes got home from the shop late in the afternoon.

"Did Owen find you?" Jo asked.

"Yeah." Agnes threw her bag down on the floor by the door and kicked off her boots.

"What happened to his face?" Jo asked.

"It got pounded by Claude Doucette," said Agnes.

"Why?"

"Oh, you know. Boys'll be boys."

"Be serious, Agnes."

"I told Owen that I thought Claude was cheating on me, and he went after him."

"Wow, it's like a movie or something," said Jo.

"He could've gotten himself killed," Agnes replied.

She went into the bedroom and came right out again.

"I've got something for you." She held out the bag of beads that Kookum had sent to her.

"I can't take those," said Jo. "They're yours."

"I'm giving them to you. I want you to have them. It's the least I can do. Use them for your project. They're *very* Saskatchewan."

"Thanks, Agnes, that's sweet. But I don't think there's going to be a project."

"Yes there is," Agnes replied. "By the way, we're moving to Owen's tonight."

"What?"

"Owen invited us to stay at his place for a while. You know, in case Torris comes back. And I decided to take him up on it."

"Without asking me?"

"Yes."

"But I don't want to move. And I don't want to impose on Owen."

"We're not imposing. And I already told him we would. He'll be here any minute with his car. We need to start packing."

Owen lived in a tiny house about halfway between the practice arena and the town center. The front hall was flanked on one side by the guest bedroom, where Agnes and Jo would sleep, and on the other by the living room and kitchen. Owen's bedroom was off the living room. The kitchen was small but clean, probably because Owen didn't really cook. A bright orange, second-hand sofa was the focal point of the living room, along with a beat-up sofa table and a huge TV. On the other side of the room there was an empty space where a dining room table should have been. Owen told Jo to go ahead and set up her mannequins, worktable, and sewing machine there, and she attacked the task with more energy than she'd mustered in a long time.

Agnes carried her bag into the guest bedroom. After a while, Owen appeared in the doorway.

"Hey, Ag. Can I come in?"

"Sure," she said.

He didn't actually go in, though—the room was so small that there wasn't any place for him to go. There was only about one step between where he was already standing and the first of the two twin beds, so he just stood in the doorway. Agnes was on the far side of the room, pulling some of her things out of her bag and putting them into a dresser drawer. Between them, under the low ceiling, a light fixture glared.

"Is this going to work out for you?" he asked.

"Of course it is, O. It's so kind of you."

"Nah."

"It *is*."

"It's nothing."

"Is there anything we can do for you while you're gone?" she asked. The Prairie Wolves were leaving tomorrow on their final road trip of the season.

"Nah. Just do your usual thing. Everything's pretty plug-and-play."

"How's your face feeling?" she asked.

"It's been better," he said, with a shrug and a beat-up version of his trademark smile.

She didn't smile back. Although she never would have advised it, he'd gotten himself beaten up on her behalf. Did that mark him, now, as hers? She said, "I feel really bad about it, O. Is there anything I can do to make it better?"

"I can think of a couple things," he said, and he winked at her with his good eye.

He was surprised that she had no sarcastic comeback to offer. She didn't even roll her eyes.

She asked, "Are you going to play tomorrow?"

"Yeah, I'm going to play."

"Are they going to make you wear a cage?"

"I guess, probably."

"That's good," she said.

Owen leaned his shoulder up against the doorjamb. He took a bite out of an apple and studied her while he chewed it. Even

164 · LESLIE SPITZ-EDSON

as fatigue and injury overtook him, he felt that he was starting to get the game in hand, that he'd driven his opponent into the boards with enough violence, and sent him deep for the puck enough times to just about have him nailed.

For Agnes, meanwhile, all she could see were the black eye and the mangled nose. They looked horrible. None of this made any sense.

"Why'd you do it, O?" she asked.

"Do what?"

"Fight Claude."

"I told you. I didn't want him treating you like that."

"I don't need you to defend me."

"Jesus Christ, Ag. Don't you think I know that much by now?"

"Then why'd you do it?"

"I don't know." He shrugged.

"It wasn't smart. You could have gotten badly hurt. You're supposed to be playing *hockey.*"

"You sound just like Coach."

"O, I want you to win. Don't you want to win?"

"I want a lot of things."

"Like what?"

"Jeez, Ag," he said.

"What?"

He shook his head.

"O," she said. "It's not that I don't appreciate what you did. I do. I mean, I know, like, fucking Claude Doucette punched you in the face—twice. Or maybe more. I don't know."

"I punched him, too, you know," Owen said. "I got a couple good ones in."

"But he's used to it."

"Do you think that makes it hurt less?" Owen asked.

Agnes looked down at the sweater in her hands. She'd really fucked things up somehow. But Owen was still here. He didn't seem to be angry with her: on the contrary.

She looked back up at him. He was wearing the same cozy old sweatshirt she'd slobbered all over that night after Christmas, that night he'd held her and told her he loved her. It wasn't even a team sweatshirt—it was just some old generic one that he'd had forever, to judge from the looks of it. That night his heart had been slow and solid, but now his chest rose and fell far too quickly. It seemed to be pumping heat into the little room. She was going to ask him if he was okay, but when she looked into his face, he was already looking at her and their eyes met—the three good ones, anyhow—and she forgot. She scrambled to think of something to say.

"Where are you going?" she asked.

He shook his head. "Nowhere." His good eye was still locked in on hers.

"No," she said, "I mean on your road trip."

"Oh. Right." He started to list the towns, but she didn't pay attention. She could read about it in the paper tomorrow, if she wanted to.

"Cool," she said, when he was done.

"It's sort of our last chance," he continued. "We have to get, like, nine, ten points out of it to make the playoffs."

"Yeah?" she said.

"Yeah. Um, do you guys want to get some dinner?"

"I don't know," Agnes answered. "You don't have to eat with us, you know. Maybe you have other plans, or something better to do."

"No, I don't," he said.

"I'd be happy to cook something." Agnes liked to cook.

"I don't think there's anything here to cook. Since I'm leaving tomorrow and all. Do you think Jo'll want to go out?"

Jo didn't want to go anywhere, which turned out to be fine. It had been a long day and it was getting late. In the end they just got take-out and sat around the sofa table together to eat. No one said much. Jo finished quickly and went over to her sewing things. Owen's head was swimming—he was tired now, really tired, and he still had to pack for the trip. He excused himself early and apologized for leaving Agnes and Jo to clean up.

Early in the morning Agnes heard Owen getting ready to leave. She stepped out of the guest bedroom and into the hall. He was kneeling on the floor, tying his shoe. The hood of his sweatshirt was up over his curls.

"Morning, O," she said.

His eyes followed her bare legs up to a pair of gym shorts and a tank top.

"Morning," he answered. Jesus. She could really juice him up first thing in the morning. Just by standing there.

When he stood up he saw black. Blood throbbed in his temples and he reached his arm out to steady himself against the wall.

"Are you feeling any better?" she asked.

He didn't answer. He was waiting for his vision to clear. She was standing so close that he thought he could feel her warmth. Her hair fell softly around her face and over her bare shoulders. He got dizzy again, and his unsteadiness showed enough so that she reached out, involuntarily, to steady him, her hands firm on either side of his ribcage.

"Are you sure you're okay?" she asked.

"Yeah."

"I can drive you over there," she offered.

"Nah, I'm good."

She took her hands away. "I'm sorry, O," she said. "About everything."

"Nothing to be sorry for," he said.

"Play good, O."

"Thanks, Ag. I'm going to try."

She picked up one of his bags and offered it to him. He took it and she walked around behind him to open the door.

"Bye, O," she said.

"Bye," he answered. He picked up his other bag and left.

✳

That evening, after dinner, Agnes and Jo stayed home at Owen's place. They had nowhere to go. Jo was perfectly content—she sat at her sewing table, intermittently sketching and browsing through her big baskets of fabric scraps and bits of buckskin, skeins of yarn and embroidery floss, beads and buttons and other things she'd collected over the years. Agnes, though, wandered aimlessly from room to room. She had a kind of sick, empty feeling inside, and it took her a while to figure out that it was because she missed Owen.

She wandered into the hall. He'd been miserably beaten up and dizzy this morning when they said goodbye. It was her fault, but there was nothing she could do. She thought of him kneeling on the floor, tying his shoes, and suddenly an idea popped into her head. She walked back through the living room again and into Owen's bedroom. She turned on the light and opened up his closet. Bingo. There on the floor rested an old, obviously well-loved pair of trainers. She carried them out into the living room.

"Jo?" she said.

"What?"

"Can I borrow some of that tracing paper?"

"Sure." Jo reached into one of her boxes and pulled out a roll of the paper she used to make sewing patterns. "How much do you need?"

"Not much. Just, like, maybe a foot or two."

Jo handed the roll to Agnes. "Help yourself. What do you need it for? Are you making something?" she asked.

"Just some moccasins," answered Agnes, shrugging.

Jo caught sight of the shoes in Agnes's hand. Her eyes narrowed. "For whom? Whose shoes are those?"

Agnes didn't answer.

"Are they Owen's?"

Agnes nodded.

"I thought you two were *just friends*," Jo said.

"It's just to say thank you, you know, for letting us stay here."

"That's a pretty serious thank you," said Jo.

"Do you think?" asked Agnes.

"Don't you?" Jo replied.

"I don't know," said Agnes. But they both knew that you made moccasins for your husband, or maybe for your brother or your father. Not for just anyone.

Jo raised her eyebrows and turned back to her sketchbook. After a minute, though, her lips twisted into a little smile and she started rummaging through one of her baskets.

"Agnes?" she said.

"Yeah?"

"Catch." She tossed the bag of beads that Kookum had sent into Agnes's hands. Right away, Agnes had the design for the moccasins in her head.

She knelt on the floor, removed the insoles from Owen's trainers, and traced their size and shape on the tracing paper. She made templates for each moccasin and estimated how much material she would need. She wanted to use smoked moosehide, which was strong but buttery soft, so she called Kookum to ask her to send some. Then she counted the beads and waited.

With about a minute to go in the second period, and down by just one goal, the Prairie Wolves pressured in front of the Royals' net. Ducks Johnson and Dougie Linklater exchanged some crisp, cross-ice passes, and cycled it back to Barbie, who, in his trademark sneaky style, out-maneuvered Crandall and won it behind the net. He chipped it up to Dougie, who got it out to Jordie Carroll at the point, who passed it across to Hammer. Hammer unleashed a cannonball of a shot that hit someone in front and came bouncing back out to him. He dished it back to Jordie, who chipped it over to Dougie along the boards. Dougie lost it for a second after the Royal's winger Kutschner slammed his face into the glass, but with Barbie's help he dug it out of Kutschner's skates and whipped it back to Hammer at the point. Hammer pounded it on goal again and this time the rebound came to Kutschner, who somehow found the legs to skate it into the Wolves' zone and put it past Bancroft into the back of the net. The Royals' fans went crazy and the horn sounded to end the period.

The Wolves trudged into the dressing room down by two. Barbie's heart was pumping from the effort of that last frenzy. "That's okay boys, we'll get it back!" he hollered.

"Just a bad bounce," said Bennie Frobischer.

Robbie Bancroft, the goalie, pulled off his mask. He dropped his ass onto the bench and his head into his hands. "Sorry guys. Jesus Christ. Sorry."

"Not your fault," said Owen, as he pulled off his helmet with the cage. He hated the thing, but he was getting used to it.

"*I* should've had him," said Jordie. "Lost my legs."

"Shit happens," said Hammer.

"But why does it always happen to us?" complained Jordie.

"Boys, we have a good game so far," said Marcel Martin, earnestly.

"Yah, great pass to Bennie for the goal," said Fredriksson.

"We're going to get it back," said Owen. "That was a monster shift just now. Gotta keep it up."

"Boys, boys," said Bennie. "Shh! I got something to tell ya. Listen: I think I saw the Queen up in section 204. Ninety percent, no, hundred percent sure it was her!"

"You're so full of shit," said Sal.

"No, I mean it, boys. She was up there making out with Prince Albert!"

"You mean Prince Philip," said Scottie Newtower.

"No, I mean Prince Albert," said Bennie.

"Prince Albert's dead, man," said Newtower.

"You should've seen 'em," said Bennie. "He had his hand all the way up her—"

"Hey, that's sacriligious," said Tommy Trumbel.

"Nah, it's just fucking disgusting," said Newtower.

"My point is—"

"Since when do *you* ever have a fuckin' point, Bennie?" asked Sal.

"My point is," Bennie repeated, "he's got his hand all the way up her little, you know, her funny little house-dress thing—"

"Aw, come on man!" Someone threw a roll of tape at him.

"My point is he's doing pretty fuckin' good for a dead guy."

"I don't know, man. I'd rather be sucking what 'er name's toes," said Freddie Brennan.

"No way. We're talkin' *the Queen*!" said Bennie.

"She's old enough to be my grandma," said Sal.

"Great-grandma," said Brennan.

"She's a hell of a lot younger than what's his name, Prince Albert."

"You mean Prince Philip," said Newtower.

"No, I mean Prince Albert."

"Okay, come on boys, let's get it together," said Don Mrkonjic, Owen's big winger.

"Yeah, guys, let's focus," said Owen.

"I just can't *believe* I didn't stop that lame-ass shot, man. That bastard Kutschner! I hate his fucking guts. I do. This sucks, it does. It sucks," lamented Robbie.

"We got twenty minutes left. We gonna win this thing," said Marcel Martin.

"Ready to go, Macker?" asked Donner.

"Ready."

"Freddie?"

"Nah, man, I'm still thinking about what's 'er name's toes."

"You're kidding me," said Donner. "You're fucking kidding me."

Freddie replied, "Well, what kind of toes juice you up? I like the girls with those long skinny feet, you know? Kind of bony and sexy and all the little toes starting big and getting smaller as you go along. Whoo-ee!"

"What the hell are you talking about?" asked Hammer.

"Don't you ever look at girls' feet, man?"

"Who cares about their fucking feet, for Christ's sake? That's the craziest thing I ever heard."

"I'm a crazy bastard, what can I say? All those little toes in a row!"

"No self-respecting girl would let you anywhere *near* her toes," said Hammer.

Freddie shrugged. "I've sucked on lots of toes, lots of 'em! Ask any girl out there. They like it. Ask ol' what's 'er name."

"Come on boys, we gotta get it together," Don tried again.

"Let's go out and get 'em," said Barbie. "We had 'em on the ropes, we can get 'em again."

"Yeah, let's kick some ass," said Hammer.

"Make Prince Albert proud," said Bennie.

One by one the guys stood up, stomping their skates on the rubber mat. Deuce shook his head, smiling. He took a tiny pinch out of a buckskin pouch and sprinkled it into his glove. Then he got up and followed the rest of the team out.

Coach started the third period with the same line that'd been on at the end of the second. They struggled a bit but at the end of their shift they dumped it in and the third line, Martin's line, came on. With Torris benched they'd been off their rhythm, but thinking about the Queen up there in the stands with old Prince Albert seemed to have inspired Bennie and he laid a big hit on the Royals' Elmer MacIntosh. He and Marcel Martin and Torris's replacement, Artie Schmidt, got a cycle going and at the end of their shift Coach sent out Owen's line. They had a disappointing time of it, though—Freddie was knocked off the puck and the Royals cleared to neutral ice. But then, with a diving poke check, Sal nudged it over to Owen, who skated into the zone with Brennan on a two-on-one. Owen dished it across— one of his trademark *gorgeous* saucer passes—but the Royals' goalie flagged down Brennan's shot.

Owen and Freddie went back to the bench pretty discouraged. Coach sent out the second line to try a set play off the faceoff, but Barbie was kicked out of the circle and the play flopped. After the third line also failed to get anything going, Coach sent out the fourth line, with a pointed glance at Claude.

"Ya wanna go?" Claude asked Big Dickie Howard, the Royals' winger.

"Uh," hesitated Big Dickie. His team was up by two and seemed to have the momentum.

"What's the matter?" asked Claude. "Worried about that pretty white face of yours?"

"Okay, Chief, you got it, let's go." Big Dickie wasn't known for his restraint.

Immediately after the faceoff the two fighters shook off their gloves and started circling each other. The crowd roared. Play stopped. Claude's blood surged like a swollen river and his heart started to race. He saw red and for a few seconds he didn't even know that he'd grabbed Howard by the sweater and pounded his fist into the man's chin three times, slashing the flesh of his own knuckles on the helmet buckle with the first blow, knocking the helmet off with the second. With the third Howard's body slackened and Claude felt that the guy was going to fall and he tried to control it and then the linesman was there to grab the guy and Claude skated off, with a nod in the direction of his teammates, who were on their feet, pounding their sticks on the boards in appreciation.

Back in the room, Sammy, the trainer, took care of the bleeding knuckles. The adrenaline was still flowing and Claude couldn't feel his hands at all, not even the sting of the antiseptic. He'd feel them tomorrow. Dimly he heard the crowd noise and the arena organ, and as soon as Sammy had finished with him, he went back out to the bench.

✳

That game against the Royals turned out to be the high point of the Wolves' road trip. They triumphed in come-from-behind fashion, spurred, no doubt, by Prince Albert, what's 'er name's toes, and Deucer's bout with Big Dickie. After the game, the mood in the dressing room was buoyant, and when the boys boarded the bus for their all-night ride to the next town, cheap beer flowed like water.

Owen was feeling better. Something about the action of the game had alleviated the throbbing of his mangled face, and even wearing the hated cage he'd had two solid assists, including one on the game-winner. Things between him and Deuce seemed to be more or less back to normal, and he felt satisfied to have made his point by punching the big guy in the head a couple of times. And then, of course, there was the memory of Agnes standing in the hall with him before he left that morning.

The next game—against the injury-decimated Mercurys— was a gift, a relatively easy win, and Owen, still flying, came away with a goal and an assist. Claude, on the other hand, always had to will his way through the first couple of games after a fight. In spite of Sammy's best efforts, his raw knuckles burned inside the glove all night. There was no ointment that could take away the sting, and no Agnes to apply it even if there had been.

Agnes. Lying back, after the game, against the cold, hard side of the bus, his legs stretched across both seats, his feet dangling in the aisle, Claude pretended to sleep. He knew that Agnes wasn't his, but in the private night of the snoring bus he could summon her memory as often as he liked. He could hold out his hand and she would run her fingers across his knuckles while chills ran up and down his spine. He could pull her close and let the cinnamon-scent of her hair scramble his soul. He could feel her body on his, her breasts pressing into him, her fingers playing through his hair, her breath, her lips, her tongue—why'd he have to open his big, dumb mouth?

He knew why. It was for the same reason that, without being too obvious about it, he'd let Macker get in a couple of good ones: it was for survival. And the price of survival was concession. He'd been forced to stand down, to relinquish his claim. It was like signing a goddamn treaty.

But Agnes wasn't a piece of territory. What did *she* think about all of this? He realized that he didn't know. At one time he'd been reasonably sure that she cared for him. She'd told him that she and Owen were just old friends. He still wasn't sure he believed her, but that's what she had said. Didn't she deserve to have him believe her? He sure as hell *wanted* to believe her.

The next game was a miserable loss to the Miners. Only Macker's line scored, and Macker had the primary assists on both goals. The next game, too, was a loss—Claude's line was on the ice for two of the four goals against, but Macker, again, had a great game.

To hell with it, thought Claude. He should have clobbered the kid when he had the chance. As the Wolves slunk off the ice that night, tails between their legs, Claude made up his mind.

In a noisy, smoke-filled tavern in some desolate, ice-cold, rain-drenched town, Claude picked up the pay phone and dialed Agnes's number. There was no answer.

In a crudely disinfected, bleak hotel room surrounded by the congealed remains of a post-game, fast-food meal, Claude held the receiver to his ear and dialed Agnes's number. There was no answer.

In a truck-stop phone booth, with Miss March shamelessly exposing herself to him from the pages of a large, glossy wall calendar, Claude dialed Agnes's number. There was no answer.

Leaning up against a cold, concrete wall outside the hushed dressing room after another pathetic heartbreaker of a losing game, Claude dialed Agnes's number. There was still no answer.

The day after the team's return, Claude woke up late in his own bed. He got up, showered, dressed, climbed into his truck, and drove to the Indian Jewel Box.

"Is Agnes working today?" he asked the woman at the counter.

"She's in the back."

He walked to the back of the store and peeked into the office. It was a tiny room with a desk and two chairs. In one corner there were a couple of brown cardboard boxes stacked on top of each other. In the other there was a metal filing cabinet. The walls were covered with posters announcing craft fairs and pow wows. Agnes was sitting at the desk with a sandwich and a *Hockey Herald* spread out in front of her.

Mac is in there somewhere, thought Claude. *Owen MacKenzie. C. 6'2", 190. Slick-skating sniper can score, work the power play, gets the girl every time.*

"Agnes?"

She looked up.

"Can I come in?" he asked.

"Sure."

He took a step inside.

"Sit down, if you want," she said, nodding at the empty chair in front of the desk. Then she looked back down at her sandwich. "How was the trip?" she asked.

"Not too good," he said. He sat down.

"I heard."

"I tried to call you," he said.

She looked at him. "I've been staying at Owen's," she replied.

Claude's heart skipped a beat. So that was the end of it. He opened his mouth to speak and closed it again. Finally, he said, "I missed you." It was irrelevant at this point, but it was true.

"Claude, get out of here," she said, softly.

"How's your brother doing? I heard he got in some trouble."

"He didn't do anything wrong. Torris hit Jo, knocked her down. You should've seen it. You would've done the same thing as Vin."

"That's what Barbie said. How's he now? Police treat him okay?"

"He went home," she said.

"That's good. To be home, I mean."

Her eyes softened. For the tiniest second everything was outlined in gold, like the sun was waiting behind a big, dark cloud.

"Agnes."

She looked down at her sandwich again.

He reached forward across the desk and put his hand on her arm. "I'm real sorry for what happened."

She shook her head without looking up at him. "Claude, you need to go now," she said.

He pulled his arm back and left.

The Prairie Wolves' season was over. They didn't make the playoffs. Barbie stayed in town to be with Hillary and Jackie, of course, but most of the guys cleaned out their lockers, met with Coach and Sammy, the trainer, and went home for the summer.

Claude was the last to finish clearing out his things. He stood staring at his stall and at his name on the plate above it. It had been a good season for him. He'd finished with better numbers than he'd seen since juniors, and he'd done it in considerably less ice time. He didn't expect to get much farther in the sport, though. Coach was still much more likely to put him on the ice to intimidate, or to teach someone a lesson, or to fire up the other guys, than for any other reason. That wasn't likely to change. There was no going back to what he'd once hoped to be.

He probably looked to all the world like a big, dumb Indian. Not so long ago, he might have believed that's all he was. Recently, though, he'd started to suspect that there was more to him. In this room, he'd found clues. Barbie, the team's beloved captain, had shown him genuine respect and kindness. MacKenzie, the hot young prospect, had seen him as a rival and a threat—something Claude couldn't have imagined a few months ago. Even Coach, in his backhanded, racist way, had made him suspect his own worth. Yes, he'd clawed his way back, upped his game—even contributed a few extra assists and a goal or two. Somehow, though, by matching his mettle to his desire—or more accurately, to his desperation—he'd unintentionally reaped some less tangible benefit as well. And while his hockey career wouldn't last, this other thing would.

Already, it made him feel powerful. Not powerful like a fighter, but rather, powerful like someone who didn't *need* to fight. Like Uncle Eddy. It was probably the same thing that had given him the courage to ask Agnes out. Hell, it was probably the same thing that made her say yes. The same thing that made her want him. But like Uncle Eddy used to say, a warrior *provides*. It wasn't good enough to use this thing for his own gratification. Rather, like an oversized haul of fish, the flesh of a bull moose taken in the peak of his summer splendor, or the money he earned playing this white man's game, it had to be shared.

7

Owen turned his key in the lock. He stepped through the door and she was standing right there, almost exactly where he'd left her. She must have seen his car pull up.

"Ag," he said.

"Hey, O. Welcome home."

"Thanks."

They stood there for a moment.

"You had some great games, O," said Agnes.

He smiled at her. "Thanks, Ag. Too bad you can't say the same for the whole team."

"You looked strong out there."

"Thanks."

"You didn't give up much."

Owen smiled again. "You and Jo doing okay?" he asked.

"Yeah."

"Listen, Ag. I've got some news."

"Well, come in," she said.

"Yeah, okay." He closed the door and followed her into the living room.

"Wow, the place looks great," he said.

"We just cleaned it up a bit. No offense, but it was a little . . . you know." She wrinkled her nose.

"It was," he said. "Listen Ag, I have to tell you something. I got called up."

"What?"

"To the big club. To the Traders."

"No way."

"Yeah." He nodded.

"Oh my God, Owen! I can't *believe* you just walked in like there was nothing—I'd be completely out of my mind!"

He laughed at her.

"Goddamn it, O, you're going to be playing for the Cup. *For the Cup!*"

"That's a little premature," he said. "The playoffs haven't even started."

"But you're *in*."

"Almost."

"Jesus Christ, Owen! *You made it!*"

He just stood there grinning at her.

"When are you leaving?" she asked.

"In the morning."

"Wow."

"Yeah." All of a sudden he felt really tired. He said, "Well, I need to unpack and pack and, I guess, get some dinner."

"We're cooking dinner," said Agnes. "We already planned it. I mean, if that's okay."

He smiled. "It's great."

Owen went into his room and sat down on the bed. All the events of the past few weeks—from seeing Agnes with Deuce at Hill and Barbie's party, to the fight, to moving the girls into his place, to saying goodbye to Agnes that morning, nearly two weeks ago—he'd mostly left those things behind when he went on the road, but now they swarmed over him again. Sitting there in the half-darkness, though, he realized that he didn't have much left in the tank and he had to be ready to leave early tomorrow, hopefully for a long run with the big club.

The Thompson Traders. He shook his head. He'd dreamt of this for a long, long time. He sat for a moment more and then got up to take a shower.

While he was shaving, his stomach started growling. He felt like he hadn't had a decent meal in years. It was almost true—except for his mom when he was visiting home, no one had cooked for him since juniors. And he'd gotten used to coming home to an empty fridge after road trips.

He put on a pair of jeans and a t-shirt. Then he went down the stairs to the basement, where he dumped his dirty socks and shirts and underwear into the washer. Back in his room, he hung up his suit jackets and pants. He hoped they'd be passable by tomorrow. There wasn't time to take anything to the cleaners.

He didn't know what to do next, so he wandered into the kitchen. He smelled bread baking. "Jesus Christ, Ag. Is that your kookum's bannock I smell?"

"No, Owen, Kookum's not here," Agnes said, handing him a beer. "It's my bannock."

"Wow," he said.

"Just wait till you win the Cup," she added. "I'll bake you the biggest bannock ever."

Jo filled three plates with chicken, potatoes, and vegetables, Agnes pulled the bannock out of the oven, and the three of them sat around the sofa table to eat.

Owen said, "Jeez, if I ate like this every night, I'd have been called up a long time ago."

Jo and Agnes smiled at each other. "Come on, O. You get to eat out all the time," said Agnes.

"This is way better than restaurant food," he said.

"It's the least we could do," said Jo.

"How's your project?" asked Owen.

"It's almost done. Do you want to see?" Jo jumped up and ran over to her makeshift design studio. One of the mannequins was covered with a white sheet. Carefully, Jo lifted it up. "Ta da!" she sang.

The dress was made of a soft but substantial buttery, tan fabric. Its length and drape gave it dignity, and its flowing lines gave it life. It was cinched at the waist and the short jacket came together in the front with a plug of white fur.

"That's the deer's tail," Jo said.

"Okay," said Owen, not understanding.

"It's modeled after an old-time, two-hide dress," said Jo.

That didn't explain much. But patches of white embroidery evoked the speckled pattern of a doe, and trim at the hem mimicked the delicate line of the doe's head and her gracefully pointed ears.

"Okay. I see the deer now," said Owen.

"See, in the old days," said Jo, "hunters would take deer for food, clothing, everything. Women made dresses of the hides, and they trimmed them to show respect for the animals. Mine's not made of real hides, because I couldn't afford them, but you get the idea."

"Yeah. But isn't it a little bit, maybe, morbid, to wear the skin of a dead animal?" asked Owen.

"Well, we do that all the time, right?"

"Not calling attention to it, like this."

"No. But remembering the animal isn't morbid. She gave her life to feed you, and to keep your children warm. That's a sacred thing. You can't forget it."

Owen stroked the soft fur of the doe's tail. "It's beautiful," he said.

"I couldn't have done it without you—both of you," said Jo.

"I'm glad it worked out," said Owen. "I guess the Wolves just have a couple of games left and then Torr—he'll be leaving town. Barbie thinks they'll try to trade him."

"Yeah," said Jo. "I mean, I haven't seen him or anything. But when everyone's gone Jamie's going to lend us his car and we'll move back to our place. It'll be fine."

After dinner Owen helped Agnes and Jo clean up. Then Jo went to bed, leaving Agnes and Owen standing face to face in the kitchen.

"O, if you're tired, go to bed. I know you have to get up early," said Agnes.

He looked into her eyes. "Ag, it feels kind of nice that you're here to see me off. Not just because of that awesome dinner, but because this is what we—you know, since we were kids—"

Agnes got goose flesh. She said, "O, if you want to go out or something like that, just go ahead. You don't have to stay here with me."

He squinted at her.

"I mean it, O."

"Ag, didn't you hear me? I said *it feels nice that you're here with me.*"

"I heard you. But, you know, Sissy's still—"

Owen's face turned red. "I told you I'm not—God *dammit*, Agnes!"

"Owen, what's wrong?"

"I'm going to bed," he said.

"What time are you leaving?"

"Early." His bedroom door slammed behind him.

Agnes watched every minute of the Traders' games on television, hoping to see Owen get his big chance. He was young, and officially not even a rookie, but when one of the Traders' forwards went down, the coach put him in. Third-line left wing wasn't Owen's usual role, but he had a beautiful assist in his first game, followed by a couple more strong games, and then, when the guy he'd filled in for was healthy again, he sat.

The Traders made it to the first round of the playoffs. They lost the first game, though, during which the same guy was injured again. With Owen back in the lineup, they won three straight, putting themselves on the cusp of winning the best-of-seven series and moving on to the next round.

Then they lost game five. Owen was still keeping up, but in the NHL the pace is fast, and in the playoffs it's considerably faster than Owen was used to down in Wapahaska. After five straight games, the two teams had built up a good amount of hatred, too, so play was getting more physical, and Owen had to really grind it out on that third line. Digging pucks out of guys' skates up against the boards wasn't Owen's specialty, and he was often outmuscled. Ditto to challenging defenders in front of the net—he'd have had it easier if he were Claude's size. Agnes winced when he got in front of a puck trying to hold a one-goal advantage in the closing minutes of a period. She'd blocked plenty of pucks in her day, and they'd hurt, but they'd been shot by kids—these were bullets.

All in all, Owen was playing hard, and Agnes was proud of him. It still hurt sometimes, though. They'd dreamt of playing for the Cup since they were little kids, but at a certain point it had hit her that only Owen had any chance to actually do it. She, lacking the Y chromosome, had none. Still, she wanted him to win.

It was time for game six and the Traders were up three games to two. Owen was gunning for glory and Agnes was sitting in her apartment with Jo and Jo's mom, eating brownies and inhaling the formaldehyde fragrance of nail polish. It was sweet of them to want to share the experience with her, but game six of a playoff series is not the optimal time to have to explain and re-explain the icing rule to people who are more focused on their fingernails than on the television. Also, with Mrs. Gervais sitting beside her, Agnes felt that she had to modify her usual game-time behavior, which included shouting things like 'For Christ's sake shoot the goddamn puck!' at the top of her lungs.

"Oh, no, I can't believe we lost another face-off!" wailed Agnes. She buried her face in her hands.

"Do you like the red or the pink?" Jo asked her, holding up two bottles of nail polish.

The other team—the Bandits—had won the puck and they shot it around behind the Traders' net, where the Traders' top-line guys battled for it.

"Come on, boys, clear it, clear it!" cried Agnes.

But the Bandits began to cycle, the Traders were hemmed in, and by the time they did clear they were dead tired and had to go for a change.

"Agnes?" said Jo.

"Rats! We'll never get anything going at this rate!" complained Agnes.

"The red or the pink?" Jo asked again.

"What?" said Agnes.

"The red or the pink," Jo repeated.

"For me?"

"No, for me," said Jo. "Unless you want me to do yours. But then you're going to have to keep still."

"Uh, the puck," Agnes said, her eyes back on the screen. "I mean, the pink."

Thanks to a couple of heroic plays by the solid, veteran defender Doug Jackson, the Traders' second line kept the puck in the Bandits' zone for a half a minute. They couldn't score, though, and the Bandits sent it deep, chased it down, and when Owen and his line hopped over the boards they were back on defense.

"The brownies are done," said Mrs. Gervais.

They held strong in their end, though, and when one of the defenders chipped the puck ahead along the boards, Owen settled it and feathered it ahead. He followed the play and helped set up the cycle, which generated a shot on goal and a rebound. The goalie got to the rebound first and covered up, but it led to a faceoff in the offensive zone for the first line.

"Nice work, boys! Now we're getting somewhere," said Agnes.

"Would you like a brownie, dear?" Mrs. Gervais asked Jo.

"Thanks, Mom. Just put it down. My nails are wet," said Jo.

"Agnes?" asked Mrs. Gervais.

"Yes! Awesome faceoff win!" said Agnes, pumping her fist.

"Agnes, would you like a brownie, dear?"

The Traders were actually cycling the puck, with fresh legs, right off a faceoff win.

"Come on, come on! Shoot the freakin' puck!" said Agnes. "Oh, I'm sorry, Mrs. Gervais. I got a little carried away."

"That's alright, dear," said Mrs. Gervais. "Would you like a brownie?"

"Yes, thank you," said Agnes, trying her best to wrest her attention from the game and smile at Mrs. Gervais. "No, no! Terrible pass!"

The Bandits intercepted the weak pass and cleared the puck.

"God—I mean, good grief," said Agnes.

The game went on like that, the Bandits desperate to force a game seven, the Traders pressing, hoping to tie it up. For four solid minutes at the game's end, they bombarded the net with everything but the kitchen sink, but when the final horn sounded they had nothing to show for it.

To say that Agnes was disappointed would be a gross understatement. Her face was hot, her pulse was racing, and she felt as if she'd been personally humiliated. They'd been up *three games to one* but hadn't been able to close the deal! Not so deep down inside her, there started to blossom the nagging suspicion that her team was weak. If the guys themselves started to feel it, they were doomed. Goaltender Agnes would have turned the tide, vacuumed up every puck that came her way, sucked the hope right out of those nasty Bandits *and* their obnoxious, gloating fans. But goaltender Agnes wasn't in the game. Like any other frustrated, puck-crazy fan, the best she could do was bear witness.

The big, deciding game—Game Seven—was in just a couple of days, and Agnes knew she had to find a way to watch it without Jo and her mom. She loved them, she honestly did, but this game was too personal. She considered watching it at T.T.'s, but that would mean having to fend off guys at the bar. She thought about calling Jamie and Hillary, but she hesitated.

On the morning of the game, Agnes walked out to Dottie's

to get milk and eggs for breakfast. A young man strolled toward her and then stopped.

"Good morning," he said.

"Hello," she answered, confused.

"Constable Aikins," he said, holding out his hand.

Now she remembered. He was one of the policemen who'd taken Vin away.

"Oh, right," she said, not shaking his hand.

"But call me Rory."

She didn't answer.

"How are you?" he asked.

"Fine."

"And your brother?"

"Fine."

"And Miss Gervais? How is she?"

"She's fine," answered Agnes.

He hesitated. "I tried to call, you know, to follow up, to see how she's doing, but—"

"We were staying with a friend."

"Oh," he said. "Well, I'm glad I ran into you." Once more, he hesitated. "Maybe I'll call again some time?"

Agnes didn't answer.

"Would that be okay?"

Agnes shrugged. "I don't know."

"Well, thanks," he said, and he continued walking.

Goddamn cop. He seemed different, though, when he wasn't standing in her apartment holding a gun on her. Almost like a regular person. Kind of shy, even. And he had a thing for Jo, apparently. She was too good for him, though, even if she wasn't a hockey fan. Good thing they'd been at Owen's—and then it hit her: *she still had Owen's key.* She could watch the game at his place. He wouldn't mind. She'd be alone and she could cheer and curse as much as she wanted. It was perfect.

✻

Claude walked into the open garage and an older man looked up at him from under the raised hood of a car. "Hello," the man said, "can I help you?"

Claude walked all the way around to the front of the car and held out his hand. "Claude Doucette. Are you Lazare Demers?" Slowly the man put his wrench down on the engine block, wiped his hands on a rag, and rested his eyes on Claude.

"That's right," he said, and he shook Claude's hand. "What can I do for you?"

"I'm looking for your son, Vincent."

Lazare's eyes narrowed and he pulled his hand away. "What do you want with Vincent? Are you a friend of his?"

"No. I mean, I've only met him once or twice. Down in Wapahaska. When he was visiting his . . . visiting Agnes. I play hockey down there for the Prairie Wolves."

"Ah, Doucette. Of course."

"Yes, sir."

"I'm sorry I couldn't place you right away."

"Nothing to apologize for, sir."

"What do you want with Vincent?"

"Well, one of my teammates, Owen MacKenzie—I think you know him—"

"Yes."

"He told me he used to play with Vincent."

"He played with Agnes. Vincent's a couple years older. Not sure they ever played together—"

"He said he plays good D."

"Used to. For a kid. He doesn't play anymore."

"I'm trying to line up some guys to skate with over the summer. Do you think he'd be interested?"

"He hasn't played for quite a while. Wouldn't be much help to a professional like you."

"I'd like to ask him, anyhow."

"Alright, come on, then. He's in the office."

Claude followed him.

"How's your mother holding up?" Lazare asked him.

"She's doing pretty well, thank you."

"She's a strong woman."

"Yes she is, sir."

The office was empty. Lazare looked out through the open door to the street and shook his head. "Vincent, quit worrying those girls," he called. "You have a visitor."

Claude asked Vin if he would ride up toward the Narrows with him before heading to the rink.

"Why?"

"Give us a chance to get out a little. Get in the right frame of mind. Anyhow, what else have you got going?"

Not a goddamn thing, thought Vin. He figured Agnes was somehow behind it all. "Well, okay," he said.

"I'll pick you up around five," said Claude.

"In the morning?"

"Gotta get a good start."

At five the next morning the sun rose over the horizon and Vin looked out his window to see Claude's red pickup towing a wooden fishing skiff on an aluminum-frame trailer. Vin stepped out of the door with his hockey bag over his shoulder, his stick in his hand.

"We going fishing?" Vin asked.

"Nah. Already been out."

"Jesus, Deuce. Do you ever sleep?"

"Sometimes."

"Where are we going?"

"We're going to pick up Tess," said Claude.

"Who's Tess?"

"Old friend of mine."

"Okay," said Vin.

"Sorry. Should've warned you, I guess," said Claude.

Vin shrugged. Normally he'd be sleeping at this hour—if he wasn't still awake from the night before. But he wasn't sleeping now, and he had nothing better to do than to go along. He threw his bag and stick in the back and climbed into the cab of the truck. They left the trailer at Claude's mom's place and headed north.

It was funny. Down in Wapahaska, among the Prairie Wolves, Deuce was a respected figure. In an arena where size and toughness mattered, he was one of the biggest and the toughest. His reserved manner set him apart, too, and no one—certainly none of those young, white kids—could be sure whether it stemmed from indifference or disapproval or what. They probably thought it was some mystical Indian thing. But here at home, Deuce just looked like one of those guys that Vin and his drinking buddies used to laugh at. He drove an older model pickup with fishing gear and waders stowed in the bed, towed a homemade boat trailer, and dressed in old army pants, work boots, flannel shirt, and hunting cap—sort of a lumberjack look.

In fairness, though, Vin had never been entirely comfortable making fun of those guys. On more than one occasion he'd been plenty relieved to have one of them pull up alongside him, and plenty grateful to accept the ride he'd been offered. Guys like Deuce were sort of the meat and potatoes of the landscape. Or should he say the moose and bannock? There was a whole fleet of them unofficially patrolling the narrow highways that connected the area's scattered settlements. They were as much a part of home as the water that traced veins of silver through the scrawny forests and down the rocky runs. It was impossible to imagine the place without them.

The real mystery was what Agnes saw in him. She had pretty high standards. As far as Vin knew, she'd never been interested in *any* guy, except Mac. And though she'd dig in and defend him to the death when Vin criticized him, there was no doubt in Vin's mind that if given half a chance, she'd find a way to give old Macker hell. That's just what she did. And MacKenzie was the golden boy. If she could nitpick *him*, he couldn't imagine the kind of hell she'd give a guy like Deuce.

A lot of girls up here would be more than happy to land old Deuce, but Agnes was different. Agnes never settled for less when she could get more. Deuce was big and strong, but that was about the end of it. He was still a good hockey player, but he didn't have half the upside that Mac had. Mac was playing out in Thompson, now, but Deuce wasn't going *anywhere* unless it was farther north. Here he was—he should've been on the ice already, or at the gym, or somewhere, but instead he was driving way out of his way to give some old friend of his a ride. And he seemed just fine with it. In fact, he was pretending that this trip was going to *help* him train. Like he had planned it this way.

The sun was just barely topping the low jack pine that lined the highway, tinging the morning haze with a yellow glow. Gradually, the sparse, roadside flora bloomed out of the shadows into a rich palette of greens and yellows, speckled with the season's earliest wildflowers. Vin looked out the window at the boggy ponds that shone like blue mirrors into the sky. It actually felt pretty good to be on the road, riding shotgun in this old truck.

Claude glanced at Vin. He looked a lot like Agnes: honey-colored skin and jet-black hair, almond-shaped eyes, smooth wide cheekbones and a slightly pointed chin. Real handsome. Like Agnes, too, he had a muscular, athletic build. They'd only skated together once so far and, to be honest, Vin was looking more than a little rusty. Claude hoped he could get a couple other good guys to skate with them. Maybe Vin would take some pleasure in it. Maybe it would open his eyes a little.

"So you played midget down in St. Cyp?" asked Claude.

"Yeah."

"Did you always play defense?"

"No, I played forward a lot growing up. Just depended on where the coach wanted me."

"What did you like to play?"

"Didn't matter. I just liked to play."

"Then how come you stopped?"

"I don't know. Lots of reasons, I guess."

Claude didn't say anything.

Vin continued, "It changed, you know? It wasn't fun anymore. Most of the guys we played didn't care about the game. They just wanted to beat us. I hated those bastards."

"Agnes said you used to get into it sometimes, with other guys."

He shrugged. "Sometimes you have to draw a line. You know how it is, right? I didn't want anyone screwing with me, and I didn't want anyone taking advantage of Agnes, or talking trash about the rest of the family. I felt like, if I didn't step up, they'd assume they could get away with anything. And a lot of times it was a guy that—everyone thought he was just great, you know, *a fine young man*, and really he was the worst son-of-a-bitch. Know what I mean?"

"Yeah, I know what you mean."

"Really gets under my skin."

Claude nodded.

"That ever happen to you?"

"Sure," Claude said.

"So what'd you do?"

"I got in some fights, but a lot of times I just went home and told my mom."

"I never had a mom to tell."

"Yeah, that's rough."

They were quiet for a while. Then Vin asked, "What did your mom say? When you told her, I mean."

"Well, I remember when I was pretty young—maybe ten years old—there was this kid named Marty Dustin. He was just this little kid. But he used to tease me all the time. He'd say stuff like, 'Oh, you're so dirty, oh, you live in a wigwam, oh, your mama doesn't know how to keep house.' I don't know where he got it from. He'd never even been to my house! I guess it was just stereotypes, you know? But I remember my mom would just kind of dry my tears and tell me not to listen when he said those things. And then when I got older she'd say, 'Be proud of who you are. We're strong. No one can hurt us unless we let them.'"

"Do you think that's true?" asked Vin, "That nobody can hurt us unless we let them?"

"I don't know. It sure makes it easy for them if we're always stuck in our own end," said Claude.

"But sometimes we have no choice."

Claude shrugged.

"It's kind of funny, right? I mean, that's your job, now: defending the other guys, being a fighter."

"That's part of it. But it's like my Uncle Eddy used to say, what are you fighting *for*? It's like circling the Red River carts, out on the prairie, going way back. There's fighting on the outside, but the inside battle is what it's about. You know, taking care of each other."

They continued in silence for a while. The highway was straight as an arrow, the land flat as a drum. After a while Vin said, "You got a big family, eh?"

"Yeah, a lot of the older folks are gone, though," said Deuce. "My dad's gone, my uncle's gone, there's only my mom and Achille left. You'll meet Achille today. A lot of my cousins have moved away. In my family, it was only my sister, my brother, and me. Now it's just me."

"What happened to your sister and brother?" asked Vin.

"My sister's living in Ottawa. My brother passed away a couple years ago," said Claude.

"Oh, man, I'm sorry. I didn't know."

"It's okay. Time passes."

"What was his name?"

"Hector."

"Hmm. Maybe I knew who he was years ago. But I lost track. Had my own stuff going on. I guess I just missed it."

"He kind of kept to himself. Especially towards the end."

"I'm sorry, Deuce."

"Thanks."

After a while Vin said, "Agnes put you up to this, didn't she?"

"What?"

"Asking me to skate with you."

"No," said Claude.

"Sure she did. And then she made you promise not to tell. That's just the kind of thing she'd do."

"She didn't," said Claude.

He turned on the radio. It was playing a coarse, tacky C&W song—the kind that makes fun of women, and men, too, and disrespects just about everything. He turned it off again.

"How's she doing, anyway?" Claude asked Vin.

"Who, Agnes?"

"Yeah."

"I was going to ask you the same question," said Vin.

"You talked to her lately?"

"No. Haven't you?" asked Vin.

"No. Last time I talked to her was . . . a while ago. She still down in Wapahaska?"

"Yeah."

"Still working at the shop there?"

"Yeah. She's thinking about moving home and going back to school, though."

"Oh yeah? That'd be good. She told me she was—" He stopped mid-sentence.

"What?" asked Vin.

"Nothing," said Claude.

"I thought you two were getting . . . you know, close," said Vin.

"We went out a couple times."

"Didn't work out?" asked Vin.

Claude shrugged. "I guess I'm not that great a catch," he said.

Vin looked at him, trying to read his expression. It sure had seemed to *him* that Agnes liked old Deuce. A lot. And Deuce seemed to like her, too. It was almost comical to see the big fighter disarmed by a girl—by his baby sister Agnes, no less. She was a great kid and Vin loved her, but she was hardly a knockout or anything like that.

Vin said, "I don't know, Deuce. Agnes seemed really into you. Seriously. It's not her usual thing. She doesn't just fall for guys all over the place. What happened?"

Claude just sighed, like a big, lovesick moose.

"You got it bad," said Vin.

"I can't talk about it with you, you know. She's your sister."

Claude kept driving. But all he could see was the sudden softening of Agnes's gaze that morning at the Indian Jewel Box. He felt her skin, warm under his cool hands. He'd better get his eyes back on the road. He shifted in his seat.

"You hungry?" he asked Vin.

"Yeah, a little."

"We're almost there. We'll see what kind of breakfast they got for us."

They pulled into a dirt parking lot with a couple of gas pumps and a non-descript, white, frame building that in a different setting could have been an ordinary house. When Claude pulled the door open a bell jingled. The place was small and cluttered, with beadboard paneling, a lunch counter that had probably been there since the days when Fred Sasakamoose was the only Indian in the NHL, and four wooden stools. To the left, three booths lined up under a window along the outside wall. The right side was a small convenience store with a couple of rows of shelves offering everything from magazines, pop tarts, and cigarettes, to mosquito netting, bait, and ammunition.

At the sound of the bell an older man looked out from behind a shelf. He was wiry and bent, but he moved easily. His dark hair was flecked with silver and his brown face wrinkled up when he smiled.

"Eh, Little Brother," the man said, holding out his hand. "You grow some more? Or did I shrink?" They shook hands and then embraced. "How you feeling, Claude?"

"I feel good, Achille. Can't ask for more than that. How are you?"

"Very good, very good."

"Achille, I want you to meet my friend Vincent Demers."

"Ah, Vincent, welcome! I remember you. Where you been? I miss watching you play. And how're your dad and grandmother? And your sister—Mary Agnes, right? She was a hell of a player, too."

"Everyone's well, thank you, sir," Vin answered. All the old-timers kept track of the local families, but Achille's memory of Vin's career in minor hockey, not to mention Agnes's, was somewhat surprising.

Achille called into the back room. "Eh, Tezzie, look who's here!"

A woman's face looked out from around the doorjamb, and then the whole woman appeared. She was definitely worth a second look. Striking and well-built, she was probably about Claude's age, or maybe a couple of years older. She was wearing blue jeans, lots of silver bracelets, and her hair hung down in two long braids. Her eyes reflected the grass-green color of her t-shirt.

"Claude. I thought summer'd never come."

"Hey, Tess."

They embraced, and she kissed him on the lips. Then she narrowed her eyes at him. "You been okay? You look different."

"I've been good. You?"

"Missing you."

"Miss you, too."

"Who's your friend?"

"Tess, this is Vincent Demers. Vin, this is Tess."

"Good to meet you, Tess."

"Good to meet you, Vincent." They shook hands. "What're you boys up to?"

"We're going to get a little skate in, Tess. Remember? You coming?"

"I thought you said Thursday," said Tess.

"It is Thursday," Claude replied.

"Oops, I guess I'm off by a day." She smiled. "Yeah, I'm coming. But you boys need to eat. Sit down, okay? I'll put on some breakfast."

"I got a couple perch out in the truck," said Claude.

"Want me to cook those up for you now?"

"No," said Claude. "They're for you. Come on out. Before I forget."

Claude held the door for Tess and they walked outside. Vin watched through the window as Claude took a cooler out of the truck-bed. Tess grasped the handle, and he was slow letting it go, so that they were sort of linked for a moment by the fish and the ice and the cooler. They exchanged a few words. Then he let go and followed her back inside.

"By the way, Claude," Tess said, "Randy Mortimer was in here a couple days ago asking for you. I got his number in back."

She took the cooler into the kitchen and returned with the phone number. Claude took it and walked over to the pay phone.

Tess winked at Vin and gestured toward the counter. "Have a seat. Can I get you some coffee?"

"Sure," he said. "Thanks." He sat down.

She walked back into the kitchen and came back with a cup and coffee pot. "Cream and sugar?"

"No, thanks."

"Hungry?"

"Yeah," he said.

"What do you want?"

"Whatever Deucer's having."

She nodded and walked back into the kitchen.

Vin hunched over his coffee and Claude came back to join him. Tess came out of the kitchen with the coffee pot, a cup, and some cream for Claude. Vin watched her as she filled Claude's cup.

"More?" she asked Vin.

He pushed his cup towards her, watched her as she poured the coffee, and then watched her walk back into the kitchen.

"What're *you* looking at?" asked Claude.

"Nothing," said Vin.

Claude gave him a look.

"Nothing!" Vin protested.

"Just take it easy. She's my cousin."

Vin laughed. "She's not your cousin, Deuce."

"Cross cousin?" Claude winked.

"Jesus, Deuce. What the hell? She's old enough to take care of herself."

Claude poured some cream into his coffee.

Vin asked, "Did you make your call?"

"He wasn't in yet," said Claude. "I'll try again before we go. Tess can help him better than I can, anyhow. I don't keep track of the young players anymore. She just likes to keep me in it."

Claude sipped his coffee.

Vin asked, "So, Achille is your uncle, then?"

"No," said Claude. "Might as well be, though. He and my dad and Eddy were real close. Like I said, he's the only one left, but he's not my uncle."

"Does he really remember me?" asked Vin. "That was a long time ago."

"Sure, he remembers. Achille's the biggest fan there is. He watches all the kids' games, men's games, too. Even women's games. Hockey season he practically lives at the rink. He's got another guy to help him here. And Tess, of course. Tess is like his daughter, adopted daughter. She lost her parents when she was real young. She's been with Achille ever since."

Tess came out of the kitchen with a plate for each of them, piled high with steaks, eggs and potatoes.

"Wow," said Vin, "that looks great."

Tess winked at him. "You boys eat, I'm going to get my gear together." She disappeared again.

"Is she really going to skate with us?" asked Vin.

"Yeah."

"But—she's a girl."

Claude nodded.

"I mean, she doesn't look like a hockey player. Some girls do. She doesn't."

"She's running some clinics today, for some of the young kids. But she'll skate with us for part of the session. I kind of owe her. Anyhow, it'll be good to have a fourth skater. Otherwise it's just you and me and Billy."

When they'd finished eating, Tess came to clear their plates.

"I'll meet you out at the truck, boys," she said.

Claude went to try his phone call again, while Vin said goodbye to Achille and went outside. In a couple of minutes, Tess came out, too. She put her bag and stick in the back of the truck. Then she walked over to Vin and stood really close to him and looked him right in the eye. He hadn't noticed before, but she was just as tall as he was—which wasn't very tall for a guy, but it was pretty good for a girl.

"What do you play?" she asked him.

"D, mostly, but it's been a long time. Not sure I'll be much help to old Deuce."

"Sure you will," she said. "Anyhow, you can help me. Between the two of us, we'll find some use for you. How do you know Claude, anyway? I haven't heard him mention you before."

"I met him in Wapahaska this winter when I was visiting my sister."

"Your sister?"

"Yeah."

"She a friend of his?"

"Yeah."

"Hm," Tess said. She was still standing very close to him. The conversation seemed to have narrowed to an uncomfortable point, but neither of them took a step backwards. She was still looking him in the eye, too, and he was looking back, unblinking.

"What's her name?" asked Tess.

"Agnes."

"Agnes," she repeated. "Okay."

She turned away from him abruptly and looked across the road, in the direction of the lake. It was really close, but you couldn't see it through the trees.

"Where're you guys from?" she asked, without looking back at him.

"St. Cyp."

Vin heard a door slam. Claude was coming towards them. "Ready to go?" he asked.

"Ready," said Tess.

The three of them got into the cab, with Tess in the middle, and Claude pulled out onto the highway.

Claude said, "Achille's looking good."

"He's doing okay," said Tess. "Just turned eighty, he told me."

"No kidding," said Claude.

"Born just after the war started, he said."

"Wow." Claude looked at her and then back at the road.

After a while Tess said, "Why'd you want to bring me out here, Claude?"

"What do you mean?" he asked.

"What do you want from me?"

"What do I want from you?"

"Yeah. What's this all about?" she asked.

Claude kept his eyes on the straight line of the highway. "Wanted to see you. Thought you might need a ride. Wanted you to meet Vin."

"Okay," said Tess.

A while later Tess asked, "So, what's she like, Vincent?"

"Who?" Vin asked.

"You know, your sister," she said. She turned toward Claude and put her hand on his thigh. "We were talking about Agnes just before you came out," she said to him.

"No, we weren't," said Vin.

"It's okay," said Claude.

"How long have you known her?" Tess asked.

"Me?" asked Vin.

"Not you. She's your goddamn sister," said Tess. "Claude."

"Not long," said Claude. "Just met her this winter, after I got traded. She's dating one of the other guys, one of the Wolves."

"No, she's not," said Vin.

"She is," Claude said. There was resignation in his voice.

"Oh," said Vin. "I didn't realize."

Claude sighed. "Yeah," he said.

"Jeez," said Tess. "You just can't win, can you?" Her smile was both mocking and sad.

Tess was a force on the ice. She wasn't the skater that Agnes was, but she was bigger, and just as ornery. She wasn't afraid to use any advantage, either. One time she and Claude were coming up the ice with speed. Vin didn't want to take her to the boards, since she was a girl and all, and he kept a little too much distance. She tipped the puck into her skates and kicked it to center ice, where Claude took it and shot it into the net. Tess hooted with satisfaction and mugged Claude up against the glass just the same as any guy-teammate would have done in a real game. Billy, the other defenseman, just grinned at Vin and shook his head. Apparently he'd skated with Tess before. After that, Vin didn't hesitate to subject Tess to the peskiest D moves that he, in his rusty condition, could deliver. It didn't seem to faze Tess at all.

They worked up a sweat and then Tess said, "I've got to get ready for my clinics. Come find me when you're done, Claude. Vincent said he'd help out today."

"I didn't say that," said Vin.

"Yes, you did," said Tess.

"You're in trouble now," Claude said to Vin.

"Not as bad as you are," Tess said to Claude, grinning.

"What'd I do?" he asked. He looked like the ref had called him for tripping or something.

"I don't know, but I'm going to find out," Tess said.

"Come on, let's go," Claude said to Vin. "We still got a couple minutes left."

Vin skated after him as Tess stepped off the ice.

Owen tossed his bags into the trunk and slammed it shut. No reason to spend the night alone in the goddamn hotel, not sleeping. He stood looking at his car, and it shone back at him, glazed by the cold drizzle.

Most of the guys lived right here in the city. They were going home. Some would be sliding into bed alongside a warm, soft body, which, if they were lucky, might provide a temporary distraction from the wreckage of their manhood. Others planned to seek solace at one of the local watering holes. Maybe he'd join them for a consolation round or two. Maybe not. He didn't know yet.

He walked around to the driver's side. His quads quivered like jelly as he lowered himself into the car. The cold vinyl seat burned through his thin dress pants. He shut the door, pulled his tie over his head and dropped it onto the empty seat beside him. Then he leaned back and sighed. The white puff of his breath dissolved quickly in the damp April night. Quiet filled the car with its grand presence, serene and indifferent after the overwrought noise of the arena and the heavy hush of the losing dressing room.

Owen fastened his seatbelt and the dome light faded. He was left to the yellowish glow of the parking lot light, its cheap plastic fixture chipped and clouded with an accumulation of moth corpses. He turned the key in the ignition and his headlights hit the car parked in front of him. He backed out, exited the lot, and made his way through the tired, disappointed city. But when he pulled up to the bar, its neon signs glowing with the promise of booze and smoke and guys who had nowhere else to go, he didn't stop. He had no appetite for a night on the town with a bunch of losers, even if he was one of them. Especially if he was one of them. He kept driving.

The streets were dark and shiny. A giant raindrop burst out of nowhere and splattered onto the windshield like a bug spilling its guts. A couple of blocks ahead a car slowed and turned, its brake lights bleeding red onto the wet pavement. Otherwise there wasn't much to see but the robotic motion of the windshield wipers, right, left, right, left. Owen stopped at a traffic light and a pickup pulled up alongside, throbbing with a bass beat. He just kept staring straight ahead. His turn signal ticked cheerfully, out of time with the music and unmindful of the evening's events or outcome. Finally he got the arrow. It wasn't long before he saw the sign pointing to the highway. Without giving it a thought, he turned.

Now it was pretty much a straight shot across the empty prairie. It was dark as hell, and Owen drove like a madman, trying to put the game behind him, to make it shrink, like the city in his rearview mirror, from the present into the past. After a while he noticed that the city lights behind him had disappeared, and without really wanting to, he started to replay the game in his mind.

Who could explain why his team had stumbled while the other had risen to the next round of play? Had fate simply decreed in advance that they would be the losers tonight?

No, it wasn't fate. They'd had the power to win. They'd held it in their hands. But somehow, at some crucial moment, they'd surrendered it without even realizing.

Words of explanation were pointless—shameful, even. Nothing but empty excuses. The game had been so close, so *infinitely* close, but in the end they had failed to make a play, failed to get the puck on their sticks, failed to shoot it into the net, and, instead of one of *them*, some miserable bastard on the *other* team had done it. Then *those guys* had erupted with cheers, poured off the bench, thrown their gloves into the air, and piled on top of one another in one big celebratory scrum. Meanwhile, *us guys* were suddenly undone, undressed, unraveled and revealed to be nothing more than twenty-some-odd graceless arrangements of used-up limbs and pulverized flesh flung haphazardly across the ice and slumped over the boards.

What if he—the *great* Owen MacKenzie—had managed to win the puck in the corner that one time, from that gigantic monster son-of-a-bitch what's his name? Yeah. What if. The fact is, he hadn't done it. He couldn't do it. The guy had been *planted* in the ice. Fucking *frozen* into it. So goddamn big and heavy it was impossible to move him.

There you go again, Owen fucking MacKenzie. More bullshit excuses.

Jesus Christ! Why did he have to fail? Why hadn't he been able to draw on some secret reserve of strength, like some kind of miracle hockey superman? Hadn't he wanted it enough? What kind of weak-ass loser was he?

He hadn't been tired. He was never tired on the ice. Off the ice was another story. It had been a long few weeks. Little by little, the fatigue had begun to sift down, its drowsy weight filling the endless hours spent on planes and shuttles, in hotels and restaurants and bars. It never lightened. It never lifted. A nap was never enough. A night was never enough. A day off was never enough. And now the whole goddamn summer wouldn't be enough.

Shit. The whole summer. There'd be no regrouping this time, no practice in which to fix the mistakes, no game tomorrow or the next day or the next in which to reestablish themselves as winners, as warriors, as men. They were done, dead, dormant until next year, while that other team, those other guys, those miserable smug bastards: they would continue on, they would *live.*

Owen had fully planned to win the Stanley Cup this spring. He didn't even know, yet, what it was, what it meant, or even what the game was, this man's game—how hard it was, how fast it was—but he was going to win it. Then he was going to carry that big, shiny, mythical, magical, fantastic silver chalice back home to her, to Agnes, overflowing with champagne. True, he couldn't even picture it in his imagination—it wasn't anywhere near real enough for that—but he knew he was going to do it. Only he hadn't done it. And now he was in shock. Was it really over? It couldn't be. Not so quickly. Not so finally. There must be a way back. But no, there wasn't. Only darkness in the rearview, now.

God knows he hated himself for losing. He hated himself for failing. He honestly did. But he hated himself even more for the feeling that he now started to notice bubbling up inside of him, threatening to replace the bright edge of anger with the limp pallor of complacency. That feeling was relief. He was terribly ashamed to admit it, even to himself, but the honest-to-god-damn fucking truth was, there was nothing left inside of him. Nothing. He didn't care about winning anymore. He didn't care about anything. He just wanted to lie down in his own goddamn bed and sleep and forget.

Sleep. He jerked his eyes open. Fatigue was setting in. The game was fading. Even his self-hatred was fading. The fight to win had been replaced with the fight to stay awake so as not to end up upside-down in a slough by the side of the highway—an ordinary, every-day survival instinct shared with birds and bugs and fucking bacteria, for all he knew. Glorious, right?

He remembered, as a kid, reading about some pilot or other who'd flown solo over the Atlantic in one of those tiny, old-time planes. Was it Amelia Earhart? She'd kept herself awake by opening the window to blasts of freezing air. He tried that, and it helped. Even so, sleep might have overwhelmed him had the cramping of his cold muscles and the emptiness of his stomach not conspired to keep it at bay.

Finally, with the moon rising, he reached the outskirts of town. In spite of the fact that it was the middle of the night, there were some lights on here and there. He was glad to see them—they were comforting after the vast, dark solitude of the prairie. Maybe Amelia Earhart had felt the same way when she finally came within sight of land.

He turned onto his street. Thank God he was home. He didn't even bother to get his bags out of the trunk. He was going to go inside and fall directly into bed. He wasn't going to stop to change his clothes or brush his fucking teeth, that was for sure. He walked up the front steps, fumbling with his keys in the darkness. Finally, he found the right one, turned it in the lock, and opened the door.

Immediately, he knew something was wrong. The house was missing that stale smell it got after being empty for even just a couple of days. He stood still, listening, for a moment. All quiet. He switched on the hall light. Still there was no sound. He tiptoed into the living room. The faint blue light of the TV flickered across a shape lying on the sofa, and a splotch of long, dark hair spread out across a cushion.

"God dammit," he said, with exasperation and dismay and just plain weariness.

At the sound of his voice Agnes's eyes popped open and she lifted her head.

"Owen?" she said. Her eyes were blinking in the light from the hall behind him.

"What are you doing here?" he asked. "You guys moved out, right?" He was way too tired for this.

"Yeah. We did. I just came to watch the game. I guess I fell asleep." She swung her feet onto the floor. "Tough game, O. Sit down. I'll get you a beer."

"I don't want a beer," he said. "And I've been sitting down for hours now." He felt cornered. He didn't want to deal with anyone right now. Certainly not her. He said, "Anyhow, it's my goddamn beer. I'll get one myself if I want it."

"Fine. I was just trying to be nice."

"Nice? You broke into my house! I oughta call the police."

"I didn't break in! I used the key that *you* gave me."

"Fine. Whatever. I'm going to bed."

He stumbled into his room and slammed the door. He took off his jacket and threw it onto the bed, but he didn't throw it far enough—it made it only to the edge and then it slithered off again, onto the floor. He stood there for a couple of minutes. Come to think of it, a beer sounded pretty good. He opened the door and walked back into the kitchen, ignoring Agnes and grabbing a can out of the refrigerator.

"I can't believe we lost," she said.

She had followed him. Now they stood face to face in front of the refrigerator. He opened the can, tossed his head back, and downed it by the gulp.

"Yeah. Well, that's hockey, I guess," he said.

"What do you mean, *that's hockey, I guess*?"

He didn't answer. He had no answer.

She continued, "What happened? I mean we were up *three games to one*. What a disaster. It's like the goddamn Titanic."

"Thanks," said Owen.

"Seriously. You run into one teensy little iceberg and the next thing you know you're at the bottom of the fucking ocean."

Owen stared at her.

She went on. "I just don't get it. Everything's laid out for you, you're playing in the NHL for God's sake—in the *Stanley Cup playoffs*. All you need to do is win one more game. One more lousy—"

"If it's so goddamn easy, you try it!" he hissed.

"Go to hell!" she said. She looked hurt.

"What do you want anyhow? What are you doing here?"

"I told you, I just—"

"I mean it, Agnes! What do you want from me? I did the best I could. I did everything they asked me to do. *Every*thing. *Every* day. Every *minute* of every day. Like a goddamn fucking machine!"

"O—"

"You don't believe me. You don't *know*. You'll *never* know."

Owen slammed his beer into the sink. He yanked his shirt up over his head, and the buttons popped and skittered across the floor. He pulled off his undershirt, too. Agnes stared at him, her wide eyes looking into his. He was glad if she was alarmed. He was fucking *ecstatic* if she was frightened.

"Ugly enough for ya?" he asked.

Agnes's eyes shifted downward, past the angry, bulging veins in his neck to a big, dark, purplish-blue welt on his chest.

"Jesus, O, that's a good one," she whispered. She touched it, with the pad of her index finger. Then she noticed another bruise blossoming just below the bicep on his left arm. "And this one, too. Does it hurt?"

"No," he lied.

"That's bullshit. You sure it's not broken?"

He didn't answer.

Agnes looked at his face. He'd long been healed up from the fight with Claude, but now there was a big, new scrape alongside his nose and continuing on through his eyebrow, only partly scabbed over. It must have been from that high stick in game four or five—she'd seen him bleeding on TV. He'd drawn a penalty on it and they'd scored, so it had ended up okay. Except for his face, of course.

It wasn't the first time she'd seen a cut on his face, but now he didn't look like himself at all. His lips were colorless and pressed together. His eyes were black holes and his skin was so pale that it looked blue.

"Gosh, O," she said, "You look terrible. What time is it? I didn't think you'd be back tonight. I didn't mean to—how'd you get here so fast?"

"Just got in the car and drove," he said. "Now, if you'll excuse me."

He brushed past her and out of the kitchen. She heard his bedroom door close behind him.

"Goodnight, O," she said. She knew he couldn't hear her. She picked up his shirt and undershirt off the floor. A lump burned in her throat and she closed her eyes. She wanted to think of something beautiful, comforting, and the first thing she thought of was that night before Christmas, standing under the neighbor's trees, watching Owen flicker across the ice, his blades scraping, whispering to her through the thin, icy air. She'd wanted to join him so badly, but she just couldn't. He'd seemed so perfect, so set apart from everything, like he wasn't even real. She opened her eyes and she was back in the dark, empty kitchen. His undershirt was still warm in her hands: warm from his heat, from his anger, from his pain.

She went into the living room to turn off the television and then walked over to his door. She lifted her hand and knocked.

"O?" she said.

No answer.

"O?" she tried again, a bit louder.

"What?" came his muffled voice.

"Can I come in?"

"No."

She opened the door a crack and peeked in. It must have been close to dawn, but it was still dark, and moonlight raked in through the venetian blinds. Owen was lying face down on the bed, still without a shirt, still wearing his dress pants and shoes.

"I said, no," he said.

She went in and closed the door behind her. Then she walked over, untied his right shoe, and pulled it off.

"I said, no," he said again.

"I'm just going to help you off with your shoes."

"Oh, for God's sake, Agnes," he said. But he didn't move a muscle.

She untied his left shoe and pulled it off, and then she put both shoes down together over by the wall. She peeled off his socks and tossed them in the direction of the shoes. He didn't so much as wiggle his toes.

Agnes stood there looking at him. His head rested sideways on the bed. The moon cast stripes of silver across the nape of his neck, his smooth, round, left bicep, his angled shoulder blades, his bumpy spine, and the soft curve of his lower back. His breathing was deep and slow. She crawled up onto the bed and sat on her knees beside him. She put her hands on his shoulders—they were warm and soft—and she leaned forward, her nose at his neck, to inhale the smell of him. Slowly, she ran her fingers through his hair. It was soft and fine, crazy in loops and curls. She rubbed gently around his temples and all over his scalp. Then she put her hands on his shoulders again and started to massage them.

She worked her thumbs and fingers deeply into his firm flesh and all around his bony shoulders. She leaned into his upper back where the muscles were tight between his shoulder blades—he took a deep breath and let it out slowly. She kneaded his arm from his shoulder down to his warm palm and rubbed each of his long, bony fingers. They curled limply in her hands. She did the same to his other arm, taking care to avoid that ugly bruise, and then she played with his hair some more, letting the ringlets curl around her fingers. She worked down his spine, gently circling each vertebra with her thumb, and when she got down past his rib cage, she lay down, propping her head up on her arm. She caressed the concave swoop of his lower back, which was covered with blonde, downy hair, and slid her hand around his waist. His dress pants, with the shiny black belt threaded carefully through each belt loop, made her think of a little boy dressed up for Mass.

She'd known Owen when he was a little boy, but years and years had passed since then. She tried to remember what he was like at school, or on the playground, or even at her house, eating lunch with her and Vin and Evan like he often had on Saturdays, when his mom had to work. What had he even looked like back then? When she tried to picture him, she couldn't even see his face. He was just a flash of happy energy—running, jumping, shouting—a string of motions, like a smaller, less refined version of the guy in the backyard ice rink. Back then, though, it was daytime. The sky was bright and the ice stretched to the horizon. Losing didn't matter, and winning didn't, either. Just being in the game was enough.

She woke up. The stripes of neon moonlight were gone, replaced by the soft light of dawn. Her arm was resting across Owen's lower back. His breathing was deep and even—he was asleep. The side of her that was close to him was warm, but her back was cold, so she turned over and wedged it up against him. He stirred, too, curled up around her, and draped his arm over her. Soon she was very warm. He seemed to be sleeping soundly again. No way could she sleep now, though, not with him so close around her, so she just lay there as the light in the room grew, and she felt his hot breath in her hair.

After a while he stirred again. He was waking up, and she could feel his breathing quicken. He put his hand on her arm, so gently that she barely felt it.

"Ag," he whispered.

"Yeah," she breathed back.

"Hi."

"Hi." She twisted her head back to look at him. He was still marked by the high stick, but otherwise he looked like himself again.

"I want to kiss you," he said.

"I want to kiss you, too."

His face came close to hers and she closed her eyes. He kissed her eyelids, one and then the other, and then he kissed her mouth. She wove her fingers into his hair at the nape of his neck, pulled him close, and kissed his lips, as slowly and tenderly as she could. She felt like they were bobbing around in the middle of a sunlit lake, with the cool breeze playing all around them. She wanted it never to end.

He wrapped her up in his arms. After a long time he said, "Ag, I don't want to leave you."

"Then don't."

They kissed some more.

"I can't help it. I have to drive back," he said. "Garbage bag day."

"I know," she said.

"I don't want to go," he whispered.

"I don't want you to go," she whispered back.

They kissed again.

She said, "You promise to come back?"

"God, yeah."

"When?"

"As soon as humanly possible."

"Kiss me again, before you go."

He kissed her mouth and earlobes and neck.

"Ag, I want to make love to you."

"Yeah," Agnes whispered. "Me too. But I don't have, you know . . ."

"Me neither," he breathed.

"Just hold me then, O, okay? Just hold me."

"Jeez, Ag, you're knocking me out right now. You really are."

The office door squeaked open. Vin heard footsteps coming toward him, and then he felt someone nudge the creeper he was lying on. He nearly dropped his wrench on his face.

"Hey, Vincent, is that you under there?" said a woman's voice.

He rolled out from under the car.

"Oh, hey Tess," he said. "What's up?"

"Where were you?" she asked.

"When?"

"Saturday. You said you'd help with the game."

"No, I didn't," said Vin.

"Yes, you did," Tess answered.

212 • LESLIE SPITZ-EDSON

Dad walked over. He'd been at the other end of the garage, fiddling with some old part or another. "Vincent," he said. "Why don't you introduce me to your friend?"

Vin got to his feet. "Dad, this is Tess—" he began.

"Therese Delaronde," she said, holding her hand out to Dad.

"Lazare Demers," he answered. "It's a pleasure to meet you." They shook hands.

"Likewise," she said.

"Vincent," Dad said, "if you have something to talk about with Therese, why don't you use the office? Don't make her stand out here in the garage."

"Okay," said Vin. "After you," he said to Tess, gesturing toward the office door with mock politeness.

"Nice meeting you," Tess said to Dad. Then she turned and Vin followed her into the office, closing the door behind them.

"So, what happened to you?" asked Tess. She folded her arms and her bracelets clanged together.

"Give me a break, Tess. I never said I'd be there on Saturday."

"What were you up to, on Saturday night, that was so much better than helping me?"

"I like to go out on Saturdays. I went out with some buddies."

"You went out drinking, eh?" she asked.

"No."

She narrowed her eyes at him. She said, "Okay, then, this Saturday, meet me at the rink at seven forty-five. You'll help me coach the game, and then we'll go out."

Vin didn't answer.

Tess said, "You said you like to go out on Saturdays. So we'll go out, okay?"

She was standing very close to him, the same way she had back in the parking lot at Achille's.

He grinned at her. "Are you asking me out?"

"No. I need your help with the game. Seven forty-five, got that?"

"I thought you had the hots for old Deuce."

"I don't have the hots for anyone. Seven forty-five on Saturday, right?" she repeated.

"Okay," said Vin, still grinning. He thought, *why the hell not?*

Tess said, "See you then." The door closed behind her.

On Monday morning, Claude and Vin drove to the rink.

"Agnes'll be in town this weekend," Vin told Claude.

"Oh yeah?" Claude's face brightened.

"Yeah, she's driving up with MacKenzie."

"Oh." Claude resumed staring blankly at the highway. After a while he asked Vin, "How'd it go on Saturday?"

"Pretty good," Vin answered. "Better than I thought."

"How'd you like the kids?"

"They were okay," answered Vin.

Claude smiled.

"Yeah," said Vin. "They seemed to like me. Not as much as they like Tess, but they listened to me and everything. Well, except for one busy little squirrel."

Claude chuckled. "Yeah, there's always one."

They drove some more in silence.

Vin said, "She's a little hard to figure."

"Who? Tess?" asked Claude.

"Yeah, Tess."

"She's alright. She loves those kids," Claude answered.

"I can see that," said Vin.

"She's a real strong personality," added Claude.

"Bossy," said Vin.

"That too," said Claude.

They drove for a while.

Vin said, "You and Tess . . . ?"

He looked at Claude, but Claude was looking straight ahead, completely expressionless.

Vin continued, "I mean, are you two . . . ?"

"No."

"I was thinking I'd, maybe, you know, ask her out."

The corner of Claude's mouth turned upwards just a little bit.

"What are you smiling at?" Vin asked him.

"Nothing."

"So, what do you say?"

Claude didn't answer.

"You don't want me to."

"It's not me. It's—"

"She asked me back to her place," said Vin.

"Yeah?" said Claude. "What'd you do there?"

"She made us some Indian tacos."

"Her Indian tacos are real good," Claude said.

"Yeah," said Vin.

"What else did you do?" Claude asked.

"Went out for a beer."

"What else?"

"That was about it."

Claude nodded as if to say, *case closed.*

Vin continued, "She's got this, this way of—"

"She does."

"Deuce, she's not your cousin."

Claude didn't answer.

"Right?"

"What do you want to do today, O?"

Owen looked at Agnes. She sat facing him on the sofa, cross-legged, eating scrambled eggs on toast. It was their last day together for a while—tomorrow he was leaving for the Trader's development camp down in Thompson.

"I want to eat breakfast. Or lunch. Or whatever goddamn meal this is," he said. And he gave her that crazy, lopsided smile.

She laughed. "You know what I mean."

"Yeah."

"So?" she asked.

"I want to make love to you."

"Again?"

"Yeah."

"Better not wear yourself out. Camp starts tomorrow."

"To hell with it," he said.

"Let's do something special," Agnes replied.

"Let's get out of here," said Owen. "I know the perfect place."

They stopped at Dottie's to buy sandwiches and then headed south past farms and fields on the clean, straight, prairie highway. The sky was perfectly blue. They rolled down the car windows and let the warm wind wash over them. Even the manure from a roadside cow pasture smelled sweet on a day like this. Agnes looked at Owen, settled into his familiar driving posture, his t-shirt rippling across his shoulders and chest. He'd been at the gym four days a week all summer and it showed. His face, though, was lined in a worried kind of way.

"What are you thinking about, O?" Agnes asked.

"Just wondering what camp'll be like."

"You might be the only one who's already played some games with the team," Agnes said.

Owen shrugged. "Could be." It was true—the camp was for prospects, not for guys already on the Traders' roster.

"You're not nervous, are you?" Agnes asked.

"A little."

"But you played there last spring. The coaches know you."

"Yeah. But it's not so much about the coaches. It's more the whole scene."

"What do you mean?"

"It's like juniors, remember?"

"No. I'm a girl. I couldn't play in juniors. Remember?"

"Right. But when you came out to visit that one time—"

"You completely ignored me. You left me with your *parents*. And Evan."

"I know. Sorry. But that's the thing. I was trying to fit in."

"And being with me would keep you from fitting in?"

"Yes. Definitely."

"Thanks a lot."

"Ag, you wouldn't want to fit in. Trust me."

"You did."

"I didn't have a choice."

"But—"

"I was trying to walk the line, you know. When you're with a new group of guys it's not always that easy to do."

Agnes didn't answer. Everyone had heard the stories about what went on in juniors. He was probably right. She wouldn't have wanted any part of it.

"And it was my first year," Owen added.

"But, Owen, this isn't juniors."

"True."

"So hopefully it's not like that."

He nodded.

"And you played in the playoffs. The other guys'll look up to you."

Owen smiled a twisted smile. "Yeah. I'll have a target on my back."

Agnes was quiet for a while and then she said, "I'm really proud of you, O."

"Thanks, Ag. You're nice to say it."

"I wish I could be there with you."

"I wish you could be with me, too. But it wouldn't be fun for you. They keep us busy all the time, day and night."

That wasn't what Agnes meant. She'd meant that she'd like to be there *playing* with him, as one of the other prospects. They could look out for each other, like they used to. But she didn't say it. It was impossible anyhow.

＊

They turned off the main road and followed the signs to the lake. The parking lot was ringed with small trees, brush, and wildflowers. Owen parked near the trailhead and they started walking. It was hotter and drier down here than it was in the woods back home—twigs and dead leaves popped and rustled under their feet. The sunlight seemed to cool, though, as it filtered through the green leaves, and as they came to the edge of the little woods, the breeze picked up and they stepped out into a field of dancing grasses. Beyond it, a long, sandy beach edged the dazzling turquoise lake.

"Wow, it's beautiful," said Agnes.

"Yeah, I like it here," said Owen. "Different than the lakes back home, but nice."

They found a spot away from the other people who dotted the beach and sat knee to knee as they ate their sandwiches. Owen looked at Agnes. A cool breeze shimmered in her hair. Tiny goose bumps formed on her golden skin and then disappeared again.

"You're quiet," Owen said to her.

"I'm just . . . memorizing you."

"You pretty much know what I look like by now."

She brushed her fingers over the fuzzy blonde hair on his arm. "There're just a lot of little things. I'm afraid I might forget some of them."

"I've already memorized everything about you, Ag. I swear, I can just close my eyes anytime, and there you are." He looped his finger inside the neckline of her t-shirt. "Come on, take this off, already. It's killing me the way your bikini's peeking out up here." He kissed her behind the ear and then, with his teeth, started to tug at the string that tied her swimsuit around her neck.

"Hmm, is it just me, or is it getting a bit warm out here?" Agnes said. "Maybe we should go for a swim."

The water was cold. They raced to keep warm. She was a good swimmer but he caught her every time, and then she had to pay with a kiss.

When they got cold they went up on shore and sat in the sand. They'd ended up a considerable distance from their picnic spot, and a group of four girls were tanning themselves on a blanket just a few feet away. They were all blond and pink and ponytailed. Agnes was sure that Owen had noticed them, but he had his back to them, now. She, on the other hand, could see them clearly. They were looking at her and giggling at something one of them had said.

When the giggles died down one of them said, in a stage whisper, "I think that's Owen MacKenzie."

"Who?" said another.

"You know, the hockey player."

"You're so ignorant!" said a third.

"That's not him," the fourth one said.

"I'm pretty sure," said the original girl. "It's hard to tell from here, though."

"Shh, they can hear us!"

"That's not him," said girl number four again. "Owen MacKenzie's got better things to do than hang around with a girl like *her*."

"Yeah, I mean, *look* at her," said one of them.

"I don't even care who he is," said the second girl. "He's hot! I wish he would turn around. I want another look at those abs."

"And those shoulders!"

"Let's go for a swim."

"Good idea, I'm getting hot."

"I'm extremely hot." They all giggled. Then they got up and sauntered—not directly toward the water, which would have meant walking behind Owen, but around behind Agnes, so that they were directly in Owen's sightline. Owen put his hand behind Agnes's neck, pulled her close and gave her a kiss that lingered nearly as long as it took the girls to reach the water. Then he laid back and looked up at the sky. Agnes did the same.

"I gotta tell ya, I don't appreciate being objectified like that," he said.

Agnes laughed. "Yes you do."

"Okay, maybe a little."

"You have put on some muscle this summer."

"Just following orders."

Agnes gazed up into the blue sky. "I'm going to miss you, O."

"I'm going to miss you too, Ag."

"I hope it goes really well for you."

"Thanks," said Owen, propping himself up on his elbow and playing with the pool of water in her navel.

"I'm sure it will," Agnes said.

"Thanks, Ag. But, you know, it's only a week, and then I'll be back."

"It's only a week this time, O. But you'll be going out there in the fall, too," she said.

"Maybe," he said.

"You will. You're a great player."

"Nah," he said. "But if I—what are you going to do this fall, Ag?"

"I don't know. Jo'll be here until Christmas, at least. I guess I'll stay, too. Keep working, try to save some more money. Hope . . . " her voice broke a little bit, "hope that you stick out there—"

"Aw, Agnes." He rested his hand on her bare stomach. A tear spilled from the corner of her eye. "Don't cry," he said. "It's going to work out. We'll make it work out."

"Okay," she said, not sounding convinced.

He caught another tear with his finger. She started shaking and wrinkled up her face. The tears kept coming. Suddenly he knew why she'd tried so hard to push him away. It made sense, in an Agnes kind of way.

"Jesus, Ag. I'm the biggest fucking idiot of all time, aren't I?"

She was still crying, but she shook her head and laughed. "Not quite," she said.

He scooted closer to her and cupped his hand over her shoulder. "Don't worry, Ag. Do you think I'm going to let you get away from me after all this?"

"I don't know," she said.

"I'm not, Ag."

"You don't have to say that, O."

"I mean it. Jesus Christ, Ag. You know I do."

She could feel his hot, desperate breath on her face. She knew he meant it right now. But in the fall things would be different. Or in the winter, or in the spring. There'd be some other girl at some point, that was obvious. She'd be smarter than the witty quartet here at the lake, but she'd be equally blond and, yes, she'd be white. Not because Owen was racist—he wasn't—but because it would be simpler for him that way. And he deserved that. He deserved a normal girl who didn't have a loser brother and a big, empty hole inside where her disappeared Indian mom should have been. She ran her fingers through his damp hair. The lake water had made it even softer, like a baby's hair. He lay back again.

They heard splashing. The girls were getting out of the water and walking back to their blanket. Owen said, "Let's hit the road, Ag. I want to take you out to a really good place tonight."

"You don't have to do that, O," she said.

"No, but I *want* to."

She smiled.

"Anyhow, I'm getting hungry."

"You're *always* hungry," said Agnes. "Are you sure there's nothing wrong with you?"

"Are you saying you think I'm a freak of nature?"

"Yes, that's exactly what I'm saying."

They got up and started walking back to pick up their clothes and their picnic things. A couple of the girls came running over to them. One of them thrust a pen and a baseball cap at Owen and asked, breathlessly, "Will you sign this for me?"

"Uh, sure," he said. "What's your name?"

"Cindy."

He wrote, *for Cindy, Owen MacKenzie 11.*

"Thanks!"

Owen put his arm around Agnes's shoulders and they kept walking. They could hear the girl calling to her friends, "He asked my name!"

Agnes said, "You're such a nice guy. I would've said no."

He shrugged. "They're fans. It's part of the job."

"You're right, of course."

"But I was *this close* to signing it: *for Cindy, from Donald Duck*."

8

Agnes and Jo were headed to Hillary's for dinner. They rolled down the windows of Agnes's rebuilt clunker, purchased from her dad, to make the most of the "Indian summer." The trees blazed yellow in the low sunlight, the asphalt exhaled the gathered heat of the day, and as the evening cool fell, the atmosphere trembled with a hazy glow. As they turned onto Hillary's street, the sun slid behind the trees, and they heard the sweet, clear cries of kids playing. A half dozen of them, plus Jamie, swarmed in the blue dusk, sticks at the ready, in front of a goal that was set up at the edge of the street.

"Car, car!" someone called. The kids scattered. As soon as Agnes had parked, one of them stick-handled back into the middle of the street, smacked the ball into the empty net, and threw up his arms in celebration.

"No fair! That doesn't count," came the cries from the other kids.

"Yes, it does! Empty-net goal!"

"No way! Cars are a time-out!"

"Yeah, you can't score during a time-out!"

Agnes and Jo laughed, and Jamie left the game to greet them. They started up to the house, but Jackie ran after them. "Agnes!" he shouted, panting. "Will you play goal for us? Please?"

"Well," she hesitated.

"Jackie, she's here for dinner. Maybe next time," said Jamie.

"Aw," complained Jackie.

"I guess I could for a few minutes," Agnes said. "If that's okay with you, Jamie."

"Sure, if you really want to," he said.

She smiled. "It'll be fun." There were few places she felt as much at home as on the street, playing hockey. She'd played all the time as a girl.

The kids gathered around Agnes while she strapped on the pads. There was only one girl out there now, and Agnes noticed that she was hanging back some.

"What's your name?" Agnes asked her.

"Katie."

As Agnes took her position, one of the boys taunted, "Bet you can't stop me!"

"Bet I can," said Agnes.

"Bet you can't!" He ran in and took a shot, but she kicked it back to him.

"Aw," he said.

"Try again," she said. "How about you and Jackie, on the rush?"

They tried it, and he scored.

"Great!" said Agnes. "Now you and Katie."

They went on like that for a while and then Agnes challenged, "Who can shoot it five-hole?"

After they'd each had a couple of tries she said, "Okay, guys, I'm done. It's time for me to be a grown-up now."

"Five more minutes?" they begged. "Please?"

"It's almost dark," replied Agnes. "I can barely see the ball!"

She pulled off the goalie gear. Under the pads she was damp with sweat, but it felt great. When she and Jackie got up to the house, Jackie ran off to his room and Agnes headed into the kitchen.

"Padding the stats, eh, Agnes?" said Jamie. He was wearing an apron and holding an oversize spatula and a pair of tongs for the barbeque.

Agnes laughed. "That was the most fun I've had in a long time."

"Yeah. I'd give anything to be a kid again," said Jamie.

"Again?" said Hillary. "I'm not convinced you ever *stopped* being a kid."

Jamie grinned.

Agnes said, "Jackie's such a nice boy, Hillary."

Hillary smiled. "A lot of that is thanks to Jamie. I couldn't do it myself."

"Sure you could, babe," Jamie said, "You were doing great long before we even met."

"Aw shucks, thanks," said Hillary.

"How'd you two meet, anyhow?" asked Jo.

"Well, it's a funny story," said Hillary. "Do you want to tell, Jamie?"

"No, I want to hear you tell them," he laughed. "Come on out and sit down. I'm just going to put these steaks on."

They walked out the kitchen door to the tiny patio. Hillary plugged a cord into an electrical outlet and a string of Christmas lights lit up the wooden fence. The steaks sizzled on the barbeque.

Jamie said, "Go ahead, Hill, tell them."

"Okay. It was back when my sister, Nancy, lived in town, and she was always trying to get me to go out with her to bars, which was never really my thing. But she kept hounding me, and so finally one day I said, okay, and I got a babysitter for Jackie—he was only about three years old at the time—and we went out.

"We were sitting there at this bar, and these two guys came over and started talking to us. They seemed nice. We were all just talking, and after a while one of the guys, the funny one—Jamie—asked me for my number. I put him off, but he didn't seem to get the message. Every time the conversation slowed down, he'd ask again. He must have asked, like, five or six times, and I kept saying no. I mean, I'd just gotten my first nursing job, and it hadn't been that long since I broke up with Jackie's dad, and I felt like I had my hands full. I didn't need anything else in my life. So, finally, he gives up on me and asks Nancy for her number."

"You're kidding!" said Jo.

"I'm not," said Hillary. "And, of course, Nancy gives him her number right away. Anyhow, eventually we all say goodnight, and I go home and don't think anything else about it. A couple of days later, Nancy calls me and says, 'Remember that guy we met at the bar, Jamie?' And I said, 'Yes.' She said, 'He called me last night.' And I said, 'So, are you two going out?' And she said, 'Well, Hill, we had a really nice conversation, but he didn't ask me out. He asked me for your number!'"

"I'm a sneaky bastard," said Jamie, winking.

Hillary continued. "So Nancy asked me, 'Can I give him your number?' And I said, 'No.' And she said, 'Oh, come on, if I don't he's just going to keep calling me.' So finally I just gave in. I figured I'd have to explain to him myself why I wasn't interested in dating."

"You can see how well that turned out," said Jamie.

"He hasn't changed a bit," said Hillary. "He still won't take no for an answer."

"Well," said Jamie, "sometimes the stakes are just too high. I mean, what if I'd have let you have your way, and someone else had gotten to you first? It'd be me and the jukebox singing the blues down at T.T.'s, and some other guy out here on the patio grilling your steaks, if you know what I mean."

They all laughed.

"What are you up to, Jo?" asked Hillary. "What are you going to do when you're done with school?"

"I'd like to start my own business, maybe sewing clothes for special occasions. Like baptisms and weddings and things like that."

"That sounds promising," said Hillary. "I bet there's all kinds of tailor work available. I could have used your help when I was redecorating Jackie's room, with the curtains and all."

Jo nodded. "Yeah, I guess I could do that kind of thing."

"She can do *anything* with fabric and scissors and thread," said Agnes. "She's the master."

"That's not true," said Jo.

"How's Owen doing out there in Thompson?" Jamie asked Agnes.

"He's okay. He was real pumped at first, but lately he seems kind of tired."

Jamie nodded. "It's all new out there. Here he's pretty much mastered everything. You know, you get the details down and then it's just music: timing, tempo, flow. In Thompson it's a whole new ballgame. Like, up here we're the Monkees, over there it's the Stones."

"Nice mixed metaphor," laughed Hillary.

Jamie smiled. "You get my drift."

"Yeah," said Agnes. "He just has to get over the hump, and then he'll feel better."

"It'll take some time, though," Jamie said. "It's not road hockey. It's a tough league. There's a lot of structure. You know, system stuff."

Agnes nodded.

"And Owen's not—he doesn't feed off hanging with the team the way some guys do," continued Jamie. "Even when he was here, a lot of times he'd rather be with you—or even, you know, with Sissy—than spend the whole night at the bar with the guys."

"Yeah. He doesn't like to drink that much," said Agnes.

"It's not only about the drinking," said Jamie. "He'd *rather* be with you. Down here that worked out okay. He was already our number-one guy and that first line clicked early on. Up there, though, he's just another guy trying to fit in. It's dog-eat-dog."

"I guess you're right," said Agnes.

"And up there he doesn't even have you," said Jamie.

When they got home that night, Agnes dialed Owen's number. He didn't pick up, so she left a message on his answering machine.

"Hey, O. It's me. Agnes. Just calling to see how you're doing. I miss you. Call me, okay?"

Then she opened the closet and pulled out the box with his moccasins in it. The beading was finished, and she was proud of it. The tiny, deeply colored, sparkling beads were tightly spaced—not easy to do on the tough moosehide—and they followed the contours of her leaves and flowers as gently as the prairie breeze. It was time she finished them, so that he could wear them this winter out there in Thompson. She sat up late under Jo's work light, stitching on the cuffs with the tiniest, most even stitches she could manage, wishing the phone would ring.

The next morning she was dragging. Owen hadn't called her back, and she was still thinking about what Jamie had said. It had made her worry about Owen in a way that she hadn't before. She'd always taken it for granted that he'd make it. But what if he didn't?

Jo left for work and Agnes sat with her coffee, leafing through the course catalog for the College back home.

The phone rang.

"Hello?"

"Hey, Ag."

"O? Is that you?"

"Last time I checked."

She laughed at his dumb joke. "I'm surprised to hear from you at this hour. What's going on? Is everything okay?"

"Yeah. Everything's okay."

"That's good."

"Hey Ag, thanks for the message last night."

"You're welcome."

"It means a lot to me."

"I was thinking about you. All night," said Agnes. "I miss you."

"Miss you, too," he said.

She could hear his breathing.

"Um, Ag?"

228 • LESLIE SPITZ-EDSON

"Yeah?"

"They're sending me down."

Agnes's heart jumped. He was coming back! But out loud she said, "Aw, no, O, I'm sorry. Are you okay?"

"Yeah." He hesitated. "Are you disappointed?"

"Disappointed?" Agnes didn't know what he meant. She couldn't wait to get him back.

"In me," he said. "For being sent down."

"What? No. I mean, I'm sorry if it's got you feeling bad. Are you feeling bad?"

"Sort of."

"O, they're going to call you back up again. I know they will."

"Yeah," he said. "It's just—the game's so fast out here. Sometimes I blink and the play's passed me. Or I miss some play that should be automatic by now and do something dumb instead. I feel like a stupid kid."

"O, you're not a stupid kid. Anyone can make a mistake."

"I can't afford to make mistakes right now."

"O—"

"Even the hits feel harder all of a sudden."

"O, you're still a rookie, right? It's a different game over there. You'll grow into it."

"That's what they say. But I feel like I've hit a wall. And Holub's healthy again—ready to go. They don't need me."

"I need you," said Agnes.

"I'll be there in a few hours."

"Don't drive too fast."

"Just fast enough," said Owen.

"I can't wait," Agnes said.

"Meet me at my place?"

"Yeah," she whispered.

Owen played for the Wolves that night and had two goals and two assists. Agnes had a good seat behind the bench and cheered for him like crazy. After the game they went to T.T.'s. They found a place to sit, and then Owen got up to get their drinks. He was gone a long time. A mass of people stood around the bar, talking loudly, shouting orders at the bartenders, and pushing each other to get through. They mobbed Owen, congratulating him, welcoming him back, and asking him questions about the Traders. He looked over at Agnes a couple of times, but he kept getting cornered by other people. She started feeling a little bit left out, but she tried not to let it bother her. Finally, he came back with two bottles of beer and sat down beside her.

"Phew. Sorry about that," he said.

"It's okay." She lifted her beer bottle. "To you," she said.

He shook his head.

"Come on, O!" She handed him his beer. "To you," she said again.

They drank.

"Really, really awesome game," said Agnes. "You're a stud."

"Nah," he said.

"You are. You're a total stud."

"It's that nap I didn't take. I was inspired." He winked.

She rolled her eyes. "Seriously, O, is it just a lot easier down here?"

"It was tonight. But I don't expect it to last. I mean, I was just *going* tonight."

"Yeah, you were," said Agnes.

"Does it make you hot for me?"

She rolled her eyes.

He grinned.

She reached for her beer again.

"Hey, Mac, good game." Claude leaned over them, casting his big shadow.

"Thanks, Deuce." Owen stood up and they shook hands. "Have a seat, man," Owen said, indicating his chair.

"No, thanks, that's okay. Hi, Agnes."

"Hi, Claude," she said.

"How've you been?" he asked.

"Good. You?"

"Good," Claude answered. He looked from Agnes to Owen and back again. He said, "Well, I'd better get going." He walked away.

Owen sat down again and took a sip of beer. They sat for a minute in silence. Then he said, "I'm ready to go now."

"Are you sure?" asked Agnes. "We just got here."

"I'm sure. I've had enough."

They stepped outside and T.T.'s heavy door swung shut behind them, snuffing out the shouts, the laughter, the scraping of chairs, and the clanging of glasses and bottles. The outside air was light and cool and quiet.

"It feels good out here," said Agnes. "Let's walk around the park once." She took his hand and they started walking.

After a while he said, "That felt weird, just now, with Deuce."

"Did it?"

"Have you seen much of him since I've been gone?" asked Owen.

"No. I haven't seen him at all."

Owen was quiet.

"Are you okay, O?"

"Yeah. It feels kind of funny, that's all. I mean, I know that you and him were . . . you know. It's hard not to think about it, especially when he's right here in town with you. And I'm far away."

"Owen, he's not right here in town *with me*. You know that."

"Yeah, but—"

"And Claude and I were not 'you know.' We weren't. We never were. I swear."

"You don't have to swear, Ag. It doesn't change anything between us."

"It seems like it does."

"I can't help it. I know that you're attracted to him—"

"I was."

"You were. And you two—aw, Jeez." He stopped walking and put his hands over his face.

His emotion surprised her. She pulled his hands away so she could look at him. "Owen, we never—we just like, made out one time. One lousy time, okay? That was it. We went on a date or two. That's all."

"Really?"

"Yeah. You're the only one, O. You are." She put her hands on his shoulders, put her face close to his, and whispered, "You're the first guy I ever, you know, I mean ... "

"Jesus, Ag, really?"

Now she was embarrassed.

"I'm the first ... ?" he asked.

She didn't answer.

"Gosh, Ag. I'm such an idiot. If I'd have known that, I'd have ... I don't know. I mean, was it okay? I hope I didn't, like, hurt you or anything."

"You're not an idiot. O. You didn't hurt me. It was definitely okay. More than okay."

"More than okay?" he asked.

"A lot more than okay, okay?"

Owen still looked troubled—his face was all scrunched up. It was bizarre how much reassurance he needed on this. He was a stud, for God's sake. Any girl would want him. Couldn't he tell she was completely nuts about him?

She said, "Owen MacKenzie. It was *way* more than okay. Seriously, I mean it." She put her arms around his neck and whispered in his ear: "*I love you.*" Was that the first time she'd told him? "I never loved anyone else. Not like you. Never. I mean it."

She kissed his mouth. He put his hands on her waist and they kissed for a long time, just standing there on the sidewalk. They heard someone walk by but they didn't know or even care who it was.

"Let's go back to my place," he whispered.

"Do you believe me now?" asked Agnes.

"Believe what? I don't even remember what the hell we were talking about."

By the time Claude got to the rink in St. Cyp it was past six o'clock—later than he'd intended. Hopefully she'd still be here. He parked his pickup and hopped out. A blast of wind and icy rain nearly tore his jacket off. Tonight's trip back to Wapahaska in the wee hours wasn't going to be a joy ride, that was for sure. Inside the building, though, it was dry and bright—run-down, but in a comfortable, well-loved kind of way.

"Hello, Mrs. McCallum," he said.

"Claude!" Mrs. McCallum came out from behind the desk, her soft, wrinkled face stretched into a bright smile. Claude had always been one of her favorites, ever since he was a little boy just learning to play. He bent over to embrace her.

"How are you, Claude? Are you having a good year?"

"I am, thank you, Mrs. McCallum," he said.

"How's your mother?"

"She's good. I just came from her place."

"Well, give her my best, when you see her. And Cilla, too. The little one must be really shooting up."

"He is. How's Del?" Del was the youngest of Mrs. McCallum's eleven children, and the only one that Claude really knew.

"He's doing good. Still working out in Port Georgia. Now, what can I do for you, Claude?"

"I'm looking for Tess. Is she here tonight?"

"She's here. I think she's in the office. She's got a visitor."

"Thanks, Mrs. McCallum."

"You're welcome, dear."

Claude walked down the hall and peeked through the window into the office. Tess was leaning across the desk, deep in conversation with a good-looking young man. Claude tried to duck out of sight but Tess saw him and smiled. She held up a finger and mouthed, "One minute."

Claude stepped back from the door and examined the bulletin board that hung on the wall nearby. Large, construction-paper letters in red, green, and sky-blue read *All Colors–All Bands Youth Hockey Club of St. Cyprien: Where Skates and Spirits Fly!* He smiled. That was quite a mouthful. A few years ago, the leaders of the old youth hockey program had become embroiled in some kind of scandal, and Tess had kept the program alive, renaming it and injecting it with her own considerable passion. Now, the photos on the board, featuring kids of all ages skating, scoring, celebrating, and posing with their teammates, showed plainly how much joy it brought the community—the rosters, schedules, flyers announcing social events, and sign-up sheets soliciting needed supplies and volunteers testified to the amount of work it took to keep it going.

The door opened and Tess led the young man out of the office. It turned out that he was a police constable from Wapahaska, traveling across the province to observe youth programs. The men shook hands and then the constable left. Claude asked Tess if he could buy her dinner.

"That'd be nice," she said. She closed up the office and they walked outside. Claude followed Tess's taillights through the darkness back to her place. When they got there she parked her car, and Claude got out of the truck to open the door for her.

The arctic wind roared through the trees that surrounded Tess's little cottage, invisible in the darkness. She put her hand on his arm. She said, "It's a miserable night, Claude. There's food in the fridge. Let me cook something for you here."

"Tess, you've been working all day. I said I'd take you out. Come on, hop in."

She climbed in. He got in the other side and they started driving.

"Is Buffalo House still your favorite place?" he asked.

"Yes."

They got a quiet booth in the corner. A votive candle in a glass holder illuminated the glossy wooden table top and smoothed their faces.

Claude rubbed his hands together. "Winter's here again."

They opened their menus.

"How're the Wolves, Claude?"

"We could stand to win a few. We got MacKenzie back. Maybe things are looking up."

"What're you doing here?" Tess asked.

"Wanted to see you," said Claude.

"I don't believe you. I'm nothing to look at anymore," said Tess.

"Sure you are."

The waitress came and they ordered drinks.

"It's been a while," said Tess. "I mean, since you wanted to see me."

"That's not true," said Claude.

"How's your mom?" asked Tess.

"She's doing pretty good."

"What about you?"

He shrugged. "It's better than it was."

Tess put her hand on his. She said, "Claude?"

"Yeah, Tess."

"Achille's sick."

"What?"

"Yeah. Cancer. Lung cancer."

"No." He took her hand in both of his. "He seemed good this summer."

"Well, at his age, it goes fast, I guess."

"When'd you find out?"

"A couple weeks ago," she said.

"Why didn't you tell me?"

"I don't know, Claude. You have your own life, right?" She freed her hand from his. "I could tell something wasn't right. He had a cough that wouldn't go away, and he seemed to be losing weight. He was short of breath all the time. He said it was just because he's getting old. But I told him, he's been old as long as I can remember." She chuckled. "I finally dragged him in to the clinic."

The waitress brought them their drinks and they ordered dinner.

"Have you gotten him up to the cabin lately?"

"Back in the fall we went up to take the dock out. Even then he was so weak, I had to do most of it myself."

"That's a tough job," said Claude.

"The worst part was how bad he felt about it—about not being able to help. But he's still good in a canoe. Had to help him climb in, but otherwise he did great."

"You're so good to him, Tess."

"He's always been there for me." She choked up a little.

"You think you'll get him up there this winter?"

She shook her head. "No."

"No?"

"There's no point, Claude. He could barely make it down to the water this fall. But in the winter? With the cold and the snow and him even weaker? No."

"I'm sorry, Tess."

"It just hurts, that's all," she said, and she squeezed her eyes shut and took a deep breath. When she opened her eyes, she smiled. "I wish you could visit him, Claude. He loves you, he really does. He talks about your dad and Eddy all the time, about going up there, to the cabin, when we were kids. Remember? They'd put Helen and me in charge of you and . . . Hector. But Helen always kept Hector for herself—he was easy—and I was stuck with you." She grinned.

"What's wrong with me?" laughed Claude.

"You were a nightmare. Maybe you don't remember. You were always showing off, always doing stupid things."

"Wanted to make an impression on you, I guess."

She laughed at him. "You succeeded." Then she said, "You've changed a lot since then."

"You haven't changed," he said.

"Wonder what'll happen to the land up there once he's gone?"

"We'll find a way to hang onto it, Tess. Don't worry."

Tess looked like she was going to cry again. She said, "Anyhow, I wish you could see him, Claude. One more time. He'd really like that."

"I'll try to get up here again soon. I'll go see him."

"Thanks, Claude," Tess said.

Claude asked, "How's the hockey club?"

"It's good. More and more work, though, somehow."

"How's Vin working out?"

"He's okay. He's good with the kids." She took a sip of her drink.

Claude asked, "He's still helping with the games?"

She nodded.

"That's good."

"Yeah." Tess looked into his eyes. "Listen, Claude, I have to be honest with you. Vincent and I have been seeing each other this past month or so."

Claude didn't answer.

"You know," Tess continued, "he just kept asking and asking. And I was lonely."

Claude didn't say anything.

"Vincent likes me, you know? We have fun together. He's got a lot of energy."

"He's a young kid," said Claude. "Real young."

Tess said, "Sometimes you just want a guy to hold you and tell you everything's going to be okay."

Claude studied his hand, which was resting on the table, wrapped around his glass of cola.

"Claude." Tess got up and moved to his side of the booth. He didn't want to look at her but she put her hand on his cheek and turned his face toward hers. "I was so happy to see your face through that office window tonight. It was real nice of you to come and see me." She let go of his face and he looked back at his cola.

Tess moved back to the other side of the table again, and they sat there awhile, sipping their drinks.

Finally Claude said, "And here I thought you were dating that constable."

Tess laughed. "You kill me, Claude, you really do. I mean, a cop down in Wapahaska? In what universe would I be dating some young kid cop down in Wapahaska?"

"I don't know," he said.

"At least I'm going to hold off until I've exhausted all the possibilities up here," she said, smiling.

"Well, you're off to a good start," he said.

She pressed her lips together. "Claude, take me home."

"But our dinner hasn't come yet," he said.

"I don't care. I'm not hungry anymore. It's been a long day. I'm tired. I want to go home."

Claude asked for the check, paid it, and they left.

After they got into the pickup, Claude said, "Listen, Tess. I'm sorry. I didn't mean it like that."

She shrugged. "Don't worry about it, Claude. Believe me, I know I'm not perfect."

"You don't have to be perfect," Claude said.

"Yes, I do, apparently."

"I like you the way you are," Claude said.

"I don't care if you fucking *like* me, Claude."

They didn't say anything else all the way back to her place. When they got there, he put the truck in park and pulled back the door handle.

"Jesus, Claude," she said. "You don't have to walk me to the goddamn door."

She shoved open the cab door and jumped out, slamming it behind her.

He sat shivering in the frigid air she'd let in until the light went on in her front room.

To hell with it. He didn't care if she was dating Vin *and* the policeman *and* every other guy in the province.

He should have told her, but it was too late now. The moment was gone.

The Traders called Owen back to Thompson. He'd had a great run with the Wolves and Agnes was sure he'd stick out there this time. Maybe he was, too, because saying goodbye was harder than before. But one night when they were talking on the phone he invited her to visit him. They set a date, and soon after, a thick envelope arrived in the mail. It was an airplane ticket.

Agnes had never flown before. She took her seat by the window and watched the bleak, winter landscape streak past as the plane accelerated and took off. It rose unsteadily through a layer of ghost-like clouds until all of a sudden it burst free into the sky. Forward motion seemed to cease and the plane just hung there, deep in the blue. Agnes closed her eyes and felt the sun on her face.

The blanket of cloud below started to break up, and Agnes leaned her forehead against the cold glass, watching as the snowy prairie revealed itself far below. It was funny: Driving across the prairie in a car made Agnes feel tiny in the grand circle of the horizon, and from the airplane, she could see how much wider that circle really was. But instead of making her feel smaller by comparison, the extra altitude made her feel bigger. She could see *so far*. She had imagined that flying would be frightening, but it wasn't at all. It was exhilarating.

It was only when the plane landed that her nerves surfaced again. How could she measure up to Owen's big-time teammates and all his new friends? How would she look against this new big-city backdrop? What if everything had changed? What if he didn't love her anymore?

She needn't have worried. There he was, same as ever, wearing the same old army green, wool jacket, the same knit cap, and the same crazy smile.

"Come on, let's go," he said. He picked up her suitcase, grabbed her hand, and pulled her along at top speed. His hand was hot and sweaty, and he was breathing hard. He looked over at her, and their eyes met. He pulled her aside.

"Jesus Christ, Ag. I've just got to kiss you, okay?"

He kissed her, still squeezing her hand. Then he said, "Okay, let's go."

He was still driving the same old car, too. They got onto one highway and then another, driving through neighborhood after neighborhood until finally they crossed a bridge, exited the highway, and worked their way through what seemed to be an endless maze of city blocks, shadowed by tall buildings.

"Jeez, O. This place is huge," said Agnes.

"I know," he said. "But don't worry. I know my way from the airport, anyhow. I got you a room in my hotel. We're almost there."

The city streets might have been in shadow, but Agnes's room was not. Eighteen floors up, it was almost like being on the airplane again. Outside the window, the sun pulsed its blonde rays into the cloudless sky. Agnes could see west over the city to an endless rim of sprawling, snowy mountains. And although the palatial room had a dresser, a wardrobe, a desk, a refrigerator, a television, a king-sized bed, and an entire sitting area over by the window, they could have run a peewee hockey practice in the space that remained. On the table by the window stood an enormous vase of red roses, glowing crimson in the sunlight.

"Whoa," said Agnes. "There must be a hundred roses over there!"

Owen made a funny face and stroked his chin. "Nah, only about, maybe, four dozen, I'd say."

"Jesus Christ, O. Are they from you?"

"There better not be anyone else sending you roses," he said.

"There isn't, but—"

"I just wanted to get some color in here. I think these rooms are kind of dull."

"You're crazy, O. This is an unbelievable room. Look at the view!"

He just stood there, smiling that crazy smile of his.

"How'd you even manage to get such an awesome room?"

He shrugged. "I've been living here for months. I've made some friends. And they all like free hockey tickets."

"Thanks for having me, O. And flying me out here and everything."

"It's just me being selfish. A Christmas present to myself."

She didn't know what to say. She started to sweat, standing there in her winter coat, the sun beating down on her.

"Are you okay?" Owen asked.

"Yeah. It's just—"

"Come here," he said. He unbuttoned her coat and pulled it off her shoulders. He took her hands and sat on the edge of the bed, pulling her onto his lap. Forever, it seemed, he'd been craving the warmth of her voice and her skin, her hair and her eyes, and finally she was here and the soft sweetness of her was all around him. They were in a tower above the city, with the afternoon sun beaming down on them, and he honestly didn't care what happened next, if anything. The feeling of her arms around him and her lips on his was more than he could possibly bear. It might make him cry. It might even kill him right here and now. And that would be just fine with him.

They lay in each other's arms, breathing together, and the day dissolved into twilight.

Agnes said, "O, I need to talk to you about something."

"Sure. What is it?"

"I'm going back to school."

"That's great."

"Yeah. I'm moving home right after Christmas."

"Wait, you're moving home?"

"Yeah. You know, I'm going to the College there. I can live at Dad's and maybe work, too. It'll save money."

"But you won't be in Wapahaska," he said.

"You won't, either, right O? You'll be here, I'm pretty sure, and then I'll be stuck without you anyhow. And meanwhile I'm paying rent. I'd probably have to find a new roommate, too, because Jo's moving home also."

"You could stay at my place," offered Owen.

"I'd feel funny mooching off of you—"

"I don't see it that way at all, Ag."

"I know you don't. But it wouldn't make sense anyhow. I'm already enrolled up at St. Cyp."

"Yeah. I guess it's just that, you'll be farther away."

"I know. I don't like that part of it either. And I'm not exactly thrilled about living at home, but without you and Jo it won't be any fun down in Wapahaska."

Owen didn't answer.

"It's something I need to do."

"I understand, Ag."

"Maybe I can visit you again sometime?"

"I'm counting on it."

"Thanks, O. Thanks for understanding."

"Jeez, Ag. You're welcome." He reached over and turned on the bedside lamp. "I'm going to have to go soon, to get ready for the game."

"I know," she said. "Before you go, I want to give you your Christmas present."

She pulled a box out of her bag and gave it to him, her heart pounding. He held it in his hands for a few seconds, looking at her. Then he opened it. Inside was a pair of lustrous, light-brown moccasins with fur-lined cuffs. Each had a cluster of beaded, green leaves at the instep, five curving, green stems, and five graceful, crimson lilies, highlighted in fiery orange, outlined in iridescent black.

"Wow. These are amazing." Owen ran his fingers over the beadwork and the fine stitching.

"Try them on," she said.

"They're way too nice to put on my old, beat-up, hockey-player feet," he replied.

"They're made to be worn, O."

He put them on. "They're soft."

"They're moosehide."

He took a few steps. "They fit perfectly, too."

"They should," said Agnes. "I made them just for you."

"Wait. You *made* them? Really? Like, from scratch? You sewed all these little stitches, and put the beads on and everything?"

She nodded.

"Jesus, Ag, I figured you'd bought them at the shop."

"If they don't fit right, I can fix them."

"No, they're perfect just the way they are."

He took a few steps toward the window.

"Owen, do you know what they're saying?" Agnes asked.

He looked back at her. "What do you mean?"

"They're saying, *you're my man now*. It's what an Indian woman does, you know? She sews a pair of moccasins for her man. To keep him warm when she can't be with him. She makes her own design so everyone will know that he belongs to her."

Owen sat down beside her. "Ag, I do. I belong to you."

He slipped the moccasins off and put them back in the box.

"I have something for you, too," he said.

"O, you shouldn't have gotten me anything. You already flew me all the way out here and—"

"Well, don't get all excited. You might not want it anyway."

"What?"

"If you don't, it's okay."

"Why wouldn't I?"

"You don't have to wear it if you don't want to. You don't even have to keep it. I can give it to my mom or something."

"Jeez, O, what the hell is it?"

Owen opened the wardrobe, pulled a hockey sweater off one of the hangers, and dropped it in her lap. Its lush, warm tones soaked up the last of the afternoon light and smoldered in her hands.

"It's gorgeous!" she said. It was a fantastically beautiful jersey—not an imitation, but the real thing. The bold crest was affixed with hundreds of little stitches, worthy of Jo herself. Agnes held it up, turned it around, and then she saw the back, with its big, square, appliquéd letters, M-A-C-K-E-N-Z-I-E, and, beneath them, Owen's number, 11. Her dark brown, almond-shaped eyes looked up at him over the neckline.

"You don't have to wear it," said Owen again. "I promise, it won't hurt my feelings."

"Of course I'm going to wear it, O, are you crazy? It's the most beautiful thing I've ever seen. Why wouldn't I wear it?"

"You have your own jerseys, I know that."

"Not like this."

"So, it doesn't feel strange," Owen asked, "with my name on it?"

"Why would it feel strange?" she asked.

"I don't know."

"Owen, I'm so proud of you. I'm proud to wear it."

He took her hand in his and kissed it. "See you after the game." He grabbed his jacket and was out the door.

Agnes knew the Thompson arena would be enormous, but when she found her seat, looked up, and saw a whole other tier on top of what there was in Wapahaska, she couldn't help but gasp. This place probably sat double the number of people or more. As she looked around, a woman came down the aisle and sat next to her. She had short, wavy, strawberry blonde hair and her fair skin was covered with freckles. "Hi," she said. "Judging by your sweater, you must be Agnes."

"I am," said Agnes. She offered her hand. "Agnes Demers."

The woman shook her hand and said, "Glad to meet you. Owen said you'd be here this weekend. I'm Caroline, and this is my daughter Stephanie. We belong to Doug Jackson, number eighty-one down there." She pointed down to the ice, where the players were warming up.

"Nice to meet you," said Agnes. She reached over to shake Stephanie's hand as well.

Stephanie was wearing a Traders jersey just like hers. She was probably about twelve years old, with a mouth full of braces, fair skin like her mom's, and long, auburn hair.

"Owen's told us all about you," said Caroline.

"That can't be good," joked Agnes.

"He told us you played hockey with him," said Stephanie.

"I did," said Agnes

"I play, too," said Stephanie.

"What position?"

"I play D, like my dad."

"I was a forward when I was your age," said Agnes. "Later on they put me in goal."

Stephanie gave her a gleaming silver smile. "Mr. MacKenzie said you were the meanest goalie out there."

"Oh yeah?" asked Agnes.

"He meant it as a compliment," Stephanie added quickly.

"I know," Agnes laughed.

"He said you were better than he was."

"Well, that was a long time ago," replied Agnes.

Caroline said, "Stef was amazed to hear that you two used to play together."

"We come from a small town," said Agnes. "Everybody played together."

"I'm going to play in the Olympics," said Stephanie.

"Wow," said Agnes.

"Yeah. Women's hockey'll be an Olympic sport in '98."

Caroline smiled. "Stef's so excited. It gives her something to aim for, you know?"

"Maybe you can play in the Olympics, too," Stephanie said to Agnes.

Agnes laughed. "I don't play much these days. Owen's the hockey player, now."

"You don't play anymore?" Stephanie looked shocked.

Quickly, Caroline said, "Stef, I'm sure Agnes is very busy. Sometimes when people grow up they don't have time for games."

Caroline's words struck close to Agnes's heart. Hockey was more than just a game. How could she not have time for hockey? She said, "I'm in the process of moving back home to finish my teaching degree. Once I'm settled again, maybe I can find a team."

"That's good," said Stephanie. But her brow was knitted. "All the girls keep quitting, you know? And no one even cares."

Caroline said to Agnes, "It's been huge—the interest that Owen's taken in Stef's playing. That kind of encouragement is hard to come by for a girl. I guess I don't need to tell *you* that."

"No," agreed Agnes. But she couldn't have imagined that, as the privileged white daughter of a professional hockey player, Stephanie would encounter some of the same obstacles that she had. She said, "Don't worry Stephanie, I'm not going to quit. And don't you quit either, okay? I want to watch you play in the Olympics."

Stephanie smiled at her and they settled in to watch the big boys.

After the game, Owen introduced Agnes to some of the other players. A few of the younger couples were going to a club and invited them to come along, but they wanted to be alone.

"What do you want to do?" asked Owen.

"I don't know. Are you hungry?" she asked.

"Um, yeah."

"I wish I could cook you something."

"Trust me, so do I. Let's just go back to the hotel. We can get room service or something."

They got into the car and pulled out onto the street. Christmas lights adorned the doorways and street trees, and there were lots of people out on the sidewalks, so that it actually seemed more lively now than it had during the day.

"Do you like it here, O?" asked Agnes.

"I do," said Owen. "I've been itching to get out a little and explore, though, you know? I want to check out the mountains. Maybe this summer we can go together—like a camping trip or something."

"I'd love that, O," she said.

He put his hand on her thigh and she put hers on top of it. After a couple of minutes, he had to turn a corner and he pulled his hand away.

"So you met Stef and Caroline," he said.

"I did. It was nice to have someone to sit with. Stephanie seems like a pretty serious player."

"She loves it. It's great to see, you know?"

"I hope she sticks with it."

"Yeah. What about you? When are you going to start playing again?"

Agnes shrugged. "I don't know."

"Have you thought about it?"

"Sure, I've thought about it."

"It's how I always think of you," Owen said. "You know, going to the curl-and-drag. Flagging down a wrister. Slashing the shit out of some poor bastard when the ref's looking the other way."

They both laughed.

"You were a good player, Ag. I bet you could be again, if you wanted."

Agnes frowned. Of course she *wanted*. Winning the championship that one year with Owen and the St. Cyp North Stars bantam AAA team was probably the best memory of her entire life. She'd do it again in a minute. She hoped that Stephanie would win gold in the Olympics. She wished that she could play in the Olympics, too. But most of all, she just wanted to play.

She craved that intimate back-and-forth with teammates, the thrill of creating on the ice, the feeling of competing, hard, and those moments when thinking stopped and she was outside herself, outside of real life, existing only in the game. That was the *real* reward for all the workouts and the drills, the early morning practices and the long rides to rinks in far-away towns. That reward was no longer winnable in her world, but she hoped it was in Owen's.

She said, "I was spoiled, that's all, playing with you. It was inspiring. I always had to try my hardest, to measure up at all."

"It was inspiring to play with you, too," Owen answered. "You were real different than the other guys. If it wasn't for you, I probably wouldn't be here now."

"No way," she said.

"I mean it," he replied. "You made me want it. You really did."

9

Before Agnes moved to Wapahaska, the college in St. Cyp had seemed confining. Now that she was back, cozy seemed like a better description. The campus was well off the main road in its own little park-like zone complete with flowerbeds and graceful stands of aspen trees, now covered in snow. Between the main building and the parking lot, the sidewalk broadened into a terrace where students gathered to compare notes or make plans for after class.

One student seemed different than the rest. She never lingered to talk—after class she'd bolt out of the building and disappear. One day Agnes packed up her things early, before the instructor dismissed the class, and caught up with the girl in the hall.

"Hi, I'm Agnes," she said.

"I'm Priscilla," said the girl.

"What do you think about the class so far?" asked Agnes.

"I like it. I guess I was hoping for more case studies, though—more problem solving, that kind of thing. What about you?"

"Maybe you're right. I hadn't thought about it that way. I'm just happy to be keeping up."

Priscilla held the door open for Agnes, but as soon as they'd stepped outside, Agnes knew their brief conversation was over. Priscilla was on her tiptoes, scanning the parking lot.

She said, "I'm sorry, Agnes, I have to go. See you next time, okay?"

She ran off and Agnes watched as she greeted an older woman

with a small child in tow. Priscilla dropped her book bag on the sidewalk, scooped up the little one, and gave him a big kiss on the cheek.

Next class, Agnes sat down next to Priscilla.

"Hi, Priscilla."

"Hi, Agnes. Sorry I had to run off the other day."

"That's okay. I could see you had an important date."

Priscilla smiled. "Yeah. That's Toby. He's my little boy. His kookum was watching him all day and I don't like to take any more of her time than I have to."

"She probably enjoys it."

"She does, but he's a handful, especially for an older person. And I have two classes on Mondays. It's a long day for her."

The following Monday, Agnes left class with Priscilla again.

"Are you meeting Toby again today?"

"Always."

"Will you introduce us?"

Priscilla laughed. "Sure."

They walked outside together. "I don't see them yet," Priscilla said. "You might as well get going. You can meet him next time."

"I'm not in a hurry. I'll just wait with you."

"Okay."

"How old is Toby?" asked Agnes.

"He'll be three in April."

"It must be hard to find time to study with a little one."

"Not really. I just study at night, after he's gone to bed. Getting to class is the tough part. If it wasn't for Mary Alice— that's his kookum—I couldn't do it. But she's a huge help. We're even living at her place now. It's much nicer than where we were before. Oh, there they are!"

Agnes followed her down the row of parked cars and Toby came running to meet them.

"Mama!" he said.

"Hello, little man," Priscilla answered, picking him up.

Agnes, smiling, reached her hand out to Toby's grandmother. "Hello, I'm Agnes."

"Hello, Agnes, I'm Mary Alice."

"Nice to meet you."

"It's very nice to meet you," answered Mary Alice. "I'm so glad Priscilla's making some friends at school. I don't remember seeing you before, though. Are you just starting?"

"No, I started a couple of years ago, but I took some time off."

"Good for you," said Mary Alice.

"What did you do today?" Priscilla was asking Toby. But the little boy squirmed desperately to free himself and Priscilla put him down on the sidewalk. "Hey, Toby," she said. "This is my friend Agnes."

Agnes crouched down to look Toby in the face. He had big brown eyes and curly hair. "Hi Toby," she said. "I'm Agnes."

Toby reached his hand inside his pocket and pulled out a well-crumbled piece of cookie. He thrust it at her. "Want a cookie?" he asked.

"Mmm, yummy!" Agnes said, and she popped it in her mouth.

Toby beamed at her.

The next time they left class together, Priscilla said, "Hey, Agnes, it was pretty brave of you to eat that cookie. Who knows what kind of germs were on that thing?"

"I'm still alive, so it couldn't have been too bad," said Agnes. "Toby's really cute."

"Yeah, thanks."

"Does he, I mean, I don't mean to be nosy, but, are you still together with his dad?"

"His dad is dead."

"Gosh, Priscilla. I'm really sorry. I didn't mean to bring up a hard subject."

"It's okay."

"What was his name?"

"His name was Hector. He was a sweet guy. So gentle. But he'd get so down on himself. On everything. Finally, I think, he just kind of gave up."

"Priscilla, I'm so sorry."

"Thanks, Agnes. And thanks for asking."

After a while Agnes asked, "How long has it been?"

"About three years."

Just then another student came up next to Priscilla, lightly touching her shoulder.

"Oh, hi Allan," she said.

"Hi, Priscilla. Um, we're having a study session for Developmental Milestones on Monday. Do you want to join us?"

"What time?"

"At three. In the lounge."

"I wish I could," she said. "But I've got another commitment."

"That's too bad," said Allan.

"Yeah," said Priscilla. "Maybe next time?"

"Alright then," said Allan. "See you in class."

He walked away.

"Too bad you can't join them," said Agnes.

"I don't want to ask Mary Alice to watch Toby past three o'clock."

"I could watch him for you," offered Agnes.

"I couldn't ask you to do that."

Agnes shrugged. "I'm happy to do it."

"Are you sure? He can be tough to handle."

"I'm tough, too. I love kids. I'll just take him over to the park and let him run around. Does he have skates?"

"Yeah, he's got skates—believe it or not. His uncle spoils him."

"Bring them along. We'll have some fun and meet you back here around four."

"Agnes, you're an angel!"

"Hah! That's the first time anyone's called me *that!*"

*

Agnes snatched up the receiver before the first ring ended. "Hey, O," she said.

"Hey, Ag. You see the game?"

"Of course."

"What'd you think?"

"I loved seeing you on that second line. How'd it feel?"

"Pretty good. We need to get more used to each other, though."

"You and Petersen are good together. You're both really fast, and then with Callahan going to the net, you guys could make some things happen."

"Did you see the play where Dougie shot it from the point and that big rebound went straight out to Callie?"

"Yeah, I wish he would have passed it to you—"

"Me too. I was pretty open over there."

"Next time. But that shift you guys had right before Ericson scored—that rocked."

"Yeah, we kept 'em in there a long time."

"So you're feeling better?" she asked.

"Yeah, yeah. That trip east was a killer. But I'm good now."

"You're getting enough to eat and all that?"

"I'm getting plenty to eat. It's the *all that* I'm low on."

"Me too."

"Gotta get you out here again."

"Yeah."

"What about you? Did you end up playing the other night?" Owen asked.

"Yeah."

"Was it any better this time?"

"No. Same deal. Pickup, you know? Defenders can't defend—or they don't bother to try. Lots of breakaways. No plan for clearing the zone. It was a free-for-all."

"What about the other guys?"

"Some are okay. Some are assholes."

"I still think you should try a women's league."

"I played on girls' teams in high school. Most of them are just in it for the social stuff. You know, talking about guys and getting exercise and having fun. That's not the way I play."

"Yeah, who likes to have fun?"

"Come on, O. You know what I mean."

"I'm not sure I do."

"Do *you* play for fun?"

"I get paid to play. I'm a professional!"

"And I can't *be* a professional. No matter how hard I want to work I'm still stuck on the outside, with everyone assuming I just want to look pretty and gossip and chit chat all day. And the harder I work, the worse it gets, because then everyone thinks I'm some kind of freak."

"It can't be *that* bad."

"How the hell would you know? Have you ever been a girl? Trust me—it's hard enough to keep it light playing pickup. If I were playing for points I don't think the other girls would like me very much."

"That's probably true."

"What do you mean by that?"

Owen took a breath. He said, "Ag, I love you for being intense about the game. That's the way you are. It's awesome. That's why you *can't quit.*"

"It's not that I *want* to quit."

"I bet there are some better teams out here. It's a bigger city. There are more people. More women."

"You're not supposed to be noticing that," said Agnes.

"You know what I mean. There's just more stuff going on in general. It's worth checking into. I mean, if you want to play."

"I guess so."

"I'm not just saying that to get you out here."

"I don't believe you."

"I'll call you tomorrow, Ag."

"You better."

Agnes and Toby ended up having a great time together, and so did Priscilla and Allan. Priscilla asked Agnes to watch Toby every Monday, and Agnes was happy to do it. One Monday, though, as Priscilla was rushing off to meet Allan, she said, "Oh, Agnes, I almost forgot to tell you. Toby's uncle has been watching him today, so he'll meet you instead of Mary Alice."

"Okay," said Agnes. "How will I find him?"

"He'll be in a red pickup. His name's Claude. He's a big boy. You can't miss him."

"Wait. Claude?"

"Right," said Priscilla. "Claude. In a red pickup. See you at four!"

Agnes barely had time to get used to the idea before she saw Claude pulling into a parking spot. She walked over to meet him.

Claude lifted Toby down onto the sidewalk and she bent over to give him a hug. "Hey Toby! How's my Monday buddy?" she asked. Then she straightened up and looked at Claude.

"Hi, Agnes," he said. He looked sheepish, and kind of guilty, as if it was his fault that they'd ended up meeting again like this.

"Hi, Claude."

"How are you?"

"I'm good," she said.

He just kept looking at her.

"You have a new cut," she said.

"Yeah." He fingered the little row of stitches angling up from his jawbone.

She touched the corresponding spot on her own face, and then felt stupid for doing so. "How'd it happen?" she asked.

"Fight. The guy didn't take his glove off. Seam just kind of opened me up. Looks pretty bad, right?"

"No," she said.

"How's school?"

"It's good."

"I—we miss you down in Wapahaska."

Agnes looked down at the ground.

"How's Macker doing?" Claude asked.

"Good."

"Must be. We never see him anymore."

"Yeah," said Agnes.

"I guess he'll be out there for good, now."

"Yeah, I hope so. I mean, it looks that way."

"You two still . . . together?"

"Yeah."

Claude shuffled his feet. "Well, I'd better get going."

"Wait, Claude."

He looked at her.

She said, "I want to get this straight. Toby is your nephew. Hector was your brother?"

"Yeah."

"You never told me about Hector. You never told me what happened to him."

"It's not an easy thing to talk about," said Claude.

"No, but it's part of who you are. It would have helped me understand."

"Nothing much to understand," he said.

"That's not true. As it was I sort of jumped to conclusions, you know?"

He squinted and shook his head. "No."

"Well, last winter, when we first met, you were coming up here a lot, right?"

"Yeah," said Claude. "It was a tough time."

"I didn't even know."

"No."

"You came up to visit Priscilla and Toby—"

"And my mom," said Claude.

"Just Priscilla and Toby and your mom."

"Yeah."

"Okay," said Agnes. "See, I thought—"

"Wanna go, wanna go!" interrupted Toby, tugging at Agnes's parka.

"In a minute, Toby," said Agnes. "I'm talking to your Uncle Claude." She looked back at Claude. "Remember when I ran into you and you were buying those sweatshirts?"

"What sweatshirts?"

"They were for Toby and Priscilla, right?"

"Oh yeah, I remember," said Claude.

"Well, I didn't know who they were for, you know? I was angry because I couldn't figure out what was going on with you."

"What do you mean?"

"You never called me. And you kept leaving town. And then I see you buying those sweatshirts, for a woman and a child. And so I just jumped to conclusions, see?"

Claude still looked puzzled.

"Claude, I figured you had a family up here."

"A family?"

"You know, like a wife or a girlfriend. And a kid."

"What? Me? How could you think that?"

"It seemed like a logical explanation."

"No, Agnes. No. Of course not." He caught her hair as it swam out from under her hat in back, and pulled it gently forward over her shoulder. He said, "Gosh, Agnes. I really am a big dumb Indian."

"No, I was the dumb one."

"I should have told you," he said.

"I should have asked," she answered.

They stood there for a long time. His hand was still holding her hair, resting just above her breast, over her heart. She wondered whether he could feel it beating through her bulky parka. The parking lot had emptied and there was no one around except Toby. He was throwing clumps of snow at a tree. The sun was low. The last class of the afternoon was in session and there was a sleepy feeling, a little bit like the afternoon they had spent watching kids skate at the neighborhood rink down in Wapahaska, and then at her place. She remembered the feeling of his arm around her, and of his big body under hers, and she shivered.

Claude pulled his hand away and put it in his pocket. He said, "So, Macker's out in Thompson."

"Yeah."

"He's a good kid. Pretty tough to go after me like that, too."

"No, it was stupid," said Agnes. "You could have killed him. I told him that."

Claude chuckled. "He was just telling me to back off."

Agnes thought about that for a minute. Then she said, "I'm going to take Toby to the park now."

He nodded. "Good to see you, Agnes."

She smiled. "Toby, say goodbye to your Uncle Claude."

"Bye," said Toby.

Agnes took the little boy's hand and they walked away.

A couple of nights later, Agnes's phone rang. It was Priscilla.

"Hey, Agnes."

"Hey, Priscilla. What's up?"

"Thanks again for watching Toby on Monday."

"My pleasure," answered Agnes. "Did you have a good time with Allan?"

"Yeah. We sat in the lounge and pretended to study, but really we were just talking about stuff."

"That's great," said Agnes.

"Mary Alice asked me to invite you over for dinner next Tuesday."

"That sounds nice. Will you and Toby be there?"

"Of course, but I have to tell you, Claude's going to be there, too."

"Claude?"

"Mary Alice is on a mission to find him a woman. I don't think he's dated anyone since Hector died. She really likes you. And according to her, Claude seemed to really like you, too."

Agnes didn't know what to say.

After a few seconds Priscilla asked, "Are you still there?"

"I'm here."

"It's okay if you don't like him," said Priscilla. "I understand."

"I like him."

"Well, what do you say? Do you want to come?"

"Um, I can't make it. But tell her thank you. Very much. It's really nice of her to think of me."

Agnes crouched in goal. She'd given one up already and wouldn't let it happen again. The guys skating the puck in now were the same two who'd beaten her before—a tall, unwieldy guy and a guy in an orange jersey. She knew they figured they could beat her again because she was a girl. The tall guy glanced up as if he was going to shoot. She smiled inside her mask—it was an obvious deke. He passed to orange-jersey guy, who took a shot. Agnes dished it into the corner with her left pad.

"Nice," said Jennie, one of the defensemen on her team and the only other woman in the game tonight.

A few shifts later, the tall guy stripped Norm of the puck and streaked toward Agnes, obviously trying to intimidate her. She stared him down, daring him to shoot, and when he did she kicked the puck aside again.

"She stoned you there, Jeff," called one of the other guys.

The next time Jeff—a.k.a. tall guy—was on the ice with orange-jersey guy, orange-jersey guy dumped the puck in and battled Steve for it on the half-wall while Jeff planted himself in the crease in front of Agnes. Jennie tried to shove him aside but he was bigger than she was and it was hard to get a good position on him because he kept shifting back and forth annoyingly, tapping his stick on the ice and yelling, "Brian! Brian! Here! I'm open!" Steve won the puck and tried to pass it back to Ted to clear, but another guy intercepted it and shot it on goal. Jeff tried to deflect it in, but he didn't have anywhere near the skill to do it, and he tripped himself up and fell into the net, almost on top of Agnes. She wanted to tell him off. What did he think this was? The Stanley Cup playoffs? To calm herself, she skated around a little bit while a couple of the other players reattached the net.

"Had enough for today?" Jeff taunted her.

She skated back to the net.

The next time Jeff got the puck he skated across the blue line and skyed it at her. She didn't know how he got it up so high, or winged it so fast, but somehow it eluded her neckguard and slammed her just above her collarbone. She managed to cover the puck as she fell, but she couldn't get up right away. She was dizzy and her arm went numb. Her sweat froze on her body. Everyone rushed over to her.

"Agnes! Are you okay?" cried Jennie.

"I think so," said Agnes.

"You need a hand?" asked Ted.

"Should we call it a game?" asked Jennie.

"No," said Agnes, forcing herself to breathe, feeling the blood return to her limbs. "We've still got a few minutes. Might as well play."

"Are you sure?" asked Norm. "Maybe we should get someone to check you out, make sure you're okay."

"Nah," said Agnes, getting up onto her feet. "I've had worse. It just stunned me."

Meanwhile, Steve was up in Jeff's face, haranguing him loudly. Agnes appreciated his support, but if she'd been as big as he was she'd have decked the guy.

Play resumed. Agnes was ready for another challenge from her buddy Jeff, but it never came, and the final five or six minutes ticked away. Ted hollered, "Let's call it a night, boys!" The puck rattled off the boards one last time, and Norm flipped it up onto his blade and caught it in his glove.

Agnes stepped off the ice. "Hey, sis," said a familiar voice.

"Vin, you're early," she answered.

"No. I just got here. That snowplow needs a hose. I had to improvise a replacement until we can get a new one. How was the game?"

She made a face, and under her breath she said, "What the hell is wrong with these bastards? It's just a pickup game, for God's sake."

Jennie and Ted stepped off the ice and joined them. Ted asked, "You ladies coming out tonight?"

"No," said Jennie. "I've got to get home to the kids."

"Sorry," said Agnes. "I've got class tomorrow."

"Party poopers," he said.

"Someone's got to play grown-up," said Agnes.

"But why's it always got to be the girls?" joked Ted. "Why can't it be old Marv over there? We don't want him along, anyhow."

Jennie smiled. "I'm going to change," she said.

She trudged off and Ted followed. Vin asked Agnes, "Do you need me to beat the crap out of someone for you?"

Agnes shook her head.

Vin snorted. "I'll meet you at the car."

Agnes joined Jennie in the closet that the women used as a dressing room. After she changed she lugged her bulky hockey bag through the heavy door to the outside. The sky over the parking lot was pitch black. Two forlorn light posts, wrapped in swirling snowflakes, cast their meager glow across an assembly of tired, hunkered-down cars and pickups. An icy blast set Agnes's bag swinging where it hung from one shoulder. Balanced by her stick in the opposite hand, she picked her way slowly across the mess of ice, snow, gravel, and pits of crumbling asphalt. There was no one in sight.

Vin's trunk was always full of car parts, so she threw her bag and stick in the back seat and slammed the door. A frigid gust ripped across the parking lot and pelted her face with prickly snowflakes. Inside her parka she felt the sweat crystallize on her skin like frost creeping up a windowpane. She turned around and went back inside.

Vin was in the lobby, deep in conversation with an unfamiliar woman. They were leaning against the wall, facing each other, their eyes locked together. Vin's hand was on her arm.

Agnes walked right up to them. "Jesus, Vin," she said. "Thanks a lot for keeping me waiting outside, alone in the parking lot."

"Oh, hey, Agnes. Sorry. I got held up," Vin said.

"I can see that," answered Agnes. She looked at the woman. "I'm Agnes, the forgotten sister of the parking lot."

The woman stood up straight and looked at her. "So you're Agnes. I'm Tess. Tess Delaronde."

"Hi," said Agnes.

"Vincent told me you're a goalie," Tess said, "We could use your help."

"With what?"

"Working with the kids, maybe teaching a clinic or two."

"Maybe."

"It's more fun than it sounds like," said Vin.

Agnes looked at him. "Well, okay," she said.

"Do you have a minute now?" Tess asked. "Maybe you could let me know when you're available."

"Sure. We seem to have all sorts of time," said Agnes, looking at Vin again.

Tess kissed Vin on the mouth and said to him, "See you tomorrow." Then she led Agnes down the hall to the office.

She said, "So. Agnes. You lived down in Wapahaska, right?"

"Yes."

"Why'd you move back?"

"It was just a temporary thing, moving down there."

They went into the office and Tess pulled out the desk chair. "Have a seat," she said. She handed Agnes a sheet of paper and a pen. "Just write your name and phone number and when you're available."

Tess sat down on the edge of the desk, right next to Agnes's paper, and watched her as she wrote. After she finished, Tess said, "So, Agnes, I heard that when you were down there, in Wapahaska, you dated one of the Prairie Wolves."

"I still do," said Agnes.

"You do?"

"He's mostly been with the Traders this year, though," Agnes added.

"Okay," said Tess. "So it's MacKenzie, then. Sorry."

Agnes shrugged. "It's not a secret or anything."

Tess stood up. "By the way, we have a teen game on Saturday evenings—Vincent helps me coach—and afterwards there's an open game. The All Players Game. Anyone can play—teens, parents, coaches. You should join us. It's a lot of fun."

"Maybe. At the moment I'm thinking I'll never play again."

"Why not?"

"I'm sick of these guys. These pickup guys. They don't care about the game. They just want to score on me, and if they can't they turn into psychopaths."

Tess shook her head. "Don't let them hijack your hockey, Agnes," she said.

Agnes didn't answer.

Tess asked, "Have you always played goal?"

"Since I was fourteen."

"What'd you play before?"

"Forward—right wing, mostly."

"Have you ever thought about switching back?"

"No. Being a goalie is sort of what I am now."

"Do you have to be just one thing?"

"I've been a goalie for a long time. I like stopping the pucks. I'm good at it."

"I'm sure you are. But maybe it'd be fun to shoot some, for a change," suggested Tess.

Agnes squinted at her.

"Either way, you're welcome on Saturday. Guaranteed—no psychopaths allowed."

Agnes slid into the passenger seat next to Vin. "So, why didn't you tell me? What's going on?"

"What do you mean?"

"You know what I mean. With Tess."

"The normal stuff."

"How'd you even meet her? It's been years since you spent time hanging out at the rink."

"Deuce introduced us back in the summer."

"Claude did?"

"Yeah. They're old friends. Except I think there was more to it than that. Anyhow, she needed help. So I'm helping."

Agnes didn't reply. After a while she asked, "What do you mean, you think there was more to it? With her and Claude, I mean?"

"Just what I said. Seems like they were more than friends—at one time. Don't worry, though. At the moment I'm pretty sure his heart belongs to you."

"Bullshit."

"Seriously. You should hear him sigh whenever I mention your name. It's almost fun to torture him, you know?"

"Is that why you're dating Tess?"

"No."

"I think it is," said Agnes.

"You're wrong."

"She's way too old for you, for one thing."

"No she's not."

Agnes shrugged.

"She's not!" he protested.

"Maybe not. But I think you're dating her because she's Claude's old girlfriend and you think it's really cool to date Claude Doucette's girlfriend."

"You're full of shit, Agnes."

"Maybe I am," she replied. "Maybe I'm not."

"She's a good person, she really is," said Vin.

"I never said she wasn't."

"We really … like each other."

"Right."

"I thought you'd be happy. I haven't been out with Lance and the boys for weeks."

"I am," she said. "I think it's great that you're getting back into hockey. I do. I just think you need to be more—" She stopped abruptly.

"What?" asked Vin.

"I don't know," said Agnes, slowly. "I guess it really isn't any of my business."

"You're right. It isn't," he said.

Agnes stared out the car window, into the darkness and the blowing snow.

"Come on in for a minute, Agnes, I have to get my purse." Agnes followed Jo back to her bedroom in her parents' place.

"Wow, you still have all your dolls," Agnes said.

Jo's dresser was host to a throng of characters: fairy princesses and queens and some woman politician whose name Agnes couldn't remember; Louis Riel and Gabriel Dumont, of course, complete with tiny moustaches and, in the case of Dumont, a long, shaggy beard; a Dene woman on tiny snowshoes and other Indians in traditional dress; several dolls in other national costumes—even a hockey player doll.

"Hey, you still have my Blair Atcheynum doll!" said Agnes.

"You can take him back whenever you want."

"Nah. He'd be lonely at my place," said Agnes. "He's happier here with all these pretty girl dolls."

Jo laughed.

"You should keep a couple of them by your sewing machine.

Show them off to your customers."

"I don't know," said Jo. "Most of them aren't very good. I made them when I was pretty young."

"I think they're amazing."

Jo closed the door. "Agnes, guess who called the other day?" she asked.

"I don't know. Tell me."

"You have to guess."

"Santa Claus?"

"You're hopeless. It was Rory."

"Our old policeman friend? What did he say?" asked Agnes.

"We went out for coffee," said Jo.

"You went *out* with him? Why didn't you call me right away?"

Jo shrugged.

"So he came all the way up here to see you?" Agnes continued. "Not that you're not worth it, because you are, but—"

"He was up here for work," said Jo.

"So, how was the date?"

"Good."

"Good? Come on, Jo. You're the one who brought it up. You have to tell me *something*."

"Okay. We went to Anderson's. Just in the middle of the day. He asked about what I'm doing, about my business and everything. He told me about why he decided to be a policeman. He's nice."

"Are you going to see him again?"

"I think so."

"So you like him?"

Jo hesitated. "I do. It feels awkward, though. The way we met wasn't exactly romantic."

"Jo, you've got to try to forget about that."

"I know. I'm trying. It's funny. Rory remembers it real different than I do. I mean, when we talked about it, he kept telling me how strong I looked to him. Like, that's why he remembered me."

"You are strong, Jo. Look how great you're doing now."

"But it still hurts." Jo put her hand on her heart and her voice trembled. "How could he think those things about me? I'm not *like* that. Am I?"

Agnes put her arm around Jo. "Of course you're not. Everybody knows it. It didn't come from anything you did. It all came from his twisted mind."

Tears welled up in Jo's eyes. She whispered, "I thought he loved me."

"I know, Jo."

"I even thought I loved him. I mean, I just don't know what was wrong with me."

"There's nothing wrong with you. You just made a mistake, that's all."

"I'm sorry, Agnes," she said, trying to wipe away her tears.

"Don't be sorry. Cry as much as you want."

"I guess it's just going to take some time to get back to my old self again."

"Jo, you don't want to be your old self again, right? Your old self dated Clay Torris. Your new self isn't going to make that kind of mistake."

"I hope not," she whispered.

"It's good that you're living at home for a while," said Agnes.

"It is." Jo nodded and blew her nose. She asked, "When are you leaving?"

"Thursday."

"I guess you can't wait."

"*That's* an understatement!"

"Cool," said Jo.

This was exactly why Agnes loved Jo. Her tears weren't even dry yet, but she had a huge smile on her face and she was bouncing up and down on the edge of the bed. You'd think *she* was the one flying off to the big city to visit her boyfriend.

"At least you've got one up on most girls whose boyfriends are far away," Jo said. "You get to see *yours* on TV."

"That's the worst of all!" protested Agnes. "I mean, the camera looks at him for one second and then he's gone. I can hardly stand it. But I have to watch the game because he always wants to talk about it afterwards."

"That's sweet," said Jo.

"Nah. He's just blowing off steam after the game."

"Still, he could be blowing it off with someone else," said Jo.

"Who else would want to listen to a shift-by-shift rundown of his entire game?" asked Agnes.

"Well, when you're *there* you can't waste your time on *that*. You'll have to find ways to distract him."

"That's the plan," said Agnes.

"You should get a new dress," Jo said.

"I don't wear dresses."

"That's because you don't *have* any. But you should get, like, maybe a sweater dress—something classy but also really sexy that'll, like, pop his eyes when he sees you."

"Pop his eyes?"

"Yeah, you know, like in the cartoons when a guy sees a really good-looking girl, and his eyeballs pop right out of his head."

Agnes laughed.

"I'm serious. Owen hasn't seen you in ages. You want to knock him dead, like, immediately. You want him on the floor, drooling like a dog."

Agnes said, "Okay, you've convinced me. But where do I get one?"

"Don't worry. I've got it all planned out. I've got your list right here," said Jo, pulling a piece of paper out of her pocket.

"You've got a list?"

"Yeah, I wrote everything down when we were talking on the phone the other day: coat, sweater, boots. Okay, let me add the dress. You're going to need some tights, too."

"You're crazy!" said Agnes.

"I know. But I love to shop. Let's go." She grabbed her purse from where it hung on the back of her desk chair.

"If being a designer doesn't pan out, you could be a personal shopper."

"You're right. I could," said Jo, grinning. She opened the door and they headed out.

The night before she left Agnes waited up after Owen's game. As usual, she sat right beside the phone so she could pick it up before it disturbed Dad and Kookum, who'd already gone to bed.

When Owen called he started to talk about the game as usual, but then he said, "Oh, hell. To hell with the fucking game, Ag. I'm just dying to see you. Absolutely dying."

"Me too, O."

"I better go. I've got to clean up the place. It's a hellhole right now."

"Okay, O. See you tomorrow."

"Yeah. That sounds beautiful. *See you tomorrow.*"

Agnes stepped into the terminal and Owen was standing right inside the door. He practically pounced on her. She laughed and then they kissed—a long, lingering kiss right there on the spot.

"Sorry, but I've been waiting for that forever," he said.

"Me too."

He grabbed her hand and pulled her away from the gate. "Let me carry something for you."

She handed him her coat.

He blinked. "Wow, you look fantastic!"

She smiled. She was wearing the dress that Jo helped her pick out.

"Seriously! I was going to ask if you wanted to stop on the way home and grab some lunch. But suddenly I don't feel very hungry for a sandwich, if you know what I mean." He smiled that crazy, lopsided smile.

Agnes laughed. If she'd diverted Owen's mind from food, even briefly, it was a real accomplishment. Chalk one up for old Jo.

"You're going to like my place, Ag," he said. "It's got a great view of the river. It's kind of empty right now, though. I haven't had time to fix it up yet. I'm going to need your help."

He made a big deal about wanting to show her around the place, but somehow they got held up in the bedroom and before they knew it they were kissing and he was untying the colorful scarf she was wearing around her neck. That's when he noticed the ugly bruise above her collarbone.

"What's this?" he asked.

"A bruise, silly," she said.

"How'd you get it?"

"Pickup."

"It deflected?"

"No, someone shot it from the point. Or maybe a little closer."

"You're kidding. What kind of an asshole would shoot one up there in a lousy pickup game?"

"The kind of asshole who can't handle the fact that he's being repeatedly stuffed by a girl. An Indian girl."

"I hope someone kicked his ass."

"It's okay, Owen," she said.

"I mean it, he could've really hurt you."

"It's *okay.*"

"I'll come up there and kill him myself if I have to."

"Relax, O. It's just a bruise."

"But, Ag, don't get yourself hurt, okay?"

"Don't worry. I think I'm going to take a break anyhow."

"What? From playing?" Owen didn't believe her.

"I'm sick of dealing with that shit."

"But, Ag, when we played together, those games were rough. You did great."

"It's not that it's rough. I'm fine with rough. Roughness is part of the game. It's just, I'm tired of getting singled out, kind of. Why can't they treat me like just another goalie? Maybe I *should* try forward next time."

"No. You're good in goal—and it's the best way for you to have an impact."

"An impact on what? These aren't real games."

"Next chance I get I'm going to come up there and *personally* kick the guy's ass."

"Forget about it, O," said Agnes. She pulled him close and kissed him. "Now, where were we?"

Owen was still fired up. "I will. No one'll ever mess with you again."

She sighed. "That's sweet, O. But that's not going to fix it. It's just the way it is."

"What you need is a bodyguard. Like Gretzky. Too bad I'm all the way out here."

She chuckled. "No offense, but that sort of thing's never been your strong point anyhow."

"True. Hey—what about Vin? You should get Vin to play with you."

"I don't need *him* getting into trouble, too."

"No, but he wouldn't have to really fight or anything. It'd be enough that he's there, that he's your brother, maybe."

"Hmm. You know, that's actually not a bad idea. You're pretty smart for a guy who can't even get a gig as an enforcer."

He traced around the bruise with his finger. "It's actually a nice-looking bruise," he said.

"You should have seen it at first," she replied. "It was a lot more gruesome before."

He kissed it. "It must've hurt."

"Mostly it just stunned me. I kind of went numb for a minute."

"Did you finish the game?"

"Of course I finished the game."

"I'm proud of you, Ag," he said, stroking her hair.

"Yeah, I'm such a jock, right?"

"You are. The sexiest jock ever."

"No. That distinction would go to this other guy I know."

"Who's that?"

"Owen MacKenzie. Famous hockey player. Maybe you've heard of him."

10

Vin threw his gear in the back seat of the car, slammed the door, and got in the driver's side. Agnes threw her gear on top of his, slammed the door, and got in the passenger side. Vin turned the key in the ignition and pulled out of the parking lot.

Agnes didn't know what to say to him. The first time they'd played together neither of them had played particularly well, but it had been a real kick. It'd been worth the price of admission just to see her buddy Jeff's face: not only had she come back for another game—she'd brought reinforcements. Vin had encouraged her to play the puck more, and they'd amused themselves trying to make some plays that way. The best thing, though, was that Vin had enjoyed it. He'd been hilarious, relentlessly harassing Jeff and orange-jersey guy, and offering choice commentary when he had the puck behind the net and only she could hear. She hadn't heard him carry on like that in years. Tonight, though, he'd been completely different, sour from the moment he stepped onto the ice. He'd barely communicated with her at all. Even now he wasn't talking to her, or even looking at her.

Finally she said, "What the hell is up with you, Vin?"

"I don't know what you mean."

"You totally ignored me the whole game."

"I didn't see you. Were you even out there?"

"What are you talking about?" asked Agnes.

"I saw *MacKenzie*," he said.

"What?"

"MacKenzie's *sweater*," he replied. Agnes often wore the jersey that Owen had given her—she'd worn it tonight.

"So?" asked Agnes.

"Don't you feel a little funny wearing *his* goddamn sweater?" asked Vin.

"No. A lot of girls wear their boyfriends' jerseys."

"I don't like seeing you with his name on your back."

"Jesus, Vin. It's none of your business."

"Yes it is. You're my sister. And it's like he's . . . branded you—"

"Branded me? What am I? A cow? We're talking about *Owen*. He's been my friend since forever. He gave me a beautiful jersey. I'm not going to leave it hanging in the goddamn closet."

"Why's he buying you all this stuff, anyway? Paying your way out to Thompson all the time? What is it that he really wants from you? Have you ever thought of that?"

"Are you saying I'm an idiot? Or a whore? Or both?"

"I just wonder where things are going with you two."

"Okay. Now I get it. You think that just because he's white and I'm not he couldn't possibly love me! He's just using me, is that it? Here I am worried about his friends out there and what they'll think of me. But you're the biggest fucking racist of all!"

"How dare you say that!"

"You don't believe he could love me for who I am!"

"I just don't want him to take you away and make you into something different!"

"Bullshit! You don't care about me at all. Why shouldn't I wear his jersey? Why shouldn't I visit him? We *love* each other. You're just jealous because he's making something of himself and you can't even hold down a decent job because you hang around with a bunch of losers and think that you have to be loyal to them because their skin is the same color as yours. You'd better get your shit together or you'll end up just like them."

"It's better than being a full-of-himself little mama's boy who's always had everything handed to him. You're *my* sister—"

"You're so full of shit, Vin. Owen isn't anything like that and you know it. He goes to work everyday just like all the rest of us. His family isn't rich. If they're a little better off than we are it's not because his dad's the fucking Prince of Wales, for God's sake. You're a man just like he is—maybe you could have been a pro, too, but you pissed it all away. That's on you, not on him."

"I'm a fuckup, is that what you're saying?"

"No. I'm saying you had a *choice*. And you made the choice to do *nothing*. Absolutely fucking nothing. I bet you won't even keep coaching, once Tess comes to her senses and dumps you. Come to think of it, though, maybe *that's* for the best. Because you look pretty fucking god-awful out there, you really do."

Vin didn't answer. He just kept driving. Agnes stared at her reflection in the dark window until it dissolved in her tears. Suddenly, Thompson felt very far away, and Owen even farther. He'd said she inspired him. He'd said he was proud of her. He'd said he belonged to her. Did she dare believe it?

The next time Claude was in town, Mary Alice asked Agnes to join them for dinner, and Agnes accepted the invitation. She arrived just a few minutes past five and parked her car. The house was small but inviting—it had a new coat of paint and the walk was well shoveled. When she knocked on the door, Claude opened it.

"Hi, Agnes."

"Hi, Claude, how are you?"

"I'm doing good."

"When'd you get into town?"

"This morning."

"Leaving tonight?" she asked.

He nodded.

Mary Alice peeked out from behind her son. "Claude, ask Agnes to come in. Take her coat. Come in, Agnes. I'm so glad you could make it."

"Thanks for inviting me," answered Agnes. She held out a small bouquet of lillies. "These are for you, Mary Alice. Can I help you with anything?"

"Thank you, dear, but no, Priscilla's helping. Everything's almost ready. Why don't you two have a seat in the living room? Can I get you something to drink?"

"I'll get it," said Claude. He took Agnes's coat. She was wearing her new dress, and she smiled to herself when she noticed Claude giving her a second look.

"What do you want to drink, Agnes?" he asked.

"Just a glass of water, thanks." Agnes sat down on the sofa.

When Claude came back with the water, Toby was bouncing along beside him.

"Hi Toby," said Agnes.

"Ag-nes," he said. "Wanna see my new airplane?" He skipped over to her and stood leaning against her leg, making the plane fly in loop-de-loops so close to her face that she had to put her hand up to guard against a wing taking out one of her eyeballs.

"Tobes, give her some space," said Claude.

Agnes laughed. She put her arm around Toby. "How's my Monday buddy? Will you be my buddy today, too?" All of a sudden Toby got shy and retreated to the high fortress of Claude's lap.

"I'd take her up on that, if I was you," Claude said into his ear. He bounced the little boy on his knee.

Sitting in his mom's armchair, Claude looked like he was in a dollhouse, and Toby looked like a little doll. Agnes smiled.

"You have a beautiful smile, Agnes," Claude said.

Immediately Agnes thought of Owen. He was the king of smiles. He had a game tonight, and she wouldn't be watching it.

"How are the Prairie Wolves doing, Claude?" she asked.

"We're over .500."

"That's good."

"We got a new prospect. His name's Gavin Butler. Real young kid. Pretty quiet. Barbie's getting him settled in, though."

"Jamie's great with everyone," said Agnes. "How's he doing?"

"He opened up real strong. Led the team in points and everything, but then he hurt his shoulder—I guess it was November. Missed three or four weeks."

"That's too bad."

Claude nodded. "He's okay. A guy like him knows what he has to do to get back."

"How about you, Claude? Are you happy with your season so far?"

He nodded. "Surprised they kept me. Maybe you heard—Fredriksson moved on, and we were pretty good together."

"Who're you playing with, now?"

"A couple of younger guys. It's good. Every once in a while I feel like I can help one of them out with something. Hard to believe, right?"

"No." She smiled at him. "I've been working with some younger goalies. With All Colors–All Bands."

"Oh yeah? For Tess?"

She nodded.

"Knew you played. Didn't know you'd be interested in that."

"Vin put me up to it."

Claude started bouncing Toby again.

Agnes continued, "And I love working with the kids. I was thinking I might try that All Players game, too. Tess was telling me about it."

Claude nodded. "That's real fun," he said.

"You've played in it?"

"Sure. In the summer."

"Isn't it a little beneath you?"

"There's some good players come out for that game."

"Not like you," said Agnes.

"They love to play. More than I do, most of them."

"No," said Agnes.

"They do."

"But you're a professional."

Claude shrugged.

Agnes thought for a minute. "It'd be a thrill, playing against you. Even if you dinged me for a hundred goals."

Claude laughed. "Not sure I could do that to you."

"You'd have to try."

"I guess so," Claude said.

"It'd be a good test for me," Agnes pointed out.

"Sure, why not?" he said, smiling.

Priscilla came in. "Dinner's on the table," she said.

Toby jumped off of Claude's lap and spun in circles with his airplane, making engine noises.

"Calm down, Toby," said Priscilla. "If you want to sit at the table like a big boy you have to be good, okay?" She took his hand.

Agnes and Claude followed them into the kitchen. He put his arm around her without actually touching her, just like that time back in Wapahaska when they were out looking at the stars.

"Mary Alice, the table looks beautiful," said Agnes. The long, wooden table had been pulled out from the wall and decorated with a red, woven runner and the flowers that Agnes had brought.

"We're not fancy here," said Mary Alice, "but we want you to be comfortable."

"It's just about the same as our house," said Agnes.

"Agnes, why don't you sit around that side, next to Claude," Mary Alice continued. "And then go ahead and serve yourself, before it gets cold."

After they started eating, Mary Alice said, "Agnes, I remember you telling me that you took some time off from school."

"That's right."

"To do what? I don't mean to be nosy, I'm just interested."

"I just wanted to get away for a while. A girlfriend of mine helped me get a job in Wapahaska, so I moved down there with her."

"Agnes was in Wapahaska, just like you, Claude," said Mary Alice.

"I lived there a little over a year," Agnes continued, "and then I decided to go back to school."

"But you and Claude didn't ever meet, in Wapahaska?"

"We did, actually," said Agnes.

"You did?" asked Mary Alice.

"Once or twice," said Agnes.

"You didn't tell me that," said Mary Alice to Claude.

"Sorry, ma. I—"

"He probably doesn't even remember," interrupted Agnes. "There are so many girls there, you know, hanging around the hockey team."

"I wouldn't forget you, if I met you," said Claude.

"That's nice of you to say," said Agnes.

"Anyhow, you're not that kind of girl," he said, taking a big bite of roast chicken and potatoes.

Mary Alice and Priscilla looked at each other.

"The kind that hangs around hockey teams," Claude clarified.

Everyone was quiet, except for Toby, who took advantage of the conversational lull to blurt out, "Wanna play airplanes, mama!"

"Eat your chicken, first, Toby," Priscilla said.

"I'm not hungry," he complained.

"If you eat your chicken and peas, you can have some ice cream for dessert. Okay?"

Toby picked up a piece of chicken with his fingers.

"Claude, did you grow up in this house?" asked Agnes.

He nodded. "On and off. Mom moved down here for good after dad died. But we always had a place up north. I told you about it, didn't I?"

"I think so. Blue Lake area, right?"

"Wait a second! How long have you two known each other?" asked Priscilla, with more than a hint of outrage in her voice.

"Maybe about a year?" said Claude, looking at Agnes.

"Well, I think this is fantastic!" said Mary Alice. "I had no idea! Now, there's plenty more! Claude, would you like more chicken?"

When the evening was over, Claude walked Agnes to her car. He asked, "So Vin put you up to it. Working for Tess."

Agnes nodded.

"How's he doing?"

"Better. Hockey seems to be good for him."

"That's good."

Agnes asked, "Do you think he'd have a shot at playing again, I mean, if he worked really hard?"

"Maybe. He has to want it, you know? There's a lot of young guys ready to go."

"Yeah."

"And, you know, hockey's a tough game. But it's a tough life, too."

She didn't answer.

"Agnes," said Claude. "Why'd you come out tonight?"

"Mary Alice has asked me a couple of times now."

"That's not why," he said.

"No."

"You didn't come out to see me," he said.

"I did come out to see you, Claude."

"Why?"

"I kind of missed out on getting to know you last year."

"But you're with Macker now."

"True."

"It seemed different tonight," he said.

"It was different spending the evening with you and your mother," said Agnes. "In her house. I'm sorry I acted like you didn't remember me."

He shrugged. "It was kind of funny."

She smiled. "I didn't mean to lie. It's just that … it's complicated."

"Yeah. It is." He shuffled his feet. "Hey, Agnes, next time I'm home, can I call you?"

She nodded.

She hadn't bothered to button her coat when they walked out and now he slid his hands inside it, around her waist. He bent over and kissed her just once on the lips, so softly that it could have been just a friendly kiss.

"Might be a couple weeks," he said.

She didn't answer.

He turned and walked back to the house.

The score was tied with under three minutes to go. The Traders had been stuck in their end for nearly a minute, the Millionaires pressuring hard. When the Traders' goalie, the big Swede Axel Eklund, finally froze the puck, Coach sent Owen's line out hoping they'd be able to move the play out of the zone. Unfortunately, Owen lost the faceoff and the Mills quickly moved the puck to the point. Their defenseman took a shot on goal and one of their forwards corralled the rebound, attempting a pass back out to the D. Owen intercepted it, though, and sped out of the zone with the puck on his stick, Baxter Peterson on the right wing, and J.P. Callahan bringing up the rear. When Petes made it past the Mills' D, Owen passed him the puck, and with Callahan crashing the net Petes shuttled it back to Owen, who roofed it over the goalie's shoulder. The Mills' fans fell silent as the Traders celebrated.

With their third line on the ice, the Traders won the next faceoff, but the first line lost possession and the Mills, solidly ensconced once more in the Traders' zone, pulled their goalie for the extra attacker. Just like before, pummeled with shots, Eklund finally froze the puck and Coach sent out Owen's line again. This time Owen won the faceoff, pulling the puck back to Callahan, who battled for it long and hard against the wall until somehow it squirted out to Petes. Deftly evading a looming

Mills D-man, Petes made a diving play to knock the puck out to Owen, who shot it down the ice and into the empty net, putting the game away. It was the first two-goal game he'd ever had in Thompson. Seconds later, the final horn sounded and the Traders marched triumphantly back to the dressing room.

"You coming out with us?" Kirb Rogers asked Owen.

"Gotta celebrate your big game, man," added Bo Salsnik.

"I might," said Owen. "Where're you going?"

"There's this place down by Chinatown we always go. You'll like it. I know you like those darker skinned girls," said Kirb.

"Maybe," Owen said.

"Your girl's way back in Thompson, right? Wonder who *she's* fucking tonight?" said Salser.

Owen narrowed his eyes, but he didn't say anything.

"I tell ya, they're *real* nice over there," said Kirb.

"He's not kidding. I had one last year. Whooee!" Salser exclaimed.

"I'll think about it," said Owen.

"Gotta get her out of your head when you're on the road," said Kirb.

"Yeah, live a little, you ol' pussy," said Salser.

"She doesn't live in Thompson, does she, Mac?" asked Marty Wilson, the captain. "Your girl, I mean. What's her name? Agnes?"

"That's right," Owen answered.

"She's not even in Thompson?" asked Kirb.

"Shit!" said Salser.

Still looking at Marty, Owen said, "She's going to college up in St. Cyp."

"College?" said Salser. "She'd be better off snagging you once and for all, eh, Mac? That's what they all wanna do, you know? Then it's *easy street.*"

Owen ignored him.

"How long have you been together?" Marty asked him.

"About a year. But I've known her forever. We grew up together."

"Is she good in the sack?" asked Salser. "I've heard those Indian girls really put out."

Owen felt his blood starting to churn. This guy was worse than the pricks he played with in juniors.

"Give it a rest," said Doug Jackson, Stephanie's dad, from the other side of the room, which had grown quiet as guys tuned in to the enlightening discussion.

"Maybe I heard wrong," laughed Salser.

Owen took a deep breath. "Like I said, we grew up together. Played hockey together. She's a damn good goalie, too."

"Like to see her make a stop on me," said Salser.

Marty said, "Give him a break, Sals. You never liked a girl before?"

"I've liked plenty of girls," said Salser.

"Yeah, too bad none of them enjoyed their cruise on *Lake Flaccid*," said Kirb.

All the guys laughed.

"I'm just trying to loosen him up," said Salser. "It's for his own good."

"Sals, give it a rest," said Marty.

Salser stood up and turned toward his stall, making a big deal to show how disgusted he was.

J.P. Callahan said to Owen, "He's a barbarian, Mac. If he bothers you, let me know."

"Ditto," said Jackson.

The Traders had a short homestand coming up, and at the last minute Owen called Agnes and asked if she'd be willing to fly out for a couple of days. She'd have to miss a class and one of her goalie clinics, but she heard something in his voice and she didn't want to tell him no.

When she arrived the Chinook was blowing, and they went for a walk along the river.

"So, what's up, O?" asked Agnes.

"Nothing much," he said.

"You didn't fly me all the way down here to tell me that nothing's up."

"No."

"So what is it?"

He stopped walking. "Bottom line is, I miss you, Ag. I want you to move out here. I want you to move in with me. What do you think?"

His face was scrunched up in that worried way of his. He started walking again. "I guess it's kind of a big step. You might need more time. That's okay. But I don't want to be without you anymore."

"Jesus, O. I'm getting goose bumps."

"You don't have to answer now. But will you think about it?"

"I think about it every day."

"You do?"

"Owen. I think about you all the time. It's just hard to imagine myself here. It's so different. So big. I don't know if I'd fit in."

"Sure you will. I'll help you. Big is good. You can do anything you want out here. You can go to school. You can teach. You can play hockey."

"I meant, fitting in to *your* life here."

"Ag. My life is simple. It's you, and me, and hockey. That's about it."

"I know, but—" she hesitated, "what if people say things about us because, you know, I'm not a white girl? I mean, what if—"

"*What if?* Jesus, Ag, what planet have you been living on? People say those things *all the time.* Like those numbskull girls on the beach, remember?"

"But, so, you're not afraid that—"

"No. Are you?"

She hesitated.

"Don't be afraid, Ag."

"You don't understand—"

"I understand. Trust me, I understand. I just don't care. I don't give a fuck. I'm not going to let some racist bullshit take you away from me."

Agnes didn't answer.

"Come on, Ag."

She looked out across the river.

"Don't be afraid," he said again.

"I'm not afraid, okay? I just, I don't want it to hurt you."

"Jesus, Ag. It's not going to hurt me. Not as bad as losing you."

Agnes got gooseflesh again.

Owen said, "You can fly out here anytime you want. Just tell me. I'll set it up. Even if I'm not here you can stay at my place, check things out, do whatever you need to do."

"You're too good to me."

"No. I just—I want you so bad."

"I don't know why."

"Jeez, Ag." His kiss was the same as the very first one, back in Wapahaska, the morning after he lost that playoff game.

"O," she said. "You're going to make me cry."

Owen was in a better mood after the game, and they went to dinner. They got a corner booth. Agnes scooted close to him and put her left leg over his right.

"O, can I ask you something?"

"For a price."

"What's the price?"

"A kiss."

"That's easy," said Agnes. "Deal."

"You think I'm giving away my answers too cheap?" asked Owen.

"It's too late now. We made a deal."

He grinned. "Alright then, shoot."

"You've made love to other girls, right?"

"What? No—"

"Before we were together. I know you did."

He squinted at her and answered, slowly, "Yeah . . . "

"Is it different with me?"

He nodded.

"How?"

"Uh . . . in every possible way?"

"That's a cop-out answer. In most ways, I'm just like any other girl."

"No, not really."

"So, what's different about me?"

"I don't know, Ag. You're just *you*, you know? But then, sometimes you're different. It's hard to explain. That's why I always want you—like now, for example."

"But you wanted those other girls, too."

"No . . . "

"Sure you did."

"Not like you."

"Why? How's it different?"

"It just is. With them it was because, you know, they're girls, and—"

"That's not a very high standard," said Agnes.

"I didn't mean it like that. There's always *something* I like about a girl I'm with. But with you, it's not just *something*, it's *everything*. It's always been that way. Even before I knew what a girl *was*. Even when you were down on me for my playing, or whatever—I liked that, too. Not that I want to encourage that kind of thing."

She smiled.

"Does that answer your question?" he asked. "'Cause I'm ready for that kiss."

"Are you ever attracted to other girls now?"

286 • LESLIE SPITZ-EDSON

"Oh, come on, Ag, I don't want to talk about other girls—"

"Last question of the night, I promise. Be honest. Are you?"

"Well, sure, it's not like I don't notice other girls. But why would I want anyone else if I can have you?"

They left the restaurant. The night was clear, but the lights of the city outshone the stars. Maybe they'd beckoned to Agnes's mom, all those years ago, in the same way they now winked at Agnes. But whatever they'd seemed to promise, it hadn't been enough. Whatever they'd demanded in return, it had been too much. She never could go home again. Whether she'd wanted to or not.

Agnes reached out and held Owen's hand.

He asked, "Have you heard from any of the Wolves?"

"No. Jackie and I are pen pals, but I don't get much actual news from him."

"Heard from Deuce?"

"I've seen him."

"You've seen him?"

"Yeah."

Owen let go of Agnes's hand.

"He asked about you," continued Agnes. "Said he thought you were pretty tough for fighting him that time."

"Where'd you see him?" asked Owen.

"It turns out that Toby is his nephew. You know, my friend Priscilla's little boy, the one I babysit? Claude was up visiting his family and I ran into him once when I was babysitting Toby. Turns out he didn't have a girlfriend at home after all. The sweatshirts were for Toby and Priscilla."

Owen was silent.

"Are you okay, O?"

"Yeah."

"Come on. Something's bugging you."

He swallowed. "Here's the thing. You're going back up there

tomorrow, and he's up there and your whole life's up there and I'm stuck down here. How can I compete with that?"

"O, my whole life isn't up there, obviously. You're here. There's no *competition* for you."

"But you seem so settled up there."

"It's my home. My family is there, my friends are there—"

"Deuce is there."

"Come on, O."

"And it turns out he doesn't have a girlfriend," said Owen.

"I think you're overreacting just a little bit," said Agnes.

"It just seems like there's some unfinished business there," said Owen.

"It's all in your head," said Agnes. "He's just a friend. We have a lot in common, that's all."

"Unlike you and me," said Owen.

"I didn't say that," said Agnes.

"You're always saying it, in one way or another: that you're from a different place than I am. That it won't work between us because you're some poor Indian girl and I'm some big, white hockey star. Well, that's just bullshit. We're the same, okay? You're just like me. We're from the same place. We've always been together. We belong together. I believe that. Don't you?"

"Owen, that's not exactly true, that we're from the same place."

"Jesus, Agnes. I can't go back in time and turn myself into something I'm not!"

"I don't want you to."

"So I'm just screwed? Before I was even born, I was screwed?"

"No. Of course not. I never said that. I just have to get used to the idea—"

"Get used to the idea? Agnes, you've known me *forever*. You know who I am. You know what I want. The only question is, what do *you* want?"

＊

They walked back to Owen's place in silence. When they went to bed, Owen just said goodnight and rolled over. Agnes cried herself to sleep.

In the morning she had to take a cab to the airport so that he could get to practice on time. They stood by the front window waiting for the cab and she said, "O, you know I love you. Right?"

"I know. But I'm asking you for more than that. I'm asking you to have some faith in me."

"Of course I have faith in you, Owen. I do."

"Not in my goddamn hockey playing. In *me*."

"I do, O. I do. You're a rock."

"No, I'm not. That's the thing, Ag. You still don't get it, do you? Don't you think it would be easier for me to stay at home, too? I could get a job like my dad's, or an apprenticeship like Evan's. It would be way easier than busting my ass out here every day and coming home to a goddamn empty bed."

"Owen, *please*." Agnes put her hands on his shoulders. "I know it's hard out here right now. But you belong here. I'm not sure that I do. I want to be with you. But I need to have faith in *me*. I need to be sure that I'm not going to fuck everything up for you."

He put his arms around her. "You're crazy," he breathed into her ear.

"You're still going to call me after the game, right?" she asked.

"Of course."

They held each other, and then the cab came and she had to go.

It was Saturday, and Agnes was itching to play. The only option was Tess's All Players game. Claude had said it was fun. She laid her hockey gear out on the back porch, running her hands over the bulky goalie pads and blocker, remembering how she'd first learned to use them, and how she'd helped the team win the championship that year—they couldn't have done it without her. But when it was time to pack up again, she left her goalie stuff lying there. She pulled Owen's jersey out of the closet and threw it into her bag. At the rink, she dressed and headed out to the ice where Vin and Tess had just finished coaching the teen game. Tess waved, but when Vin saw her, he turned away.

"Glad you could join us," Tess said to her. "How was Thompson?"

"It was okay," Agnes answered. "I hated to miss that clinic. Thanks for understanding."

Tess nodded. "How's he doing?"

"He's having a rough time."

"It can fuck with your head," Tess said. "Being alone."

Agnes didn't answer.

"You'll figure it out," said Tess.

"Hope so."

"Here, have a puck," said Tess. The heavy, hard-edged object felt good in Agnes's glove.

She dropped it on the ice and started skating. After a few laps someone came up alongside her. She recognized him right away—he'd been on a team with her and Owen when they were maybe ten or eleven, and he still looked like a big, chubby kid. He was still a clumsy skater, too, but he had a big smile on his face.

"Agnes," he said to her. "Long time no see."

"Stan."

"Eh, nice jersey," he added, still smiling. "MacKenzie. He still playin'?" He winked.

Agnes laughed, and Stan maneuvered around behind her to get another look at the back. "Nice," he said again, nodding.

"Thanks," she replied.

Only one player had dressed as a goalie, so only one net was occupied. But Tess didn't even ask Agnes if she'd brought her goalie gear, she just put her on a line with Stan and a young center named Rosemary. Vin ended up on the opposing team with Tess.

The game began. Agnes's legs felt good but her brain struggled to read her new linemates' choreography. Her hands were hopeless.

"Sorry about my passing, guys," she said, when they got back to the bench.

"It'll come," said Rosemary.

"You're still a better skater than I am, anyhow," said Stan.

On the next shift, Rosemary feathered the puck to Agnes in the neutral zone and sped ahead. Agnes tried passing it back but it ended up in Rosemary's skates and before she could recover, the backchecker had corralled it and skated it out.

At the bench, Agnes apologized again.

Rosemary shrugged. "We'll get it."

She was right. As the game picked up, the warm glow of effort and sweat crept over Agnes's body and swept her into the game. Anything seemed possible now. Sitting on the bench between shifts, she couldn't wait to get back out there. On the ice things started to click, and finally they pulled off a perfect give-and-go. The goalie made the save on Rosemary's shot but Stan, parked in front of the net, potted the rebound. Everyone on the ice hollered. The first period ended.

"I think we're starting to *gel*," said Stan.

"Thanks, coach," said Agnes. They all laughed.

A few shifts into the second, Stan went to help Rosemary battle for the puck against the boards. They got it out to Agnes in the slot and, uncontested, she deked the goalie and rifled it into the back of the net. It felt great. She threw up her arms to celebrate. It was only afterwards, when she saw Vin skating back to his bench, that she realized he was the one who'd neglected to cover her. She was furious. Since when did she need *his* help to score?

When the period ended, Tess skated over to Agnes and Rosemary.

"Rosemary," Tess asked. "Do you think you could come down Tuesday night late for an hour or so? If Ruthie can make it, too, I thought we could work on a few things."

"I'll try," said Rosemary. "You know, I was thinking, what about Agnes? She'd fit in real good at Bear Lake."

"Nah, she wouldn't be interested," said Vin, who appeared suddenly behind Tess, his gloved hand on her shoulder. "She'll probably be in Thompson that weekend."

"That's not true," said Agnes. "I'm interested."

Tess slid out from under Vin's hand. "You'd fit in *perfect*, Agnes," she said. "But it's too late to sign you up. Tournament starts Thursday after next."

Vin cut in. "We still on for tonight, Tess?"

Tess looked at him. "Yeah. We're on. We need to have a little talk."

Vin looked confused. "Uh, great," he said, skating away.

Tess turned to Agnes. "What's his problem?"

Agnes shrugged. "He doesn't like my jersey."

Tess raised her eyebrows. "It's a damn nice jersey."

One shift into the third, a new player hopped onto the ice in Rosemary's place. He was sixteen or seventeen, wore no helmet, and his hair stood straight up like Vin's. He had a sort of tense energy and a sparkling way with his stick. Stan seemed to be looking out for him—he'd pass him the puck and the kid would dangle madly until someone stripped him. It was no way to win a hockey game, but he didn't care about that, and neither did Stan. They were just playing. One time the new kid dangled around a guy, looked up, accidentally made eye contact with Agnes, and was pick-pocketed again. Agnes winked at him and he shot off after the puck thief, harassing him from behind. A ref would have whistled the kid for slashing, but there was no ref, and the other guy had to fend for himself.

When the shift was over, they headed for the bench.

"I'm Agnes," Agnes said to the kid. "What's your name?"

"George," he said, looking down at his skates.

Someone called to him from farther up the bench, "Eh,

Georgie, take my shift, will you? I'm gassed," George swung his legs back over the boards.

"I see you've met my brother George," Rosemary said to Agnes.

"Barely," she replied, laughing.

"Don't take it personal. He's shy around girls."

"Where are you guys from?" asked Agnes.

"Big Lake Mission. I'm living up in Caribou now, with my sister."

"Do you come down every Saturday?"

"I try. Started out it was just going to be a little workout on the weekend—a way to look out for Georgie. Turns out, this is what keeps me in the game."

"It *is* fun."

Rosemary shrugged. "A little slow tonight. But it's different every time. Depends on who's here."

"Vin's not pushing the pace tonight, that's for sure."

"He looks okay when he's not covering you. You got him trained pretty good."

They laughed.

Tess skated towards them, hollering, "Girls! Tea time's over! Come on, Rosemary: you and me and Agnes. Let's go!"

Agnes laughed. This would be fun—the three of them against Vin and Billy. Now Vin would have to play. He'd have to acknowledge her.

But it didn't turn out that way at all. He persisted in letting Agnes beat him on every play, as if she were a little kid. Once he actually slowed down to let her by. Another time, when she stopped short to chip the puck over to Rosemary, he backed off to give her more space.

"What the hell are you doing?" she hissed at him.

He gave her the fakest smile ever. She narrowed her eyes and shoved him as hard as she could, but he just glided backwards, making a goofy face at her. She turned away and tried to clear her mind.

Billy was all over Tess on the half wall, but somehow she managed to throw an unexpected shot on net that the goalie couldn't control. Agnes and Vin converged on the loose puck, but instead of trying to clear it Vin left it lying there at Agnes's feet. They glared at each other. The game seemed to stop, the ice to splinter, and something else came crashing through.

"What the hell's *wrong* with you?" Agnes barked at Vin.

"What do you mean?" he taunted.

"You know what I mean," she said, up in his face.

He shoved her away.

"Don't push me," she said, shoving him back.

He thrust his glove into her face and she reciprocated. He spat onto the ice—not normal spitting, but disgusted spitting.

"What was that for?" She shoved him again.

He turned to skate away. "Answer me!" she hollered. She followed him and cross-checked him, hard. "I said, answer me! Or are you afraid of me?"

He spun around.

"Maybe you're afraid of *MacKenzie*."

He threw down his stick. She thought he was going to slug her, so she flung her arms around him to hold him in check. They lurched around as he struggled to get free.

"Why won't you play the game?" she snarled.

"To hell with the goddamn game!" He hooked his leg around the back of hers and they both fell, Vin mostly on top of Agnes. She floundered, trying to gain some traction on the slippery ice.

"Jesus, Vin. Let me go!"

She hauled back her arm and punched him, bypassing the hard-shell pads for his uncovered face. He held up his hands in defense, and she managed to squirm free and climb on top of him.

"You think I'm going to go away and never come back?" she snarled. "Like Mom?" She punched him again, but her knuckles crashed into his helmet. She didn't even feel it. "Don't you know me at *all*? *Shame* on you! Goddamn thick-headed loser brother of mine!"

"Agnes—"

"I said, shame on you!" She got him again, on the nose. She was panting and sweating and her knuckles were bleeding, but she kept pounding him until they pulled her away.

11

Claude pushed his mom's refrigerator back against the wall, mopped the kitchen floor, and put away the cleaning things. He put the cooler and some camping gear into his pickup. Then he took a quick shower and got dressed.

Mary Alice was thrilled that he had a date with Agnes, but, of course, she didn't know about their complicated history, and she also didn't know that Agnes was officially someone else's girlfriend. Claude had been uncertain about asking her out, but in the end, he couldn't think of a compelling reason not to. He had nothing against Macker. Macker was a good kid. But if he were in Claude's place, he'd do the same thing.

Agnes stood waiting on the sidewalk outside the College and Claude pulled up alongside her. She climbed into the truck. "Hey, your scar's looking good," she said, pointing to her own jaw.

"Yeah," he answered. "I'm going for the Frankenstein look. The Indian Frankenstein."

She laughed.

He said, "The sun's out. I was thinking we could grill some steaks out by the river."

"Really?" she said. It was inching toward April and the days were lengthening, but it wasn't exactly warm. There was still plenty of snow on the ground and the river was iced over.

He said, "We don't have to. We could go to a restaurant. But it's real nice out there. If we get cold we could come back to town for coffee or a drink or something."

"Well, okay, that sounds good."

"Are you dressed warm enough?" he asked.

"I think so."

"I've got blankets in the back, just in case."

They drove north along the river. The road was nearly deserted. Slim pines zipped past them, glistening. Their snowy tops, where the sun raked across them, were apricot, but in the shadows they cooled to a dusky blue. Finally, Claude turned onto an unmarked drive that led down to a little clearing with a fire pit. He backed in and parked. As soon as Agnes hopped out of the cab she felt the cold creep up around her, but once they had a fire going it wouldn't be too bad. Claude spread a heavy, woolen camping blanket on a log by the fire pit and invited her to sit down, but she walked past it, down to the edge of the frozen river. He took some charcoal out of the back of his truck and got a fire going. Then he joined her on the riverbank. Their shadows stretched out long and blue across the ragged ice.

"Claude, I want to be real straight with you," she said.

He didn't say anything.

"You know I'm still with Owen."

He nodded.

"I care about him a lot."

He took her gloved hands in his bare, sooty ones and drew her close and kissed her.

"Claude, I—"

"Sorry," he said.

"Don't be sorry," she said. "I just need to know—"

He kissed her again, a longer kiss this time.

"I'd better check on the fire," he said. She followed him back up the shore and sat down on the log. He stirred the coals and then went to get some things out of the truck.

"Can I help you?" she asked.

"No thanks, I got it."

He sat down next to her, and they stared into the fire. The flames shrunk, and the heat, concentrated in the little pile of glowing embers, melted the air and wicked the moisture from their faces.

"Do you do this often?" she asked.

"What?"

"Come out here like this."

"Whenever I can. Not too much, these days."

"Do you come out alone?"

"Used to come with my brother. Or my dad."

"Did you ever bring a girl out here? I mean, before now?"

He hesitated. "Yeah."

"Who?"

"A girl I used to date. We came out here a few times."

"What was she like?"

"What do you mean?" Claude asked.

"You know, was she short, tall, fat, thin, funny—?"

"She was taller than you. Nice-looking. Not really *funny*."

"What happened?" asked Agnes.

"What do you mean?"

"Why'd you break up?"

Claude looked into the fire. "It was a hard time. I was coming off a rough season, lots of injuries. My dad died. Hector was sick. She was real good to me. But then I had to get serious again. Training. I got a chance out there with the Steers. I had to go."

"She didn't want to go with you?"

"Nah. She's got her own life here, you know? She's got a job, and Achille—he's like her dad—he's getting older. It'd be tough for her to leave him."

Claude pushed a couple of potatoes into the embers and set up the grill.

"You warm enough?" he asked.

"Yeah. The fire feels good."

He said, "I used to roast deer out here. Or moose, even. Can't hunt when I'm playing, though, so it's been a long time. In the summer I like to fish, but this'll have to do for now."

Agnes said, "It'll be great."

After a couple of minutes, she asked, "Claude, what happened to Hector?"

He looked at her. "To be honest, I don't know exactly. Like I said, it was a hard time. And how was I supposed to know that he, you know . . . ?"

"You couldn't know, Claude," Agnes said.

"He was the good twin. Always good in school. I was the troublemaker. He was going to be a winner."

Claude unwrapped the steaks. He continued, "The doctors said it was depression. Maybe they were right, but their medicine didn't work. It just kind of made him go cold. Stole his spirit. He should've—maybe he should've been happy about Cill. I mean, sure, she was young, just a kid, but that's the way it was. And you know Cill. She's solid. She's a good mom."

Agnes nodded. "She is."

"Strange. Dad died, and then Hector finds out he's going to be a dad, and he just kind of bails out, too."

"Are you angry at him?" Agnes asked.

"He's dead. How can I be angry at him?"

Agnes didn't say anything.

"Are you hungry?" Claude asked.

"Yeah." She nodded.

He put the steaks on the grill. They sizzled and Agnes's mouth started watering.

"So what do you two do out in Thompson?" asked Claude.

"Oh, you know. I go to the game. We walk around town, look around."

"I bet it's nice out there, eh?"

"It is. It's really different—lots of tall buildings. There're tons of people out at night and the lights are amazing. There're a lot of restaurants and clubs and things."

"Do you go out a lot when you're there?"

"No. Sometimes we get dinner after the game."

"What does he do when you're not there?"

"He calls me. Maybe sometimes he goes out. I don't know."

Claude flipped the steaks. He got a couple of camping plates, knives, and forks out of the truck. "Want something to drink?" he asked.

"Thanks. What about you, Claude? What do you do after games? You never used to meet up with the rest of us at T.T.'s."

"I'm trying to be more a part of the team now. Last year it was like I was in two places at once."

Agnes said, "I kind of miss those days, last year. It was fun."

"I remember the first time I saw you."

She smiled, remembering that day at the Wolves' practice when Claude looked up at her and put that hard shot past Bancroft.

He said, "And the time we went out to the river and saw the Chepuyuk and looked at the stars."

"Yeah. How come we always end up going on these cold, winter dates?"

"I don't know. It's kind of funny how it keeps happening, though." He looked into the fire again. The embers glowed a hot, rosy orange. When he looked back at Agnes, she was glowing, too, from the heat, and her eyes were shining. He felt again how young she was, and it awed him.

He said, "You know, Agnes, there aren't city lights, or restaurants out here, but if it was me instead of him, I'd always keep you warm."

"I know you would, Claude."

Heat washed over their faces and the fat hissed softly as it dripped into the fire. The smoke stung their eyes.

"Looks like it's time to eat," Claude said.

They ate and then they piled snow onto the fire. Agnes helped Claude put everything away and then they sat in the back of the pickup, their legs dangling over the tailgate. The sun was setting behind them, over the crisp, frosted forest. The sky above the river turned lavender and violet and blue, and the stars started to pop out, first just a handful and then scores of them, multitudes, getting thicker and brighter by the second.

"Did you sit like this with the girl you dated that summer? You know, and watch the sunset and everything?"

"That was real different."

"How?"

Claude thought about it for a minute. "We mostly came out here to take our minds off things. I don't think we watched the sunsets."

"So what did you do?"

"Well, she liked to sing and dance. She had these funny old French songs that Achille taught her when she was little. She'd take off her shoes and dance right down there, on the shore. You know, jigging to those old tunes. And then, you have a couple beers, and there's just the two of you, and, well, you know."

"Yeah."

"I mean, don't get me wrong. I really liked her. She has a big heart. Maybe, if things had stayed the same, maybe we'd have gotten married."

"Have you ever looked her up again?" asked Agnes.

"She's with someone else, now."

They leaned back on their hands and looked up at the sky. It was wide over the river and over the forest on the far side. The stars got brighter as the sky deepened, until they blurred together in giant masses of starlight, like piles of diamonds, mounds of shattered river ice. Agnes looked over at Claude. His broad, calm face was tilted up to the starlight, the left cheekbone marked by the white scar from the long-ago high stick. She reached out her hand and touched it, and he looked at her, and the universe flipped upside down. She pulled the silly hunting cap off his head and ran her fingers through his glossy black curls. He unzipped her jacket and slipped his hands inside, pulling her close and kissing her as if she belonged to him. It felt good to her and she put her arms around his neck and they lay back in the truck bed with the blankets and the charcoal and the camping gear. After a while she hid her face up against him and was still.

He pulled a blanket up over them and they lay like that for a long time, breathing together.

"Agnes," he said. "Are you okay?"

"Yeah," she whispered.

"Do you want to go?"

"No. Not yet."

"Are you cold?"

"No."

"I told you I'd keep you warm."

"I didn't doubt it."

Claude's heartbeat was slow and even. There were no other sounds: no wind, no water, no animals, but she could feel those things around them. The cold, winter stars, the white blanket of snow, the enormous silence of the frozen river: they lived inside her, in the very deepest part of her. She could go a hundred thousand miles away and they'd still be there, beating slow and solid like Claude's heart.

Lying in his arms, she had a vision of what it would be like to be with him, forever: their little house—or maybe if he could keep playing for a few more years, a bigger house, it wouldn't matter—Claude up and out early, fishing, hunting, a couple of kids. He'd be happy, if only because he didn't expect more. Maybe he didn't even want more. And that was okay. It was fine. It's what made Claude Claude.

But then it hit her: *no*. No, it wasn't fine. It was a lie, a story people told about him, a story they were telling themselves. It wasn't what made Claude Claude. Not in the slightest.

Claude wasn't stupid. He knew that she was in love with Owen. He'd known it since the beginning. In fact, that might be the only thing he really knew about her. That he wanted to try anyway, hoping that maybe one more cold, winter date could change things between them, made her heart sore.

She whispered, "Claude, are you asleep?"

"No. Just looking at the stars."

"They're beautiful tonight, aren't they?"

"Always are," he answered.

After a while they started getting uncomfortable lying there on the hard metal truck bed, so they packed up and got into the cab. He turned the key in the ignition and cranked up the heat.

"Do you want to get a beer or something?" he asked.

"I don't know." It would seem strange to sit with him, now, at some bar, with the harsh, inside lights glaring at them.

He said, "Let's just head back."

"Okay," she said.

He put the truck in gear.

"Wait," said Agnes. She put her hand on his.

Claude put the truck back in park. "What?" he asked.

"You need to go back and get her."

"Who?"

"You know, Tess."

"Tess?" asked Claude.

"She's the one you were talking about, right?"

"I told you, she's with someone else now."

"She still loves you, Claude."

"It's too hard, with me away playing, and her up here. She doesn't like to be alone."

"Jesus, Claude. Don't be stupid. You want her. She wants you. You can work something out."

He sat for a minute. Then he put the truck back in gear and it crept forward onto the snowy road. The trees popped up before them, called to attention by the truck's headlights, and then fell back again into the darkness. When they got to the highway, Claude looked both ways and then turned left.

"Did you ever play in Tess's game?" he asked.

"The All Players game?"

"Yeah."

"You didn't hear about it?"

"No. Hear what?"

She smiled to herself. "Someone told me, it's different every time. Depending on who's there."

"I guess that's true," agreed Claude.

"What's it like when you're there?" asked Agnes.

Claude chuckled. "Last summer a kid wanted to fight me. Young kid."

"Did you do it?"

"Couldn't really *not* do it."

Agnes smiled. "Now he's the king of St. Cyp, right?"

"I guess he is," Claude answered. "Tess ask you about Bear Lake?"

"We talked about it."

"You gonna play?"

"Maybe next year."

"That'd be good. She's always looking for new girls."

"Oh yeah? I met Rosemary. Who else plays with them?"

"Not sure anymore. They're spread out all over. My sister used to come out from Ottawa. Now she's got kids and everything so that makes it hard."

"Is it a big tournament?"

"Not too big, but they got all ages—kids, women, men, old-timers."

"You know, Rosemary's brother—his name's George—he's got some skill. Someone should work with him."

"Yeah, George—it's just good he's coming to play. Those kids've had it hard."

They were getting closer to town, now.

"Claude," asked Agnes, "what did you mean when you said that hockey's a tough game, but also a tough life?"

"I meant it's lonely. You're on the road a lot. Away from the people who care about you."

She didn't say anything.

He continued. "You asked about Vin. He's a good kid, but even if he could get his game back, if he has trouble when he's living at home, with his family, it's going to be real tough when he's away, playing for some team in Alberta, or B.C. Real tough. Trust me."

They were quiet for a while. Then Agnes said, "You don't really want to play pro, do you?"

He shrugged. "It's working out okay so far."

"You'd rather work with Tess," she added.

Claude kept his eyes on the road.

"So, why, Claude?"

"Toby," he said. "I'm the only father he's got. I've got to make sure that he and Cill have what they need. At least until she's out of school."

They drove on for a while and then Agnes asked, "Are you driving back tonight?"

"Yeah," he said. He kept looking straight ahead along the path his headlights cut through the trees. Agnes looked at his hand on the steering wheel, big and strong and scarred, but still soft.

"Claude, I'll never forget being with you tonight," she said.

"You don't have to say that."

"I'm not just saying it."

Claude pulled in alongside her car, waiting all by itself in the College parking lot.

Agnes reached over to embrace him. "Go back and get her. Okay? Please, Claude?"

She still said his name so beautiful and soft, her tongue just barely touching the roof of her mouth.

"Goodnight, Agnes."

"Goodnight, Claude."

Agnes got home towards the end of the Traders' game. She wasn't in the mood to watch, but she wanted to see Owen. He looked so *beautiful* to her, sitting on the bench, leaning forward on his elbows, chewing on his mouth guard. She loved the way his eyes darted back and forth, following the action on the ice. She couldn't wait to tell him about tonight. Maybe they could set a date for her next visit. She was dying to be with him again.

After the game ended she waited for the phone to ring.

"O?"

"Hey, Ag."

"It's great to hear your voice," she said.

"Yours too," he answered. "What'd you think?"

"You know I always love to see you play."

"Yeah?"

"You're a beautiful skater."

"I'm blushing over here, Ag!"

"Wish I could see it in person, though," she said.

"Wish I could see *you* in person so I could throw you into bed and make crazy passionate love to you."

She laughed.

He said, "It's not a laughing matter."

"Owen, I have to tell you something."

"What?"

"Remember when you told me that you know what you want, but I have to figure out what I want?"

"Yeah."

"And that it seemed like there was unfinished business between me and Claude?"

There was silence on the other end of the phone.

"Are you there?" asked Agnes.

"I'm here."

"Do you remember?"

"Yeah."

"Well, I wanted to take care of that business."

Owen didn't say anything.

"Because I want things to work out between you and me. I do. I love you, O."

Owen still didn't say anything.

"I said I love you. Are you there? Owen?"

"What?"

"Aren't you going to say you love me, too?"

"I love you, too," he said.

"Aren't you going to ask, what did I do, what happened?"

"What did you do?" he said slowly. "What happened?"

"I went on a date with him. Just one date."

Owen was quiet.

"Are you okay?" Agnes asked.

"What do *you* think?" Owen replied.

"I think you're scaring the shit out of me. Are you *okay*?"

"No. I'm not okay. Last spring or fall or whenever it was, you said that it didn't work out between you two, and now, like a million years later, you're going out with him again! How am I supposed to be okay?"

"Because you said, you thought we had unfinished business."

"And I guess I was right!"

"Maybe you were *then*," Agnes said. "But it's finished now."

"How the hell am I supposed to believe that?"

"You've got to believe it! Listen to me! This is a good thing. We talked, I got to know him a little better, where he's coming from and everything—"

"Jesus, Ag. What are you trying to do? Kill me?"

"No! Owen, please, just listen to me—"

"Let's just say goodbye for now. We'll talk about it some other time—"

Owen hung up, and Agnes just sat there, at the wrong end of the line, holding the receiver in her hand.

A thick cover of clouds lay between the earth and the sky. Tess had had a restless night, one of a string of restless nights since Vincent had gone. She'd been sympathetic after his fight with Agnes—he'd looked like he'd been through a wood pulper—but she'd needed to speak for Agnes, too, and that was more than their precariously constructed relationship could bear. Now her heart, swollen with hurt and worry, refused to let her rest. Just before dawn, though, she'd slipped into unconsciousness and, inexplicably, dreamt she was with Helen, Claude's sister. The two girls were together on the lakeshore up at the cabin, and Helen was laying out her plans for looking after "their" little brothers—the twins Claude and Hector. They always called them "their" brothers even though they weren't Tess's brothers at all. They were only Helen's.

The air was light and delicious, scattering sun-flecks like snowflakes across the lake. Helen's dreamy eyes and the sprinkle of freckles across her nose were in soft focus, up close to Tess's face. It was a sweet, wonderful dream, a gift from heaven, or wherever such precious fragments come from. Helen had moved away years ago, but in the dream they stood together on the shore, Helen with a commanding, sisterly hold on Tess's wrist, Tess in thrall not to the hand that held her, but to the monstrous beauty of the girl herself—the sister she didn't have, the sister she wasn't. Helen's presence flooded Tess's being like some crazy, hallucinatory drug. It cradled her, lulled her, for a little while.

When her alarm sounded, Tess rolled out of bed. She drank her coffee while she was getting dressed, put the half-emptied cup in the kitchen sink, and got into her car. She wanted to preserve the long-ago, summertime atmosphere of the dream so she drove the miles between her place and Achille's without turning on the radio. She pulled into the lot and parked in her customary spot to the left of the building.

Was she early? She wasn't, but thanks to the clouds it was dark enough, still enough, so that she might have believed it. Also, there were no lights on inside. The "closed" sign was hanging in the window, and the door was locked.

"Achille?" she said out loud, to no one. "Where are you, old man?"

Her feet crunched across the gravel and she peered through one of the windows to the left of the door, the ones that looked in over the booths inside. It was even darker in there than it was out here.

She tugged at the door again, but it was just as locked as it had been a moment ago. Still she fought with it, yanking it again and again. Then, suddenly, she panicked and started to pound on it with her fist.

"Achille? Achille!" She ran around behind the store and down the short path through the trees to Achille's tiny one-room dwelling.

There was no answer when she knocked. She turned the knob and opened the door a crack.

"Achille?" she called.

His voice came to her, filtered through the room's jumbled collection of old traps and snowshoes, the dusty fiddle, the canoe paddles and hunting knives and other odd bundles of objects, some known to her and some mysterious. He was singing.

Luron, luré
Luron, luré
C'est la bel-le Françoise, lon gai,
C'est la bel-le Françoise.

Tess stepped inside.

"Achille?" she said again.

"Tezzie?" came Achille's voice. "I thought you would never get here." He coughed. It was a dry, unsatisfying cough. She was used to it.

"It's the same time as always," she answered, as she stuffed her keys into her pocket.

Achille was lying on his back on his cot. His right arm, hanging over the edge, was wrapped around an old, wooden hockey stick.

"It's time to go, Tezzie," he said. "Get me my paddle."

"What?"

"My paddle. You know where it is." He pointed a shaky finger toward the far corner of the little room.

Tess sat down on the edge of his cot. She laughed at him. "What are you talking about, Little Papa? You're not gonna paddle today. It's time to open up. It's a work day."

"No, Tezzie," said Achille. "Not for me. Help me sit up." He tried to sit up but fell back again in a spasm of coughing. "On second thought," he whispered, wheezing like the squeaky broomcloset door at the rink, "just get me my paddle."

Tess put her hand on his forehead. It was hot and clammy. "You're weak. Let me get you some breakfast," she said, standing up. "Maybe a drink of water."

"No. My paddle, girl. That's all I need," said Achille.

"Okay, old man." She smiled at him. "Rest. I'll be back soon." She heard him singing as she left the cabin.

Qui veut s'y marier, ma luron, lurette,
Qui veut s'y marier, ma luron luré.

Tess used her key to get into the back, kitchen entrance of Achille's. She pulled out the eggs and milk and bread, chopped up some ham, and cooked him a nice little breakfast. It would give him strength to get up and start the day. She poured him a glass of water, too, and carried it all back to him.

"Tezzie, what are you doing here?" Achille asked her.

"I brought you some breakfast," said Tess.

"Good girl, put it on the table," he said, patting his little bedside stand with a shaking, wizened hand.

She did as she was told. "Achille," she said. "Let me help you sit up, so you can eat."

"I'm not eating," he said.

"Just one bite," she said.

"Sing with me," he begged.

"But it's time to open up."

"We sang it when you were small. It's about *la belle Françoise*, who wants to marry. But her man is going off to war. You remember." Achille lifted up the hockey stick and held it as if it were a paddle, his left hand cupped around the butt end, his right holding the shaft. His voice shook, but he paddled in time.

Luron, luré
Luron, luré
C'est la bel-le Françoise, lon gai,
C'est la bel-le Françoise.

"Tezzie, sing with me!"
She sang while he wheezed and tried to paddle as best he could.

Qui veut s'y marier, ma luron, lurette,
Qui veut s'y marier, ma luron, luré.

Exhausted from the effort, Achille dropped his arms. The hockey stick slid to the floor.

"Little Papa, are you alright?" asked Tess.

He nodded, his eyes half closed, and he drew a shuddering breath, like a puck clattering to death along the boards.

Tess reached out to hold his hand. "Rest, now," she said.

They sat like that for quite a while, his eyes closed, his breathing tortured.

Just when she thought he must be asleep, he opened his eyes. "Have you talked to him, Tezzie?"

"Talked to whom?"

"Claude."

She let go of his hand. "I'm going to help you eat something," she said.

"Tezzie, listen to me—"

"Let me help you sit up," said Tess.

Achille was light in her arms and damp with sweat. She got him propped up against the wall with his pillow.

"Are you cold, Little Papa?" she asked.

He didn't answer. She held the plate in front of him and scooped some scrambled eggs onto the fork. He nibbled at it.

She watched him try to swallow. It was hard for him. Maybe his throat was too dry. He pushed away the plate and the fork.

"I can't eat," he said.

"But I cooked it just for you."

He shook his head. "Tezzie. Where's my paddle?"

Tess put his breakfast back on the nightstand and picked up the hockey stick from where it lay on the floor. She laid it across his lap.

His hand shook crazily as he picked it up. "What's this?" he asked. "I'm going far away, Tezzie. I'm going to shoot the rapids. I'm going to hunt the buffalo. I'm going to catch the sun."

"No, Little Papa, don't go. Stay here with me."

"Get me my paddle," he said.

"No," she answered. "I won't."

"Yes," he said. "Do it for your old Achille—we been together so long."

She couldn't tell him no this time. She took the trembling hockey stick out of his hand and walked across the room, through a curtain of tears, to fetch the paddle. It was a beautiful paddle, simply carved in blonde wood, polished smooth, sensuous in its curves, darkened where his hands had gripped it. She laid it across his lap.

"That's the one," he said. He stroked it fondly and smiled up at her, a bright, gap-toothed smile. "I remember a day when the sun sparkled through the leaves, by the water. And you slept on a blanket, like this." He flung his arms up to mimic a child, sleeping with abandon, and Tess grabbed the paddle to keep it from sliding to the floor. He laughed. "My little one! You slept, and I smoked, and the river sang, and the paddle danced. You don't remember. But you'll have many more days like that one and I've seen my last. It's only fair that the memory is mine."

Tess shook her head. Tears slid down her cheeks.

"Now, Tezzie. Therese. Listen to me. It's all written down and signed, sealed—but I'm gonna tell you anyway. The store is yours, and this little place, of course. The cabin is yours. Everything is yours. Do what you want with it."

She shook her head.

"There's one other thing," he added.

She sniffled. She was wet with tears.

"It's Claude. He's a good man, Tezzie. A very good man. Just look at him. He's big, he's strong, he's—" The old man convulsed with coughing. Tess held the water glass up to him and he wet his mouth. He continued. "It's a shame—no?—that I can't leave him to you, the way I leave those other things—"

"But, Little Papa—"

"Now, girl, none of that is important."

They heard knocking on the door.

Achille continued, "Promise me you'll talk to him."

"No," Tess replied.

"Promise me you'll do what I say."

"No," Tess said again, hoping her intransigence would keep him alive somehow.

"You're a stubborn girl," said Achille, shaking his head.

They heard the knocking again.

Achille raised his voice, "Father, is that you? Come in."

Tess heard hard footsteps on the wooden floor, and Father Aubichon emerged from the gloom, his face as white as his frock was black.

Tess stared at him in horror. Achille wasn't just *playing* the dying old man—he was ready to go. Otherwise, Father Aubichon? Really? Achille had never once been to church in Tess's memory. The next figure to come through that door would be death itself.

"Tezzie, be a good girl and give us a couple minutes," said Achille.

Tess got up and left the little house. Not knowing what else to do, she went back into the kitchen to clean up the modest mess she had made cooking Achille's breakfast. She thought of calling Claude. She thought of calling Vincent. But in the end she just sat down on the stool by the back window and tried to conjure last night's dream. She closed her eyes. If it weren't for Helen standing beside her, holding her wrist, she'd never make it through this.

She jumped. Father Aubichon was rapping on the kitchen door. "He's asking for you," the priest said.

When she returned Achille was lying just as she'd left him.

"I'm ready," he said.

"No."

"You don't need me anymore, Tezzie. Let me go. If I stay, I'm only gonna hold you back. I can't eat. I can't drink. I don't belong here. We gotta go our separate ways." He coughed again. "Now get me my bottle from that cupboard over there."

"Achille—" began Tess.

"What's a little drop of whiskey gonna hurt a dying man?" asked Achille.

She hadn't intended to deny him his drink, anyhow. She brought him the bottle and helped him hold it while he wet his mouth.

"Now." He lifted his paddle and held it at the ready. "You too, Tezzie," he said.

She picked up the hockey stick.

"*Dis bon voyage*," he said.

"*Bon voyage*, Little Papa," she whispered. She kissed him on the forehead, and she sung him to sleep.

Ah! Qu'a vous donc, la belle, qu'a vous tant a pleurer?
On m'a dit hier au soire, qu'à la guerr' vous aliez.
Ceux qui vous l'ont dit, belle, ont dit la vérité.
Au retour de la guerre, je vous épouserai.

Ah! What is it, my love, that makes you cry so much?
They told me tonight that you must go to war.
The ones who told you, they spoke the truth.
When I return from the war, I will marry you.

✳

He'd come in spite of himself. It wouldn't feel right not to. It was Saturday—lots of clinics today. When Vin walked in, Mrs. McCallum greeted him kindly and handed him a small, folded piece of paper. He opened it and read to himself:

Dear Vincent,
Achille died this morning.
Please take my place this week. The kids need you.
Thanks.
Tess

"When was she here?" he asked Mrs. McCallum.

"Yesterday."

Vin folded the note and put it in his pocket. "Thanks," he said.

"You're welcome, dear."

He walked down the hall to the office, opened the door, and turned on the light. He sat down at the desk and read the note again. She was a piece of work. Worse than Agnes. She'd always had a way of manipulating him, of making him do what he'd had no intention of doing, and making him like it, too. He hated that. He crumpled up the note and threw it into the trash.

It was quiet now, but soon he'd hear doors opening and closing, the excited chatter of kids, and then the clatter of sticks and pucks, the shrill whistles and coaches shouting instructions over the din. And Tess—Tess wouldn't be here. She was somewhere, alone. She hated to be alone.

He picked up the phone and dialed her number. It rang again and again and again. He hung up and dialed the number of the pay phone at Achille's. A man's voice answered.

Vin said, "This is Vin Demers. I need to talk to Tess."

"Just a minute."

Tess's voice came on. "Hello?" She sounded far away.

"Tess. It's me, Vin."

"Vincent."

"I got your note."

"You did."

"I'm sorry about Achille."

"Thanks, Vincent."

"When are you coming back?" he asked.

She didn't answer.

He said, "Don't worry. I'm here."

"Thank you," she said.

"Do you need anything? Do you want me to come over tonight?"

"Vincent, no—you're so sweet. But no. I'll be fine."

"Yeah. Goodbye, Tess."

Agnes saw Owen crumple, crunched against the boards just as he dished the puck out to Petersen, but the camera shifted ahead to follow the play.

"Wait, go back!" urged Agnes, who was sitting in the living room in St. Cyp, watching the game with Dad and Kookum.

The whistle blew. The play-by-play announcer said, "There's a man down behind the play. It's MacKenzie, the Thompson rookie."

They showed Owen curled up on his right side, on the ice, facing the boards. His gloves lay abandoned on the ice and he was clutching his leg in obvious pain. The trainer was already bending over him, his hand on Owen's back, his face down close to Owen's.

"What are they saying?" asked Agnes.

The announcer said, "This is bad news. The Traders are outside of the playoffs, looking in. They need all hands on deck."

On screen they were rolling a stretcher out onto the ice. "Not a stretcher!" cried Agnes. "Come on, O, you can stand up, right?"

The trainers worked to slide a board underneath him, propping his leg up and tying it down, and then they lifted him onto the stretcher. The camera showed the other players tapping their sticks and the fans applauding as they wheeled Owen off the ice.

"I'm going out there right now," Agnes announced, standing up.

"No you're not," said Dad.

"But it looks like he's really hurt."

"You can't drive out there all by yourself," said Dad.

"Yes I can."

"Don't you have an exam tomorrow?"

She did.

He continued, "Agnes, he's not going anywhere on that leg. Wait until he's out of the hospital."

"Do you think he's going to be in the hospital?" asked Agnes.

Kookum said, "Why don't you take your exam tomorrow, and then call the MacKenzies? Maybe they're driving out there, and you can go with them."

Uneasily, Agnes sat back down and watched the rest of the game. They showed the replay again and again, from different angles. It looked like Owen's knee or shin had been smashed between the other guy's knee and the boards.

Agnes decided that she would drive out to Thompson the next day, after her exam. She packed her bag and got ready for bed, hoping the whole time that Owen would call. Of course, he didn't. They weren't speaking to one another. Or, anyhow, *he* wasn't speaking to *her*. She sat up at the kitchen table and looked over her notes for the exam, trying to calm herself down.

It didn't work. When she got into bed, she was wide awake. She pictured Owen crushed, fallen, in pain, alone in some sterile hospital room. Yes, she was angry with him for hanging up on her, but that didn't matter now. He'd only hung up because he was hurting. Now he was hurting even worse. She was hurting, too. It wasn't just about his broken leg—if, as she assumed, it *was* broken—it was about their broken friendship. Their broken love. Quietly, so as not to wake Kookum, she slid out of bed. It was time to go to Thompson and try to put things back together.

By the time Agnes reached the outskirts of Thompson, it was late in the morning. She stopped to get gasoline and a map, and then she worked her way across town to Owen's place. She didn't know if he was there. Maybe he was at the hospital, or at the arena, or at some doctor's office in another part of the city. She found a parking spot on the street, but she didn't get out of the car right away.

About an hour into the drive last night, it had suddenly occurred to her that Owen might have a new girlfriend. It hadn't been very long since their fateful phone call, but as the example of Sissy had plainly shown, Owen wouldn't have much trouble finding a girl if he wanted one. What if she arrived at Owen's door only to find herself face to face with the second coming of Sissy?

If the situation were reversed—if it were Agnes who had found a new boyfriend—Owen would probably just beat the shit out of him. That's what he'd wanted to do to Claude, right? But Agnes couldn't see herself punching some poor girl in the head. She'd be more inclined to throw a few punches at Owen himself: number one, for refusing to listen to her on the phone that night; number two, for ever doubting her in the first place; number three, for being such a ridiculously good hockey player that he'd had to move far, far away; and, number four, for even considering any other woman but her. But beating Owen up wasn't an option either—it wouldn't be right to pick a fight with someone who was already hurt.

So, what would she do if some new girl answered the door? She didn't exactly know, but she wouldn't let herself be put off, that was for sure. She'd labored over those moccasins— the leather was tough, the needle keen—and every stitch was binding, every bead a sparkling facet of her love for him. She'd given them, he'd taken them, and he'd worn them. He was hers. Hers to love, hers to care for. She wasn't going to give up on him, no matter what.

All through the night and into the morning, as Agnes sped across the prairie under the starry sky, watching the heavens warm to the rising sun, she'd imagined one crazy scene after another. But now that she was here, in front of his place, in the light of day, she felt calm. No matter who opened that door, Agnes knew in her heart that Owen loved her—only her. And she knew that she loved only him.

She got out of the car and walked up to his door. She knocked.

Nothing.

Maybe he hadn't heard, so she tried again, louder this time.

Still nothing.

She waited. He was hurt. Maybe it was hard for him to get to the door. Then, just as she lifted her hand to knock again, the door flew open and there he was.

"Whoa," she gasped.

"What do you mean, *whoa*?"

Owen was looking down at her with a supremely irritated expression on his face. His sandy curls flew wildly around his head, and his bare muscles were flexed, straining to hold himself upright on a pair of crutches.

She didn't answer him. He looked like a Greek god in boxers, carved in white marble, glowing in the morning sunshine, but she wasn't going to *tell* him that.

"Do you always answer the door in your underwear?" she asked.

He said, "What the hell are you doing here?"

"That hit looked pretty ugly. I thought you might need some help."

"Well, I don't, so you can go right back where you came from."

"I've been driving the whole goddamn night. Can I at least come in for a minute and get a glass of water or something?"

With some difficulty he turned himself around on his crutches and lurched into the living room, leaving her to close the door and follow him in. He set the crutches aside, lowered himself onto the sofa, and lifted his injured leg up onto the table. She couldn't see what it looked like because it was all wrapped up in a bandage.

She dropped her car keys on the table. "Have you had breakfast?" she asked.

"No," he said.

She went into the kitchen. There were a few eggs in the refrigerator, a few slices of bread, an ancient-looking onion, and a marginally edible green bell pepper. No sign of a woman in here.

"Do you want an omelet?" she called to him.

"Sure," he answered.

Agnes put on some coffee and started cracking eggs into a bowl.

"There's no milk for the coffee," she told him. "Do you want to drink it black?"

"Okay," he said.

"Do you want some juice?"

"Sure."

She brought him the last serving of orange juice. Then she went back to the kitchen. By the time the coffee was done the omelets were, too. She put his on a plate with some toast and half an apple that was lying around and did the same for herself. She brought him his plate and coffee, and then she went back to get hers.

"Mind if I join you?" she asked.

He shrugged. "Make yourself at home."

She pulled a chair over to the sofa table and positioned it so that she was facing him.

He was already halfway through the omelet.

"O, I'm sorry that you got hurt. It really sucks."

"Yeah," he said, taking another bite.

"Does it hurt a lot?" she asked.

"Not too bad."

"What's the deal with it? Do you know?"

"It's broken. They're going to look at it again today and then decide what to do."

"What are the options?"

"Surgery or cast, I think. But I was pretty out of it last night."

"I bet."

"Yeah, they gave me something for the pain and it really knocked me out. Corey'll know the deal."

"Corey?"

"The trainer."

"Oh, right. Do you want another omelet?" Agnes asked. The first one was long gone.

"Sure," he said. "Thanks."

Agnes put her plate down and got up.

"Jesus, Ag. Finish yours, first," he said.

She ignored him and carried his plate back to the kitchen.

When she came back with the second omelet he said, "Thanks, Ag."

"You're welcome."

He wolfed it down nearly as quickly as the first.

"Sorry I wasn't too nice when you first got here," he said.

"That's okay. I can think of a million reasons you wouldn't be happy to see me."

"But you came anyway," he said.

"Just to piss you off," she answered.

He said, "I've got to get dressed. They're going to pick me up soon and take me to see the doctor." He lifted his leg down to the floor and hoisted himself up off the sofa. She handed him his crutches.

"Breakfast really hit the spot," he admitted.

"Yeah, well, you gotta eat."

*

The doctors scheduled Owen for surgery the next morning. They planned to insert a pin to hold the fractured bone together. He wasn't allowed to eat anything before the operation, so Agnes promised to visit him at the hospital that evening to take his mind off his empty stomach. When she peeked into his room his face brightened, and she couldn't help but smile. She'd missed him.

"Hey, Ag," he said.

"Hey, O. Are you doing okay?"

"Yeah, yeah," he said. "Sit down." He patted the edge of the bed next to him, and she came and sat down.

"Ag," he said, "I'm not looking forward to this."

"That's understandable," she replied.

"I've never had big surgery like this before."

"You'll be okay."

"I mean, I had my tonsils out, but that's about it."

"They'll take good care of you," she said.

He looked up at her. His forehead was all wrinkled. "Ag, if, like, anything happens to me—"

"Nothing's going to happen to you, O."

"My Mom said you skipped an exam to drive out here," Owen said.

Agnes shrugged. "Yeah, well, it was just a goddamn exam, you know?"

"Still, it was really nice of you."

"Well, I knew you weren't going to call me, so how else was I going to know what the hell was going on with you?"

"My mom asked . . . she wanted to know if you're planning to stay for a while, after I get home from the hospital."

"I don't know. Do you want me to?"

He nodded. "Yeah. I mean, if you can."

"I can."

"Will you call her and tell her? She was worried that I'd be alone."

"I wouldn't leave you alone," said Agnes.

"I know."

"Even when you *want* me to leave you alone, I won't leave you alone."

Owen smiled. He was starting to look woozy, though. They must have given him something to help him sleep.

"Don't worry about anything, O," Agnes said. "Just get some rest and I'll see you tomorrow, okay?"

She stood up, and then she bent over and gave him a little kiss on the lips. He was nearly asleep, anyhow. He smiled a drowsy, little-boy smile, and closed his eyes.

When Owen came home from the hospital, he was accompanied by jars of pills and a pile of papers with instructions on them. At dinner he barely managed three bites before his head started to drop and Agnes had to help him to bed. She figured she'd better bring him his medicine before she did the dishes—before he fell asleep. She read the instructions, gathered the prescribed pills, and poured a glass of water. Then she went and stood in his doorway.

"O?" she said. "Can I come in?"

"Yeah."

"Are you comfortable?"

"Sort of." He was on the bed, half lying, half sitting. He looked awful, all pale and puffy and cross-eyed.

"Here's your medicine."

He swallowed the pills and drank the water.

"Thanks, Ag."

"You're supposed to keep your leg elevated. Let me help you." She put down the empty water glass, pulled his blankets back, and tried to help him move his leg so that she could position a pillow underneath it.

"Ouch, *shit*, goddamn it!" he cried out.

"Jeez, O, I'm sorry," said Agnes.

"It's okay," he said, grimacing. "It's just a little tender, that's all."

"I'm sorry, O. I'm not too good at this," she said.

"No, you're perfect. Just what the doctor ordered."

She smiled. The dumb joke was vintage Owen, and it reassured her to hear it. Together they managed to get his leg up on the pillow, and then she pulled the blanket back up to his chin. "Sleep well, okay?" she said.

"I'll try."

"If you need another pain pill or anything, just yell. I'll be on the sofa. I'll keep the door open a crack."

Owen's face got all scrunched up. "You're sleeping on the sofa?"

"I'm afraid I won't be able to hear you from the guest room."

"Why don't you just sleep in here, Ag? The bed's plenty big. We've done it before." He winked.

"Owen, you're angry with me. Remember? You hung up on me and never called back. You don't want me in here."

"I'm not angry with you."

"Well, that's nice. But I don't want to sleep with some guy who wouldn't even hear me out."

"I won't try anything. I promise." He grinned.

"No," she said, annoyed.

"Oh, come on, Ag. Now's not the time to teach me a lesson. You know we're going to work it out."

"No. I don't know that."

"You're here, right?"

"I came here to look after you, to keep you from *starving* to death, because you can't even fucking *cook*—even on *two* legs. But that doesn't mean I'm automatically forgiving you for acting like a jerk. Anyhow, that isn't even the point. This same thing keeps happening, every time the subject of Claude comes up."

"Look, I'm sorry."

"Sorry's not enough. We've got a lot to talk about. But this isn't the time. You couldn't even sit through dinner."

Owen pouted.

"Go to sleep," said Agnes. "I've got to clean up in the kitchen. If you need anything, yell. I'll be on the sofa."

Claude didn't even have to think about it. As soon as he heard the news, he knew exactly where she'd be. He knew exactly what she'd be feeling, too. He'd felt the same thing when his dad died. He'd been plunged into nothingness, like falling off a cliff, an endless fall, with nothing to brace himself against, nothing to hold on to. He'd waited for the crash that never came. He was still falling.

Leaving was easy: death in the family. He put some groceries into the cooler, got into his truck, and headed north. Soon, the elements of his every-day life—the morning skate, the upcoming game, and even his teammates—had sunk behind the last of the town's car dealerships, RV lots, and equipment rental outlets.

The vast dome of the sky was Easter-egg blue, trimmed at the horizon by a wide band of white, feathery clouds. Beneath it, alive and softly breathing, stretched the prairie, its last patches of snow giving way to dancing wildflowers. Claude's eyes followed the line of the highway. Everything was simple now, stripped clean of meandering turns and roadside curiosities. There were just two people and the long, straight line that connected them. He rolled down his window and the sun-scented wind blew the cap off his head, tousled his hair, and caressed his face like a woman's breath.

After a couple of hours, Claude stopped to stretch. By the side of the road, the new grass trembled, each tender blade etched with tapered ribs that caught the sunlight in prisms of emerald and violet. A cool current swept past, heavy and moist as water. It lay across the blades, bending them like a lover, and then was gone. In the roadside ditch there was a film of ice—soon it would be gone, too, and the water below would seethe with life until the summer prairie drank it down. Claude climbed back into his truck. He had hours more to go.

Claude's great-grandmother was born in the north and she lived her entire life there. From her grandmother, she learned how to set snares, sew moccasins, and make snowshoes; to paddle, cure pelts, and gather food in the forest. But Claude's great-grandfather rode in the last of the buffalo hunts, tall in the saddle, broad-shouldered in his beaded buckskin jacket and crimson sash. His body rippled with the movement of his horse, but his arms were steady, his aim clean through the billowing dust. He fought with Dumont and Riel, too, before moving west and north again, in search of liberty. But during that first winter, liberty was worth far less than a warm bed and a woman to share it with. The strapping young fighter who straggled into the post after the bitter defeat at Batoche, ragged and bloody, was satisfied to be claimed by the strong and capable Marie Hélène, and to be adopted by her numerous kin. He never once regretted it, for the whole of his long and prosperous life.

Claude knew the road well, from the prairie town of Wapahaska to the north, his home, but most often he'd driven it at night. The brilliance of the day, or the novelty of it, seemed full of meaning somehow, and with time at his disposal, he tried to puzzle it out. His thoughts came and went and swirled around each other, and he couldn't decide, finally, whether the wide prairie, laid open to the sun, was an ache, a wound, a revelation, or a promise.

He started to feel giddy out there on the prairie, just him and his pickup—like a kid skipping school on the first day of spring. He thought about Jamie Barber, the Wolves' captain, who, just a few days ago, had asked about Uncle Eddy again. Then he'd surprised Claude by confiding that he was thinking about retiring. He felt like he had a couple more years in him, but management had hinted that they might deal him over the summer, and that had scared him. He didn't want to leave Hillary and Jackie, and he didn't want to ask them to uproot themselves for some unstable, short-term deal, either. He'd been lucky, he said, and he was right. He'd been with the Wolves for a lifetime in hockey years, and that stability had allowed him and Hillary and Jackie to become a family. Still, it wouldn't be easy to leave hockey, his first love, or to figure out what kind of work an old, beat-up, retired minor-league hockey player could qualify for. That was the puzzle they'd all have to face, eventually. Lucky for Jamie, he had a good woman to face it with.

After a while, trees started creeping onto the prairie, mostly jack pine, but here and there a stand of birches raised its limbs in a brilliant white chorus. Far ahead, Claude saw a dot, dark against the soft pastels of the land and sky. As he approached, it acquired shape, and color, and, finally, words announcing the pavement's imminent end. He rested his foot lightly on the brake and then, with a rush and a swirling cloud, his truck burst onto the rough surface.

The going was slower here, and both the road and the distance that it must cover seemed suddenly to stretch like an elastic band into a true line, that geometrical abstraction of infinity. Claude began to grow impatient, anxious even, like those desperate European sailors, who, oddly, had feared falling off the earth's edge. But he had one up on them. He didn't ride the periphery. He sought the center. He was going home.

Claude left the gravel, turning onto a muddy road that descended gently with the land. The birches and pines gathered more closely around him, and he rolled his window down to feel himself in the forest, where the bracing coolness soothed his skin and bluish snow still slithered along the forest floor in shapes that echoed the shadows. The road narrowed, grew uneven, and made a sudden sharp swing to the right. He bumped along, slowly now, always looking to his left for the turn-off. It had been so long, he was afraid he wouldn't know it when he came to it.

But there it was. No doubt. The truck itself even seemed to know it, and stopped. All was quiet as it hadn't been since he left

Wapahaska. Or, rather, since he left this place the last time—he couldn't even remember when. Claude turned and drove on until he came to the little wooden cabin. Her car rested there already, in the clearing. He parked his truck beside it.

He could see her footsteps in what was left of the snow, leading from the car to the cabin door. He followed them and knocked. While he stood waiting he fingered the trim around the door and the little window to its right. The cheerful red paint had peeled and faded, and the wood was splintered. Down by the ground the doorjamb was rotting. It had probably been some years since Achille was strong enough to take on these simple chores—now, the old place cried out for some care. Claude knocked again, and, hearing nothing, slowly opened the door.

"Tess?" he called. "Tess? It's me, Claude."

He walked in. A small black suitcase, with a parka thrown over it, sat on the rough, pine floor by the door. A grocery bag and some keys graced the big table. There was no other sign of her. Claude walked outside to the woodpile, which was sizable, probably untouched since autumn. He carried a couple of arm-loads inside and laid them by the fireplace. Dad, Uncle Eddy, and Achille had been extremely proud of that fireplace—they'd hauled the stone themselves from some far-away quarry and then built it, along with the hearth and chimney, over a couple of summers. It was the second thing they'd built here—the first was the modest, wooden dock—and little by little, they'd assembled the rest of the place around it.

After he'd left the wood inside, Claude took a quick walk around the outside of the cabin. It looked shrunken and old and run-down, much like Achille himself that time Claude had visited him at Tess's request. But Achille hadn't mentioned the cabin then, or even his own illness. He'd only talked about Tess.

Claude saw the footsteps leading from the cabin down to the path, and he followed them into the woods, toward the lake. He felt layers of pine needles, years and years worth, springy under his feet, under the snow. They used to chase each other—he and Hector and Helen and Tess—barefoot, down the bouncy path, through the stumbly sand, onto the sun-warmed dock, their feet pounding faster and faster, until they reached the end of it and launched themselves into the sky, hollering with joy, and splashed down into the cold, blue lake. The path had seemed longer, then. Already, now, he could see the lake through the trees, but it wasn't blue today. Today it was hard and flat and frozen.

When he came to the narrow strand he stopped, just under cover of the trees. Down the beach a few yards, at the end of the land, a woman stood looking out across the expanse of ice. She wore blue jeans and boots and a big, grass-green sweater. Her long, black hair fell in two braids down her back. Claude's eyes locked onto her, a patch of green against the ice and the ragged, dark line of trees beyond. Whatever doubt had remained in his mind evaporated.

"Tess," he said.

She turned toward him.

They caught each other, and held each other, and didn't let go.

Owen hadn't anticipated the slow, plodding nature of the days as they, somehow, straggled past. It took a couple of weeks for his head to start clearing, and when it did, he almost wished it hadn't. He couldn't stand this feeling of being broken and in pain, of being hindered in everything he tried to do. He also hated feeling like people were looking at him—not, as they had done before, because he was Owen MacKenzie, the hockey player, but rather, because he was some invalid on crutches who couldn't manage to cross the street quickly enough, or make it through a goddamn door by himself. He'd hoped that the regular routine of rehab would make him feel better, but it had some definite downsides. The physical therapy hurt like hell, and the modified strength and conditioning crap was excruciatingly dull. He had little choice but to do exactly what the trainers told him to do—the team was hoping to have him back in the fall, and they didn't want him losing a step. He didn't want to lose a step, either. Where would he be then? He tried to stay positive at his workouts, but sometimes when he got home, he crashed. He couldn't help it.

Agnes was great. She was doing everything for him—cooking, making sure he took his medicine, doing all kinds of other stuff around the house. Ever since the night he got home from the hospital, though, when they'd argued about where she would sleep, there'd been a dark cloud between them. No, he wasn't a total idiot. He knew that it actually originated with that phone call, and her date with Deuce, and as time passed those things became harder to ignore. But he couldn't bring himself to ask about them right now. So he shoved them aside.

One day Corey took him to an appointment with the specialist. On the return trip they mostly talked hockey: the minor league playoffs, possible off-season trades—maybe the team would get rid of that prick Bo Salsnik—and other team gossip.

When Owen got home, Agnes was in the living room.

"Hey, O, how was your appointment?"

"Good. The doc says I'm right on schedule."

"I'm not surprised. You've been doing everything they say."

"And you're such a big help, Ag," he said. "I don't know what I'd do without you."

She smiled at him indulgently and finished braiding her hair. She was clearly headed out for some exercise, wearing gym shorts and a t-shirt, and all he wanted in the whole world was to run his hands along those warm, smooth arms of hers and maybe steal a kiss. But even if the crutches hadn't been holding him back, he knew she wouldn't have it. She picked up her house key and gave him the stingiest little hug ever.

"I'm going for a run, okay?" she said.

"I'll miss you," he answered.

"Yeah, I'm sorry. I meant to go earlier, but I lost track of the time," she said. "I'll get dinner going when I get back."

"Okay," he said. "Take your time. Oh, by the way, did you hear? Corey told me on the way home—the Prairie Wolves made it to the second round."

"Yeah, I saw it in the paper," said Agnes.

"I guess Deuce is excited," said Owen.

Agnes squinted at him. "One would assume," she said.

"Have you talked to him?" Owen asked.

"No, I haven't."

"Really?"

"Really. But what if I had? What business is it of yours?"

"It's my phone."

"And you're going to tell me who I can and can't talk to? Really, O? Have you fucking lost your mind?"

"I didn't mean it that way," he said.

"How *did* you mean it?"

Owen didn't know what to say.

Agnes continued, "And why are you so obsessed with Claude, anyway?"

"I'm not obsessed with Claude. You're the one who's obsessed with Claude," Owen said.

"No," said Agnes. "You're the one who's always bringing him up. It's weird. You never ask me about anyone else, only him."

"Who else should I be asking about?"

"Oh, I don't know—maybe one of the million other people we know in common? You could even ask about me. But no. It's always Claude. You're obsessed."

"That's ridiculous," said Owen. "Why would I be obsessed with him?"

"That's a question for you to answer," she said, walking out of the room into the hall. "I'm going for a run."

He called to her, "And why are you always going running these days? You never used to run."

"Because my goddamn skates are in fucking St. Cyp, that's why," she called from the hall, as she shoved her feet into her trainers.

"Jesus, Ag, if you want to skate, we can get you a pair of skates," Owen yelled back.

"I can buy my own skates, thank you very much," she shouted, "if it turns out I'm sticking around. Which seems less and less likely by the minute." She walked out and slammed the door behind her.

Shit. He really didn't want her to go. Even if she wasn't sleeping in his bed, even if she did have a ridiculously short fuse these days, it was still way better than not having her here at all. And it wasn't because he needed her to cook for him. He could cook a lot of things. It just wasn't that easy to do it on one leg.

He sat down on the sofa and put his leg up and brooded while he waited for her to get back. He'd never in his life felt so stupid and helpless. He could tell Agnes wasn't happy, but he didn't know what to do about it. He wasn't in the mood to joke around the way he usually did, but even if he had been, he doubted he could get a laugh out of her at this point. And it was no wonder she didn't want to get near him—he could barely walk. And what if his leg didn't heal right? What if he couldn't get his playing back up to the level it was at before? What if they sent him down to the minors forever? Then he'd be no use to her or to anyone else. He'd be no competition for Deuce, that was for sure.

He did wonder about their date. When he closed his eyes he could still see the two of them sitting together at Hill and Barbie's party. They seemed so comfortable together, their faces were so close, her hand was on his knee. It still made him feel vaguely ill. Maybe he *was* obsessed.

✳

It was forty long minutes before he heard her key in the lock and she walked into the living room. He took a deep breath.

"How was your run?" he asked.

"Good," she answered, still breathing hard. "I love that bluff overlooking the river up there. The strip along Oxen Ave. is fun, too."

"You ran a long way," he said. He stood up, grabbed his crutches, and followed her into the kitchen. "You're tough."

"And sweaty," she answered.

"I always loved you sweaty. Stinky hockey gear and all."

"You couldn't even smell mine because yours was a hundred times worse," she deadpanned.

"True enough," he said. "Ag, I'm sorry about what I said before. It was just stupid. Of course you can talk to anyone you want."

"Gee, thanks." Agnes filled a glass with water and drank it down.

"By the way," asked Owen, "how's Jo doing?"

"She's okay." Agnes filled the glass again and drank.

"What about that constable? Didn't you tell me that that constable from Wapahaska was trying to get her to go out with him?"

"Yeah."

"How'd that turn out?"

"Good so far. She seems to like him."

"Nice."

"It is, if it turns out that he's a good guy." Agnes put her empty glass down and continued, "I'm going to take a shower." She started walking toward the guest room, where she'd been sleeping since Owen stopped needing her at night.

"Ag, wait."

She turned around.

"How's, uh, your kookum?"

"She's fine," said Agnes.

"I haven't seen her in ages."

"True."

"And your dad?"

"He's good."

"I guess they must be glad to have you at home," Owen said.

"Yeah, I think they are."

Agnes turned toward her room again.

"How's it been for you, you know, living at home?" Owen asked her.

She stopped and turned around again. "Well, I feel like I'm a little old to be living with my dad and my kookum, but it's been working out okay."

She started to turn away again, but Owen asked, "What about Vin? Did you ever get him to play with you?"

She shook her head. "It was a disaster."

"Why? What happened?"

"He didn't appreciate seeing me in your Traders' jersey. He made a big stink about it."

"Why?"

"He thinks that you don't really love me. That you're just using me."

"That's bullshit."

Agnes didn't say anything.

"Ag, you know that's not true. You know I love you."

Agnes looked down at the floor. She said, "I know. Don't worry. I set him straight." But she didn't look back up at him.

"Ag, are you okay?"

"Not really."

"Ag, I'm sorry. I really am."

"For what?"

"For, like, hanging up on you. For being obsessed with Deuce. Now, come on, please forgive me. I'm hurting over here." He smiled, one of his damn-near irresistible smiles.

She shook her head. "Jesus Christ, Owen. You've got a broken leg. No one beat you up, no one put you down—it was an accident, that's all. The doctors and trainers are swarming all over you like you're the fucking Queen. You're going to heal as good as new. Or better. I don't feel sorry for you one bit."

"I don't want you to feel sorry for me. I just want—"

"Jesus Christ, Owen. Be a man. Or, better yet, use your goddamn brain and be a woman. Grow *up*, for God's sake. I'm going to shower."

She walked away. Owen stood there for couple of minutes, then he leaned his crutches against the wall and worked his way, on one leg, over to the refrigerator. He opened it and took out some leftover chicken and some cheese. He sliced the chicken up on a plate and arranged the cheese next to it. There was half a loaf of Agnes's bannock, too, and some butter. He cleaned some lettuce, sliced a tomato and some cucumber, and found some salad dressing. He took out a couple of beers and a bag of chips and arranged everything on the table.

When Agnes returned, her wet hair was combed smooth down her back. Her face was still glowing from her run.

"Hey, Ag."

"Hey."

"Will you have dinner with me?" he asked, balancing on his crutches and gesturing toward the table with his head.

She looked at the table and smiled just a little bit. "Sure, thanks, O."

He maneuvered over to the table and pulled out a chair for her. She sat down. He sat down next to her and opened the beers. He'd never seen her look so sad.

He asked, "So, it didn't work out with Vin, but you're still playing, right?"

"Yeah, I'm playing."

"Pickup?"

"No."

"So . . . what?"

"All Colors–All Bands has this game on Saturday nights. It's real different. It's hard to explain."

"Yeah?"

She looked at him.

"Tell me about it," he said.

"It's called the All Players game. It's for parents, teens, coaches—anyone, really. So it's all different people, all different levels. But somehow we make it work."

"Like shinny."

"Sort of. But more purposeful, I guess. Not just for fun."

"I know you don't play just for fun," he said.

A second passed. Then she smiled. "No."

He said, "Ag, I know we have to talk about that date you went on with Deuce. I've been wanting to ask you about it. It's just hard for me, that's all."

"Why, O? Why is it so hard for you?"

"It's just, I know how much you admire him—how much you admire that kind of player. You know, that big, strong warrior type."

"I do," she said,

"The way he's always, like, camped out in front of the net, taking all that abuse. The way he never turns down a fight. He's really tough."

"He is." She nodded. "He's awesome."

"See, I can't measure up to any of that," said Owen. "Especially now."

Agnes shrugged.

"And I know you're attracted to him. You always have been. I can understand that. He's maybe not the most handsome guy out there, but—"

"I think he's *real* handsome," said Agnes. "I never got as good a look as I'd like to, though." She winked.

Owen sighed. Even though he liked old Deuce, and respected him, it pained him to remember the Wolves' dressing room, and being up close and personal with the big guy and his goddamn perfect muscles and his huge, fighter's hands and his golden skin and all the rest of it. And to imagine Agnes noting all those same special features. He sighed again.

336 • LESLIE SPITZ-EDSON

Agnes laughed at him. "O, I'm not, like, putting together a hockey team or anything. Or the Mr. Universe pageant."

"I know. But I want to be *that guy* for you, Ag."

She said, "There are a lot of other things I admire about Claude, Owen. You know, he probably wouldn't even be playing hockey anymore if it weren't for Toby and Priscilla. He's pretty much supporting them while Priscilla's in school."

"Really?"

"Yeah."

"I didn't know that," Owen said.

Agnes took a sip of beer and then put the bottle down. She looked into Owen's face. "Do you know what we mostly did on that date, O?"

He shook his head. "No."

"We talked," Agnes said.

"You did?"

"For the most part."

"For the most part?"

"Yeah. For the most part."

Owen swallowed. "Where'd you go, anyway?"

"One of those little beaches down-river."

"Seriously? Wasn't it kind of cold?"

"It was cold. But it was nice. Sunny. He cooked a couple of steaks, we talked, watched the sunset—"

"Did he kiss you?"

Agnes nodded. "Yeah."

"Did you kiss him?"

"Jeez, Owen. It doesn't matter now."

"But you did?"

"Yeah."

"Did you two—?"

"No. We didn't."

"No?" asked Owen. "Are you sure?"

"Of course I'm sure!"

Owen's forehead was all wrinkled.

"Owen," Agnes said. "I never slept with Claude."

"Yeah. Okay."

"Anyhow, it's not even about that. Is it?"

"Well ..."

"You think it is, because you're a guy. Because guys are all about keeping score, and marking their territory, and worrying about some other guy sleeping with their girlfriend because it'll reflect poorly on their manhood or some such bullshit. But it's not about any of that. It's about who belongs where, and who belongs with each other, and who doesn't."

Owen squinted at her.

She said, "Owen, it was beautiful out there. I wondered why I'd ever left. I wondered how I could ever leave again. The sun was setting, and it painted the snow in all the colors of the rainbow. And after it got dark, there were so many stars that there was hardly room for them all in the sky. And it was so quiet, so still that you couldn't even ... you couldn't even feel the time pass. Do you know what I mean, O?"

Owen's mind flashed back to that weekend at Sebby's parents' place. He remembered the two of them standing in the lake together, he and Agnes, at opposite ends of the little beach, for that one endless, timeless moment. That moment stretched all the way until now.

"Yeah, Ag. I know what you mean."

"I really thought about what it would mean to have that life. With the snow and the stars and the river ice. With the fishing gear and the camp stove and the sticks and skates and stuff always ready in the back of the pickup, ready to go anytime."

He nodded.

She said, "I'm not talking about having that life *with Claude*—I'm not in love with Claude—but just to *have that life*. Just to be *home*. And to hell with everything *outside*."

Owen said, "Ag, if you need to go home, I understand. I'll miss you. But I don't like to see you sad. It's not worth it. I'm a big boy. I'll find a way to make it work down here. And maybe, you know, I won't be playing hockey forever. Maybe—"

She leaned over and kissed him. "Yes you will."

"Ag—"

"Owen," she said. "I love my home. More than ever. But I can't go back there right now. There's a whole world out here. Maybe there's a teaching job, and a hockey league I need to try."

Owen didn't say anything.

Agnes asked, "Remember when you said that I'm just like you? That we belong together?"

"Yeah."

"You were right."

He didn't answer.

"If you still want me," she said.

"I want you."

"But you've got to believe me, O. Listen to me. I love hockey. You know I do. I love the drama and the speed and the force of it. I love to play it, and I love to watch all different kinds of players, including Claude. Including you. You're amazing. But I don't love you for your hockey playing. I don't love you for your muscles or for being tough or for fighting Claude or any of that."

"I know, Ag," he said.

"And I'm not going to stop loving you when you get old and can't skate anymore, you know?"

"I know."

"Or if some bigger, tougher, faster guy comes along."

He raised his eyebrows.

"Or if your leg doesn't heal right—which, by the way, it *will*."

He looked into her eyes. She said, "I love you just because of the way we are together. So you don't have to do anything special. You don't have to prove anything. You don't even have to win the goddamn Stanley Cup. Although that would be pretty cool."

"Yeah," he said. They both smiled.

"Just be *that guy* for me," Agnes said. "Like you always have."

"Okay, Ag. I'll try."

Agnes held up her beer. "Cheers," she said.

"Cheers," he answered.

They drank to themselves.

Owen put his beer down. "Ag, forgive me for saying so, but you look so goddamn beautiful right now. I really want to take you out."

"Take me out?"

"Yeah, you know. On a date."

"But—"

"Come on, Ag. Let's go."

She narrowed her eyes. "Are you looking for a hot date," she asked him, "or a hot meal?"

"Both?" he answered.

She laughed and got up from the table. "Okay, let's get this stuff put away."

They did, and then they headed out into the twinkling lights of the city.